Blue Flame

by

Trish Finnegan

Book Four in the Blue Bird Series

Burning Chair Limited, Trading as Burning Chair Publishing
61 Bridge Street, Kington HR5 3DJ
www.burningchairpublishing.com

By Trish Finnegan
Edited by Simon Finnie and Peter Oxley
Book cover design by Burning Chair Publishing

First published by Burning Chair Publishing, 2025

ISBN: 978-1-912946-42-6

Also by Trish Finnegan

The WPC Sam Barrie Series

Blue Bird

It is the blisteringly hot summer of 1976, and WPC Samantha Barrie is Wyre Hall police station's newest recruit. When young girls start to go missing, Sam finds herself at the centre of an investigation which goes far deeper than anyone expects.

Blue Sky

No longer the fresh-faced new cop in the station, life should be getting easier for WPC Samantha Barrie. She is settled into her job, is well liked on her beats, and is on track to pass her probation and become a fully-fledged police constable. However, when her colleague and best friend, Steve, is arrested for apparently trying to smuggle drugs into the Isle of Man, Sam is determined to prove his innocence.

Baby Blues

WPC Samantha Barrie has survived her first few years at Wyre Hall police station in the Peninsula. Station politics, sexist colleagues and belligerent busybodies are just some of the things she has to deal with on a daily basis, and that's before the day job itself. But now comes her toughest test yet, as a series of cases thrust her right into the heart of the action – but this time Sam, and those close to her, are the ones under investigation.

Dedicated to all emergency workers. Ordinary people doing extraordinary things. Most people don't realise how lucky they are to have you.

Prologue

Music boomed and lights bounced around the walls. Reflections from the mirror-ball overhead slid across the floor. People danced, paying him no heed. When he first arrived at the club, he'd thought that he would be able to strike up a conversation and maybe walk a girl home, but he had been rebuffed several times. He watched the women who rejected him respond to overtures from other men. What was the difference? He had bathed and taken care to select suitable clothing. He even wore aftershave. Why was he treated differently?

An attractive blonde slipped through the crowd towards the bar. He moved closer to the woman and slipped an arm around her waist.

'Can I buy you a drink?'

She turned cold eyes to him. 'Move your damned arm before I break it!'

He moved his arm. 'I'm only trying to be friendly.'

'Go and be friendly somewhere else.' She turned back to the bar to place her order.

'Let's dance,' he said.

'Let's not,' she ricocheted back without looking at him.

As she turned back with drinks in her hands, he saw her wedding ring. His patience snapped. He stepped in front of her, blocking her path. 'Does your husband know you're here? You're a disgrace. Flaunting yourself, leading men on when you have a husband.'

She stepped around him.

He grabbed her arm, causing her to spill a drink. 'Don't you walk away from me.'

She snatched her arm back. 'Get lost or I'll scream.'

'All right, love?' called the barman.

'This berk grabbed me,' the woman called back.

The man stepped back half a pace and held his hands up. 'A misunderstanding.'

The woman hurried off to her friends, who all turned towards him, scowling. Curling his lip at them, he turned and walked towards the door. What was the point of staying to be rejected and reviled by harlots? Besides, he'd noticed the barman signal to one of the security team. He'd rather leave under his own steam.

Outside, he stood and watched women in the street screeching like seagulls fighting over scraps. Some ran over to a patrolling policeman, who allowed one of them to wear his helmet, grinning as they made lewd jokes about his truncheon. How was a man in uniform supposed to gain public respect when he allowed that behaviour? He considered this for a moment. It was the uniform. The uniform commanded the respect. The man could allow outrageous behaviour from these females and still maintain respect because of his uniform.

A couple more women almost fell out of a taxi outside the club. They tottered past him on skyscraper heels, giggling like schoolgirls. Neither so much as turned her head to him. He looked along the queue to get into the club. Girls clinging to men, girls arguing with men, girls kissing men. Nobody looked at him. Nobody ever looked at him.

The women now walked along the road arm in arm with the policeman. They la-la-la-ed their way through *New York New York*. Kicking their legs high. Finally, the women released the policeman and ran over to join the queue. The policeman continued his patrol, still grinning. Wasn't he going to do something about this immorality? What about the men, weren't they going to control their women? The Bible was very clear about proper conduct for women and this scene was very far from that. The man could not allow this shamelessness to continue.

'*"The head of every man is Christ, and the head of every woman is man."* Corinthians 11:3. Get home, women!' the man shouted.

A woman in the queue shouted back, '*"There is no male and female, for you are all one in Christ Jesus."* Galatians 3:28. Now buzz off, weirdo; you're not the only one who went to Sunday school.' Several people laughed.

'You tell him, Carol,' urged her companion. 'Her dad's a vicar. She knows The Bible,' she yelled to anyone who cared to listen.

The man was outraged. A woman, a daughter of a vicar if her friend was to be believed, used the Holy Bible to mock him. It was beyond disgraceful. Also, why was she there? The only reason he could think of for a woman to go to a nightclub was to find a man. A vicar's daughter putting herself on show for men. Well, The Bible looked harshly at women like her. Just wait until he told his brothers. Only this week they had talked about this exact thing.

He spotted the policeman coming back. He must have heard the exchange, yet he did nothing! He condoned this wanton behaviour. When he went to court, how could he swear on The Bible if he could not uphold its teachings?

'Harlots! You're all harlots leading men on.' He pointed at the vicar's daughter. 'And you are the worst of all!'

She raised two fingers at him whilst continuing her conversation with her friend. It was too much! He clenched his fists, but the policeman approached him before he could take a step towards her.

'I think you should move on,' the policeman said.

'I'm not doing anything wrong,' the man protested.

'I heard you shout at the women. You're evidently upset by their presence, so if you don't move on, I will have to arrest you to prevent a breach of the peace.'

The man flung out his hand towards the queue. 'You think this is acceptable?'

'They are being orderly, unlike you. Now move. Last chance.'

The man hesitated but, noting the hardening of the

policeman's voice, nodded and turned away. The policeman watched him go.

The man didn't go far. He crossed the road but then stood in a doorway, seething as he watched proceedings. He spotted a woman, slipping into an alley beside the club. On impulse, he followed her. When he caught up, she was down a short flight of steps trying to open a rear door set into a recess.

'You shouldn't sneak in without paying,' he said.

She jumped when she saw him. 'Jesus, you scared me. I thought you were the bouncer.'

'God loves you and, if you repent, He'll forgive your sins. Come with me and we can pray together for guidance to protect your eternal soul. I'll even buy you a drink.'

'Get lost, arsehole,' she snapped as she worked at the door.

He felt annoyance rise in him. She hadn't even looked at him as she insulted him, just like that other trollop.

'You will show me respect,' he demanded.

'Why?' she turned and cocked her head. 'Because you have a dick, and I don't? Well, let me tell you, that doesn't mean anything.' She hurried back up the steps, paused by the man and said, 'Loony!'

All his frustration and outrage of the evening bubbled over. He grabbed her shoulders and threw her back against the wall. She lost her footing and fell down the concrete steps. He heard the dull thud and a soft crack.

She didn't move. He crept down the steps and felt her pulse. Nothing. Her head was tilted at an impossible angle. He picked up her handbag and tossed it to one side to feel the pulse at her wrist. Still nothing. He looked at the discarded bag. It was made of plastic, manufactured to look like patent leather. His fingerprints would now be on it. Why hadn't he thought of that and left the bag where it fell. He had to dispose of it.

'Linda? Are you there?' someone called.

Stopping only to pick up the handbag and stuff it inside his jacket, he ran behind the club and climbed over the wall into a dark, stinking entry that ran behind a row of shops. The barbed wire along the top caught on his clothing. It was generic, department store clothing. The material would match a hundred similar suits, so it was unlikely to be traced back to him, but he'd destroy the clothing later to make sure.

He had taken only a few steps on the other side of the wall when he heard the scream. He ran as fast as he could along the entry until he burst out into a, fortunately, empty road. Anyone nearby was now homing in on the commotion at the club. He slowed his pace and walked away. He didn't want to draw attention to himself, and running always drew attention.

Once he felt he was far enough away, he went to drop the handbag into a nearby wastebin but then realised that next time someone put something into the bin, the bag would be spotted and maybe the police would get his fingerprints from it. He had no criminal record, but they would hold the prints in their systems and in the future, if he had his fingerprints taken for any reason, he would be linked to the dead woman. He checked the contents of the bag. A lighter, good quality that conflicted with the cheap handbag. It was engraved with the initials *L.F.* Linda…something? A purse with a small amount of money, which he pocketed along with the lighter. She, Linda, wouldn't need them anymore.

He didn't feel guilty; it had been an unfortunate accident. If she hadn't been trying to break into the club, or if she had gone with him when he told her to, she would have been enjoying a chat and a drink with him now. He put the bag back inside his jacket again then hurried home. Once there, he would burn it.

His thoughts returned to the policeman. Ineffective as he was, women noticed the policeman. Men noticed the policeman. Nobody noticed him. That would change.

Chapter One

I sat in my place next to my mates, Steve Patton and Andy Broad, ready to start parade.

'All right, Sam.' Steve said.

'All right,' I replied.

Everyone else on B Block had been on lates since the previous Wednesday, but I had been on my month-long police driving course and had only returned to Wyre Hall police station today. I opened my pocket notebook and wrote, *"Monday, 28th August 1978"*. I underlined it then underneath I wrote *"1500: Parade"*. Obviously we were on parade, the briefing that everyone had before starting their patrol, but our notebooks were actually legal documents, subject to regulations and checks, that could be produced in court. Imagine attending court to give evidence about an incident that had happened maybe six months previously, having dealt with a million other incidents since then. Nobody has that good a memory. That's why we were expected to write everything into our pocketbooks, even that we were on rest day or leave. Want to know what I was doing last October 17th? Check in my pocket notebook.

In the old days, parade had been an actual parade where everyone stood to attention for inspection. Now, we sat in a dingy, smelly room lined with ancient posters and cobwebs. So many cobwebs. They had got worse since the cleaners had been refusing to go up ladders to reach them. The caretaker had had to add that to his long list of jobs, which meant it was hardly ever done.

Andy Broad, one of our latest probationers, or sprogs as they were more commonly known, leant towards me.

'Did you pass, Sam?' he asked.

'Of course,' I replied.

'Does that mean you'll be driving a panda?'

I heartily wished that passing the course did guarantee me getting my own patrol car.

'It doesn't work like that, Andy,' I said. 'I will be a spare driver in case of sickness or something. You don't get a panda just because you're a level three driver.'

Andy looked disappointed. 'At least you've got your CID Aides' course to look forward to. Do you have a date yet?'

'Not yet. It might be months away,' I replied.

'Have you seen the new pandas?' Steve asked.

'Blue Vauxhall Vivas. I got a quick look at them when I was doing the maintenance classes in the garage,' I said.

'I'm not sure about the colour,' Andy said. 'Pale blue all over with no markings on the doors. It'll confuse the public. What if there's a chase?'

'They have the illuminated sign, and blues-and-twos on them; that should be enough to identify them as police cars,' Steve said. 'Also, the traffic division vehicles all have livery. They're the ones doing the high-speed chases and vehicle stops.'

'Maybe so, but anyone can buy a pale blue car. They could pretend it's a police car,' Andy insisted. 'And the new signs are so narrow; even lit up, they're hardly visible until you're practically on top of the car.'

'That particular shade won't be available to the public,' Steve said.

'Pale blue is pale blue no matter what fancy name you want to give it,' Andy retorted.

'Where's Ken?' I asked to ward off any argument. Ken Ashcroft was one third of the B Block "three musketeers", the other two being Steve and me.

'He had to take Gaynor to the hospital,' Steve said. 'Her blood pressure is a bit high. I spoke to him earlier. He thought the doctors were being cautious more than anything else.'

Ken's wife, Gaynor, was in her third trimester and Ken had been getting more anxious day by day. Despite his apparent nonchalance to Steve, I could imagine Ken's head exploding with this new development.

'I'll give him a ring during break,' I said.

'Have you had your report back yet?' Charlotte Leader, our other sprog, called across the parade room to Andy.

'Not yet,' he replied.

'I've got mine.' She pulled it from her bag and waved it in front of her. 'I got an O again.'

An O was a decent achievement. Each quarter, sprogs were graded on various criteria such as Knowledge of Law, and Manner with the Public. It went A to E, with A being Excellent and E being Poor. If a sprog did particularly well at something, they would get an O for Outstanding. Despite my turbulent probation, I had managed to maintain mostly As with some Os and Bs, which was more than enough to keep the big bosses happy.

Frank Morton, who had been Charlotte's tutor constable, took the sheet from her and preened. 'O for Knowledge and A for the rest. That's because I tutored you.' He passed it along so Andy could look.

I rolled my eyes. Being proud of a result is fine, but we didn't normally pass our reports around the parade room for everyone to have a look. Also, I doubted Frank's tutoring was up to the standard of my—and Andy's—tutor, Phil Torrens. He had been brilliant. The exact right mix of teacher, big brother, and backside kicker. He had gone to Tynvoller Division on promotion to sergeant, and I missed him.

When the report reached me, I had a quick read of the comments, which told more of the story than just the grades. I then passed it on to Andy who viewed the grades before passing it back.

'I don't know how she does it,' Andy complained. 'It's not

as if she does anything especially outstanding. In fact, in my opinion, Frank has taught her to cut too many corners. Phil wouldn't have it.'

'She isn't the only one here who's gained an O. You got one in your last report, didn't you?'

'Yes, but I don't go on about it. I don't want to seem like a big head,' Andy replied.

'Look, modesty is okay, but don't downplay your achievements. Spider never does,' I said, using the nickname we had given Charlotte. 'Did you see what the Inspector wrote?'

'I didn't really notice, I was looking at the grades,' Andy said.

'Did you notice the phrase, "Confident of her own abilities"?' I asked.

Andy shook his head.

'In reports, some phrases are a code. For "confident of her own abilities" read "cocky cow". You don't ever want to get "lacks enthusiasm". That means "lazy".'

Andy sniggered. 'I always feel better after speaking to you.'

'My pleasure,' I replied. It was too. Andy was a nice lad. He'd be a good boss one day.

We all stood as our block inspector, George Benjamin, came in with Bert Mason, the station sergeant and Shaun Lloyd, our patrol sergeant. I had worked with Inspector Benjamin on an operation before he came to B Block. As a result, I still thought of him as Benno. He occasionally called me Sally, the name I had used on that operation.

'As you were.' Inspector Benjamin sat at the small table at the front. We all sat and waited for our duties.

'Welcome back, Constable Barrie,' the Inspector said.

'Thank you, sir,' I replied.

'Did you enjoy it?' he asked.

'I did, especially the skid pan,' I answered. 'Everyone should have a go on a skid pan. The winter accident rate would plummet if people could practice before encountering slippy conditions in real life.'

Several others murmured agreement.

Bert Mason passed Andy his assessment report. 'Two Os. Well done, lad.'

Andy beamed as he read the report. I was pleased that he had outdone Spider. Andy's Os were for Manner with the Public and Enthusiasm. He was outstandingly polite and keen. A good combination. Everything else was an A. The comments were equally praising of his efforts. I clocked Spider's jealous sidelong glance towards Andy.

'Look at Spider,' Steve murmured into my ear. 'Mouth pursed up like a cat's arse.'

'It does her no harm to realise that other people have ability even without a degree,' I whispered back.

'Care to share?' Shaun Lloyd called to me.

'Sorry, Sarge,' I said and concentrated on the duties that Bert was giving out. As expected, I got a foot patrol. Town centre, not my usual patch. It seemed that Bert's idea of working all over the division was still in force. I preferred to work one beat and get to know the people there, but it wasn't my call.

Bert looked around the room. 'I know some of you are concerned about Ken's wife. I spoke to him a short time ago and he told me that everything seems to be all right. The doctors are checking her weekly from now on. The child is a good size, so even if she goes into early labour, it should be okay. Ken has been given a couple of days compassionate leave. He'll be back on earlies.'

A murmur of approval went around the room.

'The other bit of news I have is that we're getting another sprog,' Bert said. 'A young lady again. She'll be here next week.'

I was surprised to hear that, seeing as it wasn't that long ago Andy and Charlotte arrived, but then I remembered that I had been the third of three. Steve Patton, Ken Ashcroft, then me. Maybe this new person would end up being the sprog as long as I had been. Until Andy and Spider had arrived, I actually thought that I would be confirmed as a regular officer whilst still being the sprog.

'Do you know anything about her?' Trevor asked.

'Only that she wouldn't be interested in the likes of you,' Bert shot back.

Everyone laughed and Trevor sniffed. 'I was only trying to find out if I'm likely to be puppy walking.'

Probably not, was my guess. Trevor wasn't exactly dynamic.

'Moving on. A young woman, Carol Shilling, has been reported missing. She's described as twenty years old, white, five-six tall, slim, fair haired. Last seen wearing jeans and a purple blouse. Keep your eyes open,' Bert said.

I scribbled the description into my pocket notebook.

'Bet she's stayed out with her fella,' Trevor said aloud.

'Shut up, Trevor,' Steve said.

'All I said—' Trevor began.

'Shut up, Trevor,' we all said.

Trevor shut up.

After parade, we crowded into the tiny control room to collect our radios and do our test calls. I hated feeling crowded, so I moved into the enquiry office next to the control room. I could do a test call just as easily from there, or even the yard.

I saw Spider approach Andy.

'Let's see the report then,' she asked.

Andy pulled the report from his pocket and handed it over. Spider gave it the once over.

'O for Manner with the Public, and Enthusiasm,' she nodded in an approving manner. I actually thought she was going to congratulate him. 'Not for Knowledge of the Law though. That's important.' She passed the report back to him.

Spider was on form. She regarded herself as a princess amongst peasants. She was a graduate entrant, which meant she had joined an accelerated promotion scheme. A fact that she had announced on our first meeting. She also let it be known that she was not looking for friendship because she would be our boss one day. Nobody here was prepared to put up with her nonsense.

Andy took back his report and put it in his pocket. 'Knowledge of the Law is important, and you will note that I got an A for that. However, it's pointless knowing the law if you lack the enthusiasm to deal with jobs properly or to generate your own work.' He looked her full in the face. 'Or if you're a complete bitch with people.'

I held back a laugh. Spider had deserved that. Andy had grown in confidence, and I was pleased to see it. Spider's jaw dropped at this pushback from one of the peasants. Before she could say anything, I approached them.

'Come on, Andy, I'm on the next beat to you so let's walk out together.' I took his arm and pulled him towards the door. He willingly followed me.

'I'll come too, I've got the shopping centre,' Steve said. He did his test call, and the three of us left.

'Well done for standing up to Princess Bitch,' I said, using Spider's unofficial nickname.

He grinned. 'She's been asking for that since training school.'

We walked past the nightclub in The Square. It was a decent place; they didn't allow entry to bucks, the local undesirables, so there was little trouble. The doormen took care of most skirmishes and only called on us if things were escalating.

'While you were away, a woman fell down the recessed steps behind the club and died.' Steve said. 'Dark alley, high heels, steps. They think she was trying to sneak in without paying.'

'How sad to die just to save a fiver,' I said.

'Yeah. It's odd, though: her handbag was missing,' Steve said.

That threw a different light on things. Not many women went on a night out without a handbag. Had it been an accident, I'd have expected her handbag to have been found at the scene.

'Could be a robbery gone wrong,' I suggested.

'Or a straightforward theft. Someone spots the handbag and just makes off with it without realising the owner was dead a few feet away,' Andy added.

'Anyway, enquiries are ongoing, but nothing much is coming

up. The CCTV was on the blink, and the only evidence they have is from her sister, who found her.' Steve said. 'She noticed the bag was missing.'

Sometimes, crimes were not solved for want of evidence. Unfortunate but it happened.

It was a pleasant afternoon. Not too hot. We walked in companionable silence until we reached the edge of Andy's beat. He peeled off and began patrol. Steve and I continued at a leisurely pace. There was no point in rushing, we'd be walking several miles over the next few hours, and who knew what incidents would occur.

'Emma and I have booked a holiday in October,' Steve said,

'Lovely. Where are you going?' I asked.

'Benidorm. The five S's.'

'Sea, sand, sun, Sangria…Spain?'

Steve wiggled his eyebrows.

I clicked on. 'Oh right, sex.'

Steve laughed. 'Speaking of which, I'm surprised you haven't been out to visit the boss yet. You must be missing him.'

Gary Tyrrell, my fiancé, had been our block inspector before his posting to Hong Kong as part of the ongoing corruption enquiry. Steve was having a hard time remembering that he no longer had to think of him as our boss.

'I can't afford to fly to Hong Kong. I expect he'll get some leave and come home before long. Anything else is not your business,' I said.

A distressed woman clutching a small toddler ran into the road causing a car to slam on. The driver, evidently shocked, got out and shouted at her. The woman shouted back but I couldn't make out what she was saying. She held the child out to the driver.

'What the hell?' Steve said.

We hurried over to the scene. The man saw us coming first.

'She just ran out,' he called.

'We saw,' I replied. 'What's going on?'

The weeping woman thrust the child at me. 'He's choking!'

The child was perhaps eighteen months old. He was floppy and saliva drooled from his mouth. His face was red and appeared swollen. I smacked him on the back, but he was still struggling. Steve grabbed his ankles and held him upside down. Still nothing. While the child was still upside down, I tipped his head back to extend the airway and whacked him hard on the back. It was bound to leave a bruise, but we were past the time that mattered. A small, metal object fell from his mouth and he drew a deep, long breath and coughed hard. I grabbed the object while Steve righted him and nursed him as he coughed.

The object was a jingle bell, the type of thing found in rattles or sewn onto teddies. I made a mental note never to have such things in the house if I had a baby in the future.

I'm sorry,' the mother said to the driver. 'I just saw a blue Viva and thought you were in a police car and you'd know what to do.'

Steve and I exchanged a look. Maybe Andy had a point about pale blue cars.

'Don't worry,' the driver said. 'Thank goodness these two were around.'

The child started to cry and held out his arms for his mother, who enveloped him in a hug.

'I think we should call for an ambulance, get him checked out.' I said. The mother nodded and I radioed the control room to arrange the ambulance.

'You get on and I'll deal with this now,' Steve said to me. 'No point us both being tied up here.

'I'll do my report at scoff for you.' I said.

'See you at scoff time.' Steve turned his attention back to the mother and child.

I walked on to my own patch, thinking about the sheer good fortune that we had been nearby and able to help the child. My patrol took me past the fire station. The doors were up, and a swarm of firemen were cleaning the appliances. I don't know why, but firemen got a bit sniffy when we called them fire engines. They didn't like us calling the fire station *Trumpton*, either. I had been very pleased when I found out that one of their men was named Pugh. They seemed to accept some of our lads calling them water fairies. All blue light workers were proud of their organisation and had a good-natured insulting name for the other services.

'Hey, Sam.'

I saw Chris Atherton waving to me and waved back. We had first met at a traffic accident a couple of years previously. I had been covered in muck and petrol and was coming down from an adrenaline high which, together with the fumes, was making me vomit. Not my best look. We ran into each other from time to time at various jobs, and occasionally he would invite me into the fire station for a cuppa if I was passing. When the firemen had been on strike, they had let me warm myself by the braziers they had by their picket line. I really needed a cuppa right now.

He came over. 'Haven't seen you for ages. Have you managed to keep out of hospital?'

I laughed. 'It must be at least a week since they admitted me. Actually, I've been away of a driving course for a month.'

He smiled. 'So how is it going? Is your chap enjoying Hong Kong?'

'He seems to be. He says the food over there is nothing like the Chinese food we get here. You know how the Chinese restaurant in town has a little fishtank by the door? They do that in Hong Kong but bigger.'

Chris said, 'I heard it's supposed to attract money.'

'Over there, it's also the menu. And they have cages of live toads by the door. They eat toads!' My insides rippled at the thought.

'That doesn't surprise me. When's his posting over?' Chris asked.

'March 1981.' Suddenly that seemed an awfully long way away.

'Blooming heck, and he still took it although it would take him away for so long? I'd never leave a girl for that long.' Chris shook his head.

I had to defend Gary's decision. Our decision. 'He asked me to go with him, you know. I chose not to go because I wanted to build up my career here.'

The sound of a klaxon from inside the station drew my attention. Firemen abandoned buckets and sponges and scrambled for the fire engines. Appliances.

'Got to go,' Chris said and sprinted into the station.

I stepped back out of the way as the first of the engines pulled out onto the road. A second followed closely behind. I hadn't heard anything on our radio, but they would only call on the police if they needed a road blocking off or crowd control; something like that.

'Where are they going?' a woman slurred behind me.

I turned around and saw Ruthie Pritchard standing there. She didn't look much better than the last time I'd seen her, but she wasn't as smelly today. She must have had a bath at some point. Also, she was wearing a different coat. Red. Not new. The frayed lapel and the top button sewn on with different coloured thread gave that away, but it was better than what she had had. She probably had visited the mission hall and been given it from the donations box. She probably had had her bath there, too. It was the handbag that really caught my eye. It was a vile, pink plastic thing that clashed with her coat.

'Hello, Ruthie. I bet you're on your way to the shopping centre. Don't you be begging there; you know it's not allowed. And stay out of the stores that have banned you.' I knew that pretty well all the stores in the shopping centre had banned Ruthie. In fact, she couldn't be far off a ban from the entire town centre. She was a hopeless addict and funded her habit with a mix of prostitution. shoplifting and begging.

'That's nice, isn't it. Can't even go shopping without coppers accusing me of stuff.'

'Just behave yourself,' I called over my shoulder as I resumed patrol. When I was out of earshot, I radioed the control room. '4912 to control.'

'Go ahead,' Ray shot back.

'Could you inform Steve when he resumes that Ruthie Pritchard is heading to the shopping centre. She's wearing a red coat.'

'Will do.' Ray then relayed my message to the shopping centre patrol. I knew that Ruthie would probably be in the bridewell before the end of the shift.

Chapter Two

I had been on patrol about two hours when the call came from the control room.

'All patrols, Wilfred's done one again.'

Ray knew that we'd all understand. Wilfred Wainwright was a retired policeman and veteran soldier of WWI. According to the older bobbies at the station, Wilfred had been at the end of his service when they had started out on their careers, and he had been a top bloke. A good copper, a father figure and a great help to sprogs. He'd never been hungry for promotion, unlike some. He had been content to remain a beat bobby, where he felt he could be of greatest use. Now in his eighties, dementia was stealing his mind, and from time to time he believed he was still in the job. We'd find him patrolling his old patch.

Sadly, Wilfred's wanderings were happening increasingly often and his wife, Kitty, who was a similar age to him, was finding it more and more difficult to keep him safe at home. When he managed to slip away, she would ring the control room, knowing that he would be traced and returned home full of tea and toast. We could all see that it would not be long before Wilfred would need to go into a care home. Something Kitty vigorously resisted.

Wilfred had a strong protective instinct and often would be found by the primary school on my patch. A Victorian building that Wilfred would know well from his police days. Whatever the time of day, he would stop outside, ready to do crossing duty just as he did when he had been a policeman. Luckily, the school staff knew Wilfred was harmless and would ring us if they spotted him there. I headed out that way and, sure enough, he was walking up the road that led to the school. I radioed in my sighting and asked for Mike Two to meet us.

I hurried over and called out. 'Hey, Wilfred. Hang on.'

He stopped and turned around. 'What is it?'

I caught up. 'It's time to go back to the station.' I could see he was a little confused. 'It's me. Samantha. I normally work out by the park.'

'Oh yes, Samantha.' He looked me up and down. 'What are you wearing, girl? The woman superintendent will have a fit when she sees how short your skirt is. You'll be put on a fizzer. You don't want that on your record.'

I looked down at my knee length skirt and chuckled. 'It's the new uniform, Wilf. I told you about it last time we spoke.' It was hardly a new uniform, but I had learnt to just go with the flow where Wilfred was concerned. I wasn't even going to try to explain that the policewomen's department had been scrapped.

He shook his head. 'It's barely decent.'

'Never mind, Wilf. A car will be here to collect us shortly,' I said.

Wilfred laughed. 'A car for the likes of us? The brass won't have that.'

From the way he was talking, I estimated that Wilfred's mind had slipped back to the 1930s, when only the elite would have had access to a motor vehicle.

Mike Two came around the corner and pulled up beside us. John Batt, the driver, opened the window.

'Hop in and I'll give you a lift back.'

Still locked into police mode, Wilfred took shotgun beside John, and I climbed into the back.

'Ray's got the kettle on so we can have a nice brew when we get back,' John said.

'That sounds good.' I took it for granted that I was included in that.

Wilfred looked around and I could see uncertainty in his

body language. He turned and stared at John's flat cap.

'What rank are you?' Wilfred asked.

'Just a constable, Wilf,' John replied. He was also well used to Wilfred.

'Ah, you must be the driver for the brass. Don't let them know you're letting plods in their car.'

'Don't worry, I won't.' John caught my eye in the mirror. I grinned back.

'Is that part of the new uniform?' Wilf nodded towards John's hat.

'It is, Wilf,' John replied. 'Only for drivers and senior officers.' Which was true. The foot patrols and patrol sergeants wore helmets.

Wilf accepted that and settled into his seat for the ride back.

We arrived back at the station, and Wilfred was greeted as an old friend. Wilf stood to attention when the inspector entered the control room, as would have been expected in his day. The rest of us did the same so he didn't feel awkward. Normally the boss had to make do with a distracted, 'sir,' in acknowledgement of his presence. He glanced around, no doubt gauging if we were winding him up.

'Stand easy,' he said. We all relaxed. 'Mr Wainwright, we haven't met. I'm the inspector of B Block. George Benjamin.' He held his hand out to Wilfred.

Wilfred shook the inspector's hand. 'Pleased to meet you, sir. Constable Wilfred Wainwright, Shale Road Station.'

Shale Road police station had been abandoned following bomb damage during the war. It had remained empty for several years before being demolished. New houses stood on the site now. However, to Wilf, Shale Road was still a working police station. I wondered if there was such a thing as cop heaven. When his time came, would Wilfred's ghost return to the site of Shale Road Station to look after the town alongside his old workmates?

Then my imagination really ran with the idea. I thought

about all the other dedicated bobbies' ghosts walking their beats for eternity. Over the years, a few people, police included, swore blind that they had seen apparitions of police officers in old fashioned uniforms. Most older police stations were rumoured to have a resident ghost. I shook myself, that was too creepy to contemplate. They were probably stories designed to scare the sprogs. Also, if there was a cop heaven, it probably involved the police club.

Bert sat Wilf in the sergeant's office and while they chatted, I was dispatched to make some toast to go with the tea.

Benno came to the kitchen after me, which spoiled my plan of making myself a slice of toast too.

'What are your thoughts on Wilfred?'

'I think he's getting worse, sir. This is happening more often; twice this week so far, I'm told.'

Inspector Benjamin nodded. 'I think you and I will take him home. We should have a chat with his wife about bringing in social services.'

'She won't like that,' I warned him. It had been suggested before and hadn't gone down well.

'Maybe not, but she's also elderly and it's clear she is finding it more difficult. I think we'd be neglecting our duty if we left one of our own without support. She might be more receptive if you suggested it.'

'I could try, sir,' I said. The toast popped and I buttered it. 'I'll get this to him while it's hot. There's a spare piece in the toaster if you fancy it.'

The words had barely left my mouth before Benno pounced on the toaster and fished out the spare slice. What was it about toast that was so irresistible?

'Thanks. See you in about twenty minutes.'

*

Half an hour later, the inspector and I pulled up outside a

gleaming, bay-fronted house in a quiet road by the King Streets. Unsurprisingly, an area where all the roads were named after kings.

Wilfred's wife came to the door. 'Thanks so much for looking after him.' She spoke in a Scottish accent, despite having lived in town for over half a century.

'You're very welcome,' I said.

'Can we come in and have a chat, Mrs Wainwright?' Inspector Benjamin asked.

'Put the kettle on, Kitty lass,' Wilfred boomed. He ushered us inside.

Inspector Benjamin took a seat in the sitting room, while I followed Kitty into the kitchen, ostensibly to help. Something Kitty and Wilfred didn't find at all odd.

In the kitchen, Kitty set about filling the kettle and spooning tealeaves into a brown, ceramic pot. I set out a tray with cups, saucers and a glass sugar basin.

'May I call you Kitty?' I asked. I hadn't dared ask the last time we had met.

'It's my name,' she replied.

I took that as permission. 'Kitty, everyone at the station is getting a bit worried about Wilfred.' I paused to draw breath.

'Och, is he getting in the way?' she asked. 'He enjoys the blether. He's always in good spirits when he comes home.'

'No, no. We enjoy a chat, too. It's fascinating to hear about the old days. It's just that he's wandering off more often and we're worried he'll get himself into a dangerous situation or maybe even forget how to get home,' I said. 'I want to make sure you're getting the support you're entitled to.'

'And what support would that be?' Kitty knew where this was leading.

'Somewhere safe for Wilfred—' I started to say but Kitty cut me off.

'No! We married in 1920, and I promised to stick by him in sickness and in health, and he promised me the same. I'm not having him put in a home while I'm able to look after him.'

'But you're getting on, yourself…' I inwardly cringed. I could have worded that so much better.

'Cheeky wee bairn!'

I smiled. 'You remind me of my nan. She's fierce too. I think you'd get on.'

Kitty smiled back. 'Aye, maybe.'

'Would you at least think about having someone in to do an assessment, Kitty? Please. You don't have to accept their suggestions, but it would be useful to have their input. You'd get the final say.'

'I'll think about it, but I'm no' promising anything.'

That was the best I could do for now. The kettle started to whistle, and Kitty poured boiling water into the teapot.

'I'll carry it in for you,' I offered. Kitty accepted.

I put the tray on the coffee table and Kitty started to pour the tea through a small sieve. No teabags here. She evidently had views on how things should be done properly. Just like my nan.

Wilfred pointed at my bare fingers. 'How come a nice-looking girl like you hasn't been snapped up by a young man yet?'

I didn't take offence; Wilfred was a product of his time.

'I am engaged, Wilf. I don't wear my ring to work in case I lose it. You know what this job can be like.'

Wilf nodded. 'Very wise. I wouldn't have thought of that.'

'That's because yer a thick-heided man,' Kitty said. Despite her words, I could hear the affection in her voice. Almost sixty years married and still in love. I wondered if that would happen for me.

I looked around the room. Family pictures hung around the walls, and on the heavy mantlepiece was Wilfred and Kitty's wedding photo. Kitty's bouquet almost reached the floor. They both looked sombre, but photographic processes were prolonged then. Next to it was a photograph of a young sailor. I could see the resemblance to Wilfred.

Kitty watched me looking at the pictures. She gestured

around the room. 'Our daughter and her family. She married an American and went to live over there after the war. Boston. She phones and sends us photos so we can keep up to date with what's happening. We became great-grandparents last year.'

'How lovely.' I dutifully turned to look at the photo of the baby on the window ledge.

'Do you get to see them often?' Inspector Benjamin asked.

'We only went out there once, and she came to see us a couple of times. It's so expensive,' Kitty said.

'It is,' the inspector agreed. 'My older brother, Douglas, lives in Portland, Oregon. I haven't seen him in ten years.'

They all shook their heads at the price of air travel.

'Who's that handsome chap?' I pointed to the sailor on the mantelpiece.

'Our Wilfie.' Kitty stared at the photograph, but said no more.

'He was twenty when his ship was destroyed in 1944,' Wilfred added.

I'd put my foot in it again. My cheeks burned. 'I'm so sorry.'

'He were a braw lad. Our grandson looks like him.' Kitty fished a tissue from her sleeve and briefly dabbed it against the corner of her eye.

I seized my opportunity. 'Do you have any family left in the UK?'

'Not for a long time,' Kitty said.

I caught her eye. 'Everyone needs some support.'

'Maybe.' She looked away.

'Come on Samantha. Let these good people get on.' The inspector stood up. I followed suit.

'Thank you for the tea,' I said.

'Och, it's no trouble. Call in if you're passing,' Kitty said. My blunders apparently had been forgiven.

I followed the inspector out. I wanted to get a definite 'yes' from Kitty about getting help, but it looked like I was going to have to wait for that particular seed to germinate for a while.

In the car, Inspector Benjamin said, 'I could contact the Welfare Department, ask them to look in on Wilf. They might decide to contact the social services.'

'Kitty would not thank you for that. She was firm that she wanted to think about things. I think we should respect that and wait a while,' I said.

He quirked his lips as he thought. 'Okay, give it a little while longer, but if he continues to decline, I'm going to go to Welfare, with or without her say-so.'

Chapter Three

Trevor was already by the snooker table when Steve, Andy and I arrived for scoff. Judging by the position of the balls, he'd been there several minutes. I glanced at the clock which showed it was just one minute past six. How did he manage to sneak in early?

We claimed our seats at the big Formica table. It's funny how people stick to the same seats. It's like some unwritten rule that you stick to your own place.

Bert and Ray came in. Bert turned the radio onto his favourite channel, which wasn't ours, but Bert outranked us. Ray went over to play snooker with Trevor and Bert sat next to me and took his sandwich box out of his knapsack. Two hard boiled eggs, a Tupperware pot of salad, an apple and a banana. This was a change from his usual doorstep-sized sandwiches, crisps and family-sized chocolate bar. I tried not to stare but he caught me looking.

'The missus said I needed to eat healthier.'

'Oh.' I couldn't think of anything else to say.

'Be careful, Sarge. You don't want to lose weight; you need to fit into the Father Christmas costume,' Steve said.

Due to his generous girth, Bert was first choice for the divisional children's Christmas party Santa.

He shuffled closer to me and whispered, 'Do you get on okay with Trevor?'

Steve and Andy leaned in to hear.

'Fine. Why, Sarge?' I replied.

'I have to arrange the sprog's tutor,' he said.

'I don't think Trevor's ever had a sprog,' Steve said. 'He's also inclined to coast along.'

'What about Frank or John?' I suggested.

'John Batt hasn't had enough service. Frank Morton has only just had a sprog. I want to try to spread the load,' Bert said.

'Bill on Mike Four?' suggested Steve.

Bert laughed out loud. 'He's a good copper but I don't think he has the temperament to be a tutor. He's retiring at the end of the year anyway, so his heart won't be in it.'

'Is he?' Who would be offered Mike Four? Not me, I had only just passed my course. Ken might get it, though. Steve should really be the next in line, but a spell of sick leave following a serious injury had pushed him back a little way.

'I might have spoken out of turn. Pretend you didn't hear that,' Bert said.

'Hear what?' I asked.

'Good lass,' Bert said.

Trevor and Ray came over to eat their sandwiches and the conversation moved on. I was glad I hadn't had Trevor as my tutor. He wasn't a bad person, he was just after an easy life, but given the trouble I had had, I probably wouldn't have passed my probation with him tutoring me. Perhaps having a sprog would make him sharpen up his act.

Andy furtled in his pocket and pulled out a strip of card filled with blocks in various shades of blue.

'Look at this.' He laid the card on the table. 'All the shades of blue available to the public. I called into the car showroom and got it.'

'You are getting far too agitated about this,' I said.

He pointed to one block of colour. 'That is identical to the panda colour.'

'What shade of blue are police cars, Sarge?' I asked Bert.

'Dunno. You'd have to ask the garage,' he replied. He stared down at his meal and sighed loudly before picking up an egg and pushing it into his mouth whole.

'I'd bet my pension that one of these shades is identical,' Andy insisted. 'Come on, let's check.'

Bert thought Andy was overreacting and preferred to stay and eat his meal, so Steve, Trevor and I followed Andy downstairs into the yard. Andy held the card against a panda.

'That is very close,' I admitted. I could see why Andy was so worked about the new pandas being a plain colour; the public didn't always look closely at the police be it uniforms or cars but as lowly plods there was little we could do about it, so there was no point worrying about it.

'It's a bit darker,' Trevor said.

'No, it's the same,' Andy said.

'Everyone sees colours slightly differently, I've been told,' Steve said.

'Which is why I maintain that police cars should be conspicuously marked,' Andy said. 'Even a stripe down the side would help.'

I patted his shoulder. 'Okay, you've proved your point. When you're Chief Constable, you can paint the pandas with rainbows, if you like. Meantime, we just have to accept the decisions of the current senior officers. I'm going back to finish my scoff.'

'Me too,' Steve said.

I led the little group back up the stairs. Bert was already gone but Ray was just finishing his sandwiches.

'Well?'

'I was right,' Andy said, evidently pleased to be vindicated.

'There is a shade that's very close,' I agreed.

'There's some discussion that people see colours differently,' Trevor added.

'That's true,' Ray said. 'That's why when we take statements, one person will describe a blue car, someone else will say it's turquoise or green. They're not lying, they're just seeing differently.'

I sat down. 'Anyway, I'm tired of discussing it now.'

Andy rolled his eyes and also sat down. 'One day, they're

going to regret not having proper livery.'

*

After break, I was covering the control room with Ray while Derek, our call handler, went to eat.

'How are you getting on with your degree?' Ray asked.

'Okay, thanks. I'm starting the foundation course.'

'How are you fitting it around everything?' Ray asked.

'I'm not tied to a set time, which is the great thing about the Open University,' I replied. 'I've bought a video recorder, so I don't miss the programmes.'

'What's the subject?' Ray asked.

'I haven't decided yet; it can go a few ways,' I replied. The only thing I had decided was that I wanted to get more than a 2:2, because that was what Spider had, and it would annoy her that I had outdone her.

'You didn't go for the promotion exams?' Ray asked.

'I was going to, but I don't want to overdo things with that and the OU,' I replied. 'I'm still young enough that waiting to finish my degree before going for promotion won't matter too much.'

Spider came in as I finished speaking. 'You're doing a degree?'

'Yes.'

'You? You're doing a degree?'

'Yes. Why?' I felt vaguely insulted.

'You were just a...'

I raised an eyebrow daring her to say it. After school. I had worked in my uncle's restaurant in Canada before returning to the United Kingdom and joining the police. Or as Spider had once said, I had been 'just a waitress'.

She exhaled. 'Never mind. What in?'

It was beginning to feel like an interrogation, but I knew she didn't like anyone threatening her elevated view of herself.

'I haven't decided yet. I'm just doing the foundation course. I can decide which direction to take it when I finish that.'

'Ah, just a foundation degree,' Spider said.

I forced a smile. 'It's not a foundation degree; it will be a BA with honours. The foundation course is just the first year and is a springboard to several different subjects. It turns out that I'm not as thick as some people like to think.'

Spider ignored my barb. 'What's the point? You're already in the police.'

'So? You have a degree and so does my fiancé, so why not me? A degree might help my career,' I said.

'I'm guaranteed promotion, you won't be,' she said.

Ray coughed politely. 'Actually, that isn't strictly true.'

Spider folded her arms. 'You'll be calling me ma'am in very few years.'

'It isn't just handed to you on a plate,' Ray insisted. 'You still must pass the exams, and the force still have to recommend you for the special course, otherwise no graduate would work. They'd just sit back and wait for the pips to land on their shoulders.' Ray turned back to the radio to acknowledge a call.

Unable to argue back, Spider changed tack. 'Why have I never seen your fiancé?'

'He's in Hong Kong,' I replied.

'Is that why you reacted so badly to that dead Chinese baby a few months back? I thought you were having a nervous breakdown.'

Enough was enough. I gripped the hole puncher but resisted the urge to throw it at her.

'Shouldn't you be upstairs having your refs by now?' I thought I was very restrained given the provocation.

Spider huffed and left the room.

Earlier in the year, I had been getting somewhat stressed. I had dealt with a couple of difficult jobs, including the sudden death of a baby. At the same time, my family were coping with a horrendous situation, I had the press on my back, and everyone I was close to seemed to be moving away or recovering from injury. Maybe I had been headed for a nervous breakdown, but my good friend, Ray, had talked to me and helped me navigate my way to peace.

A few days' leave then going on my driving course had meant a month non-operational, which had been just what I needed to finish the job Ray started, and to get back on an even keel. However, Spider had the ability to wind me up within moments of interacting with her. It was as if she deliberately looked for a potential weakness in someone, then poked it. The trick with her was never to reveal a weakness.

'You know what I think would be funny?' Ray said when she was gone.

'What?' I was still imagining the hole puncher bouncing off Spider's head.

'Imagine if she failed the exams. Without the exams, she wouldn't get promoted, graduate or not.' He slapped his knee as he laughed. 'Don't tell her I said so.'

I laughed with him. 'Even better, imagine that she passes but isn't recommended for the special course. She'd have to compete for promotion like the rest of us.' I stopped laughing. 'It's unlikely though. She got an O for Knowledge on her last assessment. Also, if she was failing, she'd be given tutoring with the training officer to get her through.' Spider must have realised she wasn't the most popular person on the block, and I might have felt sorry for her if she wasn't so consistently obnoxious and dismissive of other people's achievements and efforts.

The phone rang and I picked up the receiver. 'Wyre Hall police station. How can I help you?'

'My daughter has been stopped in her car on her way home from work by a policeman. He didn't flash his lights or anything, he just pulled up in front of her forcing her to brake sharply. He then had the nerve to ask her out. He got nasty when she refused and threatened to wait for her and stop her every day. It's not right. You lot shouldn't be using your position to do things like that.' The woman sounded furious. I would be too.

'I absolutely agree with you. Can you tell me the constable's name and where this happened?' I asked. The boss was not going to be happy when he heard about this.

'He didn't give his name. It happened about an hour ago on Civic Boulevard.'

'Hold on a moment please.' I put my hand over the mouthpiece. 'Ray, who was in Civic Boulevard about an hour ago? A stop/check?'

Ray flipped through the job sheets. 'Nobody. In fact, the panda covering that area was at a job in Town Road then.'

'Okay, thanks.' I removed my hand. 'We've just checked the sheets, and we had nobody in that area at that time. Can you describe—'

'What do you mean by that? Don't you keep track of your patrols? A bloody copper is out harassing young girls, and you can't tell me who he is? What sort of Fred Karno's outfit are you?' The woman shouted.

I was a little offended at the suggestion that we were a shambles, but I remained calm.

'If you allow me to finish, our patrol covering that area was busy with another incident at that time, so if you can give me a description, I will make enquiries for you to find out who it was. Was he in uniform?'

'Yes, he was in uniform. I don't like your tone. I want to speak to the inspector. Put me through right now.'

I sighed and transferred the call.

'What was that?' Ray asked.

'A woman complaining her daughter was stopped by a policeman. She didn't like me telling her we had nobody there and insisted she spoke to the inspector.' Another complaint for me, probably.

'That is odd,' Ray said. 'We didn't even have a foot patrol there because he had gone to the job in Town Road too.'

'If she had given me a description, I would have an idea who it could have been,' I said.

'Maybe it wasn't one of ours,' Ray suggested.

'It's too far away to be Docks or Tunnels Police,' I said. 'Even British Transport Police wouldn't be operating there.

'I'll contact the force control room and see if they've had any courtesy calls from foreigners.'

I smiled at Ray referring to officers from other forces as foreigners. On the occasions we had to visit another force area, out of courtesy we would contact the control room of that force area to inform them of our presence. Usually, other forces returned the courtesy. The force control room was different from the divisional control rooms. They oversaw all the divisions, motorways and the departments that we would not normally deal with. They also received the 999 calls and calls from other forces then filtered the information down to the appropriate division or department. They would know if we had out-of-force visitors.

The internal phone rang. 'Control room,' I answered,

'Sam, it's Inspector Benjamin. Come to my office before you go back out.'

'Of course, sir.' That was me in the mire with the boss.

Ray said, 'Nobody has said they're visiting.'

'Then who?' I was at a loss.

'Imposter?' Ray suggested.

I had a thought. 'She said he was in a car, so it has to be someone with access to a police vehicle.'

Ray nodded. 'It does look that way.'

*

When Derek came back, Ray updated him on events while I went upstairs to see Inspector Benjamin. I tapped on the door and waited for him to call me in. Once in, I stood in front of the desk and waited for him to invite me to sit. He didn't invite me to sit. Not good.

'What can you tell me about your call with Mrs Edwards?'

he asked.

'Is she the one upset because a policeman stopped her daughter?' I asked. I wasn't trying to sound flippant, but I had taken several calls for various things and I wanted to be sure it was her seeing as I never got the angry woman's name.

Inspector Benjamin's mouth tightened. 'Yes. What did you say to Mrs Edwards?'

'She was pretty upset as I'm sure you know, sir. I checked who was in the area and both the panda and the foot patrol had been engaged in Town Road at the time her daughter was stopped. I asked her for a description in case it was one of the other patrols or someone from another force passing through, although we hadn't been informed of incomers, but all I got was that it was a male in uniform. She became terribly angry, said it was a Fred Karno's circus and demanded to speak to you.'

'Is that it? You didn't tell her to shut up?'

I blinked in surprise. 'Absolutely not, sir.'

'You didn't call her a liar because there was no patrol in the area?' Inspector Benjamin cocked his head.

'I didn't! I told her our patrol had been engaged and asked her for a description so I could make enquiries. She went off like a bottle of pop and I stopped her mid rant to try to get the description. Sir, I was trying to help her.'

'How did you stop her?'

'I said, "If you allow me finish," because she cut me off mid-sentence. I was trying to be helpful. Ask Ray.' I was furious at the lies. There was no need for it.

'Okay, I'll talk to Ray later. Dismissed.' Inspector Benjamin picked up a sheet of paper and began to read.

I left the office, careful not to slam the door behind me as I wanted to, and went down to the control room. What did the inspector mean, he'd talk to Ray later? Was it a threat? Tell the truth because I will find out? Let him speak to Ray, I had nothing to hide. Damn these people.

'What's up,' Ray asked when I went into the tiny office.

'That woman who rang about the harassment has complained about me. She said I told her to shut up and called her a liar. I didn't but she is a liar.' My lip felt quivery, not sad, just bloody angry.

Ray cocked an eyebrow. 'The nearest you got to sharp was asking her to allow you to finish.'

'Thank you,' I said. 'When the boss comes to speak to you, perhaps you can tell him that. Meantime, I'm going out.'

Ray smiled. 'Have a cuppa and calm down first. No point in going out and facing the public while you're angry. Make us one while you're about it.'

Despite my annoyance, I laughed. 'You just want me to make you a cup of tea and are using this as an excuse, aren't you?'

'Of course,' Ray admitted. He lit a cigarette from the stub of his last smoke, leant back in his chair, and rested an ankle on his knee. I went into the cupboard-sized telex room behind the control room and switched on the kettle.

As I was spooning sugar into the drinks, Inspector Benjamin came into the control room. I kept my back turned and pretended to be busier than I was stirring the mugs.

'Why are you still here, Sam? I won't have you hanging around the station when you should be out,' he snapped.

I turned around but before I could answer, Ray said, 'I asked her to make us a brew before she went out, sir.'

I appreciated Ray stepping in, but I resented that he had had to. I wondered if Trevor ever got that speech. He spent more time in the station than out of it, hence his nickname, Torchy. The Olympic torch that never went out.

Then I thought I had better make the inspector a drink too because, cross as I was, when it came down to it I wanted him on my side. However, he had made me feel like rubbish, so I would have my revenge. I dug out one of the old, tannin-stained mugs from the cardboard box in the battered, grey cabinet, put a teabag in that and added hot water.

'There's one for you too, sir.' I held out the old mug that

probably hadn't been washed in weeks.

He took it and thanked me. No apology though. Ray clocked the old mug and blinked once at me. I ignored it and gave a mug to him and to Derek, then I carried two to the sergeants' office on the other side of the enquiry office for Bert and Shaun.

I was just coming back for my own drink when someone came through the front door. Nobody on our block was permanently covering the enquiry office, the control room staff were managing it between them. I put my head around the control room door.

'Want me to deal with this?' I asked.

'Oh, yes. That would be helpful,' Ray said. He turned to Inspector Benjamin. 'Is that okay, sir?'

'Sure,' the boss said. 'In fact, Sam can stay in the enquiry office unless you're short staffed outside?'

That was a turnabout. Perhaps he was feeling guilty for being so snappy after all. I didn't regret giving him an old mug though.

'No, we're okay at the moment,' Ray said.

'Would you mind, Sam?' the inspector said.

'Of course.' I went to the desk and saw a teenaged girl with an angry looking middle-aged man.

'How can I help you?' I asked.

'I want to speak to your boss. One of your lads has harassed my daughter,' said the man.

This sounded familiar. 'I'm sorry to hear that. What happened?'

'Look, no offence, sweetheart, but I don't want to discuss it with you, I want someone who can do something about it.'

I didn't take offence, even at the "sweetheart". 'What's your name please.'

'Elliot.'

'I'll see if Sergeant Lloyd or Sergeant Mason is free, Mr Elliot.' I moved towards the sergeants' office, but the boss stepped into the enquiry office.

'I'll deal with this, Sam.' He turned to the desk. 'I'm Inspector George Benjamin. Would you like to come to my office to discuss this?'

'Aye, I would,' Mr Elliot said.

Inspector Benjamin went to the side door of the enquiry office, admitted Mr Elliot and his daughter, and walked them upstairs.

I went to the control room. 'Another one complaining about their daughter being harassed by a policeman.'

Derek rested his hands on his broad belly. 'Did he harass her, though? Policemen are prime targets for girls wanting a steady boyfriend with prospects. Maybe he rejected them, and this is their retaliation.'

It wasn't the first time he had expressed such opinions. I once overheard him say something similar about me.

'You're talking rubbish as usual, Derek.' I turned to Ray. 'Are you still thinking imposter?'

Ray shrugged. 'Hard to know what to make of it.'

I made a non-committal noise and returned to the enquiry office.

Chapter Four

I got back home just before midnight. I could hear the phone ringing as I closed the door. I knew who it would be. Gary rang regularly to catch up on the gossip, and to whisper filthy nothings into my eager ear. I rushed to answer the phone.

'Good evening,' I said. 'I take it you're on your lunch break.'

'I am. I hoped I would catch you,' Gary said.

'I've just got back. And you know I like to chill out for an hour before I'm ready to go to sleep.'

'Did you have a good shift?' Gary asked.

'Not bad. Wilfred got out again. Spider was her normal unpleasant self. We're getting another sprog. Oh, and there's someone in uniform, in a police car, going around harassing women.'

'What?! He needs an appointment with C and D!' Gary exclaimed.

C and D, Complaints and Discipline, would be the department to deal with this, if he was indeed a policeman.

'The weird thing is, he can't be one of ours. We don't know who he is, or where he's from. Ray reckons it's either someone from another force or an imposter,' I told him. 'I'm leaning towards imposter because the car described matches our pandas.'

'Bloody hell. Keep me posted on that,' Gary said.

'What's happening on your side of the planet?' I asked.

'Nothing out of the ordinary. I've got leave booked, so I'll be coming home for three weeks next month,' he replied.

'What date? Which airport?' I'd have to get my hair trimmed and book a manicure. A waxing session wouldn't go amiss either.

'October eleventh, Manchester,' Gary replied.

'I'll try to get leave too,' I said.

'Hold on, don't use up all your leave. I get more than you, also I was hoping you could fly out here at some point,' Gary said.

'Maybe a week then. The end of October so we can celebrate Halloween before you go back,' I suggested.

'That would be great, but I'm not walking up and down the street wearing a sheet over my head, shouting "Boo!" to strangers.'

I laughed. 'Alternatively, we could go to the Berni Inn overlooking the river. A prawn cocktail starter, steak. Black Forest Gateau and floater coffee, then back home for afters.'

'I like that idea better. I was thinking you could come out to Hong Kong at Easter next year,' Gary said.

'Easter's not until April fifteenth next year. We have a lot to discuss before that.' I reminded him. When Gary flew to Hong Kong, we had agreed to wait a year before deciding on our future.

'It's only a little while longer. Let's leave it until you come out, then we can talk properly,' Gary said.

'I'll have to get saving up for the air fare,' I said.

'You know I'll cover that for you,' he said.

'I love you,' I whispered.

'And I love you. So, how are you going to make me feel welcome when I get home?' he whispered back.

'Well, you remember that lingerie ensemble I wore when we went to London, the one with the balconette bra and French knickers?'

Gary sighed and I grinned. I was going to enjoy telling him my plans for him.

*

Next day, I walked past the fire station in the hope I would be invited in for a cup of tea. The doors were open, and I could see men moving around inside.

Chris Atherton waved at me. 'Hey, Sam.'

I waved back. 'Hi, Chris.'

He jogged over to me. 'I can't invite you in for a cuppa, the brass are here,' he said.

Well, that was disappointing. I'd have to try the children's hospital.

'Would you be interested in tickets for our charity dance in October?' Chris asked. 'It's on Saturday the fourteenth. We've rented the old dance hall on Manor Road.'

'Yes, I would. Gary will be home. I'll take two,' I said. 'Do you want the money now?'

'That would be great,' Chris said. 'We've got a competition going on who sells the most tickets. Winner gets a *Party 7*.'

Chris was referring to the large can of beer that was popular amongst the male population. It held seven pints and was useful for raffle prizes, gatherings and parties, hence the name.

'Oi, Atherton, stop chatting up the local fuzz,' someone called over to him.

'I've sold my first tickets,' he shouted back. 'Bring a couple over will you, Walter?'

The fireman came over to us. He didn't so much walk as rock from foot to foot, rather like one of the *Weebles* I had brought my cousin's little daughter for her birthday. This man would be forever etched into my memory as Walter the Weeble. I surmised from his great size that he was based in the office.

'Here you are.'

'Thanks, Walter.' Chris got a couple of tickets and passed them to me. I handed over the money.

'Walter used to be a bobby, didn't you, Walt.'

'Aye,' Walter replied.

Walter wasn't tall, probably just about the minimum height for police, and I guessed that he had put on weight since working in the office for the fire brigade.

'Where were you based?' I asked.

'Egilsby,' he replied.

'What's your name? Maybe I know someone who remembers you?'

'Walter Hodgeson, but I don't think anyone will remember me, I just did the training.'

That was possible. There was a fairly high dropout rate as people realised what the job actually entailed. Maybe I should have let it go there, but I pressed on because I was getting slightly hostile vibrations from Walter and that always made me curious. I wondered if he had left under a cloud. Perhaps he had jumped before he was pushed; a resignation on a CV always looked better than dismissal.

'Where did you train?' I asked.

'Egilsby.' Walter replied.

'That's a station, not a training school.'

He exhaled. 'Well, that's where I went. A senior officer spoke to us. I thought I'm handy in a fight so the police would be a good fit for me.'

'I take it you were unsuccessful when you applied.' A little spiteful, but my status as a qualified police officer was hard won and I resented him trying to pass himself off as a former police officer without even the training.

He looked behind him as if someone had called, although they hadn't.

'Got to go.' He weebled back into the station and disappeared.

'He wasn't in the police, was he?' Chris said.

'My guess is he went to a recruitment event, applied, and they knocked him back. I'm not surprised, if he thought being good in a fight was all he needed to be a policeman.' I put the tickets into my bag. 'I'll let you get on, Chris.'

'Come back later on when the brass have gone and I'll make you a brew.' He lowered his voice. 'Walter will be off duty after six.'

'I might take you up on that,' I said and resumed patrol.

'Tell everyone back at the station about the tickets,' he called after me.

An hour later, Ray transmitted, 'Mike Two from control.' The radio beeped as John Batt responded. 'Thanks, John. Can you attend Charles Street? Report of a fire. Persons reported trapped. Fire Brigade and Ambo are making.'

Something like people being trapped was serious enough for all three emergency services to be called out.

The radio beeped.

'Mike Sierra Two,' Ray continued. More beeping. 'Did you get the last? Fire Charles Street, persons trapped.'

Beeping.

'Roger thanks.'

I wasn't far away from Charles Street. '4912 to control, I can also attend.'

'Roger, thanks,' Ray responded.

Beeping signalled that someone else was calling up.

'Roger, Andy,' Ray said. 'Just wait for someone else to arrive before taking any action.' Ray paused. 'Mike Sierra Two, Con Broad is only in James Street and is backing up.'

A burst of beeping ended the exchange.

I jogged to the location and arrived just as two fire appliances drew up. Chris waved at me from one. I nodded an acknowledgement. The house was well ablaze. Flames licked up the walls and black, thick, acrid smoke rose into the sky. I could feel the heat from where I stood.

The fire crews leapt out and, with a speed born of practice, got the hoses out and directed the spray into the broken windows on the ground floor while other firemen, including Chris, suited up ready to enter the house. Another fireman advised the neighbours either side to stay away until a building inspector gave them the all-clear. The ambulance crew checked out a couple of soot-streaked men. Meantime, residents stood by their doors watching events, apart from the few who held back a woman who was screaming and kept trying to break away towards the house. Two other women spoke urgently to her, no doubt trying to make her see sense. I started out towards her.

Mike Sierra Two and Mike Two arrived at that moment. Shaun hurried over to me.

'Where's Andy?'

'I haven't seen him, Sarge,' I replied.

'He was only in James Street; he had to have been here first!'

I tried not to feel hurt at Shaun's sharp tone. It was a stressful situation; I knew Shaun's tension was not directed at me.

'I've only been here a couple of minutes. He wasn't here when I arrived.'

As one we turned towards the burning building.

'Oh no,' I said.

'He knows not to rush in!' Shaun cried.

One of the men with the ambulance crew jogged over to us, still with dirt-streaked clothing and blood on his face. 'There's a child in the back bedroom. We couldn't reach her. A young bobby went in and hasn't come out.'

A crash from inside told us part of the upstairs floor had collapsed. Were Andy and the child lying dead, or even worse, alive under burning debris? I gulped. The mother sank to her knees, her screams louder than the pandemonium around us. Her companions crouched beside her, stroking her hands, her hair, anywhere they could reach that might calm her. She had to have been heard for miles. Wilfred and Kitty didn't live far away. I knew Wilfred's policing instincts would drive him to find out what was wrong, and I hoped Kitty would be able to contain him. The last thing we needed was for him to appear.

I ran over to a nearby fireman. 'We think one of our lads has gone inside after the kiddie.'

He waved an arm to the fire crews and shouted, 'Possibly two casualties!' He held two fingers up to confirm his words.

A second later, Andy, blackened and scorched, staggered from the entry a little way along the road. An equally filthy, small girl clung to his back like a koala. Both were coughing fit to bring up a lung each. The Ambos, Inspector Benjamin, Shaun and I raced over to them. The mother grabbed the girl, but the Ambos eased the child from her and began work clearing her nose and mouth and administering oxygen. The mother clutched at Andy, babbling her thanks. Inspector Benjamin gently detached the woman and took her over to the ambulance, where her daughter had been taken.

Shaun, whether from fear or relief, yelled at Andy. 'What the hell do you think you were doing? You were told not to act until someone else arrived.'

Andy bent forward as another bout of coughing immobilised him. Once he had stopped, he spat black gunk onto the ground, wiped his mouth and straightened up.

'What the hell was I supposed to do?' he shouted back. His voice sounded raspy. 'I was first on the scene! Mother was hysterical and trying to run into the fire. The neighbours were holding her back. Two men were trying and failing to get inside. I couldn't just stand there waiting for you while a child burned to death!' Andy coughed up more black gunk.

Shaun stood with his mouth flapping. Andy had never been heard to raise his voice to anyone before.

'How did you get out?' I asked. 'We heard a crash.'

'I went out of the bathroom window, shinned down the drainpipe then came around the entry.' He held out his hands, which were bloody and burnt. 'My hands hurt.'

The incident continued around us as we spoke. The firemen slowly brought the fire under control. Another ambulance arrived as the first ambulance whisked the mother and child to the general hospital.

Shaun touched Andy's shoulder. 'Come on, let's get those hands looked at. I'll feel happier if you get some oxygen, too.' He walked Andy to the ambulance. A few neighbours came over and clapped Andy on the back. He winced but took their show of appreciation.

I felt somewhat surplus to requirements, so I went over to

the inspector, who had been liaising with the senior fire officer.

'Sir, the mother and child are on their way to hospital. Andy's hands are burnt and he's coughing up black. Shaun has told the Ambos to check him out, too.'

'Are the burns bad?' the inspector asked.

'I'm not sure,' I replied truthfully. I wasn't medically trained, so something that looked bad to me might be trivial. 'What do you want me to do now?' I asked.

He looked around then turned to the senior fire officer. 'I think everything is under control?'

The senior fire officer nodded. 'Actually, if you can persuade a couple of the neighbours to provide cuppas for the lads, that would be great. Maybe some biscuits too.'

So that's what I did. Most of the neighbours wanted to help in some way. I enjoyed the idea that, in an office somewhere, someone was scratching their heads at the sudden localised surge in demand for energy as multiple kettles were filled and boiled. Now everyone knew the kiddie was safe, the mood was a lot lighter, although we were concerned when the ambos insisted that Andy be taken to the general hospital too.

I spotted Chris near the front door of the destroyed house. He beckoned me over. I could still feel heat from the building. Steam mingled with black smoke and slowly rose. Water dripped from exposed, charred beams.

'If anyone asks, I didn't tell you. This wasn't arson. The fire investigators will have to look at it before it's official, but it wasn't deliberate. Don't go inside, but take a look,' Chris said.

I peeped through the ruined front door and into the blackened hallway. 'How can you be so sure this was an accident?'

'Accidental fire usually smoulders then burns. It flows up and out in a V pattern.'

I looked at the devastation around me. I couldn't make out a V pattern, or any pattern. 'I can't see a V.'

'Just inside the kitchen door at the end of the hall.'

It wasn't well defined, but when he pointed it out, I could

see it.

'If accelerant is used then fire will not smoulder, it will go straight up, so no V pattern. If a lot has been used it will flare or burst, possibly injuring the offender. If accelerant has been spread over a wide area, the fire will jump. This has none of that.'

'I can see lots of areas that have been burned. Won't the original seat of the fire become part of the whole fire? Won't the fire just destroy everything, even with accelerant?' I asked. I believed Chris when he said it wasn't arson, but I was playing devil's advocate.

'That can happen, which is why we need to find the origin. If you know what you're looking for, you can usually find it. I think it'll be something shorting out in the kitchen.' Chris moved closer to me and pointed to the floor. 'Have you noticed anything else?'

I let my eyes wander over the floor, but much of it was covered by the fallen ceiling. 'No.'

'As fire burns in the upper levels, debris will fall from the ceiling. If there is fine dust, it shows that the upper levels burned longest and therefore started first.'

'There's no fine dust,' I said.

'Exactly.'

I stared around, open mouthed. 'I had no idea firefighting was so technical.'

He grinned, 'I think this is all fascinating. I want to specialise in fire investigation.'

'You would be like a detective.' I turned towards him and caught him studying me. He didn't look away. Neither of us spoke for a moment and I felt my cheeks grow warm, but that might have been residual heat from the fire.

'What colour do you think of when you think of fire?' he asked.

'Yellow or red,' I replied, glad the awkward feeling was gone.

'Did you know flame can also be blue and even green?'

'I know they use chemicals and stuff to make different

coloured fireworks,' I said.

'Yes, but it's not just a chemical thing, flame changes colour with temperature. A blue flame is the fiercest, a red flame the coolest.'

'Come to think of it, the flames on a cooker are blue, but white is hottest of all, isn't it?' I had a vague memory of an experiment we did at school. Physics and chemistry had been my worst subjects, so I had dropped them as soon as possible.

'Yes, but it's unlikely you'll encounter that outside of an industrial setting. Blue will be the hottest you'll see in a domestic setting,' Chris said.

'You'll make a great fire investigator. You're halfway there already.' I meant it. I was impressed.

Chris beamed. 'Thanks.

'Sam!'

I turned towards Shaun. 'Sarge?'

He waved me over.

'Got to go. Nice speaking to you, Chris.' I hurried over to Shaun and the others.

'We're resuming. Steve and Mike Two are going to take over the scene for now. The road will be blocked for some time yet.' Shaun paused. 'I'm going to recommend Andy for a commendation.'

'That's a great idea. He certainly went above and beyond,' John said.

Inspector Benjamin nodded. 'I'd endorse that.'

'How about the two men who tried to get to the child? Their efforts should be acknowledged, too,' I said.

'I'll put all three forward for recognition,' the boss said. 'Do we have their names?'

'We can soon find out,' John said. He went to speak to some neighbours and came back in no time with their details.

'Right. That's decided then. You lot get on and I'll go to the hospital to check on our lad,' Inspector Benjamin said.

*

We didn't meet up again until knocking-off time. We stood in the corridor outside the bridewell, waiting for the boss to sign our pocketbooks and to dismiss us.

The boss came out of the sergeants' office. 'All right you lot?'

'Sir,' we all replied.

'Andy is being kept in hospital due to smoke inhalation,' the boss said.

We all knew that that could be more serious than it sounded. Pulmonary oedema was an unpleasant and sometimes fatal side effect.

The boss continued. 'He'll be signed off sick for a couple of weeks to give his lungs and hands a chance to heal.'

'Is he badly burned?' I asked.

'Not too bad as it turns out. His legs were a bit singed too, but he'll be okay if his lungs behave.'

We breathed a collective sigh of relief.

'What about the kiddie?' John asked.

'Doing well. A few superficial burns and scrapes, but she'll go home once they've dealt with the smoke inhalation. Mum hasn't been admitted, but she and the father are camped out beside the child. She's traumatised but not enough to warrant calling the duty psych. Once the child has been released, they should both be fine.'

A good result. It could have been so much worse without Andy's intervention.

'Wilfred's gone again,' called Derek from the control room.

Inspector Benjamin looked at his watch. 'Let the night crew deal with it.' He turned his attention back to us. 'If any of you spot Wilf on your way home, find a phone box and ring it in. By the way, Carol Shilling is still outstanding. If you spot anyone fitting her description, ring that in too. Dismissed.'

As we made our way out, a couple of bobbies came out of the parade room. No doubt they were going to get Wilf. They nodded as they passed us. We nodded back and went home.

49

Chapter Five

Nights started fairly uneventfully, apart from the usual arrests, the odd fight, and disorderly behaviour outside the pubs and clubs. After break, it was tranquil. We could catch up with paperwork or silently patrol, looking out for suspicious people who might be thinking of burgling somewhere, and at four in the morning anyone skulking about was worthy of a stop/check.

Carol Shilling still hadn't turned up either, which was worrying. Most mispers were long back by now. Her file had been passed over for further investigation by another department, but we still had to keep our eyes open for her. Would she still be wearing a purple top, or had she planned to stay away and had taken a change of clothing with her?

On the Friday, after my break, I was patrolling by the church in a pleasant, recently built area known as "The Med" as all the roads there were named after Mediterranean islands. Most areas of town were named along a theme chosen by the town planners of the time. Perhaps, in this case, the town planners were thinking of their holidays, or maybe they wanted to brighten the town up. We, and the public, quickly adopted nicknames for the places. If we weren't sure of the name of a road, we could at least pin down the area.

As I approached Cyprus Road, I spotted a panda car flit past under a streetlight a short distance ahead, heading away from my direction. Probably, it was Mike Two. Unusually, the roof light was not on. John was normally quite particular about things like that. I didn't have time to wonder about that, because

I smelt something burning. I hurried towards the source of the smell and stopped in dismay when I saw a car burning on a driveway. All lights were off, so I had to alert the occupants. As I ran, I radioed in the job. It wasn't a scramble call as I didn't need everyone here, but I needed to get the fire brigade ASAP.

'4912 urgent.'

'Go ahead,' Ray replied at once.

'I need the fire brigade to Cyprus Road. There's a car on fire on a driveway.'

'What number?' Ray asked.

'Not sure yet but they won't be able to miss it,' I radioed back. Stupid question, it wasn't a long road. 'Fifteen,' I transmitted as I drew closer.

I listened to Ray directing patrols and supervision to my location. Derek would be on the phone to the fire brigade. I needed to get to the door without frying myself on the burning car. I went through the next-door neighbour's garden and banged on their door as I passed, then hammered on the door of number fifteen. I wasn't trying to be quiet, and the next-door neighbour opened a bedroom window and looked out.

'Bloody hell!' he exclaimed.

'You need to get out,' I shouted.

'4912, Fire en route,' Ray transmitted.

Finally, the occupant of number fifteen looked out. It was Mr Elliot, who had come with his daughter to the station. I didn't have time to discuss that with him just then.

'You need to get out! Evacuate now!' I called to him. He ducked back inside. 'Go through the back,' I shouted at the open window. I didn't know if he heard me.

Other neighbours came out in their nightwear.

'Stay back,' I shouted. The flames were getting higher, and I didn't know if the car would explode. The heat was uncomfortable, I wanted to get away from it. Where the hell was Mike Two? He hadn't been that at far away when I'd seen him, he should be here by now.

I ran to the house next door on the other side to warn them, but met them as they trooped out in their dressing gowns.

'Stay on the other side of the road,' I called.

A fire engine turned into the road and pulled up a short distance from the car. I left the crew to do their thing and went to see the Elliots, who were coming from a pathway a little further down the road. Mrs Elliot and daughter went to the opposite side of the road as instructed. Mr Elliot came over to me.

'It's him, isn't it. The copper that stopped my daughter. Why wasn't he locked up?' Mr Elliot demanded.

'I don't have the answer to that. I'd have to speak to the inspector.' I replied.

Mike Sierra Two arrived. Shaun got out and came over. 'Did you see anyone?'

'No. I smelt the fire and came to check it out.' I paused. Shaun needed to know about Mr Elliot's theory. 'Mr Elliot came into the station a little while back to complain about a policeman harassing his daughter. Apparently, he made threats because she refused to go out with him,'

'You must have heard about it,' Mr Elliot said.

'Yes, but we still don't know who it is. We don't believe he's one of ours so we're still making enquiries.'

'Bloody hell.' Mr Elliot ran a hand across his head and turned towards his destroyed car. Flames were now reaching for the fence.

Mike Two pulled up and John came over to us.

'You took your time,' I complained.

'Wind it in! I got here as fast as I could,' he objected.

I pointed towards the road I'd seen him. 'I saw you up there just a minute before I found this fire.'

'I've come straight from the station.' John pointed in the opposite direction and frowned.

I looked at the panda. The sign was lit, unlike the other panda I'd seen, but that would only take a flick of a switch, however…

The fire crew had extinguished the fire and had started putting their equipment away. One came over to us, interrupting my thought process.

'This was deliberately started. It looks like an accelerant has been poured around the bonnet.'

'We need to get the car removed for investigation,' Shaun said.

I radioed up and made the arrangements, but Ray was so efficient, I wouldn't have been surprised if he had already done that.

'What now?' Mr Elliot asked.

'We and the fire examiners will conduct an investigation on the car. Meantime, enquiries are ongoing about this mystery policeman. You need to let your insurance know what's happened,' Shaun said.

A car came into the road and a familiar figure climbed out.

'What do we have, m'darlin'?' DC Eamon Kildea called to me. I loved that man's rich, Irish voice. I'd forgotten he was the night detective, or "jack" as we called them.

I pointed to the wreckage. 'Arson.'

Eamon came over. 'And would you be the owner?' he asked Mr Elliot

'Aye,' Mr Elliot answered.

'Grand. I'll need to have a chat with you if you don't mind. Just let me talk to the fire crews for a wee while.' Eamon went over to the fire appliance.

I noticed that Inspector Benjamin hadn't arrived. Normally he'd attend anything like this.

'I'll go and speak to the neighbours. See if anyone heard or saw anything,' I told Shaun. He nodded in an absent-minded manner and continued to speak with Mr Elliot.

Nobody had heard anything much less saw anything. Hardly surprising given that it was only just five a.m. now and they had been asleep.

I heard the radio in the fire appliance chattering away. The fireman monitoring it picked up the handset and said, 'We can make that. We're just about finished here.'

He came over to Shaun. 'There's a bin fire got a bit out of control on the industrial estate. We've spoken to your detective. Are you okay here now?'

'Fine,' Shaun answered. 'The car will be shifted shortly. Our detective is speaking to the family.'

'We'll pass everything on to the Fire Investigator. Liaise with them.' The fire crew boarded the appliance and moved on to the next job.

I remembered the mystery panda car. I waited for Eamon to finish speaking to the Elliots then approached him.

'Eamon, this might be nothing but, just before I found the fire, I saw a panda car headed away from me. It didn't have the roof light on. It wasn't John because he said he came here straight from the station.'

'You're sure it was one of ours?' Eamon asked. 'The yellow streetlights can alter the look of a colour.'

I'd seen enough panda cars to recognise the colour, yellow sodium lights or not. 'It was a plain colour, just like ours and the shape was the same as ours. The sign wasn't illuminated if it was there at all. I was too far away to tell.'

Eamon thought for a few seconds then transmitted, 'DC Kildea to control.'

'Go ahead, Eamon,' Ray responded.

'Do we have any out-of-force visitors in the area?'

'Not that I'm aware of,' Ray replied.

'Thanks. Out.' Eamon rubbed his chin. 'It won't be the force next door because their pandas aren't plain blue.'

'Ports Police and British Transport Police have liveried vehicles, and Tunnels Police use jeeps,' I said.

'It's something to think about,' Eamon agreed.

*

By six-thirty, the car had been removed and residents had

returned home to their homes. The Elliots' house had suffered some scorching around the door and the fence, but the rest were undamaged. I accepted a lift back to the station in John's panda and settled myself into the report writing room to get the paperwork done on the arson. I was supposed to be off duty at seven, but I knew I was going to have to stay on if I was going to get this report submitted in good time. Then my input would probably end, as CID would take over our side of the investigation. I would only be required if the offender was found and pleaded not guilty at court.

I felt a little guilty that I had hardly given Carol Shilling a thought, but I had been busy and I could not be everywhere all at once. I just had to trust that those not involved with the arson were keeping a look out for her.

Eamon came in a short time later. 'Mr Elliot said he recognised you from the front desk. What's this about a rogue bobby? Is that why you were so bothered about that panda you spotted?'

'We had two complaints in quick succession about a bobby in a car harassing girls, but it wasn't our patrol. Speak to Ray, he created a job sheet for it.'

'No clues?' Eamon asked.

'Not a sausage,' I replied.

Eamon rubbed his chin. 'Mr Elliot isn't entirely convinced that we're not covering up for one of our own.'

'Did you tell him that we go harder on our own than with outsiders?' I asked.

'I did, m'darlin', but I don't think that helped.'

Derek came into the room. 'Sorry to do this to you so close to knocking-off, Eamon, but fire have been on the line. They're at a bin fire that has turned out to be more serious than expected.'

Eamon groaned. 'Let me guess. There's a load of property that is connected to a nearby burglary.'

'Worse,' Derek said. 'There's a body.'

My jaw dropped. 'Do you need me to go back out?' I was tired and busy, but I felt I should offer. The morning crew were only just arriving for parade.

'No, it's on Mike One's patch. We've already asked Frank and Charlotte to remain on duty until their relief arrives,' Derek said.

'What's the circs?' Eamon asked.

'Apparently it was one of those big dumpsters. When they checked it after the fire was out, they found a body in there. It's a bit of a mess. They can't tell what injury was there before or what was caused by the fire. Ray's on to the duty DI.'

'Jesus!' Eamon stood up. 'Right m'darlin', I'll have to leave you. If you get any more information about the mystery man, let me know.' He followed Derek out.

It occurred to me that Spider was going to have to get her hands dirty. If it hadn't been disrespectful to the deceased, I would have sniggered.

*

Once everyone who was going off duty had had their notebooks signed off, Steve popped into the report writing room with Bert, who wanted to sign my book in lieu of Inspector Benjamin, who was still not back. I wasn't going to go back out now, so I quickly jotted that I was engaged with paperwork for the remainder of my shift and Bert signed it. I would make a note underneath of my actual off duty time.

'Do you know anything about the body in the bin?' I asked.

'Very little so far,' Bert replied. 'The jacks are thinking she might be one of the cows.'

A prostitute from the docks. I wondered if I knew her. 'Any name yet?'

Bert shook his head. 'And remember, this isn't for public consumption yet.'

We all knew well enough not to spread what we heard in the station.

'Has Carol Shilling been found yet?' I asked. I had a nasty hypothesis forming in my mind. If the body wasn't one of the girls from the docks, maybe it was Carol.

'No.' I could tell Bert knew what I was thinking but he chose not to explore it. 'Right, get off home. Sleep well.' Bert returned to the office.

'What are you working on?' Steve asked.

'Paperwork for that arson in Cyprus Road,' I said.

'Do you think there could be a connection with the bin fire?'

I shrugged. 'Eamon's the one to speak to about that.'

'It's in a different area. It might just be a coincidence,' Steve said. 'Right, I'll let you get on. See you tonight, Sam.'

Steve left, and I plodded on through the paperwork.

*

It was approaching eight when I finally was able to leave. I was just going into the locker room when I saw Frank and Spider coming in from the yard.

'How was it?' I asked.

Frank shook his head. 'A mess. We still had to wait for a doctor to confirm death.'

'It's bloody ridiculous,' Spider declared. 'It was obvious she was dead; she wasn't even in one piece. Apparently, the heat caused her to swell so much, her insides burst out.'

My lip curled involuntarily at the image that came to my mind.

'But nooo, we're not trained for that,' Spider continued, 'We can't declare life extinct even when it's bloody obvious.' Spider tugged at her perfectly-fitted jacket. Not for the first time, I wondered whether she had paid to have it altered. 'I stink of burnt rubbish and death. I'll have to get a chitty for a new uniform. I can't be expected to wear this again.'

'Most of us just put our uniforms in for cleaning after a messy job,' I said. And were more respectful of the dead.

'Some of us have standards.' She sniffed her sleeve. 'I don't think there's enough bath oil in the world to get this smell out of my nose.' Spider stalked off towards the locker room.

'She really doesn't like getting her hands dirty,' I commented to Frank, who wore the long-suffering expression of a parent watching their child throw a tantrum.

'She didn't get her hands dirty. We just had to stand nearby to keep the scene secure. Charlotte was so far back she was standing practically in the next division. The morning crew came before the doctor arrived to confirm life extinct.'

I couldn't help but think that Spider was in the wrong job; she'd have been much better off staying with the civil service.

'Frank, what was the body wearing?' I asked.

He shrugged his shoulders. 'Impossible to say. It was all burnt.'

We'd have to wait for the pathologist to do his report, then. I hoped I was wrong.

*

That afternoon, I woke up earlier than normal. My mind drifted to the woman in the bin. The case had nothing to do with me, but it played on my mind. Who would put someone in a bin and set fire to it? I wondered if she had been identified yet. If she was one of the cows, I knew who to speak to about that.

I got up, showered, and had a quick cup of tea. Then I went to see my friend, Karen Fitzroy, who had a stall in the market. I didn't want to just pass her name on to Eamon, I was sure she wouldn't appreciate that. Before starting her sewing business, Karen had worked on the docks. She had been, and to some extent still was, an advisor/advocate and shoulder to cry on for the girls still there. If anyone knew about a missing girl, it would be her.

I found her in her stall, sitting at the sewing machine. I slipped behind her stall and turned on the kettle as she finished the piece she was working on.

'I take it business is good?'

'Growing nicely.' She finished her piece, shook it out and folded it before placing it on the table next to her. 'I'm moving into the main hall of the market. It's a bigger stall and I'll have space for a proper changing room.' She accepted the cup of tea I held out to her.

'That's great!'

She smiled. 'Yeah, I'm quite pleased.' She sipped her brew. 'Also, I've put a deposit down on a two bedroomed house by the priory. Benedict Street. It's an easy walking distance from here, and in a nicer area than my current hovel. The rent's a bit more, but I can manage that.'

'Your house is not a hovel, you've got it looking lovely, but I'm glad you're moving. You'll get a good view of the river from Benedict Street,' I said.

'Yeah. It does have a nice view from the back bedroom. I might make that my sewing room so I can watch the boats while I work. The kitchen is bigger, and I'll have a separate dining room. I've never had a dining room before.' She beamed. 'You'll have to come for your tea once I'm sorted out. I might even bake a cake for afters.'

'Sounds lovely,' I said. I had always known Karen could do well for herself if she could get away from the docks. I wanted to ask about the girl in the bin, but I knew I had to be careful about what I said. 'Karen, do you know, is everyone all right? Have any of the girls been missed recently?'

Karen laughed without humour. 'Half those girls don't have anyone who would miss them. Pimps wouldn't admit to a missing girl, in fact a good proportion of them are likely responsible for any disappearances. Bonk them on the head with something heavy and dump them in the river.' She took another mouthful of tea. 'I haven't heard of anyone dropping off the radar recently. Ruthie Pritchard hasn't finally overdosed, has she?' Karen asked. I caught the fleeting look of concern that crossed her face.

'We all know Ruthie, it isn't her. I can't say anything more.' I replied. 'If you do hear of anyone who hasn't been seen for a little while, would you ring it in, or phone me?'

'I will, Sam.'

Good enough. I trusted her not to speak about anything I mentioned to her.

We chatted for a while longer, mostly about colour schemes. Karen was leaning towards lime green for the kitchen walls. I preferred more neutral colours, but Karen said they weren't fashionable.

After half an hour or so, I stood up. 'I'd better let you get on.'

'I'll keep my ears open about that girl,' Karen said.

'Yeah, thanks. It isn't my job but I'm curious. If you do hear anything, is it okay if I pass it on to the jacks?' I asked. Karen had had enough dealings with police over the years to understand jargon.

'Sure. Try to keep me out of it though,' Karen said.

I was satisfied that I had done all I could do for now. If the girl in the bin was not Carol Shilling, Karen's help would give us more information to identify her.

Chapter Six

'Job for you. Wilfred's done one again.' Ray handed me a job sheet.

This was not good. It was three a.m. Kitty must have woken up and noticed him gone. How she must have panicked. Normally, she would notice within a few minutes, but now, he could have been gone for hours Wilfred seemed to stick to places that were familiar to him from his policing days. I decided the best thing I could do was to go to the school.

I crossed the empty road and walked up the hill beside the school. As was common in Victorian times, the building was designed to separate girls and infants from rowdy boys. The solution here was to have two playgrounds, one either side of the building, which were still segregated at playtime.

I was walking past the boys' playground when I spotted Wilfred standing like a statue by the school gate. He was peering into the empty girls' and infants' playground, one hand resting on the railings. He had put his coat on over his pyjamas but was barefoot. I felt deeply uneasy at this development.

I walked up to him. 'Hello, Wilfred.'

He jumped. 'Oh, hello.' He turned back to the playground. 'Where are the children? I have to make sure they're safe.'

'In bed, I hope. It's the middle of the night, Wilf,' I said as gently as I could. 'The crossing patrol will be here on Monday morning. He'll make sure nobody gets hurt,' I said.

Wilfred looked around as if surprised to see the streetlights and the stars in the sky. Apparently, Wilf had been a tall man, six foot four inches in his day. He had lost some of that height now, but I still had to look up to talk to him. A tear ran from his eye. Somehow, it always seemed extra sad when a large man cried.

'What's happening?'

I wasn't sure whether he was referring to his own situation or if he was confused by the empty playground. I put my arm through his. He felt cold.

'It's time for us to get back now. Kitty is worried about you.' I radioed in and asked for a car to meet us. I knew Ray would ring Kitty so she could stop worrying.

'How long have you been out, Wilf?' I asked.

He stared back at me as if I'd asked him to dance a waltz in the road. I wasn't even sure he recognised me. This was the worst I'd ever seen him.

Mike Two arrived and John opened the door. 'Hop in Wilf. I'll take you back to the station. You can warm up with a nice cuppa.'

Wilf got in the car. 'Actually, I think I would like to go straight home.'

Something had changed in Wilf; he was never normally so low, and he would never pass up a chance to go back for a brew and a gossip. I needed to tell the inspector it was time to bring in the Welfare department. Kitty was not going to like it, but needs must.

'Yes, let's get in the car and get you home,' I said.

Wilf took shotgun while I climbed in the back. He still appeared to be oblivious to his attire.

As John drove us towards the main road, Ray gave out general observations for a blue Vauxhall Viva, the driver of which had harassed a female member of the public.

'Do you think it's our phantom patrol?' I asked John.

'What's that, lass?' Bert asked.

'Nothing for you to worry about Wilf,' I said.

'Don't talk down to me, girl,' he snapped.

'Sorry, Wilfred.' I couldn't tell if he was in the present or still working in the past, but whichever it was, he knew when he was being patronised.

'There's someone in a blue Vauxhall Viva that's been pulling over young women and trying to get a date. He gets nasty if they refuse,' John said.

'Someone needs to teach him a lesson the old-fashioned way,' Wilfred said. 'Have you got a marble in your glove?'

'What!?' I exclaimed. I had always thought that stories about marbles in gloves were urban legends.

'We'd get into trouble if we did that, Wilf,' John said.

Wilf stiffened like a pointer terrier. 'Go back!'

John braked sharply. 'What is it?'

'Go back. I'm sure I saw a blue Vauxhall Viva tucked into the alley beside that shop,' Wilfred said.

John reversed a short way. Sure enough, in an alley between two shops was a light blue Vauxhall Viva.

'Well spotted,' John said.

'I think there's someone in the driver's seat,' I said.

Wilfred opened his door ready to get out.

'No, you stay here and watch the car,' John said to him. I was pleased to hear John give Wilfred a role instead of making him feel surplus to requirements.

'You can't expect the lass to deal with someone like that,' Wilfred objected. 'Let her mind the car.'

'John will deal with this. I'm just making up numbers. You watch the car, like John said. Anyone trying anything with the panda will be far more intimidated by you than me.' I got out before Wilfred could object any more.

Before we had taken more than a step, the Vauxhall Viva engine roared and it shot out of the alley and skid-turned up the road with its lights out. John and I jumped back into our panda. I shouted up a description and the single letter of registration number I had seen.

'Get after it!' Wilfred cried.

'I can't, Wilf,' John said.

'Ah, we've got a lass with us. Never mind, the others will get it,' he said.

I caught John's eye in the mirror. We couldn't chase with Wilfred in the car, but neither of us wanted to tell Wilfred that.

'You're right. Let's get you back, Wilf, then Sam and I will update the job sheet,' John said.

We dropped Wilf off at home. Kitty, wrapped in a red dressing gown with tasselled, tartan slippers on her feet, was in full flow about his 'thick heid'. Wilf just held up a hand.

'Please don't start, Kitty. I'm going to bed.'

We all watched him climb the stairs as if each foot weighed a ton.

'Kitty, have you given some thought about what we spoke about?' I asked.

She pursed her lips. 'It's my job to look after him.'

'You can't stay awake all day and all night. Nobody can,' I argued.

'I'll just lock the door and hide the key,' she said.

I upped the ante. 'He was by the school again, but what if he had gone to the docks? He might have fallen in, and we'd never have known. There are so many dangers out there. Please, Kitty, consider having some help. Or at least an assessment.' Whatever she said, I was going to speak to Inspector Benjamin.

She didn't reply for a minute and I thought she was going reject my suggestion again, but she said, 'Some say policing is a calling. It was for Wilf. He was born to be a policeman. It broke his heart when he finally had to leave.'

I smiled. 'My old sergeant was like that. He hung on as long as possible.'

Kitty remained silent for a moment then said, 'Maybe an assessment.'

'Great! I'll speak to the inspector. He'll contact the Welfare department. I don't know if they'll come out or if they'll contact social services. Maybe both.'

She nodded. I knew she wasn't happy, but she had begun to accept the inevitable.

'He was joking about the marble, wasn't he?' I asked as John drove us back to Wyre Hall.

'I'm not sure to be honest,' John admitted.

'Blooming heck, that's only one step away from a snooker ball in a sock.'

We went straight to the control room when we got back to the station.

'Have we had other reports of someone stopping females?' I asked.

Ray passed two job sheets he had left to one side from the previous shift. Same story as the rest.

'It's got to be that car Wilfred spotted,' I said to John.

'Shame we had to let him go,' John replied.

'Hey, Ray, in the old days, did you really put a marble in your glove?' I asked.

Derek and Ray chuckled.

'I didn't. I take it Wilfred has been reminiscing,' Ray said.

'A couple of the older chaps did apparently,' Derek answered.

I was stunned. 'But that's so dangerous.'

'So is whacking someone with a wooden stick,' Ray pointed out. 'If people behave, they needn't worry about either.'

I shook my head. 'I'm glad we don't do that now.'

'I'm a bit thirsty, I could just go a can of pop,' Ray nodded towards my bag.

'You normally like tea…' I began. Then the penny dropped. 'Oh. That's different,' I snapped.

'Is it?' Ray was persistent.

'Of course it is,' I insisted. 'Where else am I supposed to put my drink?'

I didn't have anything with which to defend myself other than my soft, leather handbag. In our force, females were not given a truncheon or even a little baton as in some other forces. Carrying a drink with me would add some heft to my bag if I ever needed to swing it at someone. Actually, when I thought about it, a marble in a glove was not dissimilar to me carrying a can of pop in my bag, just less explainable. It was not unreasonable to have a drink with me, given the miles we walked each day.

'Never mind, I'm still thirsty, so pop the kettle on, will you?' Ray asked.

I sighed and went into the telex room. My life in the station revolved around making tea in the telex room.

When everyone was served, I carried the boss' tea upstairs. I needed to update him on Kitty anyway. I tapped on the door but got no response. I knocked a little louder and Inspector Benjamin yanked the door open.

'What?!'

I was taken aback by the sharp response. I stepped back and stammered my first few words, but he cut across me.

'What are you doing back in? Your shift finishes at seven. If you need more work, I can soon find you some.'

I was still standing in the corridor and did not want a rollicking in public. Okay, it was nights and there was nobody around, but it was the principle.

'Have I done something to annoy you, sir? If so, I would appreciate discussing it in your office, not on the corridor.'

He exhaled loudly and stepped aside. 'Come in.'

I entered his office put down the mug and stood "at ease" in front of the desk staring into the middle distance. I thought formality was the way to go while he was in this mood.

He sat down. 'No, you haven't done anything that I'm aware of. I'm not at my best on nights so I'm sorry if I came across as irritable. Stand easy.'

I relaxed my stance. 'Thank you, sir.' I hadn't previously seen evidence that he was not at his best on nights.

'What did you come to see me about?' he asked.

'Wilfred. He's back home. I had a chat with Kitty and she's agreed to an assessment.'

Inspector Benjamin smiled a genuine smile. 'That's great. About time. I'll leave a message for the morning inspector to give Welfare a ring.'

'I'll resume then, sir.'

'Have a brew before you go back out,' he said, not knowing I already had one waiting for me downstairs.

'Thank you.' I accepted that as an olive branch.

Derek nipped to the loo and, while he was out, I said to Ray, 'What's up with the boss?'

Ray shrugged. 'He crossed the border for an hour earlier and he's like a bear with a sore arse now.'

Ray was referring to the boss going into the neighbouring force area. If he'd only been gone an hour, he must have visited a nearby station rather than the HQ. What had happened there to irritate him so much? Not my business. I finished my tea and went back out.

Chapter Seven

I was given the area we referred to as The Andes. It had nothing to do with street names; it was a hill that rose from the banks of the river. It wasn't high, three hundred feet at the most, but it was steep. Some of the streets in The Andes had steps instead of normal paving.

Parking was a bit of an issue because of the gradient. Following an incident a few years previously when the handbrake on a car failed causing it to roll downhill—fortunately, nobody died—a flattened parking area had been cut into the hillside, near the top.

The view from the top was pretty good. I could see into the shipyard and across the river, and even across the city. I wondered if I was looking into another force area beyond the city. Unsurprisingly, the view was best after dark, when innumerable lights came on and it all lay before me like gemstones on black velvet.

Before Bert's idea about moving the foot patrols around, this had been Spider's regular beat. It wasn't an especially wealthy area, but it was nice enough. People liked living in this area because of its proximity to the shipyard, a major employer in the town. We had little trouble in these parts. No wonder Spider liked it. She was currently working my former beat from the park to the docks. Judging by the radio transmissions, things were a bit lively there tonight. She would not be enjoying that. Meantime, I was able to stroll around and enjoy the peace.

I liked nights. Sound travelled further in the silence; my footsteps seemed to ring out. The town even smelled different without all the traffic streaming through. We could meet on the borders of our beats and have a chat without worrying about bosses driving past or the public ringing up to complain we were wasting time. Sometimes we could nip into the fire station or the nearby ambulance station for a cup of tea.

'Oi, you there!'

Nobody else was around so he had to mean me. I adopted a pleasant expression and turned around. 'Can I help you?'

A man strode towards me. 'Did you stop my daughter in a car about half an hour ago?'

'I haven't stopped anyone so far tonight,' I replied.

He looked around. 'Where's the cruiser?'

'Cruiser?' I echoed. We were too far from the river and too high for him to be referring to a boat.

'Your car. And where's your partner?'

'I don't have a partner. I work alone,' I answered.

'Every cop has a partner. There's no way they'd let a girl out by herself on nights. I bet he has the cruiser, and it was him who stopped my daughter. Where is he?'

It sounded like our mystery policeman was out and about.

'Sir, I have no idea what you're talking about. I'm a foot patrol; I do not have a car and I regularly patrol alone on nights. I would be interested to hear about your daughter being stopped, though.'

'My daughter was driving home and a cruiser stopped her by braking in front of her. She almost ran into him. I bet she'd have been blamed if she had. He took her details then he followed her home. He only left when she woke me up because he wouldn't leave. Your job is to serve and to protect, not harass and frighten young girls.'

'I'm sorry that happened. Did you see this person? Can you give me any sort of a description? Did you see the car?' I asked.

'He was in his uniform. The car was blue. A typical cruiser for here.' He sighed. 'I don't know why I'm bothering to talk to you. I should have called 911 or gone to the precinct to report it.'

This chap spoke with a local accent but had learnt everything he knew about policing by overdosing on *Adam 12* or *Kojak* or some other American cop programme. It wasn't uncommon. Meantime, I needed to get the incident out for observation. The offending vehicle could be miles away by now. I radioed it in for Ray and passed on what details I had. While Ray relayed my description, I turned my attention back to the man.

'I could do with speaking to your daughter. What is your address?'

'What's the point? Even if you find the perp, he'll just plead the fifth.'

I had to say something and perhaps stop him talking like a badly written New York detective.

'We're in the United Kingdom, we don't have a fifth amendment. We don't even have a codified constitution to amend. You do realise that England has a different policing system to America, don't you? Also, we dial 999 here.'

I could almost hear the cogs turning in his head as he tried to process what I said. What did I know? He'd seen police on the telly while I just did the job.

'What is your daughter's name?' I asked.

'Look, I don't want a foot patrol, I want to see someone with a gold badge,' he said.

'Nobody here has a gold badge,' I replied.

'Detectives have a gold badge. I want to speak to a detective, someone with a bit of authority,' he insisted.

'I can request a DC for you, but they'll just be a constable, like me,' I pointed out. 'And they don't have gold badges,' I added. I may as well have kept quiet.

'Yeah, get me a detective.'

I requested a jack, but Ray replied, 'It might be some time. The night jack is tied up with an incident in Egilsby.'

'Roger. Thank for that.' I turned my attention back to Yankee Doodle Dandy. 'The night detective is tied up, so to save time, I'll take the report. Meantime, the control room is giving out observation.'

He nodded and walked me towards his house.

'What number is your precinct?' he asked.

I started to give him our phone number, but he cut me off.

'Not the bloody phone number, the precinct number.'

I grasped what he was asking and resisted the urge to tell him Precinct 13. 'I'm from Wyre Hall police station.'

He rolled his eyes. 'To serve and to protect,' he muttered.

Another Americanism. I wasn't going to waste any more breath explaining to him that we were not an outpost of NYPD. It was more important that I got to speak with his daughter about our mystery panda.

*

Later, I viewed the given description with dismay. It looked like the key to this case was going to be the car, because such a generic description was not going to cut it. Average height, average build, average looks. Local accent, hair colour uncertain under the cap. If there was ever a "Most Average Looking Man in Britain" competition, our suspect would probably win it. Unsurprisingly, there had been no sightings of the suspicious car after the observations had been given, which made me wonder if our offender was able to nip home and hide his car. I submitted the suspicious incident report.

'It sounds like he's getting bolder,' Ray said.

'That's not a bad thing,' Derek said. 'They get cocky then they make mistakes.'

'It's also when things go badly wrong,' I added. 'It's when people get hurt.'

Nobody could argue with that.

*

Bert gripped me after scoff.

'Sam, I need you to take a car over to the city, collect Mr Hunter and take him home,' Bert called.

Mr Sidney Hunter QPM was the Chief Superintendent of our division, and the nearest to the Chief Constable that most of us would get. A veteran of WWII, he was well-liked and respected. Many thought he should have been Chief Constable.

I found his rank intimidating. There was something about the double braid on his cap and the crown and pip on his shoulder that cowed me. That, and his physical appearance. He was an imposing figure that radiated authority. His silver hair was still thick and cut with military precision. Even his eyebrows were intimidating.

'Me?' It wasn't that long since I'd completed my driving course, I didn't even have my own panda, so I was surprised that I had been asked. I had always assumed that the traffic department ran Mr Hunter around.

'Yes, you. St Margaret's Street station. Just go to the reception and he'll come out to you.'

'Should I take a marked car or a plain car?' I asked. 'And if I'm in a marked car, should I deal with any incident should someone stop me?'

Bert looked me up and down. 'Thought so. That is a police uniform you're wearing. Should you be stopped, try to radio in and get a local patrol to RV with you to deal with it, or if it's something urgent, you'll have to deal. Use your professional judgement.'

I thought Bert's response was unnecessarily sarcastic. I'd never ferried a senior officer around before. I decided to stop fretting and just get the job done. I checked the board and found a spare panda car, signed out the keys and went into the yard. The first thing I did was check the outside for bumps and scratches, so I didn't get blamed for anything I had not caused. Then I checked the inside of the car. I wanted it to be pristine for Mr Hunter. Someone had eaten chips in there. I'd have to leave the window open as I drove to dissipate the smell. I didn't worry about topics of conversation. He wouldn't want to chat with the likes of me. I signed the logbook then set off for St Margaret's Street.

Half an hour later, I pulled into the station and went into the front office. Several policemen were hanging around. The other drivers. I didn't know anyone else there, so I reported to the front desk and found myself a quiet corner to sit and wait.

After a few minutes, a side door opened and a number of senior officers came out dressed in dinner jackets. Some of the officers looked a little red-faced and seemed extra jovial. No women, so I wondered if this had actually been a social do.

'Looks like they've had a good time,' murmured the bobby next to me.

'Where are their wives?' I wondered aloud.

'I believe this was a reception for senior officers and members of the council. They had a meeting about the redevelopment of the city.' He stopped speaking for a moment as more officers appeared. 'There's mine.' He stood up and left with his Chief Superintendent.

I spotted Mr Hunter and stood up, but he looked through me and went outside. I wasn't surprised; he probably expected his usual driver.

'Mr Hunter?' I called after him. No response. I hurried out just in time to see Mr Hunter getting into another panda. Completely baffled, I went over and knocked on the window. The driver rolled down the glass. 'Mr Hunter should be travelling with me. Our car's over there.' I pointed to our panda.

'Miss Barrie.'

I straightened up and looked towards the voice. An imposing, silver-haired officer hurried towards me. He looked like Mr Hunter. He sounded like Mr Hunter, but Mr Hunter was sitting in this panda. I looked in the panda. Yep, there he was. Twins? I didn't know any senior officers had a twin serving in the same area.

Panting from the exertion of running after me, the other Mr Hunter stopped beside us and burst out laughing.

'We got another one, Malcolm.'

The first Mr Hunter got out of the panda and the two Mr Hunters stood side by side, laughing. Even with them standing together, I found it difficult to tell them apart. People started to gather around, including one very senior officer. The Assistant Chief Constable was witnessing my humiliation! I almost fainted.

'You're twins?' I stammered.

'No, we're not,' Malcolm said. 'We're not related at all. We just look alike. We had great fun in the training school, didn't we Sid?'

Mr Hunter wiped his eyes. 'We certainly did. They used to call us the "terrible twins". Oh, the stories we could tell.'

'Best not, though.' Malcolm winked.

I briefly wondered if one of their fathers perhaps had a story to tell. I wisely did not say anything out loud and mentally chastised myself for having inappropriate thoughts about the parentage of senior officers.

People began to drift away to their own vehicles.

'I apologise, sir. Sirs,' I said.

'No need,' the real Mr Hunter said. 'You're not the first to be fooled and you won't be the last. Let's get back.' He shook hands with Malcolm and walked with me to the car.

I held the back door open for him but he grabbed the front seat. Okay then, I wasn't going to argue with a chief superintendent, so I closed the door and climbed into the driver's seat.

'Just wait until I tell Edith about this,' Mr Hunter said as we drove away from St Margaret's. 'Edith is my wife,' he explained.

'It'll make her laugh, sir,' I commented as I negotiated a tricky roundabout by the tunnel that ran between the city and the peninsula.

'It certainly will. Everyone said Malcolm and I would stop looking alike as we aged, but it didn't happen.' He chuckled. Then he tipped his seat back and closed his eyes. That didn't surprise me, it was very late; it was the cowboy songs he sang for the rest of our journey that left me flabbergasted.

I dropped him at his home, then made my way back to Wyre Hall.

'How was it?' Ray asked when I got back. Derek was busy on the phone.

'He seemed to have had a good time,' I replied. 'I met his twin, then he entertained me with a selection of cowboy songs.'

Ray smiled. 'They've caused a few mix ups. Mr Hunter is a nice bloke, and he does love country and western music.'

'Right. So, is there anyone else that needs collecting or should I hang up the keys and go out?' I asked.

Ray glanced at the clock. 'You go out. It's been a bit lively out there, so we might need you.'

I hung on for a second, waiting for the request for tea, but it never came. I replaced the batteries in my radio and went out.

*

The phone was ringing as I got in from work. I dropped my bag and picked up the receiver.

'Hiya,'

'Hi,' Gary replied. He sounded a bit flat.

'What's up?'

My leave has been cancelled. I won't be home for Halloween. The good news is that I will definitely be home for Christmas.'

I was pleased about Christmas, but I was disappointed about Halloween.

'We're supposed to be going to the charity dance,' I said.

'I know. I'm sorry. You can still go, can't you?' Gary asked.

'I'm not sure I want to without you,' I said.

'Steve and Emma are going, aren't they?'

'Yes, a few are going from our place,' I replied.

'Then you must go. You'll have a good time, even without me.' I could hear the smile in his voice.

'I'll think about it.'

'Anything interesting happen last night?' he asked.

'I got to drive Mr Hunter home after a function and he sang cowboy songs,' I said.

'Was it an official function?' Gary asked.

'Of course it was. He wouldn't have got a ride home just for a night out,' I replied.

'Any news on the bogus bobby?' Gary asked.

'Nothing. We're still getting reports, but we still don't know who he is.'

'Disappointing.' Gary went on to tell me a story about someone he worked with, who I'd never heard of, doing something that I didn't understand, and how everyone in the office had laughed at him. I dutifully chuckled when he'd finished, but my brain was still whirring about the rogue bobby. Then something struck me. When I'd been at the training school, one of our instructors had commented that in times of crisis, the public will turn to anyone in any uniform.

'Our bogus bobby might be someone in another uniform,' I said. 'Firemen have a similar uniform shirt to us. Ambos too. And even security men and bus inspectors wear similar jackets to us. I'll pop a note in to Irene. I'm not sure if Eamon is dealing with that, or if it's someone else.'

'Good idea,' Gary said. 'But I'd be surprised if somebody hasn't already thought of that. Right, I'll let you go and relax after work. Love you.'

'Love you too.' I replaced the receiver and kicked my bag across the floor. I wouldn't need that waxing session now.

Chapter Eight

Andy was greeted by a round of applause when he returned on lates. He bowed and took his place beside Steve Patton.

'Nice to see you back,' I said. 'How are the hands?'

'Much better, thanks.' He held his hands and Steve, Ken Ashcroft—who sat on my other side—and I inspected them.

'You'll have a few interesting scars,' Ken said.

'They're war wounds to impress the grandkids,' said nineteen-year-old Andy. 'How's Gaynor? She must be getting close to her time.'

Ken smiled. 'She's fed up but doing well. Not long now. Thanks for asking.'

'Are you on light duties?' I asked.

'No,' Andy replied. 'They say I'll be fine now. I'm glad the weather is holding up, though; gloves still chafe a bit.'

The door opened and we all stood as the boss, Shaun and Bert came in to start parade.

'As you were,' Inspector Benjamin said. We all sat. 'Nice to see you back, Andy.'

'Thank you, sir,' Andy replied.

'I have some good news for you. The Chief Superintendent wants to thank you personally, and the local paper is going to send a photographer. If you prefer not to do that, let me know, but it's good publicity for the job,' the boss said.

'No. It's fine, sir. I'm just surprised,' Andy replied.

'Good. He has also sent the recommendation for a commendation to the Chief Constable.'

'The Chief Constable?' Andy's voice sounded unsteady.

'And what's more, Chief Superintendent Hunter has endorsed your nomination for a Humane Society award, and for the two men who tried to rescue the child.'

'Oh.' Andy looked like he needed to lie down.

Bert said. 'Not bad for a sprog in their first year. It'll look excellent on your record.'

We all applauded. I looked over to Spider. She was clapping in a rather half-hearted, overly genteel way.

I whispered to Steve, 'Spider's not happy.'

He grinned. 'She's got a cat bum mouth again.'

The applause died down and parade continued.

'I have some sad news about our outstanding misper, Carol Shilling,' said Inspector Benjamin. 'She is the girl in the bin. It seems she was already dead when she was dumped, so that's something to be grateful for.'

That brought down the mood, but the inspector was right; at least she hadn't burnt to death. I couldn't imagine anything worse.

'Have family been informed, sir?' asked Steve.

'Yes, but no speculation, and no talking to the press or anyone you suspect of being connected to the press. This is an ongoing investigation and the CID will take care of any information release via the press department.

He moved on to a couple of observations, including the blue Viva. Another girl had been stopped and another family was unhappy. The driver of this car seemed to like them quite young. My first thought was that he too would be young, but then an unwelcome memory of the late and unlamented Sergeant Lewington shoved its way into my head. I shouldn't make assumptions, and neither should anyone else.

Bert gave out the duties and observations. Parade ended and we got our radios and did our test calls. Steve, Ken, and Andy left to start patrol just before me, so I hurried to catch up with them.

'You know the big boss hates us walking around in packs,' I reminded them.

'We're all headed in the same direction,' Ken argued. 'What do you want us to do, march in single file like in the old days?'

'Perhaps you should just walk behind us then the boss won't think you're part of the pack,' Andy said.

'I was only winding you up.' I drew up alongside them. 'I'm calling off at the market, there's someone I need to speak to.'

'Anyone interesting?' Steve asked.

'Karen Fitzroy, the one who does the sewing,' I replied.

'Getting a wedding dress made?' Ken asked with a glint in his eye.

'Not yet,' I replied deadpan. I wasn't going to rise to the bait. 'You could do worse than getting a christening gown on order. She does lovely christening gowns.'

Ken thought for a moment. 'Actually, that's a really good idea. It can become an heirloom. My grandkids can be christened in it.'

'Won't Gaynor want to help choose?' Steve asked.

'We have similar tastes. She'll be fine with what I choose,' Ken replied.

Steve raised his eyebrows. I smiled. Ken and Gaynor were besotted with each other. She really would be fine with his choice.

'Can I come too?' Andy asked.

'Are you after a christening gown too?' I joked.

'Hell, no! I'm just being nosy.'

Steve tutted. 'Right, I'll toddle off, all on my own.' He turned towards the main road while the remaining three of us cut through the entry that would bring us out by the market.

I led the lads towards Karen's stall. A few stallholders stopped and stared as we walked past them. They probably didn't see three police officers together in the market very often, not unless there was trouble. I made a point of smiling in their direction so they knew we came in peace.

'Here.' I stopped by Karen's stall. She had put up a poster that read, *"If you're happy, tell your friends. If you're not happy, tell me."* Karen was engrossed in a piece of embroidery and jumped when I called her name. She looked from Ken to Andy, then to me.

'What's happened?'

'Nothing. Ken wants to order a christening gown so I brought him to you. Andy's just being nosy,' I replied.

Karen grinned. 'Come on in and we can talk colours. Is it a boy or a girl?'

'We don't know yet. My wife is due very soon though,' Ken replied.

'Everything okay, Kaz?' a stallholder on the opposite side called.

'Yes thanks. I'm getting an order for a christening gown,' Karen called back.

'My wife is having a baby,' Ken added.

'Go for oyster. Much classier than plain old white,' the stallholder called back to us.

'Thanks.' Ken put his thumb up.

'Oyster then?' Karen asked him.

'Sure,' Ken said.

Karen pulled out a couple of rolls of oyster-coloured material. 'What do you think?'

Ken looked from one to the other. 'I don't know. What do you think, Sam?'

I ran a finger over the materials. One was a lovely satin, but I preferred the feel of the silk.

'This one.'

Ken stroked a finger over it and smiled. 'Yeah. This one definitely. It feels great.'

'Okay, that was easy. What pattern did you have in mind?' Karen asked.

'I hadn't thought about it,' Ken said.

Karen went to a box and pulled out some patterns and held them out to Ken. 'I've got some pictures here.'

Ken shuffled through the patterns and passed one to me. 'What do you think?'

'It's lovely. I like the lace on the bottom and the ribbons,' I said, and passed the pattern back to him.

'That's short sleeved. We're coming into winter so you might want something a little warmer.' Karen took the pattern from him and studied it for a moment. 'Long sleeves. A soft flannel petticoat, detachable I think so it can be used in the warm weather too if you have another little one. I'll just put loops on it so you can change the ribbons as you please. Come back in a couple of days and I'll have drawn up a few ideas for you.'

Ken beamed. 'I will. I might bring Gaynor, but she's so big and uncomfortable at the moment she'll possibly prefer to stay at home.'

Karen smiled. 'It's a difficult time for a woman.'

I knew the sadness that lay behind her smile. Karen would never have her own child, following a terrible beating that almost took her life. I would never reveal that to anyone. 'Right, lads, let this woman get on. Thanks, Karen,' I said.

Ken and Andy moved away.

'Tell your friends,' she called after Ken and Andy. 'Thank you for bringing me so much new business, Sam,' she said to me.

'I just wondered if you'd heard anything?' I asked.

'Nothing. Sorry. Everyone seems to be accounted for. I will ring you if I hear anything, promise.'

'Thanks.' I hurried after Ken and Andy.

Ken began patrol on his beat, which wasn't far from the market. Andy and I walked on to ours. After a couple of minutes, he nudged me. 'Look, that's what I'm talking about. That car is the same colour as our pandas.'

I looked at the vehicle approaching us. The same make and apparently the same colour as ours, just as Andy said. I recognised the driver. Walter the Weeble. He was dressed in a uniform shirt, no epaulettes or tie.

'I know him, he's a fireman,' I said.

'He could get out of the car and pretend to be a policeman, and nobody would argue with him,' Andy said.

'He hasn't tried to stop his car, never mind get out and impersonate a police officer,' I argued.

'No, but just because he isn't trying to impersonate a policeman, doesn't meant that somebody else won't.' Andy watched the car go past. 'How's a member of the public supposed to know that's not a police car?'

'The absence of a police sign or lights?' I suggested.

'Look back,' he ordered. 'Just look back before it's gone.'

I turned and looked at the car disappearing into the distance.

'Now how easy it is to say it's not a police car?'

It wasn't easy at all. 'Maybe it's not a bad thing for the public to think there are more police cars on the road.' I pressed on. 'I've said it before and I'll say it again: This is not our call. We just have to put up with whatever the bosses decide. You're getting far too caught up in this. Stop carrying on.'

'I think I might submit a report on it,' Andy said.

'If that makes you happy,' I said. 'Anyway, this is my beat. See you at refs.'

'See you,' Andy replied.

He still seemed distracted. I thought he had a point about the car colours, but I did think he was overreacting about the potential danger. Surely the public would notice if a car didn't have blue lights and a sign on the roof. Then I remembered the mother of the choking child. In times of stress, maybe they wouldn't.

*

A couple of days later, at first refs, we crowded around the kitchen window looking down on Andy and the two men from the fire, shaking hands with Chief Superintendent Hunter in the front garden of the station as the press photographer snapped away. Some of the lads tried to distract Andy by pulling faces, but he steadfastly gazed at the photographer.

When it was all over, the Chief left with the two men and Andy returned to the refs room.

'Hollywood rang and wondered if you were free,' Trevor said.

'Oh, I suppose so,' Andy replied, getting into the spirit of things. 'Farrah Fawcett is being a bit of a pest phoning all the time. Tell them I expect my own jet to transport me around and champagne in every dressing room.'

I was surprised that he hadn't already featured in some recruiting posters. He ticked so many boxes. Mixed race. Tick: that was race relations covered. Handsome. Tick: it was always good to have handsome people on recruiting posters. Good teeth and a healthy glow. Tick: stops possible recruits thinking about the effect shift work would have on their looks and energy levels. Now, Andy was a real-life hero. Double tick.

'He's done well, hasn't he?' Ray commented. 'That lad will go far.'

'He has. I can see him being a superintendent in the future,' I agreed. I wouldn't mind Andy being my boss.

Chapter Nine

Next day, as I drove into work, I spotted Bert coming out of the corner shop near the police station. He was holding a family-sized bar of chocolate and a couple of sausage rolls. Being mischievous, I pipped my horn and waved as I passed. He almost dropped his loot. I was still laughing as I pulled into the station car park.

Fifteen minutes later, I was tapping on the door to the collator's office. Sergeant Irene Kildea, our collator and Eamon's wife, waved me in.

'Hi, Sam. What can I do for you?'

'Did you get my note? Has anyone considered that our mystery bobby might not be a policeman at all? He might be in another uniform, driving an ordinary blue car that looks like one of ours.'

'That young sprog, Andy, has been going on about civilian cars looking like police cars,' Irene said.

'He has a point. I saw an off-duty fireman I know driving home in his car, which is a pale blue Vauxhall Viva. From a distance, it was difficult to tell it apart from a panda,' I said.

'What time did you see him?' Irene asked.

'Half-three to four. We were walking out to our beats. I know he's not our man. He has a distinctive appearance, which doesn't match any of the descriptions given.'

Irene said, 'I think it's a given that he isn't a real policeman. They're already working on the idea that he might not be a police officer but might have access to a real uniform. I'll mention about other uniformed professions, but that's probably already on the table.' She looked at the clock. 'Parade in fifteen minutes; you'd better get moving.'

'Thanks. See you.'

I heard Bert call to me as I left Irene's office to get my jacket and hat from my locker.

'Sarge?' I said.

'About earlier. I would appreciate it if you didn't say anything. The wife wouldn't be pleased.'

'I won't say a word,' I promised. Not that I'd have the chance. I had only met Mrs Mason once in passing.

'Good girl.' He patted his belly. 'Some people are not meant to be thin.'

'I think Mrs Mason is more concerned with keeping you healthy, rather than having you lose weight,' I said.

'Maybe. Still, let's not take that chance.'

'Yes, sarge.'

I went to the locker room, where I met Andy. We gathered our things and walked together to the parade room. As we passed the sergeants' office, we saw a very young policewoman sitting on the chair by the key cabinet, listening to Bert as he spoke to her. Evidently straight from the cadets, a cadre of school leavers who had been too young to be sworn in as constables but had shown potential. They were signed up, given further education and some basic training until they were old enough to go to the training centre.

Andy abruptly stepped back out of sight and whispered, 'It's Pixie! She must be the new sprog.'

'Is Pixie her real name?' I whispered back. I'd never heard of anyone called Pixie before. It also looked as if Pixie had been told to report to the sergeants' office before parade. Nobody had told me that, or Andy. Perhaps word had filtered through that not everyone knew what they were doing or where to go on their first day.

'It's actually Pandora. Pandora Millington-Dow to be precise. In the cadets, we called her Pixie because she looks a bit like a pixie,' Andy said.

That sounded equally strange to me. Who would name their baby girl after the woman who opened a box and released all the woes into the world? But I saw what he meant about her appearance. She reminded me of a female Peter Pan, with an upturned nose and slightly slanted eyes. Definite Asian ancestry, but not full-blooded. Her straight, dark hair was cut short, which accentuated the pixie features.

'A double-barrelled name. Is she posh?' I asked. 'What's she doing in a place like this if she's posh?'

'Spider's posh,' Andy said.

'No, she's just pretentious.'

'Pixie isn't at all posh or pretentious,' he replied. 'Her family do live in a nice area, though.' Andy stepped back into sight.

Pixie looked over to us and beamed. 'Sexy-Kecks!' She had a local accent.

Andy squirmed. 'Hi Pixie.'

Bert turned to us. 'I take it you know each other?'

'We were in the same cadet intake, Sergeant,' Andy said.

'Right. You two get to parade, I'll bring Pandora shortly.' He turned to Pandora. 'Would you prefer to be known as Pixie?'

'Yes please, Sergeant Mason,' Pixie replied.

'Sexy-Kecks?' I asked as Andy and I went to the parade room.

'She always called me Sexy-Kecks. I thought I had escaped that when I came here.'

'What's it worth not to tell anyone else?' I joked.

'Nothing, because everyone will know by the end of the shift.'

We took our seats in the parade room and waited for parade to begin. A few minutes later, Inspector Benjamin, Bert, Shaun and Pixie came into the parade room. We all stood.

'As you were,' said the inspector.

We sat back down.

'This is our newest member, Pandora Millington-Dow. She's known as Pixie.'

A couple of heads shot up, but nothing was said about her

unusual name.

Bert turned to Pixie and said, 'Seeing as you already know Andy, go and sit over there.'

She came over and sat on a spare chair behind us. She put her hand across my shoulder.

'I'm Pandora but everyone calls me Pixie.'

I shook her hand. 'Samantha. Everyone calls me Sam,' I replied.

'Right, let's get on, we can do proper introductions later.' Bert said. 'Trevor, you're puppy walking.'

Trevor looked back at Pixie who gave him a little wave. I caught Steve's eye. Bert was taking a chance. Trevor was going to have to pull his finger out, if Pixie was going to learn everything. I wondered if he had what it took to tutor a sprog.

*

After parade, as usual, we all piled into the control room to collect our radios. Pixie and Bert were walking up the corridor together.

'Trevor, I'm taking the sprog to see the boss. We'll call you back when she's ready to go out,' Bert called.

We all knew that Trevor would hang around the station until actually sent to a job, and use Pixie as the excuse.

Spider marched up to Pixie and held—no, thrust—out a hand. 'Charlotte Leader, graduate entrant. That means I am going to be an inspector before long. If you need to know anything, don't be afraid to approach me.'

Pixie shook Spider's hand. 'Pandora Millington-Dow. Pixie. Former cadet but also ambitious.'

'You're still very young, but you'll learn that if you want to be taken seriously, you need to insist you do not have a silly nickname,' Spider said with all the experience of five minutes service.

'I like my nickname,' Pixie said. 'Don't you have a nickname?'

'Spider,' someone called from the control room.

'Ah, I get it. Charlotte's Web.' Pixie grinned. 'I'm surprised that nobody has named you Prof or Einstein, seeing as you have a degree. Perhaps they're wary of doing that seeing as you're going to be a boss.'

Was Pixie digging at Spider? Good on her.

Spider paused before answering, possibly wondering the same thing. Eventually she replied, 'Yes, so it would be in people's interests to treat me with some respect. There are some people here I won't forget as I ascend the ladder.' She looked right at me. I sent a big, cheesy grin back.

Pixie glanced at me then said, 'My dad always says, "Respect the rank".'

I almost laughed out loud. My dad said that too. I knew the follow up to that was, "If not the person". I liked Pixie.

'The problem with that is she doesn't have any rank,' I said.

'Yet,' snapped Spider.

'Come on, Pixie.' Bert led Pixie to the stairs to speak to the inspector.

'She seems okay,' Spider said to me. 'Very young but promising. Try not to teach her your maverick ways.'

'You think I'm a maverick? Wow! That makes me almost cool,' I said.

'Mavericks are liabilities,' Spider retorted.

We had a couple of known mavericks at Wyre Hall, who thought of everyone as sheep, while they themselves were real cops who cut through the rules to get the job done. However, we had protocols and procedures for good reasons, and there was a danger they could render evidence inadmissible. They were indeed liabilities, but I would never agree out loud with Spider. I didn't consider myself on a par with those people. I sometimes got myself into situations, but I wasn't normally a liability. A bit of a nuisance at times but nothing more.

'Get your arses out,' Shaun shouted from the office.

'Just going, Sarge,' I called back.

Chapter Ten

After break, Bert called me into the sergeants' office.
'How do you feel about Specials?' he asked.

Special constables were volunteers, receiving only expenses for their time. Some police officers resented their presence and viewed them as overtime thieves, but sometimes an extra pair of hands was useful, especially when pubs and clubs kicked out.

'I have no strong feelings about them,' I replied.

'Good. I want you to take one out with you. He's in the Specials' office upstairs,' Shaun said.

I could have done without having company. I hadn't had time to speak to Chris about returning the dance tickets, and I'd intended to go to the fire station after break. I couldn't with a Special in tow.

'Yes, Sarge,' I replied and went upstairs.

As I passed the CID office, DC Eamon Kildea called to me through the open door. 'What are you up to, m'darlin'?'

'Just going to collect a Special. Anything interesting going on here?'

'Not much. How come you've got a Special?'

I shrugged. 'Nobody else to do it, I suppose.'

'Stamp your authority early on,' Eamon advised.

'Why do you dislike them?' I asked.

'I don't dislike 'em, m'darlin'. There are some who would make great coppers but they're too short, or they just don't want to do the job full time. Some have been Specials a long time and might not take kindly to a young woman leading them around.'

'They'll have to learn to live with it,' I said. I would take the lead, but I was not above using someone's experience if it was useful.

The door to the Specials' room was open so I went in. A Special stood by the window. Mousey hair and matching moustache. He was probably close to the minimum height for men, but Special constables didn't have the same criteria as regular officers.

The Special sergeant came out of his cubby hole of an office. 'Ah good, you're here.' He gestured towards the Special by the window. 'This is Tony Fleming.'

I smiled at Tony. 'I'm Sam. Are you ready to go?'

Tony looked from me to the sergeant and back again. When neither of us said anything, he said, 'Ready.'

I led the way from the Specials' office, past the CID office, pausing only to return Eamon's wave, and out onto the street.

'Where are we going?' Tony asked.

'Around the park and down to the docks,' I replied. I was getting vibes off Tony. Not hostile, but he was not comfortable.

'Isn't it a bit rough around there?' he asked.

'If you're unhappy, you can go back to the station,' I said.

'No, I meant for a girl.'

I smiled. 'I've done this beat for a while. I've got to know the people quite well. How long have you been a Special?'

'Not long. I recently finished my initial training. I'm still learning the practical stuff.'

'There's more to it than people realise,' I said. 'Not everyone takes to it.'

We walked on in silence. After a short time, he asked, 'What made you want to join the police?'

'I wanted to help people. To make life better,' I replied. It sounded glib but it was close enough to the truth. I was not going into the traumatic incident that had led me to that decision.

'Have you done that?' he asked.

'Not as often as I would like,' I replied honestly. 'Sometimes, I have made a difference, and that's great, but sometimes people don't want help. They just want someone to blame when the bad decisions they make come back to bite them.' I took a couple more steps. 'So, what about you? Why the Specials?'

'I wanted to do something worthwhile. Like you, I wanted to make a difference. I applied, but there's a bit of a backlog they need to clear. I figured Specials was a good stop-gap until I reapply. I'd prove my commitment.'

I hadn't heard there was a backlog of new recruits, but then the training department didn't need to update me on current conditions and policy. It all sounded plausible. There were only so many places in the training schools.

'What's your day job?' I asked.

'I'm a security guard,' he replied.

'Is there a conflict of interests there?' I was concerned that policing an area he would normally guard would blur the lines. A Special constable had conditional police powers, but a security guard never had police powers, despite some of them thinking they did.

'No, I'm based in the city and I police here,' he replied.

That made life less complicated.

'Do you live locally?' I asked.

'Not too far,' he replied.

I didn't care enough to ask for a more specific answer.

'Do you find it hard to socialise when working shifts?' Tony asked.

'I do a bit,' I admitted. 'I suppose that's why emergency workers stick together. How about you as a security guard, and now a Special?'

'I don't go out that much,' he replied. 'I go to my men's group once a week but that's pretty well it.'

'What men's group?' I asked.

'A Christian men's social group. We book a meeting room in the Middleton Hotel. We have speakers most weeks. Some are pretty good; they make you think. Afterwards we have a buffet supper and a natter and play dominoes or cards or something like that.'

It sounded like a boys' night out without the pub.

'Do you find it hard, being a woman in the police?' Tony asked. 'I mean, do you find that people won't take you seriously? A woman ordering a man around goes against nature. You can't command the same respect.'

Tony appeared to be oblivious to the thin ice on which he was skating. Instead of smacking him across the head with the nearest hard object, I paraphrased one of my dad's favourite sayings.

'Respect the uniform, if not the person.'

He nodded as if I had said something incredibly wise. Perhaps, to him, I had.

'The uniform confers authority, even to a woman.'

Without answering, I turned towards the Ship Streets, a dismal maze of narrow roads and tiny, terraced houses. I spotted Ruthie Pritchard heading towards the docks. I welcomed the distraction.

I pointed her out to Tony. 'That's Ruthie. Have you met her?'

Tony shook his head. 'I've never been by the docks.'

'She's well known to us all. She's a serious addict and funds her habit by prostitution and begging,' I explained.

'Aren't you going to arrest her?' he asked.

'She isn't doing anything criminal at the moment,' I replied.

'Part of our remit is to prevent crime. You know she's going to commit crime so why aren't you arresting her?' He paused then said, 'If you're not going to, I will.'

I didn't like his tone. Instead of snapping back I decided education was the way forward.

'For what?' I asked.

'For being a prostitute.' He thought for a moment. 'CPL: Common Prostitute Loitering.'

'She isn't loitering or soliciting, she's on her way somewhere. On the occasions she does commit crime, I will arrest her, and I have done so many times,' I explained. 'Taking money for sex isn't a crime, it's the soliciting in a public place, pimping and kerb crawling that are illegal. Ruthie's going onto a ship or three. She isn't soliciting in public. If the docks police don't like her going on the ships, they'll deal with it. It might be a good idea to brush up on prostitution laws if you're going to work around here.' He was going to get into trouble if he acted unlawfully.

Ruthie saw us and tottered over; her scuffed boots flapped against her bony legs.

'He's new,' she slurred.

'He is, Ruthie. This is Tony,' I replied.

Ruthie gave him a gappy smile. She had lost another tooth since I had last seen her. Had she been thumped or was it lost because of her appalling diet and dodgy health? I'd probably never know.

Tony literally recoiled. His lip curled. I was embarrassed by his blatant disgust. Ruthie didn't seem to notice, but from the state of her eyes, I surmised she was high on something.

'Sam's a friend of the family,' she slurred. Tony's head spun towards me. 'She sent me mother down and sent me sister away.'

'It was the courts that did that, not me personally. I did explain it to you, Ruthie,' I pointed out. 'And your mother should be out of prison now. Haven't you heard from her?'

Ruthie shook her head. I also shook mine. I had never rated Elsie Pritchard as a parent, but I thought she would at least contact Ruthie when got out. Not least because her name had been on the rent book, and I was pretty certain Ruthie wouldn't have had the nouse to get it changed, but then Karen or one of the more switched-on girls would probably have taken Ruthie under their wing and helped with the transfer of tenancy. A pound to a pinch of dust, Ruthie was getting housing benefit to cover the rent.

'Have you heard from our Bernadette?' Ruthie asked.

'Haven't you?' I dodged the question. There was no way I was going to tell her that Bernie occasionally wrote to me.

She shook her head again. 'I hope she's happy.'

For a moment I felt sad for Ruthie, but her sister Bernie was thriving in Manchester. She had started training as a hairdresser, and she wrote of her long-held dream to run her own salon. She had no intention of returning to this town to be dragged into Ruthie's sad, chaotic world.

Ruthie shook herself and arranged her horrible pink handbag on her arm. 'I can't stand here nattering with coppers. I've got work to do.'

I watched her go for a moment, then led Tony towards the park.

'Filth,' Tony spat. 'Can you honestly tell me that the world wouldn't be a better place without them?'

I decided to stir the pot a little. 'If you mean prostitutes, no I don't. They serve a purpose. I would rather a lonely man went to a prostitute than take out their frustration on a woman who might not welcome their advances. In fact, I think we should have legalised prostitution like they do in some other countries. Then they would have to pay tax, and they would have to have proper healthcare to make sure they're not diseased.'

'I believe that God made someone for everyone and if women obeyed God's plan for them, every man would have a partner and the need for those degenerate knob jockeys wouldn't exist. Legalised or not.'

'Knob jockeys. What a quaint turn of phrase,' I murmured, trying to ignore the unpleasant mental picture that had created.

He blushed. 'I'm sorry. I feel strongly about this. The world was better when everyone knew their place. Hitler was a madman, but wasn't wrong when he said, *"Kinder, Küche, Kirche"*. Children, kitchen, church. What more does a woman need?'

And right there we had the likely reason Tony Fleming had been rejected by the police. I was surprised the Specials still accepted him, with such overt misogyny.

'Wouldn't you be happier sitting at home, nursing your baby instead of walking around the backstreets, mixing with the likes of that?' He cocked his head in the direction Ruthie had gone.

I did want a baby one day, maybe, but I couldn't let this slide.

'Firstly, children are not always placid little cherubs. From what I see, they bring a lot of work and worry. Secondly, I believe that women have the right to choose their partner, or if they even want a partner. Believe me, there are some men out there that most women wouldn't touch with a bargepole.' I now counted him amongst them.

'Women were created to be wives and mothers,' he argued. 'They should be married.'

'I read somewhere once that marriage is just a social construct designed by men to maintain the subjugation of women. A wedding is one single day where she can dress up and feel like a princess, but it's really just a formal exchange of ownership from father to husband. It's poor compensation for the decades of drudgery that follow.' Blooming heck, I'd have to be careful or I'd talk myself out of my own wedding, but I had finally found a use for the sociology lessons I had taken at school, and the rather intense feminist views held by our teacher.

Tony's jaw dropped, which had been my intention. 'How can you say that?'

I thought of Wilfred and Kitty and my own parents. They had traditional marriages, and it seemed to suit them. I loved Gary, but our marriage would be a meeting of equals. I would not promise to obey him, nor would I give up my career unless I chose it. Thank goodness times had moved on.

'Men are the guardians, the leaders,' Tony added.

'Yet here we are, with me leading you around.'

'But still single,' he muttered.

I pretended I hadn't heard. Who cared what he thought.

We didn't talk much after that. I deliberately walked him down the worst areas and stinkiest back alleys and entries. He was a male version of Spider. He kept his arms tight against his body in case he touched something. I told him it was a good way to find drug dealers. Just as well he couldn't see my evil grin as I walked ahead of him.

*

When we got back to the station, Tony returned to the Specials' office to sign off without a word to me.

I went to the sergeants' office. 'Bert, please don't sent me out with that misogynistic wazzer again,' I pleaded.

'You lasted longer than the last person who took him out. They didn't even last an hour. Someone off A Block. He bollocksed a job they attended,' Bert said. 'Where is he, by the way?'

'Gone back to the office to sign off.'

'Okay, I'll try to send him out with one of the lads if we get him again,' Bert said.

Good enough.

I left the office to get ready to go off-duty and, through the window, I spotted Tony walking across the yard to our car park, shrugging on a motorcycle jacket whilst juggling a helmet. I couldn't read the writing on his back. My eyesight was pretty good, but I always had trouble with red on black. No matter. I didn't care if he belonged to a club, or bought named merchandise. If I never worked with Tony Fleming again, it would be too soon.

Chapter Eleven

A couple of days later, I walked past the fire station, hoping to see Chris so I could give back the tickets. I was pleased when he spotted me and trotted over.

'You look glum. What's up?'

'Gary's not coming home until Christmas now. Sorry, Chris but can I return these?' I opened my bag and fished out the tickets.

'I was looking forward to grabbing a dance with you,' Chris said.

'Sorry.' I held out the tickets. 'It would have been a good night out.'

Chris didn't take them. 'Come with me instead. Don't worry about your chap. Tell him you'll be with me and there are several other coppers coming, including your mate, Steve and his girl. You won't be alone.'

It sounded reasonable to me. 'Okay, I'll tell Gary I'm going with you. He did say I should still go because Steve and Emma are going.'

'Great. So put your ticket away and I'll refund you for the other one. I'll meet you outside the hall at eight?'

'That'll be fine. Thanks.' I put the ticket back in my bag. 'Have you noticed the new panda cars?'

'Yeah. Rather plain if you ask me. You should have something with a bit more zizz,' he replied.

'One of our sprogs is worried that it's hard for the public to tell them from ordinary blue cars. What do you think?'

Chris rubbed his chin. 'I suppose from a distance it might

be difficult, but if everyone drives properly, I don't see that's a problem.'

'That's what I thought. Walter Hodgeson drives a car that resembles our pandas; has he ever complained about people flagging him down or anything?'

Chris laughed. 'It wouldn't do anyone any good flagging that dead leg down, but he hasn't mentioned it happening. Is it a problem for some people?'

'I just wondered. Andy's put in a report about his concerns.'

'It will be filed under B—for Bin,' Chris said.

'Probably,' I agreed.

'4912 from control,' Ray transmitted.

'Go ahead,' I replied.

'Can you make a domestic disturbance at eight Hazel View? Informant Martin Duggan.'

Before I could respond, the radio beeped, telling me that someone was talking to the control room.

'Mike Two, go ahead,' Ray said.

More beeping.

'I'll let you get on.' Chris went back into the station.

'Roger,' Ray said. '4912.'

'Go ahead,' I responded.

'Mike Two will RV with you. What's your location?'

'I'm by the fire station,' I replied.

'Remain there. Mike Two, she's by the fire station.'

Beeping

'Roger.'

I stood by the kerb, waiting for Mike Two. Normally, a domestic dispute would not need more than one person, at least to start with, but this had been described as a domestic disturbance. Two people would probably be needed. Three or more if it all kicked off. I knew the other patrols will have heard Ray and, as far as their own calls allowed, would be moving towards the parts of their beats that were closest to the address, just in case they had to lend a hand.

Mike Two drew up beside me and I hopped in.

'Know anything about this address, John?' I asked. We didn't get many calls from Hazel View. It was in an upmarket part of town, and they liked to keep themselves to themselves.

'Nothing. I don't think I've ever been to a call there,' John replied. 'Do you want to take the lead?'

'Sure.'

We arrived at a long, wide road of detached houses surrounded by generous gardens.

I knocked at the door of number eight, and a teenaged boy opened it. I could hear shouting coming from the back room. John adjusted his truncheon, so it was easily accessible if necessary.

'Come in. It's a bit calmer now. I don't think any damage has been done.' He held the door wide and stepped back. We stepped into the hall.

'Are you Martin Duggan?' I asked. He nodded. 'How old are you, Martin?'

'Eighteen.'

An adult. He looked a little younger.

'Are your parents also called Duggan?' He nodded. 'Right, what's the story,' I asked.

'My dad stole my bike. We only just found out. I got money for my birthday. I'm an apprentice at the shipyard so I bought a bike to get to work. Dad went ape and told me it would be stolen and I'd have nothing to show for my money. He took it to prove his point.'

'Who is it, Marty?' a female voice called.

Without answering, Martin led us into the large back room. A man and a woman were standing either side of a dining table nicely set for a meal. Both were red in the face. Their jaws dropped when they saw us.

'I called them,' Martin said. He flopped onto an armchair by the fireplace. I could feel the waves of anger coming from him. He gestured for John to sit on the other armchair.

I sat on a dining chair and looked from one parent to the other. 'Who wants to start?'

'I'll start,' said Mrs Duggan. 'This pathetic excuse of a man has stolen his own son's bicycle.'

'For his own good,' Mr Duggan cut in.

I raised a hand. 'You'll get your chance to speak in a moment, Mr Duggan.'

'How do you know my name?'

'Martin told me,' I replied. 'Please continue, Mrs Duggan.'

Mrs Duggan jerked her chin towards Mr Duggan. 'He wanted Martin to open a savings account with his birthday money.'

Mr Duggan interrupted again. 'I'm a bank manager and I could get him favourable rates.'

'Please, Mr Duggan. Be patient. We'll hear your story shortly,' I said.

'I reported the theft to the police last week,' Mrs Duggan continued. 'Today, my mother-in-law phoned to ask when the bike was going to be moved out of her shed. I put two and two together and confronted him.' She jabbed a finger towards Mr Duggan. 'He admitted hiding the bike, but that's not the best of it. He said he was selling the bike to someone else. It isn't his to sell!'

I shifted in my seat. 'Mr Duggan?'

'I was going to give him the money I got for the bike. The boy hasn't any savings behind him. He spends everything he earns. He needs to be more responsible.'

'That's not fair!' Martin exclaimed. 'I pay my keep and I take Sharon out on Saturday. Taking your girlfriend out once a week is hardly being irresponsible.'

'You're always skint,' Mr Duggan countered.

'I'm an apprentice! I earn pennies! That bike meant I could get to work for free! It doesn't help my financial situation when I have to pay bus fares because you refuse to give me a lift, even though it's on your way. Mum can't help me because she's got nothing spare. You control the housekeeping money the way you control everything else. She can't even get her hair done unless you say so.' Martin turned his attention to me. 'Now this. All because I won't follow his petty orders.'

In training we were taught to keep control of the direction of an argument and keep the parties on track. However, I sometimes found it useful to let an argument run on a while, as long as it didn't become physical. A lot of information came out of an unfiltered "discussion". I was getting a picture of a domineering husband controlling his family for his own benefit. My sympathies were with Martin. He seemed like a nice lad.

'It's bad enough you left school to go to the shipyard like one of the oiks from the estate. You don't have to look like one of them too,' Mr Duggan shouted.

'I told you, I didn't want to go to university, but you wouldn't listen, as usual,' Martin shouted back. 'I want a trade then I'm off.'

'Bloody New Zealand again!' Mr Duggan snorted. 'I bet that Sharon has put you up to it. A bloody gold digger she is.'

'Shut your mouth! Sharon is not a gold digger. She earns more than me at the moment,' Martin said. 'If I need a degree later, I'll do one.'

'If Sharon will let you. She needs to be gone,' Mr Duggan growled.

This was getting a bit too far off topic. We needed to return to the bicycle.

'Mr Duggan, did you believe you had the right to take the bike?' I asked. I was trying to see if he had a defence. Mr Duggan sat down on the seat opposite me. He half smiled and shrugged, which told me little.

'I knew Martin wouldn't be happy, but I did it with the best of intentions. I'm sorry my concern for my son has caused such upset.' I had never heard a more insincere apology. He didn't actually say "dearie" or "sweetheart", but they were there in spirit. I felt he had figuratively patted me on the head and was sending me on my merry way.

I didn't smile back. 'So, what happened?'

'I'm selling it—'

'It's not yours to sell!' Mrs Duggan shouted.

'Please, Mrs Duggan,' John said on my behalf.

Mrs Duggan was shaking with rage, but I turned back to Mr Duggan. 'Please continue.'

'I intended to give the money I got for the bike back to Martin, so he could make the more sensible choice.'

'Do as you say, more like,' Martin said from the armchair. 'And you do know that you won't get what I paid for it? Did you intend to make up that lost money?'

He had a good point.

Mr Duggan flapped his hand dismissively. 'As I said, I was going to give him the money. I really don't see the problem.'

I turned to John and raised an eyebrow, silently asking for confirmation of the offence. He nodded. Good enough.

I rested my elbows on the table. 'Mr Duggan. This is actually theft.'

'No, it isn't,' he argued.

'It is,' I replied.

'It's not theft and you're wrong if you say it is,' Mr Duggan insisted.

I didn't bother replying; we'd sound like pantomime characters.

'Martin, do you want to make a formal complaint?' John asked.

'Yes,' said Martin and Mrs Duggan in unison.

'I don't believe he'd have given me any of the money back. It's not the first time he's tried something like this,' Martin said. 'Tell them about the earrings you got for you twenty-first birthday, Mum.'

'That's not important now, Martin. Why don't you go to your nan's and get your bike back now,' Mrs Duggan suggested. Martin left and Mrs Duggan turned back to me. 'Will we have to cancel that crime report? Martin's got the bike back, but I do want this worthless insect to face the consequences for what he's done.'

'Of course it can be cancelled. It wasn't theft, it's at his nan's house,' Mr Duggan shouted.

'It can't be cancelled because a crime has been committed. However, it will be marked off as resolved,' I replied. 'We'll need to take statements from Martin and you, Mrs Duggan.'

'I'll be back in a moment.' Mrs Duggan left the room and I heard her pick up a phone.

I turned to Mr Duggan. 'I am arresting you on suspicion of theft. You are not obliged to say anything unless you wish to do so, but anything you do say will be taken down in writing and may be given in evidence.'

'You can't arrest me. There was no crime.' He folded his arms like a petulant toddler.

I sighed. Here was a man used to having his own way.

'I can, and I have arrested you, Mr Duggan. If you care to research the definition of the offence of theft, you will see that you have fulfilled all the elements.'

Mrs Duggan came back in and quietly stood by the door.

'Been whinging to your bitch sister again. Telling her more lies,' Mr Duggan sneered. 'Everyone knows how you exaggerate. Nobody is going to believe you.'

Mrs Duggan kept her voice even as she said, 'If they don't believe me, it's because you tell people that I lie and I exaggerate. You insist I am overreacting to things, and you deny things that I know you have done. Since the day I married you, you have believed you control everything. You've ridden roughshod over my wishes and Martin's wishes. I've always taken it and even covered for you. It stops now.'

Ignoring his wife, as I suspected he did whenever she said something he didn't like, Mr Duggan said, 'I shall contact the Chief Constable.'

'If you wish.' I deliberately kept my voice calm. I heard this threat almost every day. It never failed to underwhelm me. I took one of his arms and John moved to take the other.

Mr Duggan grew redder until he finally exploded. 'Fine! You've made your point; I'm sure you have more important matters to attend to.' He looked at Mrs Duggan. 'Tell them it was all a misunderstanding and they can go now. I've learnt my lesson.' He said the last in an irritating, sing-songy voice.

'No,' said Mrs Duggan.

'NO?'

'No. I think this is the only way you will finally come to realise that you are not king of the world.'

Mr Duggan went past red into purple. 'You'll see me wrongly charged with theft?!' He sagged onto a seat. We remained loosely holding his arms. I didn't think he'd do a runner, but the risk was never zero.

'I manage a bank. I'll lose my job, my reputation. My house. Church!? What will people think?'

Mrs Duggan snorted. 'They deserve to know what a nasty piece of work you really are.'

'You'll regret this, you vindictive hag! You'd better get a solicitor because I'm divorcing you. And you can tell that ungrateful brat he isn't welcome in my home anymore. I paid for everything, you contributed nothing, you'll get nothing.'

'I contributed years of unpaid labour to keep the house running, and to raising our child, so you could concentrate on your career and gallivant off with your *brothers*.'

She said the last as if it was a swear word. Much as I despised Mr Duggan, I didn't see a problem with him spending time with his brothers, but it was evidently a source of resentment in this house. I wondered what lay behind that.

'I contributed to maintaining your reputation and hosting work events to advance your career. I gave up my whole life to enhance yours, but it was never enough,' Mrs Duggan continued.

'You are a leech, a sponger. You are nothing!'

'Mr Duggan!' I exclaimed. That was beyond the pale.

'Oh, trust you to side with her. Women always stick together.'

'You have brought all this on yourself,' Mrs Duggan said. 'And I have just come off the phone with my solicitor. I have an appointment. I'm divorcing you for unreasonable behaviour. I wish I'd done it years ago. I have details of all the accounts. All of them. Yes, I know about your secret savings account. I deposited a letter with those details to the solicitor some time ago. I have just authorised him to act upon it, so don't think you can hide any more money from me.'

I led an incandescent Mr Duggan outside and got into the back of the car with him.

Mrs Duggan followed us out. 'Find somewhere else to stay. You are not welcome back here.'

'This is my house!' Mr Duggan shouted. 'I'm putting it on the market, and I'll make damned sure you don't see a penny. Let's see how you manage in the real world.'

'It can't be worse than living with you.' Mrs Duggan turned on her heel and went back inside, slamming the door behind her.

*

Back at the bridewell, I processed Mr Duggan, who kept protesting his innocence. When I was almost finished and ready to get a date for court, the bridewell sergeant called me to one side.

'I think a police caution would be most appropriate here. He's a bank manager, a respectable position. It's a family matter,' the bridewell sergeant said.

'It's theft!' I argued.

'Technically, yes, but he has a clean record. I think a shot across his bows is the way forward.' He narrowed his eyes, 'And it's my decision.'

Technically, my big toe. I was unhappy about that decision, but he outranked me.

We returned to the charge office.

'Mr Duggan, would you come to the desk please,' the sergeant said.

Mr Duggan came over and stood with his nose in the air.

'Mr Duggan, Constable Barrie and I have discussed it, and we have decided that this is best dealt with by a caution.'

We hadn't decided that at all, I'd had it foisted on me. However, I remained silent like a good little constable.

'I said it wasn't a crime,' Mr Duggan crowed.

'Oh, it is a crime, but we have decided that, if you choose, this can be dealt with by caution. You understand that if you accept the caution, you are accepting the guilt?' the bridewell sergeant asked.

'I'm not guilty of theft,' Mr Duggan said.

'I cannot caution you unless you accept that you are guilty of the crime,' the sergeant said.

'Or you can maintain your innocence then you can go to trial at court, even take it to Crown Court,' I added gleefully, ignoring the bridewell sergeant's dirty look. That would be my preferred choice. Then we'd see how *technical* the theft was.

Mr Duggan remained silent for several seconds. 'I can't accept any guilt. I'll lose my job if I have any conviction for dishonesty, even a caution.'

'You understand that if you accept the caution, you will be able to return home very quickly. If you choose to plead not guilty, there is a chance that the verdict will go against you?' the bridewell sergeant said.

Mr Duggan jutted his chin like some stupid hero in a film, accepting his doom. 'So be it.'

This was one court case I was looking forward to.

Chapter Twelve

Earlies: never my favourite shift, especially as John Batt and I were summoned to the inspector's office. Neither of us had any idea why. I wracked my brains to think of something that I had done that I shouldn't have done, or not done that I should have, but came up with nothing.

John knocked on the door and Inspector Benjamin called for us to enter. We stood side by side in front of his desk while he silently read a letter. Eventually, he looked at us.

'I've received a complaint from a Mr Roger Duggan, that you were,' the inspector paused to check the letter he was holding, '"Rude and officious". You refused to allow him to speak and you encouraged his son to complain about him. Then you unlawfully arrested him.'

John and I stared at each other, our jaws slack.

'That was not the case, sir,' John said. 'Mr Duggan was condescending and arrogant, especially to Samantha. He spoke to his wife in a most disgraceful way, right in front of us.'

'He cites that the fact that as he was offered a caution is proof the arrest was unlawful,' Inspector Benjamin said.

I had to speak up. 'Sir, it was lawful as the paperwork will verify. As you know, a caution does not mean no crime has been committed. The bridewell sergeant decided a caution was the best way to deal with it but Mr Duggan refused to accept he had done anything wrong, so it will have to go to court.'

'He's an unpleasant bully,' John added. 'He believes that he will win in court.'

'I don't see how he can,' I added.

The inspector folded the letter and put it on the desk, 'Okay. I have seen the file. I doubt C and D will be interested in this. As you say, there is paperwork to back up your version of events. Hopefully, this will be the last we hear from Mr Duggan. Dismissed.'

John and I left the office and waited until we got downstairs before speaking.

'Complaints and Discipline? Why would C and D be involved!' I exclaimed.

'They won't care about this, like the boss said,' John said.

'Even so… I can't wait to get to court with that wazzer,' I said.

'Me too,' John said. 'Let's get started. I'll give you a lift out to your patch.'

Bert was holding his stomach when we walked past the sergeants' office. I stopped at the door. John peered in over my shoulder.

'All right, Sarge?' I asked.

'Bloody heartburn. Do you have any indigestion tablets?' he asked.

John felt in his pockets and shook his head. I rummaged in my bag and pulled out a pack of antacids and gave it to him.

'Will this do?'

He took it and quickly popped one into his mouth. 'Thanks, lass. I think all that salad I've been eating is disagreeing with me. My mother was a martyr to heartburn and couldn't touch cucumber. Maybe I'm the same.'

The chocolate he'd been sneaking probably didn't help either.

He held the pack out to me. I shook my head. 'You keep it in case it comes back later.'

He popped the packet in his pocket. 'Thanks. Are you off out now?'

'I'm giving Sam a lift to her patch,' John replied.

'What did the boss want?' Bert asked.

'He received a complaint from that bolshy wazzer we locked up for theft of his son's bike. It's all rubbish,' John replied.

'It usually is,' Bert agreed.

John and I went into the yard. I couldn't shake the feeling that this was not the last we would hear of Mr Duggan. He was too full of himself to allow such humiliation to pass without retaliating.

I spotted Pixie going out to meet Trevor. I seized my chance to say something.

'How's it going?'

She smiled at me. 'Okay so far, I think.'

'Listen, Pixie, if you feel that you're not getting what you need in the way of training, you must mention it.'

She eyed me for a moment. 'Is Trevor not the best person to tutor me?'

I shrugged. 'He's a nice enough bloke. A bit rough around the edges. He deals with stuff allocated to him very well…'

'But only stuff allocated to him? You mean he's lazy,' Pixie said.

'Nooo…' I paused. 'Yes. His nickname is Torchy, from the Olympic torch that never goes out,' I said.

Pixie chuckled. 'Thanks for the warning. If I feel I need more training, I'll mention it.'

'I'm not trying to cause trouble, just be aware. He'll probably make an effort now he's tutoring you, but if you need to talk, I'm here. Also Irene, the collator, gives great advice,' I said. 'By the way, I loved how you handled Spider. She can be a bit much sometimes.'

Pixie grinned. 'I've met her sort before. I did my research before I came here. One of the benefits of coming in from the cadets is that I've done attachments to a lot of the departments. I've read up on you all as far as I was able.'

Uh-oh. My face must have dropped.

She continued. 'Oh, don't worry. I'm impressed by you. Commendations while still in your probation, and an arrest for murder, no less.'

'I'm just a copper, same as everyone else,' I said.

'And humble with it. It takes more than a degree to be a role model.' Pixie smiled.

'Thanks, Pixie.' I felt quite moved. Nobody here had ever said anything so nice to me.

'I'd better go. Trevor will be waiting.'

I stood staring after her. She'd also be a brilliant boss one day, unlike a certain human arachnid. I would love it if our two youngest members did reach high rank whilst graduate Spider languished at Inspector, unable to go any further. I'd go and find Ray, who would have retired by then, and tell him all about it, and we'd laugh and laugh.

*

Later on, Wilfred wandered off again. Those of us that were free headed off to his favourite places on our beats. In my case, it was the school, but he wasn't there. I kept my eyes open, but it was only as I was going in for scoff that Ray transmitted that he'd been found.

As normal, Wilfred was in the control room gossiping to Ray and Derek when I got back to the station.

'Hello, Wilfred. Where were you?' I asked.

He looked like a rabbit in the headlights.

'It's me, Samantha. I kept an eye open for you, but I didn't see you,' I said.

'Oh, hello, Samantha. I went to check on the YWCA, it's surprising how often you find men hanging around there trying to spy on the young ladies.'

The YWCA building was no longer a YWCA, it was now more of a community hub and a meeting place for brownies, girl guides and scouts. Wilfred had forgotten again.

'I bet you'd have given them short shrift if you'd found them, Wilf,' I said.

'I would that, lass,' he said and chuckled.

'I'll leave you chaps to talk. I'm going to get my scoff.'

110

I was surprised to see Spider in the report writing room as I passed.

'Hey, Spider, was it you who found Wilfred?' I was trying to be friendly.

She rolled her eyes. 'Stop calling me Spider.'

'It's only a nickname. Loads of us have them.' I wondered what she would say if she found out her unofficial nickname. 'Was it you who found him?'

'Yes, damned nuisance he is.'

'Don't be like that; he's a nice bloke when you chat to him. He just thinks it's 1940,' I said.

'I don't know why you encourage him.'

'He's an ex-cop so he's one of us, and he's interesting. He spotted that sus car a little while back. He remembers this town from before we were born. He remembers how local families are linked. It's interesting to get another perspective, and you never know what's going to be useful.'

Spider snorted. 'There is no comparison between policing then and now. He and his kind are obsolete.'

'That's harsh, even from you,' I said. 'He's us in the future.'

'That is definitely not me in the future.' Spider picked up her report and walked off without further comment. I mentally shrugged and went for my break.

*

When I came down from scoff, Wilfred was still in the control room. Usually someone had driven him home by now, but perhaps it had been too busy.

I wasn't scheduled to work the control room this shift, so I swapped my radio batteries before going out again.

'Mrs Hayes is complaining about her neighbour, Bessie, again,' Derek said to me.

'Bessie's been quiet recently,' I commented. I'd actually thought she had died but that was not the thing to say in front of Wilfred.

'She has been quiet recently, but she's back again.' Ray turned back to the radio to acknowledge a caller.

'What's going on?' Wilfred asked. He appeared to be in the present.

'Bessie turns up at Nellie Hayes' house and tries to barge in. For some reason, she thinks that Nellie has kidnapped her sons. Those boys would be in their fifties by now and I'm sure if they were in Nellie's house, they could get themselves out if they wanted to. She's only about four feet ten and six stone wringing wet.'

Wilfred shook his head. 'Be kind to Bessie. She suffered more than most in the war.'

'How so?' I asked. Many people suffered in the war, but any new information was helpful in this dispute. Previously, bobbies got Nellie to agree to Bessie looking around her house to convince her that Nellie had not kidnapped anyone. Understandably, Nellie was fed up with this. More recently, patrols just tried to shut Bessie up and get her back home.

Wilfred took another mouthful of his tea. 'Nellie has five boys and two girls. The girls worked in a munitions factory. Three of the boys joined the army and the other two went into the navy. They all came home after the war. Bessie wasn't so lucky. She was widowed while her children were still small and was left with three boys and three girls. The two oldest girls joined the Land Army. The youngest, Freda, was still at school. The oldest boy joined the Royal Navy and the other two joined the Army. Only the youngest boy came home, and he became a *ten-pound pom*.'

Wilfred was referring to the scheme where Australia only charged ten pounds for people to move there, a fraction of the normal price. It was unlikely that Bessie had seen her remaining son since. I felt a pang of sympathy for her.

'That's sad, but lots of mothers lost sons. It doesn't give Bessie the right to barge in on Nellie.' I avoided mentioning Wilfred's own son.

'That's true,' Wilfred agreed. 'However, not long after her second son died, there was a terrible munitions accident at RAF Fauld in Staffordshire, near to where her daughters were working as Land Girls. Many people were killed in the surrounding area, including, it's presumed, Bessie's girls.'

I was drawn in by this tragic tale. 'They didn't find their bodies?'

Wilfred shook his head. 'They've never been heard from since that day. The crater was over a thousand feet wide and a hundred feet deep. It destroyed a reservoir and farmland, animals and buildings. People are still listed as missing from there. It was the last straw for Bessie, she lost her mind. She spent some time in hospital. Eventually young Freda had to leave school to take care of her.'

Poor Freda lost her family, education, and opportunities. Another casualty of the war.

'The poor woman. I've never heard about RAF Fauld.' I turned to Ray. 'Did you know any of this?'

Ray shook his head. 'It does explain a lot.'

I decided that this new information would go into my report, once I had dealt with the incident. That way, other patrols would perhaps be more understanding instead of becoming exasperated.

'Why did she focus on Nellie?' Ray asked.

Wilfred shrugged. 'We all thought it was because she'd see Nellie's boys and then she'd remember that her sons had gone to war with them. Somehow it all got mixed up in her head.'

'That's useful to know. Thanks Wilfred,' I said.

Bearing this in mind, I attended the address, a tiny, terraced house in Victory Street, one of a number of residential streets just off the main shopping street. They were all named after the ships that took part in the battle of Trafalgar, so there was Neptune Street, Brittania Street, and so on. We nicknamed the area after the battle.

An elderly Bessie was trying to get into Nellie's house while a pale, middle-aged woman, her youngest daughter, Freda, tried to pull her away.

'Mam, stop it! The police are here now.'

Bessie looked at me, shrugged off her daughter and ran to me. 'Help them! She's got them in there. Make her send them out.'

'Bessie, I guarantee that your sons are not there,' I said.

'You haven't even looked!' Bessie pointed an accusing finger at me. 'You're in on it too. You're hiding them.'

'I'm so sorry,' Freda said. 'She's been getting agitated for days. I've been able to keep her in, but she waited until my back was turned and rushed out.' She wiped the back of her hand across her heavy, baggy eyes. She looked tired to the bone.

The front door opened, and Nellie came out.

'Nellie, I'm sorry. I tried to stop her,' Freda called.

Bessie rushed for the door, but Freda and I grabbed an arm each. Bessie screamed and dropped to the ground.

'Freda, this is the worst I've seen her. I think I should call the doctor.' I radioed in my request to Ray. I didn't have to ask who her doctor was, everyone in the area used the same surgery.

'I'll ask the Father to come too. He calms her down,' Freda said and ran off towards the church a short distance away. The local priest was an important figure in this area, and often the first person people turned to in times of trouble. Nobody around here had a phone in the house, and it was as quick to go to the presbytery as it was to the phone box.

Bessie continued wailing on the ground. Several neighbours had come out and were standing on their doorsteps watching with their arms crossed over their ubiquitous wraparound pinnies. I crouched beside Bessie ready to move if she tried to get into Nellie's house again.

Nellie knelt beside Bessie and put an arm across her shoulders.

'Look, Bess, I've told you before. Your boys are not in there.'

'Liar!' screamed Bessie.

'No. Remember, Bess, they fell in the war. They were heroes.'

Bessie stopped wailing and stared at Nellie. 'The war?'

'Yes, they died to keep us safe from the Jerries. Your boys were heroes,' Nellie said. 'And your girls. They worked to keep us all fed.'

I saw something click behind Bessie's eyes. She was back with us.

'My children were heroes,' she said to me.

'They certainly were,' I answered. 'Wilfred Wainwright has told me about your brave boys and your hardworking girls.'

'You know Mr Wainwright?'

I nodded, a little surprised that she remembered him, although perhaps I shouldn't have been. 'He's retired now but he's still a regular visitor to the station.'

'He was a good copper. He cared, not like some of them.' Bessie struggled to her feet, aided by me and Nellie. I saw Freda hurrying back down the street with the parish priest jogging beside her.

'Bessie, Bessie, what's happening, my lamb?' he panted as he arrived. He nodded at me and I nodded back. I had an ambivalent relationship with religion and felt a bit awkward around the clergy in case they thought I was judging their career choice, or that they knew how I felt and were judging me.

'She's feeling better now, Father, aren't you, Bess?' Nellie said.

Bessie nodded. 'Thank you for coming, Father. I was confused.'

'4912 from control,' Ray transmitted.

'Go ahead,' I responded.

'Doctor en route.'

'Roger.'

The priest heard the transmission and took Bessie's arm. 'Come on, Bessie, let's get you home and wait for the doctor to arrive. Freda can make us a nice cup of tea while we chat.' He and Freda walked Bessie to the house.

'I don't blame her; I think I'd have gone crazy if my children had died,' Nellie said to me. 'I try to be understanding but it gets a bit much. I have my own life and I've got two boys still at home.'

It wasn't unusual for unmarried children to remain in their parents' house, but elderly Nellie was actually looking after two middle-aged men who should have been well capable of taking care of themselves. It wasn't my place to pass comment.

'I'm concerned about Freda,' I said. 'She looks so drawn and tired.'

'Little wonder. That girl gave up school and her whole life for Bessie. She could have gone to university, you know. She had the brains, but she didn't even stay long enough to get her school certificate. Now she's got nothing. No qualifications, no husband or children. Her useless brother buggered off to Australia, so she gets no help from anyone.' Nellie sighed.

'I'll hang around and have a chat with the doctor before he sees Bessie. Maybe he'll take a look at Freda too. She looks at the end of her tether.'

Nellie nudged me. 'Hey, when you've finished here is there any chance you can take a look at Annie Hodgeson's house?' Nellie pointed out a house a couple of doors further down from hers. 'She died a few months back. I don't know who lives there now, but it's looking really run-down and it's beginning to smell. And there's rats. Big, vicious ones. My son, Donald, found one in the privy a couple of days ago and it went for him when he cornered it.'

'It got into your house?' I would be annoyed too if I'd found a rat inside my house.

'No, we don't have an indoor bathroom. My husband always said the kitchen's good enough to wash in. He's gone now, but I can't afford to get it done. At this rate, though, it won't be long before the rats do try to get into the houses. And sometimes, when I'm in the yard, I can hear noises like crying coming from the house. I think there's animals getting in there.'

'Have your neighbours mentioned anything?' I asked.

'No, but they're hardly ever there. They're a young couple and they both go out to work. The people on the other side of

Annie's house haven't mentioned anything either.'

'It sounds like an environmental health issue more than a police issue,' I said. 'You should ring the Environmental Health people about the rats and the smell. Maybe the RSPCA too. In fact, I'll pop a note in for the council.' I wrote the house number on the back of my hand.

'Annie would be horrified if she thought her house was smelling. I mean, I'm a houseproud woman, but she put me to shame.'

'Any patrol please. PA Peninsula Bank,' Ray transmitted.

Personal attack alarm. The bank was on my patch. I glanced around the street. The doctor was still not here.

'Sounds urgent. Never mind Annie's house, you get off. I'll tell the doctor about Freda,' Nellie said. 'I'll let the police station know what he says.'

I was mildly surprised she had followed the transmissions. It could take a few days to attune your ears to the radio. Most members of the public could only pick out odd words.

I trotted towards the main road, at the same time I transmitted, '4912 to control. The priest is with Bessie and her daughter in their house and the doctor is on his way so I can assist. Would Mike Two be able to pick me up, I'm on Town Road?'

I heard the radio beeping.

'Roger,' said Ray. 'Mike Two from control, pick up Con Barrie on Town Road. Mike Three is also making.'

The radio beeped briefly, then silence. The bank wasn't on Mike Three's patch but with PAs at banks, we didn't know what we'd find so we always backed each other up.

I heard a siren approaching and Mike Two roared towards me. He pulled up and I jumped straight in. I barely had time to close the door before John took off again and raced to the bank.

John flung the car into the kerb, part mounting the pavement. We ran into the bank to find the cashiers quietly working. One cashier met my eyes but quickly looked away.

'Dear, oh dear. Did I interrupt your tea break?'

I recognised that voice. I turned around and saw Mr Duggan standing at the door to his office, ostentatiously checking his watch.

'Where's the emergency?' John asked.

'I decided it was about time we tested the response we receive from the local constabulary. Fifteen minutes from when I pressed the alarm. What if there really had been armed robbers? We could all be dead by now. I'm afraid I will have to lodge a complaint against you.'

I thought that fifteen minutes from when he pressed the alarm wasn't bad. It would have gone to the monitoring station. They would have phoned it through on the emergency line, the red telephone that sat beside the green and grey telephones next to Derek. He would have written a job sheet then passed it to Ray who transmitted it to us, and we almost broke our necks to get to the bank.

'You deliberately set off the personal attack alarm?' I was still confused.

'How else was I going to get a genuine response?' he replied. I wanted to slap that smug grin off his face.

Trevor from Mike Three ran into the building, followed by Pixie. They stopped and looked around.

'What's going on?' Trevor demanded.

'Mr Duggan was testing our response,' John replied.

'You what!?' Trevor cried. 'That is misuse of the system. It's dangerous. You have caused patrols to be diverted from other incidents and to drive at high speed to get here.'

'Not fast enough, though. We'll just have to see if things improve after a complaint,' Mr Duggan said. 'I will need to see evidence of improvement. In fact, I might implement regular testing of the system.'

John snorted and turned away. 'Come on, Sam.'

'Be careful,' Trevor warned him. 'Don't forget the boy who cried wolf. We'd hate to have to withdraw response because of persistent misuse of the emergency system.'

'You wouldn't dare,' Mr Duggan snarled.

Trevor's smile told Mr Duggan that he absolutely would dare and would definitely not hate it.

'I'm complaining about the poor response and I'm complaining about you all personally,' Mr Duggan called after us. 'Especially you two, Constable Batt and Constable Barrie. You have a personal grudge against me.'

I turned back. 'That is untrue. We have a problem with anyone who misuses the emergency system. By the way, I do hope you will be able to arrange leave for your day in court. I'm looking forward to seeing you there.' Catty, I know. 'Give my regards to Mrs Duggan and Martin.' Mr Duggan looked ready to explode as I left the building, and I'd probably earned myself another complaint for mentioning it in front of the cashiers, but he asked for it and I regretted nothing.

'You know why he's done this, don't you,' John said as I got back into the car.

'Oh yes, he's still cheesed off about that domestic. Wazzer. He's just a bully who thinks he looks bigger if he intimidates weaker people. Did you notice how cowed those cashiers looked? He's too used to throwing his weight around. Well, he's met his match and I'm going to enjoy our day in court.'

John looked sideways at me. 'I love an assertive woman.'

I knocked his shoulder. 'Shut up, Batt.'

We both laughed. I knew he wasn't serious.

*

Wilfred was gone by the time we got back to the station. I went into the control room and started to shuffle through the rolodex next to Derek.

'What are you looking for?' he asked.

'A number for the security department of the bank. The manager is a complete wazzer and I'm going to report him for deliberately setting off the alarm,' I replied.

Ray picked up a laminated sheet and handed it to me. 'That number will be on here with the more important numbers.'

'Thanks.' I took the sheet into the report writing room and dialled the number. I didn't know how it would be dealt with at their end, but Mr Duggan was not the only one who could make a complaint.

Once I had dropped Roger Duggan in the mire, I completed a full report on the incident with Nellie and Bessie. I made sure to include the information I'd got from Wilfred. Maybe the next patrol would find it useful. As promised, Nellie had phoned the station from the phone box. She reported that the doctor had agreed that Freda was exhausted and had arranged for Bessie to spend some time at a residential home. Freda had been resistant, and had only agreed when the doctor said it was in her mother's best interests and the priest agreed. People in that area didn't argue with the two most important men in their community.

I was glad that Freda, and Nellie Hayes, would get a break now. I was also glad that I had spoken with Wilfred before attending the incident. It had been useful to have all that background information. I had been able to acknowledge Bessie's debilitating grief, and I felt that I had been able to deal with things better that I would have normally. I'd have to tell Spider that obsolete or not, Wilfred had helped.

Chapter Thirteen

Rest day. I stretched out in bed and thought about what to do with myself. Karen would be preparing for her move to the main market hall. I was so happy her business was taking off that I decided a visit was in order. I showered, had a cup of tea, then drove to the market. I pulled in on the cobblestones that surrounded the market building and skipped up the steps to the inside stalls. Karen was bent over embroidering a piece of material.

'Hi.' I slipped behind the workbench and turned on the kettle. 'Getting ready for the big move?'

Karen put the material down and rolled her shoulders. 'End of the week. The lease on this expires and I take over the new stall.'

I peered at the material. Karen had been sewing tiny rosebuds in pink and light blue. 'That's lovely.'

She picked it up and held it out so I could see the full effect. 'It's a yoke for the christening gown I'm making for your friend. Suitable for a boy or a girl.' Karen examined her embroidery. 'Once the baby is born, they can emphasise the colour they want by using ribbons.'

The kettle clicked off and I made us a mug of tea each. Karen put the sewing down and accepted the mug I held out.

'Do you have a date for your CID Aides course yet? It seems ages since you applied.'

It had been ages, but these things took time. That course would be the first step to becoming a detective constable. I had long felt that I was being funnelled towards the CID, and I tended to resist if I felt pushed towards something. However, I had come to realise that this was where my interests lay.

'It can't be much longer. I think it'll be a case of being told Friday and starting the Monday.' I slurped some of my tea. 'Any plans for the weekend?'

'I'm going to make some curtains for my new house. It's fab, Sam. I've got so much room. I love it.'

We chatted for about half an hour, then I left her to finish Ken's embroidery while I popped over to my parents' house in High Lake. They, and my nan, had moved to Aberdeenshire to be closer to my dad's work on the oil rigs, so I was keeping an eye on the place until it was sold. I waved to our ex-next door neighbour, Henry, who was mowing his lawn.

'Any interest?' he called to me.

'Some. We've had a second viewing,' I replied.

'We miss you Barries. You were decent neighbours,' Henry said.

I was quite touched. 'Thank you, Henry. That's a lovely thing to say. You were good neighbours too.'

I unlocked the front door and went in. It felt strange walking through my childhood home now it was empty. I walked from room to room, checking the windows and stopping for a moment to enjoy memories. In the kitchen, I ran my hand over the worktops. Mum and Dad had left some of the larger items, such as the cooker, for the new owners. I didn't exactly feel sad, they had made the right decision for them, but in a few weeks, someone else would be living here. A strange child would be sleeping in my room. I hoped they would be happy.

I suddenly remembered Nellie telling me about Annie's house. Dammit! I had intended to go back after the alarm, have a mooch to see if I could hear any animals then get Ray to ring the council. I had completely forgotten after the bank incident. I had three choices: forget it and trust that Nellie would ring the Environmental Health; leave it until my next shift and submit a report then; or drive past now and check the number seeing as it had washed off my hand and I couldn't remember it, then ring it in to Environmental Health myself. I didn't want to ignore it or leave it, so a drive past was in order.

It was only a fifteen minute drive to Victory Street. Kids playing in the street stopped and stared as I drove past. I don't know why, my car was nothing special, but possibly the only people in cars that went around there were police or social services or the doctor.

I wrote the number of the house on a piece of paper and carried on to a phone box a short distance away and phoned it in. The council would deal with it in their own time, but that wasn't my problem. Satisfied that I had done what I could, I returned home. I wanted to enjoy my off-duty weekend. We didn't get many. I would use the time to do some OU work, catch up on sleep and watch telly. I knew how to live the high life.

*

'Chris who?' Gary asked when he phoned that evening.

'Chris Atherton. He's that fireman I told you about,' I replied. 'Remember, I told you, I felt awkward going alone? I was going to return the tickets like I told you, but he said I could go with him.'

'Mm,' Gary didn't sound impressed.

'Now don't you start getting all jealous. You said I should go. He knows I'm spoken for. Steve and Emma and a lot of others will be there too, and I'll be wearing my ring.'

'Okay,' Gary said, but I caught the edge to his tone.

'If you're unhappy then I'll give Chris my apologies.'

'I don't want to stop you having fun,' Gary said.

'But you're okay with making sure I feel bad whilst I'm doing it?' I countered.

'I don't want you to feel bad.'

'Gary, if you don't want me to go, I won't, but don't say you don't mind then get all huffy about it.'

'I'm sorry if I made you feel bad. You should go. Enjoy yourself.'

I remained silent for a few seconds. 'You do trust me, don't you?'

'Of course I do,' Gary declared.

'Okay then. I'll tell you all about it next time we speak,' I said.

'I look forward to it,' Gary replied.

I decided not to read any negativity into his reply.

*

My next shift was nights. I was put into the control room as Derek had booked time off.

'Where's Derek tonight?' I asked Ray.

'Oomies,' he replied.

'Where?'

'His old regiment reunion. They're getting older so they've christened themselves the Oomies.'

I still didn't get it.

'As in "Ooh me back. Ooh me knee." And so on,' Ray explained, which made me laugh.

'Can you mind the radio, I need to nip for a jimmy riddle,' Ray asked.

Hardly surprising as he drank about forty-seven cuppas in a day. Between the tea and his heavy smoking, his insides must have been dyed deep, mahogany brown.

Typically, not a minute later, Steve shouted up on the radio, so I moved over to Ray's seat and acknowledged him.

'I'm on Micklestane Drive. The alarm has just gone off at a house named Phuket. I'm about to check it out. Could you create a job sheet for me, please.'

I knew the house. It was in a wealthy area and surrounded by vast, green lawns. I would never be property hunting up there.

'Roger.' I replied and swiftly scribbled out the address on the sheet 'By the way, Steve, that's not how you pronounce "Phuket".' Lucky we were on nights. The brass sometimes monitored the radio and would have a fit if they had heard what Steve had said.

'It's how it's spelt,' he argued. 'Anyway, the front appears okay. I'm making my way around the back.'

'Roger, but stand by for back-up.' It wasn't good for a lone foot patrol to be mooching about a large house in the small hours. Who knew what he'd run into.

I jotted details so far on the sheet then asked Mike Three to back Steve up. Pixie was still in company with him, so a couple of extra officers were a good idea.

'Roger control. Making from the park,' Trevor said.

'Roger, thanks for that, Mike Three. Steve, for your information, Mike Three is backing up.'

No response. I left it for a minute, if Steve had ignored me and was sneaking up on a burglar, he wouldn't thank me for giving him away. However, if he was in trouble… I dithered for another minute but couldn't leave it any longer.

'Con Patton, respond please,' I transmitted.

Nothing.

'Mike Two to control, do you want me to make Micklestane Drive too? I'll bring Andy with me.'

'Thank you, John,' I replied and added his call sign and Andy's number to the sheet. Nobody could relax while a colleague was not responding.

Ray came back so I shifted over to the phones.

'Anything happening?' he asked.

'Steve came across an alarm on Micklestane Drive and now he's not responding. Mikes Two and Three are making to back up with Pixie and Andy. I've done a job sheet. Should I let the inspector know?'

Ray's forehead creased as he read the sheet. 'He keeps a radio in his office, so he'll have heard it. Okay. Let's leave it a few minutes, see what the patrols say.'

He had barely finished speaking when Mike Three called up. I could hardly understand a word he said.

'Is he laughing?' I asked Ray. 'I think he's laughing.'

'It sounded like he was strangling a goat,' Ray replied.

'Try Pixie, you might get some sense out of her,' I suggested.

Ray called up both pandas but despite hearing several attempts at transmission, all intelligible because of the snorting and cackling sounds, he gave up.

The boss came into the control room. 'What the hell's going on?'

'Uncertain, sir,' Ray replied.

'Steve came across an alarm in Micklestane Drive. He went to check it and Mikes Two and Three backed up when he failed to respond. We haven't been able to understand a word since. I think they're laughing,' I said.

The boss grabbed the mic. 'Anyone at Micklestane Drive. Report.'

After a few seconds, Pixie came on air. 'Con Millington-Dow, sir. I think it would be best to explain what's happened when we get back.'

'Explain now,' Inspector Bejamin demanded.

'Yes, sir. We are at the rear of Phuket on Micklestane Drive.' She pronounced it properly. 'There is a covered swimming pool and Steve has fallen in. He's okay. Mike Two is bringing him back to the station. They left a short time ago so should be with you soon. We are with the homeowner now and everything is in order. He believes the alarm was triggered by his cat.'

'Roger.' The inspector replaced the mic and shook his head. 'He fell in a damned pool?'

The sound of a car engine in the yard signalled that Mike Two had arrived.

'This is going to be interesting,' Ray said.

I heard the door to the yard open and a squelching sound approach the control room. Steve, dripping wet and bareheaded, came into the office with John Batt who looked ready to burst into laughter at any second.

Steve tossed his radio down onto the desk. 'It's Donald Ducked.'

'What happened?' I asked. 'Pixie said the pool was covered.'

'It was covered, with one of those plastic sheets you pull over from a roll. I didn't see it in the dark and when I heard someone, who turned out to be the owner, I ran right onto it. Every time I tried to stand up, it sank down and filled with more water. I finished up having to crawl to the edge so someone could pull me out.'

John started to crack up. 'Stop it. My sides hurt.'

'Wazzer!' Steve rolled his eyes.

'He'd almost reach the edge then he'd lose his grip and slide down to the middle again.' John leant against the door jamb and wiped the tears from his eyes. Even the inspector grinned at the image that gave us. John regained control and continued. 'That wasn't the best of it though. When he finally got to the edge, it dipped right down and he rolled into the pool proper. It took three of us to pull him out.' John completely lost it and gasped for breath against the door.

'My helmet's still in the pool. The owner said he'd try to get it back in the morning.' Steve added. 'And I don't know if my pocketbook is usable anymore. Thank the Lord it's a new one. Worst case scenario, I'll only lose a couple of days' evidence and I don't think I've dealt with anything that will end up in court during those days.'

'Right,' the boss said. 'John, are you okay to drive?'

'Yes, sir,' John replied.

'Okay, in that case, please take Steve home to get changed. Steve, get that uniform in for cleaning. You can't go out without a helmet so you're in the control room when you get back. Sam, you can go out when Steve gets back.'

John looked at Steve and burst out laughing again. I could hear Steve moaning at him until they went into the yard. Ray, Inspector Benjamin and I burst into laughter.

*

Bert was already in the refs room when I got there, a Tupperware pot of ham salad in front of him.

'That looks nice,' I said to him. I meant it. The ham wasn't the plastic-wrapped supermarket ham; it was thick cut and a nice, deep colour that promised lots of flavour. The salad was crisp and the tomatoes a rich red. Mrs Mason was looking after her man.

Bert rubbed his stomach.

'Are you okay?' I asked.

'Bloody heartburn again. It's driving me mad,' Bert said.

'Have you told your wife you're getting heartburn?' I asked.

'No, she'll only nag me to go to the doctors.'

'Bert, perhaps it is time to visit the doctor. You might have an ulcer or something,' I urged.

'Aye, you might be right,' he admitted.

'I am right. You need to tell your wife, and you need to go to see the doctor.'

He remained quiet for a minute. 'Okay then.' He stood up. 'I'm going to find some milk to drink.'

I ogled Bert's salad and considered offering to swap it for my sandwiches, but if he was trying to shift heartburn, cheese was probably not a good idea. I resolved to go shopping in the morning and make myself a nice ham salad for tomorrow's tea, instead of resorting to old faithful, cheese sandwiches. Tasty as they were, it was not good to eat them every day, at least not with as much cheese as I liked to put on them.

*

After scoff, I returned to the control room until Steve got back. It was the quiet time that Ray used to make sure the batteries were charged and admin completed. I was sorting the day's job sheets when Ray looked over my shoulder towards the front desk. 'Customer.'

I turned around and saw Karen. I jumped up and went to greet her. 'It's the early hours! What's happened?'

'I'm glad I got your shifts right. I remembered you said you often looked after the office after your break. Have you seen Ruthie Pritchard recently?' she asked.

I shook my head. The last time I had seen Ruthie was when I was with that wazzer Fleming. Ruthie's bony legs had been stuffed into baggy, scuffed boots. The neon pink, plastic handbag that looked as if it had come free on the front of a teenager's magazine, clashed horribly with her red coat. Her clothes were dirty and unironed, her lank hair crawled with lice. The bad skin and the gaps in her teeth added to the picture of neglect, and no doubt added to Fleming's disgust. She was belligerent, defiant, but at the same time, so vulnerable and frail.

Karen's brow wrinkled. 'I've been to visit some old friends. Two different people have told me that she hasn't been seen for days. You know she was always down by the docks or the supermarket.'

Thinking about it, it had been a while since our patrols had mentioned seeing her at the supermarket or the shopping centre. I'd have to check to see if anyone from another block had seen her.

Karen continued. 'To be honest, I wondered if she'd finally OD-ed. I went around to her house but I got no answer. I looked in the windows but saw nothing. I've got a bad feeling, Sam.'

So did I. Ruthie was a fixture in the town and was always spotted around and about the shopping centre when she wasn't working on the ships or begging outside the supermarket.

'Do you want to report her missing?' I asked. I knew nobody else would.

'I'm not sure. I might be making a big fuss over nothing,' Karen said.

'Okay. I'll start a job sheet and get the address checked out to begin with. If I put it down as a concern for welfare job, the patrol can enter the house.'

'Great idea. You know I prefer my name not to feature, don't you?' Karen asked.

'It would be better if it did,' I said.

She shook her head. 'I'm known to police, so anything I say will be dismissed because of my past. Put me down as anonymous.'

'Okay, for now,' I agreed. 'But you know none of us here will judge you or dismiss your concern about Ruthie.'

'I'm sure you won't, but others…' Karen smiled. 'I'll let you get on. I'll contact you if I hear anything.'

'Likewise,' I replied.

Karen left and I returned to the control room and picked up a job sheet.

'What was that about?' Ray asked.

'Ruthie Pritchard hasn't been seen for a while,' I replied. 'I said I'd log it as a concern for welfare, but I wonder if I am better listing her as missing.'

Ray puffed smoke from his nose. 'Given Ruthie's known drug addiction, I think you should start it as a concern for welfare.'

I filled out the form and passed it to Ray, who passed it to Trevor on Mike Three, who was not impressed.

'She'll be off her head on some ship or other,' he said.

'We still need you to go into the house and check it out.' Ray used his "get it done" voice. One of three or four tones he used that we all had come to recognise.

'Roger,' Trevor responded. I had never heard anyone sound so unenthusiastic. Perhaps Karen's judgement was not so far off the mark.

'So, we'll see what happens,' Ray said to me in his normal voice.

*

About half an hour later, Trevor called up.

'Mike Three to control.'

'Go ahead,' Ray responded.

'Right, I've been to the address. It's a complete midden. I wouldn't have said anyone has lived there at all but knowing Ruthie, she probably calls it home. There's no sign of her anywhere.'

'Roger, thanks,' Ray transmitted.

'So, escalate it?' I asked.

'Let's see what Bert says.' Ray reached for his phone and dialled Bert's extension.

Bert said to escalate it. Ruthie's description was passed out to patrols, not that it was needed, everyone knew her, and Ray sent out an APB. Meantime, I completed a misper form and that was circulated to other forces. I rang the women's prison to try to find out where Elsie, Ruthie's mother, had gone after her release from prison in case Ruthie had gone looking for her. However, once she had fulfilled her requirement to report to probation, Elsie had dropped off the radar without contacting either of her daughters. I hesitated to contact Ruthie's little sister, Bernie. She was not yet an adult and was settled in a foster home in Manchester. Ruthie had mentioned that Bernie had not maintained contact with her. Luckily, Bert agreed with me. Bernie would only be contacted when it was absolutely necessary.

Steve returned and took over in the control room. I updated him on the Ruthie saga then went out for the remaining few hours of our shift. I was not covering any of Ruthie's usual haunts, but I still kept an eye out for her.

Despite our efforts, the shift ended without any sighting of Ruthie. As I drove home, I wondered if she was going to be one of our long-term mispers, some of whom had probably gone into the river and would never be found. She spent enough time by the river, so it was not unlikely that she might have fallen in whilst under the influence of something. I hoped that she would pop up again soon. She was a nuisance, but she didn't deserve to just vanish.

Chapter Fourteen

Lates again. I was scheduled to cover for Derek after refs, again. I didn't mind taking my turn with this, but it seemed to be happening most days now. It was time to have a word with Bert about it, again.

We were also covering the front desk. Something else to bring up with Bert. We hadn't had a regular front desk officer since Steve had returned to full duties. A middle-aged couple came in and stood patiently at the desk. I went to speak to them and clocked the dog collar around the man's neck.

'Good evening, how can I help?' I asked.

'Good evening. I am Reverend James Shilling and this is my wife, Margaret.'

My stomach sank. They were Carol's parents. I nodded greetings to Mrs Shilling who looked frail and broken.

'Our daughter, Carol, was recently found deceased in your area,' Reverend Shilling said.

'May I express my deepest sympathy to you both.'

'Thank you,' Reverend Shilling said. It sounded automatic. 'We have two reasons for our visit. First, we want to personally thank you all for your efforts in finding Carol, even though the outcome was not as we hoped. Secondly, Carol was wearing a bracelet and we wondered if it had been found yet. It was given to her by her grandmother who passed last year, and has enormous sentimental value, especially now.'

Mrs Shilling spoke, her voice quiet and unsteady. 'It's silver, with her name engraved on it… She was wearing it when she went out… that night…'

'I don't know of any bracelet being handed in, but I'll check our property book for you. If you care to take a seat, I'm sure our inspector would like to speak with you.'

'You're very kind.' Reverend Shilling took his wife's arm and gently led her to our plastic seats. It occurred to me that we should get some more comfortable seats in a private area for victims.

I put my head into the control room. 'Ray, would you ask the boss to come down, Carol Shilling's parents are here.'

Ray picked up the phone without comment. I returned to the front office and flicked through the found property book.

A couple of minutes later DI Webb entered the front office from the corridor and shook hands with the couple. I hadn't expected him to come down, but thinking about it, it made sense.

'Reverend and Mrs Shilling. I'm DI Norman Webb. I'm so sorry for your loss, would you like to come through for a chat?'

Mrs Shilling looked at me.

'I'll continue checking the book and I'll let you know if I find anything,' I promised.

She allowed her husband to lead her through the door from the enquiry office. She seemed almost childlike. Probably the doctor had given her something to help her cope with such a terrible loss.

I couldn't find anything remotely resembling the bracelet in our book. I wasn't surprised. Not many people around here would hand in a silver bracelet. The Shillings would have more luck going to the pawnbrokers. That's where we went if we needed to look for property. The pawnbrokers around here were pretty good and would have rung us if anything had looked a bit off with a customer. I wouldn't say that to the Shillings though, they had enough on their plate. I might take a stroll past and look in the window when I went back out. Actually, DI Webb would probably think the same and dispatch someone to the pawnshop in the morning with the order to go through their inventory.

The side door opened and DI Webb showed the Shillings back into the enquiry office.

'I'm afraid I couldn't find anything. I'll enter it into the system; then, if it does arrive here, I'll leave a note for you to be contacted straight away,' I said in answer to the unasked question. I could do a lost property report and add that to the crime file.

'Thank you. Bless you. Bless you all,' the reverend said, and guided his wife out.

Most organisations lump lost and found property in together. Not in the police. Found property and lost property had separate systems. The property officer would then try to marry up lost and found items. Much of the found property linked back to crimes.

*

I stopped at the pawnbrokers on my way out, but the bracelet wasn't in the window. There was lots of interesting stuff, but no bracelets. Maybe the morning jacks would have better luck going through the inventories. I was walking back out to my beat, thinking about the Shillings, when the boss pulled up beside me.

'Hop in, I'll peg you here.'

I wasn't going to turn down a lift, even if it was with the inspector. I got into the passenger side. Once a shift, we were visited by supervision who signed our books. We called these visits: pegs. I got my pocketbook out for the inspector to sign. It was all up to date, so no frantic scribbling was needed.

The boss signed my book. 'Do you know where people around here meet their dealer?'

'Often, it's by the park main entrance. I do know that the dealer will scarper before I get close. I think he has lookouts posted around the park. They must signal each other.'

'Let's park up in the entry by the furniture shop, we might see something.'

I guessed the boss had been getting a bit stir crazy in his office. He seemed quite excited at the prospect of bagging a dealer. It made a nice change; he'd been so grumpy recently.

'Mike Sierra One from control.'

Normally as the passenger, I would pick up the handset and reply. However, this was the inspector's car so I hesitated.

The boss picked up the handset. 'Go ahead.'

'Call from a Mrs Archer. She says she needs to speak to you urgently.'

'Roger.' The inspector placed the handset and swore under his breath. Without another word, he pulled over by a phone box and went to make a call. I was intrigued. What was so urgent that he couldn't even wait to get back to the station? What about Ruthie's dealer?

Eventually, he returned to the car and picked up the handset.

'Mike Sierra One to control,'

'Go ahead, sir,' Ray ricocheted back.

'I'm going over the border. Please give them the usual courtesy call. I'm not sure how long I'll be. Also, I'm taking Constable Barrie with me.'

'Roger, sir.'

I assumed we were now not going dealer hunting. The boss hadn't given Ray an address, so how did he know where he was going? Why would he need me with him?

'What's happening, sir?' I asked.

'I don't want this to be general knowledge, do you understand?' the boss stated.

'Yes, sir,' I replied. My pulse increased at the thought I was being brought into a secret.

'My mother is suffering from Alzheimer's; she lives in a supposedly secure unit, but she's learnt the key code and keeps wandering off. She's wandered again only this time they can't find her.'

'Have the local police been informed?' I asked.

'Yes, but I need to speak to the staff at the unit.' The boss turned on the engine and set out to the unit.

It was interesting going into another force area on duty. There was no danger of the public mistaking us for a local police patrol as our car was so plain compared to the liveried cars of the other force. This was a good thing as it made it less likely we would be flagged down to assist with something in an area we didn't know.

A car pulled up beside us as we waited at some traffic lights. It was a pale blue Vauxhall Viva. It was hard to see any difference in the colours of our cars. Light shone across the window so I couldn't see the driver.

'It is hard to tell them apart,' I murmured.

'What?' asked Inspector Benjamin.

'Just thinking aloud, sir,' I said.

The lights changed colour and the Viva turned off. We continued to the unit.

The secure unit was in an older building within the grounds of the large, modern hospital. It probably had been part of the original hospital. A major road ran along one side of the grounds, and a canal ran along another side. In my opinion, it was not terribly safe for people who might be confused.

We pulled up in the car park, and Inspector Benjamin led the way in and gave his name to the receptionist.

'Mrs Archer will be with you shortly. Please take a seat.'

The reception area was bright and lined with armless, soft chairs similar to those we had in the refs room. I perched on one while the boss paced about.

A woman came into the reception. 'Mr Benjamin, thank you for coming. Good news, she has been found. The police are returning her as we speak. Let's go to my office.'

We followed her to her cluttered office.

Inspector Benjamin said, 'That is good news, Mrs Archer, but I have to ask, how was she able to get out—again?'

Mrs Archer chewed her lip before answering. 'She has learnt

the code and she is canny; she waits until the staff are busy…'

'That has been the answer for the last three times she has absconded. Why has nobody changed the codes? Why wasn't she spotted by reception? I'm afraid this time I intend to escalate my concerns until somebody can carry out basic security measures and I can be assured that my mother is safe in your care,' Inspector Benjamin snapped.

Mrs Archer's cheeks flushed. 'You know it's not that simple. There are budgets…'

'You could at least change the codes,' the boss insisted.

The phone rang and Mrs Archer answered it. She gave a curt reply and replaced the receiver.

'Your mother is here. They're bringing her to the ward.'

'Good. Now, while we're here, please phone someone and get them to sort the codes. I do not intend to leave until this is done. My brother lives abroad, and I cannot keep running up here like this. I have to work.'

'We don't ring you every time…' Mrs Archer's voice trailed away as she realised what she had said.

'What do you mean?' Inspector Benjamin's voice was dangerously even.

'I mean if she doesn't leave the building.' Seeing the inspector's face, Mrs Archer continued hurriedly. 'She is sometimes found wandering in other parts of the building. That's not really escaping.'

'I want to see the incident reports of all those occasions,' Inspector Benjamin said.

'We don't log those. As I said, she doesn't leave the building. They don't count.'

'But she leaves the unit, so I think it does count. Who told you not to log such incidents?' the boss asked.

'I run this unit, and it was my decision,' Mrs Archer replied. 'It is only recently that your mother has become so troublesome. We are aware that you work long hours and your brother is abroad, so I think you should be more appreciative that we don't contact you as often as we could. If you are not happy with our care here, you could always try to find somewhere else.'

There are two types of rage. The red-faced, eye-bulging, profanity-laden explosion; and the more dangerous, white-faced, narrow-eyed, nostril-flaring rage that guarantees hell and revenge. The boss turned white.

'I'm going to see my mother. I expect the codes to be changed before I leave.' He paused. 'Constable Barrie, I want a statement from you about what you have seen and heard today.'

'Yes, sir,' I replied. I understood now why he wanted me to go with him. He knew a showdown was imminent and he wanted an independent witness.

Mrs Archer seemed to notice me for the first time. 'Are you family?'

'Constable Barrie was attending an incident with me when I got the call. I did not have time to return her to the station before coming here.'

'Well, I have to insist that she stays off the ward,' Mrs Archer said.

'I'll write my statement here, sir,' I said.

'No. Constable Barrie is coming with me. My mother might be distressed, and she would be comforted by the presence of a female officer.'

Utter nonsense, but I followed the boss from the office, ignoring Mrs Archer's protests.

The ward was just like any other modern hospital ward, with a comfortable day room at one end and a dining area at the other, but rather than rows of beds, actual bedrooms ran along a corridor off the dining room.

The boss went over to a woman dressed in a brown skirt with a beige blouse. Her long, silver hair was pulled back into a ponytail. She didn't look very old, mid-sixties perhaps, but dementia wasn't fussy who it affected.

'Hello, Mum,' he bent down and kissed her forehead.

'Georgie!' his mother sounded delighted. She looked past him to me. 'At last! I thought you'd be alone forever after Amanda.'

Well, wasn't that an interesting little snippet. However, I had my discreet head on so I pretended not to hear. I did wonder if Amanda had been his wife or girlfriend. He certainly hadn't mentioned her back when we were working on that past operation.

Inspector Benjamin chuckled. 'Don't get excited. We work together, that's all.'

'I worry that you're lonely, Georgie,' Mrs Benjamin said.

'I'm not lonely. I have plenty to keep me occupied. Specifically, you. You've been getting into mischief again.'

She giggled, a lovely, tinkly sound. 'I get bored here. I went for a walk.'

'Mum, you have to stop it. You're not always yourself and it could be dangerous.'

In a second, Mrs Benjamin's mood changed. 'Stop bullying me! Where's Douglas? I need him here. You stay away from me.'

The boss sighed. 'Dougie is still in America, Mum. I don't mean to bully you, but I do worry about you.'

'I hate you. It's no wonder Amanda left you. Piss off!'

Time for me to leave. I quietly moved towards the door.

'Amanda didn't leave me, she died. You were at the funeral and wore a dark grey dress,' the boss said quietly.

Amanda died! Definitely time for me to be absent. I opened the door.

'Mum, I'm going now. You need to stop getting out. I'm getting them to change the codes to keep you safe.' He bent forward to kiss her again, but she raked him hard across the face with her nails. He flinched but didn't respond.

I slipped through the door and waited in the corridor. I knew what Alzheimer's could do to someone, but I had never actually seen it before. Poor Benno, no wonder he was getting tetchy.

The door opened and Inspector Benjamin came out. His cheek was a deep red with a couple of blood-spotted scratches. He lit up a cigarette, leant back against the wall and blew smoke towards the floor. I stood silently waiting for him. I was not going to comment on his mother, and I absolutely was not going to mention Amanda.

'That wasn't really Mum,' he said eventually. 'The first part was Mum. I thought she was having a good day, but this shitty disease makes her turn on a sixpence. I used to pay a carer so I could work, but she couldn't cope with behaviour like that that and I was forced to find a secure unit.' He looked around. 'A supposedly secure unit.'

'I'm so sorry,' I said. 'Do you still want that statement from me?'

The boss finished his cigarette and crushed the butt into a sand filled fire bucket. 'I don't know.'

I had the feeling he wasn't actually talking to me. However, he had started the conversation about his mother, so I said, 'If I may speak freely as an outsider, sir, I think you should complain about the unit. They should at least have changed the codes when they realised she had memorised them. Also, the way Mrs Archer spoke to you and told you to be grateful, was out of order.'

Inspector Benjamin said, 'She felt attacked and cornered so she lashed out.'

'She didn't like you pointing out her inadequacies, more like. It's her job to keep the patients safe, and it's been pure luck that your mother didn't go onto the road or by the canal.'

The inspector looked lost. I decided it was okay to be more informal. 'Benno, I will do that statement, and I think you should arrange a meeting with social services to discuss your mother's care.'

The inspector remained silent for a while, then he said, 'You're right. I have hesitated to complain because I am grateful that my mother has care. Mostly the staff have been great with her, but this cannot continue.'

'Have you considered asking for a leave of absence while you sort this out? Please don't think I'm being disrespectful, but all this worry must be impacting on your work.' I knew I was treading on thin ice here, but one thing I had learnt during my time in the police was that sometimes you had to have difficult conversations; and the only way to say something that might not be welcome was to just say what was necessary, then deal with the fallout.

'Are you saying I'm a shit boss?' Inspector Benjamin asked.

'You're a great boss, Benno, but not having to worry about work for a while might clear your mind so you'll be better able to sort out your mother's situation.'

Benno smiled. 'Let's get back,' and he walked off towards the car park, pausing only to bid farewell to Mrs Archer and reiterate his intention to complain. We passed a man working on the locking mechanism of the door to reception. It looked like the security code was being changed. Perhaps Benno would now get some peace.

I thought that the conversation was over, but when we reached the car, he said, 'You're right. I will ask for time off. A couple of weeks maybe.'

'Benno, you know how slowly the wheels of social care turn. I believe a month might be more use. Two months even.'

Benno half-smiled. 'You're definitely trying to get rid of me, Sally.'

I liked that he called me the name I had used during our operation. It told me he was feeling more relaxed and hadn't taken offence.

'Come on, let's get back,' he said.

I followed him from the building. He must have known I had heard his mother mention Amanda, but he didn't bring her up once. I wasn't going to ask.

Chapter Fifteen

When we next paraded on, Inspector Benjamin was gone. Family emergency, Bert said, and he didn't know when he'd be back. Bert had been made temporary inspector until the boss returned or a replacement was found. I kept my promise and didn't tell anyone what I knew, although I suspected that Bert knew everything.

Bert sent me to cover the control room. Derek had an appointment and wouldn't be back until after break. I left parade and trotted to the control room. Ray would struggle to get prepared for the shift alone, whilst simultaneously monitoring the radio.

We'd just finished the prep when parade ended and the block crowded in for their radios and batteries. Ray dished out a couple of outstanding jobs, which were not well received. There was a certain pride in the control room about clearing incidents. Blocks didn't like having to pass over incidents because they'd be subject to teasing about sitting around; although really, everyone knew that wasn't the case. The incoming block disliked having to take them because they'd get their own pile of incidents during the shift and leftover incidents just delayed those.

When everyone had done their test calls and gone out, Bert came into the tiny room rubbing his stomach.

'Are you still getting indigestion?' I asked.

'Aye, a bit,' he admitted.

'Did you make an appointment to see a doctor?' I asked.

'I'm nagged at home and now I'm getting nagged here,' Bert moaned. 'Yes, Mum, I have an appointment.'

'Good. About time,' I said. 'Do you feel up to a cuppa?'

'I'm always up for a cuppa,' Bert replied.

I went into the miniscule telex room and turned on the kettle and prepped the mugs. As I waited for the water to boil, I said, 'Not long until you're Father Christmas again. Have you planned any tricks this year?'

'Nothing out of the ordinary. As far as the kids are concerned, I'm leaving my sleigh outside and walking up the stairs,' Bert replied.

'Is it true that last year, you came through a chimney?' I asked.

Bert guffawed. 'It is. Someone made a pretend chimney so I could come up through it onto the dais.' He patted his stomach. 'I got stuck and demolished the whole thing. One of the helpers got the kids singing *"When Santa Got Stuck Up the Chimney"* while the others freed me. Everyone in the audience thought it was part of the show.'

I laughed. 'I bet they loved it. It must be wonderful to be able to make children so happy.' Suddenly I had a thought. 'Bert, we should call you sir while you're acting inspector.'

Bert thought for a moment. 'Bert is fine unless any brass are around.'

So, Bert remained Bert as long as there were no big bosses in the vicinity.

Next parade, Bert had pips on his shoulders. Nobody commented, we were more concerned with Ken's absence.

'I bet Gaynor is having the baby,' Steve whispered to me. 'Her due date must be around now.'

Steve was probably right, although Bert had previously commented that the child was big enough to be okay if she went into labour early. Bert didn't mention Ken's non-appearance, so we continued as normal.

Derek spotted Bert's pips when we went to get our radios after parade.

'It's official then. Now's a good time to retire; you'd get an inspector's pension now, even though it's a temporary promotion,' Derek said.

'Aye, it's the only time I'll gain any advantage in this job,' Bert agreed.

'When's the boss back,' Derek asked.

Bert shrugged. 'Who knows. It must be bad, because his brother is flying in from America. He didn't even come back when George's wife died. He just sent flowers.'

I remembered Inspector Benjamin saying he hadn't seen his brother in a decade. It also looked like I had my answer about Amanda.

'Amanda.' I murmured.

'Aye. How did you know her?' Bert asked. 'It happened a few years back.'

'I heard her name mentioned,' I replied. 'How did she die?'

'Leukaemia,' Ray answered. 'It was probably a good thing they hadn't had children.'

'She was only a young lass. I suppose they thought they had time for all that,' Bert added.

Poor Benno, his wife gone, his brother abroad and his mother with dementia. He had no support. No wonder he got crabby sometimes. I loaded the batteries, pocketed a couple of spares, did my test call and walked out to my beat with Andy, who was covering the beat next door.

'Look! That's the type of thing I'm telling people about.' Andy pointed to a car coming towards us.

I watched the pale blue Vauxhall Viva coming towards me. At first glance, I thought it was a police car but there was no police sign, no blue light, no other marking on the car. I caught a glimpse of the driver, who wore a flat uniform cap.

'He's in uniform!' Andy exclaimed and jumped into the road with an arm raised to stop the car. The car didn't stop, it veered off and disappeared up a side road.

I grabbed my pen to note the VRM, but I only managed the last two numbers and the suffix. On the back of my hand, I jotted ….65T. Brand new. I radioed up an urgent observation to the control room and Ray swiftly passed it on to patrols. I thought it reasonable to label it a Fail To Stop incident.

'That wasn't one of ours, was it?' Andy asked.

'I'm fairly sure the car isn't a police vehicle, but the driver was wearing a uniform and a cap.'

Andy quirked his mouth. 'I said that would happen. Anyone can buy a pale blue Viva, and from a distance it looks like a police car.'

I couldn't disagree. At first glance I had thought it looked like a police car.

'4912 from control,' Ray transmitted.

'Go ahead,' I replied.

'I've created a job sheet for your sighting.'

'Thanks for that.' I jotted it onto the back of my hand. I'd add it to my pocket notebook later. The job sheet would be married up with the other job sheets that were forming the file about the bogus bobby. I turned to Andy. 'I'll put a note in for the collator.'

'If someone buys himself a lookalike police vehicle, puts on a uniform and starts driving around town, isn't that impersonating a police officer?' Andy asked.

That got me thinking, too. 'If he isn't a police officer and he's pulling people over, then definitely.' I thought a bit more. 'Playing devil's advocate, maybe he likes Vauxhalls. Perhaps he's a big police fan, or actually is a police officer. If he was travelling to go to work, it would be unusual, but not unheard of, to be in uniform.' I looked at my watch. 'Maybe he's from another division and making his way into work, but it's a strange time for anyone to start a shift.'

Andy shook his head. 'If he was going to work, or coming home, he'd wear a civvy coat over his uniform and he absolutely would not wear his hat,' Andy insisted. 'And even if he were the world's biggest Vauxhall or police fan, who in their right mind would choose one that colour unless they wanted it to look like a police vehicle? And why would they want it to look like a police vehicle?'

Why indeed? 'Good point, but I think the blue the police use is slightly different from the blue the public can buy. If we did arrest him for impersonating a police officer, that driver can pull up the colour charts and show a court that the blues have different names and therefore they were not trying to impersonate a police officer.'

'It's so close it doesn't make a difference!' Andy exclaimed. 'And how would he explain the hat?'

'It only takes a tiny technicality to destroy any case we'd have,' I said.

Shaun pulled up beside us and got out. 'All right, you two. I'll do your pegs here.'

'All right, Sarge,' we chorused and got our pocketbooks out.

'Just give me a minute to write up that last vehicle sighting, Sarge,' I said. I scribbled the details of the incident from the back of my hand and passed the book over.

'I was in the office when you radioed that in. What happened?' Shaun asked as he signed.

'We were walking along and saw a police car coming towards us, only it wasn't a police car,' Andy said.

'Did you see who was driving?' Shaun asked.

'No, but he was in a uniform, including a flat hat,' Andy replied.

'That doesn't mean it was a police uniform,' Shaun said.

'But you can't tell from a distance. Is he committing an offence, impersonating a police officer?' Andy asked.

'Possibly, probably. Let's see what Bert says,' Shaun replied. He handed back my book.

'Do you want me to submit this as a general report or a suspicious incident, Sarge?' I asked.

'Suspicious incident,' Shaun replied. 'We can't have civilians in uniform driving around pretending to be police.'

Andy smiled the smile of the vindicated. 'He agrees with me.'

*

Later, I was sitting in the control room while Derek had his meal. It had been tranquil so far, and Steve and I were discussing the rogue car before he went back out.

'He's got to be local,' I said. 'There wasn't a single sighting after he made off from us.'

'Or very lucky,' Steve said.

The phone rang and interrupted us. I answered.

'Hi, Sam,' Ken said.

'What news?' I immediately asked. Steve moved closer and Ray shuffled his chair towards me.

'Gaynor had a little girl a couple of hours ago.'

'Fantastic! How are they both? How are you?'

'Mother and baby are fine. She's a wee bit early so they'll keep hold of her a few days in case of problems, but they don't seem overly worried,' Ken said.

'Name and weight?' I asked.

'Kenneth, and I'm about twelve-and-a-half stone,' he replied.

'Wazzer. The baby,' I laughed.

'Why do women always ask that?' Ken asked. 'Seven pounds and we can't decide between Amy or Jennifer.'

'Both great names,' I said.

'Right, got to go. I'm knackered, so going to get my head down for a while. Speak soon.' Ken hung up.

'It's a girl,' I announced. 'Name to be decided. It's either Amy or Jennifer.'

'Great news!' Ray said and broadcast it on the radio to all patrols.

'I hope it's Jennifer,' Steve said. 'I like that name.'

'If they don't use it, you'll have to use it for your future daughter,' I said.

Steve chuckled. 'Don't say that to Emma. She'll get the wrong idea.'

'What wrong idea? I thought you two were going strong,' I

said.

'We are, but I'm not ready to take the next step yet,' Steve replied.

'Maybe they'll go for something totally different, Euphemia or Maud,' Ray said. Steve and I pulled faces. Ray continued, 'I had a great aunt called Maud. A nice woman. Always had mint imperials in her pocket. She died just after the war.'

That was a conversation killer, so Steve went back out and I turned back to the phones. I'd order some flowers from the florist. Perhaps I should arrange a collection for a block gift.

'When do you think Bert will put someone on the desk?' I asked Ray.

He shrugged. 'He's got other things to think about now.'

'It would be good for one of the older lads. They could just coast to retirement without getting cold, wet, or hurt,' I said.

'Who would you choose?' Ray asked.

I thought for a few seconds. 'Bill.'

'He does Mike Four,' Ray said.

'He might be happy to give up the panda,' I said. Nobody was quite sure what Bill got up to during a shift. He'd attend work given to him, but he was never seen patrolling and he didn't take sprogs. He must have been doing enough to keep the bosses happy, or perhaps they were happy to let him slack off for his last few months.

'You know you won't get Mike Four,' Ray said. 'It'll go to Ken first.'

'That wasn't my motivation,' I said. 'Especially as I'm waiting for my CID aides' course.'

'When do you think that'll come up?' Steve asked.

I shrugged. 'Nobody tells me anything. It could happen tomorrow.'

'Don't become one of those jacks that thinks they're too good to mix with uniforms. It's a role, not a promotion,' Steve said.

'I'll be an aide, lower than a worm down a hole,' I replied.

'But at least you'll be close to the action. You won't be put on guard duty or sent on pointless errands,' Steve insisted.

'Isn't that the very definition of an aide's function. Pointless errands?' I asked. 'It's something I have to do if I want to be a permanent detective.'

'You need to start thinking about what you want, young Steve. Branch out into the departments or stay as a response officer,' Ray said.

'I like motorbikes, and dogs. Maybe I can go into the traffic division, or the dog department.' He grinned. 'I could attach a dog basket to my motorbike, kill two birds with one stone. Track the baddies with the dog then chase them on the motorbike.'

I laughed aloud at that.

'Is that an outbreak of morale I hear?' Shaun called from the sergeants' office. He opened the door. 'More to the point, is that Patton still here?'

'I'm just on my way out. I was just getting an update for the latest sighting of the rogue car.' Steve put on his helmet.

'It's a job sheet, not *War and Peace*. Move your arse.'

'Yes, Sarge.' Steve winked at me and left.

Chapter Sixteen

Bert didn't seem comfortable with his new rank yet. He still used the sergeants' office, despite being entitled to use the inspector's office. As I passed the sergeants' office, I saw him popping a tablet into his mouth and washing it down with a long gulp of hot tea.

He looked up and saw me. 'New tablets from the doctor. I said I'd go, didn't I?'

I stood in the doorway. 'I'm glad you did. Are they helping?'

'I think so. I've got to go to the General for tests to make sure there's no ulcer or anything, but the pain is a lot less,' Bert said.

'Glad to hear it,' I said. 'I'm on my way out now. Speak later.'

'Speak later.'

I still hated earlies. I needed a cup of tea and a quiet half-hour to come to. Neither of which I was going to get. I passed the fire station in the hope of being invited in for a cuppa, but the doors were down and nobody called to me. Dejectedly, I trailed off to my beat, my old stomping ground from the park to the docks. I would normally drop in on Karen, except she had moved to Benedict Street, so I would have to patrol tealess, unless I was called to an incident at someone's house.

About ten o'clock, Ray called me on the radio. 'Can you attend Wherry Street. Mrs Hall at number eight. Reporting her daughter missing.'

'Roger,' I responded. Wherry Street was at the quieter end of the ship streets. We didn't often get jobs there. The houses were a little larger than the rest of the area, with a decent-sized kitchen.

I went to number eight and knocked at the door. A harassed-looking woman brought me in and sat me on an armchair.

'Thank you for coming. It's my daughter, Sharon. She never arrived at work this morning. It's the childrenswear factory, she works in the office. Her manageress rang here.'

'When did you last see her?' I asked.

'About quarter-to-eight. She put on her coat, shouted "Tarrah," and left for work. She never got there! I know we're supposed to wait twenty-four hours, but I'm too worried.'

Another one paying too much attention to American cop shows. 'We don't bother with that in England. I'm not sure they really do that in America. Ring us as soon as you're worried. The sooner we know, the sooner we can begin enquiries.' I got my form out and a pen. 'It's Mrs Hall, isn't it?'

'Yes, that's right.'

'Right, let's work through this form and we'll get her circulated. Full name and date of birth?' I asked.

'Sharon Mary Hall, the first of June 1961.' I could hear the tremor in Mrs Hall's voice although she was trying hard to remain calm.

I noted the details then moved to the description.

'Can you describe Sharon to me, Mrs Hall?' I asked.

'She's not very tall, five-two and slim. Blonde hair. She wears it in a ponytail for work. She was in her normal office clothes: black skirt, white blouse, and a blue coat.'

'Did she give any clue that she didn't intend to go to work?' I asked.

'None. She's a good girl. She's never been any trouble. This is completely out of character for her. Her boyfriend is a nice lad too. They're unofficially engaged,' Mrs Hall said.

'Does he know Sharon's missing?' I asked.

'He was the first person I called. He's got no idea where she might be. I've phoned everyone I can think of, and nobody has heard from her.'

We discussed people Mrs Hall had contacted since receiving the phone call from Sharon's work. When I felt we had covered as much as we could, I called Ray on the radio and passed on Sharon's description for him to circulate.

While Ray was circulating Sharon's description, someone knocked on the door.

'It's Marty.' Mrs Hall jumped up and let him in. 'How come you're not at work, Marty?'

'How could I concentrate when nobody knows where Sharon is?' he replied. 'I told them I had a family emergency and came straight here.'

I was surprised to see Martin Duggan come into the room, and he was equally surprised to see me. I recalled a Sharon being mentioned when I had attended his house. Martin's father, the obnoxious bank manager, Roger Duggan, was not her biggest fan. Come to think of it, I hadn't heard any more about his threats to trigger the alarm again to retest us. Perhaps his security section had had a word after my phone call.

'Have you two met before?' Mrs Hall asked.

'Yes, when Dad stole my bike,' Martin replied.

'Ah.' Mrs Hall didn't say any more.

'Any news?' Martin asked.

'None,' Mrs Hall replied.

'I've just circulated her description,' I added.

He sat on the sofa and rested his elbows on his knees. 'I'm at a loss what to suggest.'

Mrs Hall patted his shoulder. 'I'll put the kettle on.'

When she was gone, Martin turned to me. 'What happens now?'

'We just have to go through anyone we can think off who might know where she's gone. Her description is out there now, so I hope she'll be back soon.'

'I hope so too. We're going to get married and move to New Zealand together once I've qualified.'

'I remember your father mentioning New Zealand,' I said.

'He doesn't know about the marriage bit, so don't tell him,' Martin said. 'Sharon's mum knows. She might be coming with us.'

'How are things at home?' I asked out of curiosity as much as anything.

'Hard but better,' he replied. 'I know that sounds odd, but it's better since Dad left; however, money is tight because he hasn't paid for anything to force Mum not to divorce him. He thinks he's going to starve us into doing what he demands. He doesn't know that Mum's got herself a job in the supermarket. Not bad for someone who's been a housewife for over twenty years.'

'I think your mum's a resourceful woman,' I said.

'Yeah, she is. I got a Saturday job to get more money. It's hard work on top of my apprenticeship, but between us, we're getting by. Neither of us want anything more to do with that man.' He smiled, 'Maybe she'd consider coming down under with us now.'

Mrs Hall came back carrying two mugs of tea. She handed one to Martin and the other to me. 'I've been thinking of anyone else to contact but I can't think of anyone else.'

'Can you think of anyone, Martin?' I asked.

He shook his head.

Mrs Hall said, 'Sharon's friends will be at work at the factory. I'll have to phone them later on, but I really think I've called everyone else.'

I finished my tea and stood up. 'May I see her bedroom? Then I'll have a quick check around the house and garden if you don't mind, Mrs Hall.'

'Whatever for?' she asked.

'A number of times, when someone has been reported missing, they've been found hiding somewhere in the house. Usually it's kids that do that, but occasionally an adult tries it for whatever reason. It's basically a tick on my form.'

Mrs Hall nodded. 'Very well.

'When I've finished, I'll call in to Sharon's work and speak to some people there. Meantime, if Sharon returns or if you hear anything, ring us at once. Thank you for the tea. Before I leave, do you have a photograph I can have?'

While I mooched about the house and the shed looking for anything that might throw light on why Sharon had gone, Mrs Hall got me the most recent photo then saw me out.

Feeling much refreshed after my cuppa, I walked to the childrenswear factory. I updated Ray as I went.

The receptionist didn't seem pleased to see me when I entered the front door. Never mind, I wasn't there to see her.

'I wonder if I might speak to someone about Sharon Hall. I believe she didn't arrive at work this morning,' I said.

'Haven't you got anything better to do than hound people for skiving off?' the receptionist snapped.

'Has she skived off?' I asked.

'You just said she didn't come to work.' the receptionist replied.

'That doesn't mean she's skiving, unless you know differently.' I fixed her with my iciest stare.

The receptionist blushed, but said, 'That goody-two-shoes wouldn't do anything she shouldn't.'

'She's been reported missing,' I said.

'Oh!' said the receptionist. She sounded genuinely shocked.

'Oh indeed,' I said. 'So, who do I speak to?'

'I'll see if Mrs Price is in. She's the office manageress.' The receptionist picked up the phone and dialled an extension.

While she was speaking to the office, I wandered around the reception area, checking out photographs of smiling employees and cheerful delivery drivers. I wondered if this was really such a great place to work. Perhaps it was; I knew jobs here were sought after and there didn't seem to be a huge turnover of staff.

A side door opened and a smartly dressed woman of about forty came into the waiting area. She held out her hand. 'I'm Mrs Price. I believe you want to talk about Sharon Hall?'

I shook her hand. 'I'm Constable Barrie. Sharon Hall has been reported missing. Your receptionist has told me that it's unusual for Sharon to miss work.'

'It is. Let's go back to my office.' She glanced at the

receptionist. 'Mark me as busy for the next hour or so, please.'

'Yes, Mrs Price,' the receptionist said. The attitude had gone.

I followed Mrs Price through the door and into an admin office. Mrs Price's office was situated at the far end.

'Please sit down.'

I took the visitor chair while Mrs Price sat behind her desk.

'Thank you for seeing me. I believe someone rang Sharon's home when she didn't come to work?'

Mrs Price nodded. 'That was me. It is so unusual for Sharon to not turn up without notice, I was concerned that there was something wrong. I didn't mean to upset her mother.'

'I think Mrs Hall is pleased you did ring. Sharon left for work as normal this morning, so she had no idea Sharon wasn't here. Sharon wouldn't have been missed until this evening without your call,' I said.

'I feel better about it in that case.' Mrs Price smiled. 'Would you like a cup of tea.'

'Yes, thank you.'

Mrs Price pressed her intercom and ordered two teas, which arrived very quickly along with a plate of chocolate digestives.

'Did Sharon behave normally in the last few days? Did she request time off and perhaps it was declined? Has she mentioned anything to anyone you know of about going somewhere today?' I asked around a mouthful of biscuit.

'Sharon is a quiet girl. A hard worker. She hasn't asked for time off, and she was behaving perfectly normally yesterday. She has friends here, but nobody has mentioned any plans to me.'

'May I speak to her friends?' I asked.

Mrs Price stood up and went to the door of the office. 'Paula, Caroline, Elizabeth, would you come to my office please.'

Three girls, all clad in black skirts and white blouses, stood up and nervously glanced at each other.

'Chop chop,' Mrs Price said.

They came into the office and huddled together. I caught sight of the other girls in the office whispering together.

'Sharon has been reported missing. This officer is making enquiries. Please tell her if you know anything,' Mrs Price said.

The girls all began talking at once. I held my hand up to silence them.

'It would be easier if you spoke one at a time, if you don't mind.' I pointed to the girl on the left. 'Please tell me your name, and did Sharon mention anything about going away, or anything at all?'

'I'm Paula, miss. No, she didn't mention anything. She'd tell us if she was planning anything, wouldn't she?' She looked at Caroline and Elizabeth who enthusiastically agreed.

I pointed at the middle girl, who was wearing a black cardigan over her white blouse. 'Elizabeth?'

'Yes, miss. Sharon didn't tell me anything either. Have you spoken to her boyfriend?'

'I have. He's at her house with her mother, but he doesn't know anything either.' I turned to the remaining girl. 'Can you suggest anything, Caroline?'

'No miss. She was in work yesterday and everything was normal. We're all supposed to be going to the new club in the city at the weekend. She never mentioned going away and we talk about everything.'

I didn't know what else to ask, so I took each girl's details for the report.

'You will tell us when she's found, won't you, miss?' Paula asked.

'I'll make a point to contacting Mrs Price and perhaps she would be good enough to pass any news on to you.' I looked at Mrs Price who nodded.

'Thank you for your help, girls,' I said. 'If you do think of anything else at all, even if you think it's not important, please ring me, or tell Mrs Price.'

They went back into the office and at once went into a huddle. I finished my tea.

'Thank you, Mrs Price. Please let me know at once if you hear anything,' I said.

'I will. I do hope you find her quickly.'

So did I

Back at the station, I completed the file for Sharon, attached her photograph, then phoned Mrs Hall for an update. Then I went into the collator's office and had a rummage to see if I could unearth anything, but I came up empty-handed. I then went to the control room and did a check on the PNC to see if anything came up there. It didn't.

'I circulated that girl and did an APB,' Ray said.

An All Ports Bulletin would mean that if Sharon tried to leave the country, the port, or airport would be aware of her missing status. I had done as much as I could unless more information came in. The file would go to another department for ongoing enquiries.

*

That weekend was the charity dance. At 19:55 hours, I parked up and walked the short distance to meet Chris. He was waiting outside for me. He waved and I waved back.

'You look nice,' he said.

I gave a little twirl. 'Thank you, kind sir. You look nice too.'

Chris laughed and tugged at his shirt. 'What, this old thing?'

I took the offered arm and we went inside.

Chris met a couple of men at the entrance. 'Guys, this is Samantha. Sam, this is Vic and Eddie. They're on my section. Vic's a newbie.'

'All right,' Eddie said.

'Nice to meet you,' I replied.

'My name is not actually Vic,' said Vic.

'Why do they call you Vic?' I asked.

'Short for Vicar,' Eddie replied.

Vic rolled his eyes. 'My dad's a vicar, not me.'

'You work for the church, though. Doing that youth stuff,'

Eddie insisted.

'We do nicknames in the police too,' I told him. 'Do you mind being called Vic?'

He grinned. 'Not really. It means I've been accepted, doesn't it.'

'What youth work do you do?' I asked.

'The church runs residential courses for young people who need guidance. Perhaps they're going off the rails or feel isolated. They study The Bible and do activities. I supervise some of the activities. It's quite good fun actually, and most of them say they've enjoyed it.'

'That sounds great.' I meant it.

'Never mind all that. How did you manage to get a looker like that, Chris?' Eddie asked.

'My devastating charm,' Chris retorted. I waited for him to explain that we were not an item, but he didn't. 'Come on, Sam, let's sit down.'

He introduced me to a few more people as we went into the hall. I instantly forgot their names. That happened sometimes when I met a lot of people all at once.

In the corner, a DJ had set up his equipment and was playing *Monster Mash* to get people in the mood. Appropriate. as Halloween wasn't far off. Steve and Emma were already there. I spotted a couple of people from other blocks at Wyre Hall and waved. Chris and I went over to Steve's table.

'Been here long?' I asked.

'Only about five minutes before you,' Steve replied. He nodded a greeting at Chris.

I sat down at the table, while Chris went to get our drinks.

'I think you're awfully brave to come out by yourself,' Emma said. She was a sweet thing, but sometimes rather ingenuous for a nurse.

'Emma, I walk the streets at night, by myself. This is nothing. Besides, I'm not by myself, I'm with Chris, and you're all here.'

'I suppose,' she said. 'I'm safe and warm in a ward and I forget that there are people outside working in the dark. Including my Steve.' She put a hand on his knee. He covered her hand with his.

I didn't know whether to be jealous or nauseous.

Chris came back with our drinks and sat down. The DJ put on *The Time Warp*.

'*Rocky Horror Picture Show*!' Steve cried.

'Can you time warp?' Chris asked me.

'Like a pro!' I cried.

All four of us raced onto the dance floor. From now on, I would always associate this song with Chris.

I spotted Walter the Weeble as I stepped to the right. I had seen him driving a blue Viva, but I couldn't see how he could be our mystery policeman. I kept looking at him as I checked off the description of the offender in my mind, but it didn't really fit Walter. His size was the most noticeable thing about him so if it had been him stopping those girls, they'd have been sure to mention it. Nor did he resemble the person Andy and I had spotted in the blue Viva. No, I was happy that our man was not Walter the Weeble. He was a fibber, but he wasn't an imposter.

Judging by the dirty look he gave me when he caught me looking, he hadn't forgiven me for exposing his lie in front of Chris. Then I was distracted by the pelvic thrust and forgot about him.

The evening passed quickly, but eventually, it was time to leave.

'That was great,' I said. 'Chris, if you sell tickets next year, put me down for a couple.' I couldn't read the expression that flitted across his face.

'I'll walk you back to your car,' he said.

Steve and Emma wished us goodnight and went their own way. Emma nestled close to Steve, who had his arm protectively around her shoulders. For a moment, I felt jealous and not at all nauseous. I missed Gary.

Chris took my arm and brought me back from my thoughts.

'Do you want to go for a drink before you go home?' he asked. 'The clubs will still be open.'

'I'd better not,' I said. 'Gary might ring me, and he'd worry if I'm not home. Besides, I need my sleep.'

'Do you want to come for a drink another time instead?' Chris asked.

'People will talk,' I said.

'Blow other people, we know you're engaged—to a man who abandoned you,' Chris said.

'That's unfair,' I complained.

'I suppose so. Okay, I'm on nights next week, we start earlier than you do, so the following week would be better. A drink at the Gozzie Moggie. A week Friday. Say seven?'

The Gozzie Moggy or the Squinting Cat to give it its correct name, was a new pub that had opened in Odinsby. It followed the recent trend for humorous and sometimes downright bizarre names. It was a decent enough place.

I thought for a moment. 'Okay then.'

'It's a date,' Chris said.

'No, it's a drink,' I corrected him.

Chapter Seventeen

It came as a bit of a surprise to me when Bert announced on our next parade that Sharon Hall was still missing. Every day that passed meant that it was less likely she would be found safe and well. I wondered about contacting Mrs Hall, but a different team had been doing the follow up investigations and I might just be adding to her stress. Worse, I might give her false hope.

Someone had already retraced her route to work to identity any likely spots she might have come to harm. However, her route took her along a main road then onto another main road to the industrial estate then on to the factory. It would have been the rush hour, so abduction had been ruled out. Even on the estate, people would have been leaving and arriving, so any attempt at an abduction would have been spotted.

'She could have gone off with someone she knew,' Charlotte suggested.

'Yes. If she'd arranged to meet someone, she'd have just got into the car and nobody would have thought anything of it,' Frank added.

'To be honest, that's the best-case scenario,' Bert said. 'However, given the information we have so far, Sharon had not planned to leave the area. Her boyfriend's workplace has been contacted, and they confirmed that Martin had been attending work just as he should and the only time off he'd taken was after he'd received the phone call to say Sharon had been reported missing.'

'Her friends told me that they had made arrangements to go out that weekend,' I said.

'If she was planning to run away, she would want them to think everything was normal,' Spider insisted.

She had a point, but I hadn't picked up anything that showed any planned deception on her part. The receptionist actually described her as a goody-two-shoes. I wondered how long it would be before they started a full fingertip search of her route. To my mind, the most likely place she was taken would be the main road from her house with its easy access to the dual carriageway and the motorway, but she would not have gone quietly, so somebody would have noticed if she'd been fighting. Sadly, this lent weight to the idea that she had gone off voluntarily. Either way, poor Mrs Hall and poor Martin.

DI Webb collared me in the corridor by the control room. Typically for him, there were no pleasantries or chat. He went straight to the point.

'Sam, what are you doing a week on Monday?'

'Rest day, sir.' I replied. But if he wanted me for an operation, I would be there like a shot.

'We have an opening for an aide starting on that Monday. Parade on in the CID office. Nine am. I'll let Bert know.'

I almost whooped, but I managed to keep it in. 'Thank you, sir. I'll be there.'

DI Webb walked on and I went into the locker room, where I did a happy dance. My aide's course, at last. I'd miss my rest day, but who cared? It would all work out over time.

'I'll miss you,' said Andy when I told everyone at refs.

'I'm only going to be upstairs,' I replied.

'Who will you be working with?' Steve asked.

'I don't know,' I admitted. I had assumed it would be DI Webb, seeing as he had been the one to inform me, which meant my shifts would largely follow B Block, but I could be put with anyone. I hadn't thought to ask.

*

Next parade was somewhat subdued. Sharon Hall was still outstanding. This was bad. Very bad.

'For your information, nothing came of the press conference with Sharon Hall's mother, so they're filming her route to work with a lookalike in the hope it will jog someone's memory,' Bert said.

There were no quips, no comments at all. Everyone could feel that this was deeply worrying. Bert left us alone with our thoughts for a minute before continuing.

'In other news, Samantha is moving on. She begins her CID aides' course a week Monday.'

'You haven't even had your own panda yet,' Frank said.

'Not a requirement,' I retorted. 'I'll be back after six months, so maybe I can do it then.'

Parade continued but my thoughts were with Sharon Hall. And Ruthie Pritchard. She hadn't been seen by anyone since Karen had reported her missing, and I found that worrying. She was never mentioned on parade. Nobody had set up a reconstruction for her.

Once we had our radios and had done our test calls, I walked out to my beat alone. I scanned the people around me, hoping to catch sight of Sharon or a tatty red coat and scuffed boots tucked in a corner that might be Ruthie. As I wandered through the shopping centre, I struck up conversation with a couple of the security staff and asked about her. They all knew Ruthie, but nobody had seen her for a while. I found it rather sad that nobody had missed her until I mentioned it. Also, I was a little troubled that she had not received the attention that Sharon Hall was getting. Yes, I knew there were huge differences. Sharon was a good girl who lived a stable and sober life. Ruthie lived a chaotic life and she occasionally did go off for days, but never for this long. How long did she have to be gone for to get even a fraction of what Sharon was getting? Would she ever get that? I resolved to mention it when I got back. Perhaps once I had started as an aide, I could get someone to look more closely at it.

*

On the Friday, I parked in the Squinting Cat's car park and walked towards the door. Chris was already there, waiting for me. He pecked my cheek. I stepped backwards a half pace and side-eyed him.

He held his hands up. 'It was just a friendly greeting. It's the sort of peck I'd give my nan.'

'You're comparing me with your nan?'

'Of course not, just offering an explanation.' He guided us towards the lounge bar. 'You go find a table and I'll get the drinks.'

'Just coke please,' I replied.

He went to the bar and I found us a nice table in a quiet corner. We'd probably talk about our jobs, and I didn't like discussing what I did around strangers. I worried that someone who had a grudge against the police would overhear and things could turn nasty. Chris returned with our drinks and settled himself in.

'Typical copper,' he said.

'What do you mean?'

'Table in the corner, seat facing the room. It was the same at the dance. You all sat lined up against the wall. I felt like I was facing an interview panel.'

I glanced around me. I had indeed positioned myself so nobody could creep up on me and I could see everything.

'It's instinct,' I replied. 'I didn't do it intentionally.'

'Protecting yourself has become second nature. Why do you do the job if it's so dangerous?' Chris asked.

'It isn't always dangerous. A lot of the time, it's just plain tedious.'

'You seem to get yourself injured on a fairly regular basis,' Chris said.

'Says the man who fights fire. Why would anyone want to do

that?' I responded.

Chris grinned. 'I see your point.' He furtled in his pockets and brought out two bags of crisps and tossed one in front of me. 'I hope you like plain.'

'It's my favourite.' I opened the bag and tucked in.

Chris told me about his family. His parents, younger sister, grandmother, and they all lived together in what sounded like a largish house in a nice suburb of Egilsby. I told him about my family moving to Scotland.

'So, not only is your fiancé abroad, but your family have also moved away. You must feel so alone,' he said.

'I'm not alone. I'm close to my cousin and her family. She doesn't live far away,' I replied. 'And Gary will be back when his posting is finished.'

Chris remained silent for a moment, then said, 'It's unusual how loyal you are to your boyfriend. Most girls wouldn't wait that long.'

'I disagree. If you love someone, it's not difficult to let them do what will make them happy. If it is difficult, then perhaps what you feel is not love,' I said.

'Let me turn this on its head. If you had objected, would he have turned the posting down or is all this devotion one-sided?'

'He offered several times to turn the posting down. I told him to go ahead with it.' I started to feel irritated by Chris' questioning. I think he picked up on that because he didn't mention Gary again and the conversation flowed more smoothly.

'Do you want to meet for another drink when you're off next?' Chris asked. 'We could get a bite to eat too.'

I thought for a moment. I had few people I could socialise with so it would be nice.

'As friends.' I stated.

He held his hands up. 'I didn't suggest anything else.'

'Okay then.' We made our arrangements, and I went home, alone.

*

At 9am, Monday morning, wearing a smart navy blue trouser suit and white top bought specially for the occasion, with my hair in a high ponytail instead of its usual bun, I knocked on DI Webb's door. He opened it and admitted me. He wasn't alone. DI Jerome Rigby from High Lake was also there. I didn't feel warm towards DI Rigby following the disgraceful way, in my opinion, that his team had treated my cousin in an incident a few months ago. However, he was a DI and I was just a new aide, so I nodded an acknowledgement and muttered, 'Sir.' I didn't know if he recognised me.

Direct as ever, DI Webb said, 'I'm busy right now. You're on Mike Finlay's team. Tell him to find you something to do.' DI Webb turned back to DI Rigby.

I was pleased to have been put on DS Finlay's team. I saw him at the far end of the office and went over.

'DS Finlay, I've been put on your team.'

Mike smiled. 'Welcome. Eamon is going to be mentoring you.' He pointed to a pile of folders on his desk. 'You can start by sending that lot back to the records office.'

I knew I'd get the boring, routine stuff, and I knew that despite appearing disinterested, DI Webb would be watching me, so I threw myself into the task, and all the other mindless tasks that followed.

Once all the filing had been done, all records returned from whence they came, information retrieved from Irene, the collator, or from the control room, and nobody wanted another hot drink, I just hung around waiting for my next instructions. I hadn't been there long enough to have created my own jobs, so I moved from desk to desk in case someone wanted something, but I was mostly ignored. I sat at the wobbly table in the corner, where I had once seen another aide sitting. It was far enough away not to be in anyone's way, but I would still be close enough if anyone needed me.

Eamon sat close by, speaking to someone on the phone. He ended the call, chewed on a pencil for a moment then looked at me. He didn't say anything, he just watched me.

I started to feel uncomfortable. 'What's up?'

Ignoring me, Eamon called to DS Finlay. 'Mike, I've had an idea. We need someone to hang around the town because that eejit in the Viva is making a nuisance of himself again. Sam would be ideal. She can take out one of the pool cars and look out for him.'

'Has there been another incident?' Mike Finlay asked.

'Yeah, I've just spoken to the control room,' Eamon answered.

'Set a bait sort of thing?' Mike thought for a moment. 'How do you feel about that, Sam?'

I jumped to my feet. 'Fine, Sarge.'

'I'll run it past the boss. Meantime, Sam, get yourself a car, unmarked,' Mike said.

He went to the DI's office, and I went over to the board with the keys hanging from it and selected a Ford Escort. Plain beige, no markings. Perfect for undercover work and observations. I signed the space with my number.

'DI Webb agrees, so do you have a car yet?' DS Finlay called to me. I held up the keys. 'Great. If you do happen to come across a suspicious blue Viva, do not attempt to stop it by yourself. Call it in, so uniform can send a marked car to do the stop. Follow it if you can, but do not get into a car chase. Understand?'

I signed out a radio and checked the channel. Channel 2. CID often used a different channel to the divisional one, which was normally channel 1, so they didn't clutter each other's airwaves up. It was important to know which one you were transmitting on. I then drove the Ford slowly out of the yard to go Viva hunting.

*

After an hour or so, I was driving along Town Road towards the

Andes when a blue Viva came close behind me and flashed its lights. It overtook me. No sign, no blues and twos. I checked the registration plate. Last three digits were 65T. I'd seen this before. Not a police car. I saw Tony Fleming in the driver's seat. Full uniform including hat.

'Gotcha!' I said to nobody. I picked up the handset and flipped over to the divisional channel. Keeping the radio low and out of Tony's sight, I transmitted, 'DC Barrie to control, please can you confirm that Special Constable Tony Fleming is not on duty?'

'Stand by.'

I wished that B Block were on duty. It's not that I didn't trust the others, but it was always good to work with people you were familiar with. Derek would have been ringing the specials' office while Ray was going through the duty sheet and giving the CID office the heads up. I supposed that was exactly what was happening now because in a few seconds control called me back.

'Confirmed, he is not showing as on duty, nor is he due on duty,' the radio operator replied.

'Roger. Please could you have a patrol RV with me ASAP Town Road. I'm being pulled over by Special Constable Fleming. He's in uniform, in an unmarked blue Viva. I'm in the beige Ford escort from the CID pool. We're fairly close to the primary school.'

'Roger.'

I didn't listen as a patrol was dispatched to me. I slipped my radio into my jacket. Tony slowed his car in front of me and I allowed him to lead me to the kerb. I stayed put and waited for him to exit his car.

'What's the problem?' I said out of my open window as he approached.

'Can you step outside of your vehicle, please?' he asked pleasantly. He didn't recognise me out of uniform. A common occurrence.

I got out but, instead of waiting for him, I walked towards his car. I wanted to make sure he didn't have a radio hidden in there and had been monitoring our transmissions. It would explain a lot if he had been listening in.

'Where are you going? Get back here when I'm speaking to you,' he ordered.

I peered into the car but couldn't see a radio. Dammit, that would have been useful evidence.

'Move away from my car or I will arrest you for not obeying a police officer.'

'I'm pretty sure that that in itself is not an arrestable offence,' I said. I would have to bring up a concern about the training of Specials when I got back to the station.

He marched over, grabbed my arm and yanked me away from his car. 'I actually wanted to ask you out, but I won't tolerate this disrespect. You will do as I say.' He shoved me towards my car.

He hadn't been gentle. I rubbed my arm. 'Oh dear, Tony, that's assault and that is an arrestable offence.' I saw recognition flare in his eyes. I reached into my jacket and brought out my radio but before I could transmit, Tony slapped it from my hand, shoved me away and ran.

I scooped up my radio and raced after Tony. 'You might as well stop now. We know all about you,' I yelled.

Tony didn't stop. He ran into the road causing a car to slam on and sound its horn. I held my hand up in apology to the driver as I shot past after him.

Tony took the road up towards the school. I radioed in our location, but I was getting puffed out and I hoped they understood me. It was lunchtime and the kids were crowded into the playground. We were on the boys' side. They gathered at the railings. A teacher came over to see what was happening and stood with the children, her mouth open, as a policeman in uniform fled from a woman in plain clothes who yelled into a radio. Her colleague came over to join her and his jaw joined hers on the ground.

Then I saw Wilfred. He was out again had been walking

towards the school crossing point. I wondered if Kitty knew. I hadn't heard control broadcast observations because I had been on the CID channel and had only swapped to the divisional channel a few minutes previously.

Wilfred turned when he heard the commotion. I wasn't sure if he recognised me, but he must have taken in the situation in a second. With more speed than I had seen from anyone, never mind a man in his eighties, he charged into Tony like a bull and both men fell, to the delight of the children. Tony tried to get up but Wilfred had him in a death grip. Tony repeatedly punched Wilfred, but still the old boy hung on. I restrained Tony's arms.

'Let go, girl. You'll get hurt,' Wilfred said to me. He was a little more switched on than usual, because he recognised me despite me being in plain clothes.

'No, Wilf. I need to arrest him.'

Tony continued to struggle. I managed to gasp out the caution and inform him he was being arrested for impersonating a police officer and assaulting a police officer.

'Bitch! You'll pay for this,' Tony shouted.

'He's impersonating a police officer and he's assaulted a police officer? A woman police officer!' Wilfred was aghast.

'He's a Special, but coming out in uniform when he's not on duty and harassing young girls,' I replied.

'And using bad language within hearing of children.' Wilfred slapped Tony hard across the face. I pretended I hadn't seen it. Then it occurred to me that Wilfred was .a confused, elderly member of the public who was assisting me in restraining a prisoner in full view of dozens of boys and their teachers. I probably shouldn't allow him to do that.

'That's assault, I'm going to press charges,' Tony yelled.

'Belt up or I'll give you another and I won't be so gentle next time.' Wilfred pushed a warning fist under Tony's nose. Policing must have been very different in his day.

'I've got him Wilf, you relax now,' I said.

'Neglect of duty,' Wilf said. 'I'll wait until one of the lads arrive.'

With that, a panda car screeched around the corner, closely followed by another, then came a plain car containing Mike and Eamon. The officers piled out of their cars and hurried over, handcuffed Tony and threw him into the back of one panda. The children cheered.

'Thanks for the help, Wilf,' I said. 'I'll make sure you get a mention in my report.'

Wilfred was grinning. 'You're welcome. It was good to feel a part of things again.'

'Sam, what the hell are you thinking, letting a man Wilf's age restrain a prisoner?' Eamon said.

'Let him? I couldn't stop him,' I replied.

'What are you doing letting a little lass chase down prisoners by herself without even the protection of a uniform?' Wilf retorted. 'It's a bloody disgrace. I shall be speaking to the inspector.' He turned to me. 'Pardon my language.'

Eamon rolled his eyes. 'Come on, Wilf, I'll give you a lift back while the patrol takes the prisoner to the bridewell.' He looked around. 'Where's the Ford?'

'Still on Town Road by the Viva. We should get that removed,' I replied.

'I'll sort that,' Mike said.

'It's my arrest!' I called over to the patrol with the prisoner. 'DC Barrie. Just lodge him in the bridewell and I'll be along shortly.' Normally I would be assured that he'd be lodged pending my arrival, but I didn't entirely trust other blocks not to pinch my collar. We'd be having words if they did that. One put his thumb up and they left with Fleming.

Eamon held out his hand to help Wilf up. Wilf took his hand, tried to pull up, but grimaced and settled back down.

'I don't think I can, lad. There's something wrong with my leg.'

I got a nasty feeling in my stomach. 'Would you let me look, Wilf?'

'No need. I hit the kerb as I fell. I'll be fine in a minute or two. You expect some knocks in this job.'

'You might have broken your leg!' Or, at his age, broken a hip. Dammit! I radioed in for an ambulance.

'No need for that, girl,' Wilfred said.

'No argument. I want you to get a thorough examination.'

Wilfred chuckled despite the pain he must have been feeling. 'You sound like Kitty.'

'You'll be writing forever on this,' Eamon murmured to me.

Yes, I could see I would be writing a lot of reports explaining how an octogenarian with a failing memory broke his leg helping me arrest a fleeing prisoner. I hoped it wouldn't lead to a fizzer.

The ambulance station wasn't far away, so the ambulance arrived quickly, just as lunchtime ended. The teachers had a bit of trouble getting the children back inside. Wilfred waved to them as he was loaded into the ambulance. They went crazy waving back.

As we cleared the scene, I spotted a wallet on ground where Wilfred and Tony Fleming had been lying. I picked it up and looked inside for ID so I could return it. I pulled a card out and read *"PCMG"*, Tony's name and a number. It felt like cheap card and had no embellishments. I don't know why, but I felt it might be useful for something. I'd check back at the station when I booked the wallet into the prisoners' property system.

Eamon travelled with Wilf to the hospital while I retrieved my car. I had intended to go straight back to the bridewell, but instead I decided to stop off and give Kitty a lift to the hospital. It was close to her address, so I shouldn't keep the bridewell staff waiting for too long. I radioed in to inform them I would be slightly delayed and left Mike dealing with the Viva.

When I explained the circumstances, Kitty was furious with Wilfred.

'I'm so sorry,' I said to Kitty. 'I did ask him to let me deal with it, but he wouldn't listen.'

'Och, I'm not blaming you. I know what he's like.'

We arrived at the hospital and were allowed straight through. Someone had given Wilfred Entonox gas to help with the pain. I was concerned. Healing in old people was notoriously slow, so he would probably be moved to a care facility, something Kitty had vigorously resisted. She probably wouldn't have a choice this time. 'What are you playing at, thick heided man? You're too old to be playing the hero.'

'You can't switch off being a bobby, Kitty, love. I couldn't leave the girl to cope alone,' he replied.

I could see by his eyes that Wilfred was present in the here and now.

'Kitty's right,' I said. 'You really should have left that arrest to me.'

He tapped his chest. 'I might be losing my marbles, but the flame still burns as strong and blue as the lamp over your door.'

Wilf had been in great spirits since our arrest. Despite the broken leg, later confirmed by X-ray, he had had a great time. I was somewhat relieved that it wasn't his hip that had broken.

I checked my watch. It had been about forty-five minutes since Fleming had been taken from the scene. Roughly an hour would have passed by the time I got back. Not too bad. I'd probably still get earache from the bridewell staff though.

'Kitty, Wilf, I need to deal with my prisoner, so I have get back now. Eamon will remain here for a while. Wilfred, thank you so much for your help. The inspector will be coming to visit you shortly.'

Wilfred's smile dropped. 'Good. I want to have a talk with him. It's not right letting girls out alone to face who know what. I'm glad I was there to help.'

It was pointless arguing. I'd leave that for the boss.

When I got to the bridewell, I was happy to find that nobody had tried to pinch my arrest. I did get some grief over how long it had been, but I didn't regret getting Kitty to the hospital.

I booked the wallet into property and was contemplating the card before dropping it into the prisoner property bag, when the bridewell sergeant came up behind me.

'What's that?'

I showed him the card. 'I'm trying to guess what PCMG stands for. It belongs to my arrest.'

He thought for a moment then nodded. 'I've seen one of these before. It's a membership card for a men's group at the Middleton Hotel. I don't know more than that though.'

'Tony Fleming told me a while back that he belonged to a Christian men's group.' I thought for a moment. 'PCMG. Men's Group? Christian Men's Group? That fits. I wonder what the P stands for, Presbyterian, protestant, peninsula?'

'Ask him,' the sergeant said.

'I'd rather not. I don't want him to know I'm interested in this.'

'Ah, it's an operation.'

'Something like that,' I replied.

'Then don't tell me anything about it. I don't want to be blamed if anything goes wrong.'

I put the card and the wallet into the bag and updated the charge sheet. DI Webb was coming down to speak to Tony. One thing I was certain of, he would not be a Special for very much longer, nor a security guard for that matter.

Chapter Eighteen

I met Steve in the station car park the following day.

'What are you doing here? You're supposed to be rest day,' I said.

'Court.' He pulled a face. 'The annoying thing is, I know he's going to change his plea, so I won't be needed.'

'That is annoying,' I sympathised.

'Great arrest yesterday by the way. About time that wazzer was off the street,' he said.

'Thanks. I'm in a bit of trouble though. Wilf decided to lend a hand and broke his leg.'

'Oh shit.'

'Yeah. I couldn't stop him.'

'Everyone knows what he's like. You probably won't get disciplined,' Steve said.

'DI Webb has had to refer it, though. I'll just have to wait and see what happens.'

'Apart from that, how's it going?' he asked.

'Too soon to say, but it seems okay,' I replied.

'Do you want to come to the Isle of Wight with Emma and me? I'm chartering a plane next Wednesday. It's been a while, and I need to keep my hours up.'

I'd almost forgotten that Steve had got his pilot's licence. 'Thanks but I can't. I'm going to the pictures with Chris,' I replied. That and the fact I didn't like flying. I didn't even want to think about the trauma I'd experienced in a small plane. Oh, and I didn't want to be a gooseberry.

'Just the two of you? Again?' Steve asked. 'You're getting very close to this Chris.'

'What are you saying?' I demanded.

'I'm saying I've noticed how close you and Chris have become, and if I've noticed, so have others. You stop by the fire station for chats at every opportunity. You went to the dance with him, you've had drinks with him, and now you're going to the pictures. Just the two of you. By anyone's standards, that's a date.'

'Rubbish!' I snapped. 'What about all those times you and I went to places together. They weren't dates.'

'But everyone thought they were. Have you forgotten that everyone thought we were an item?' Steve replied.

He was right, they had.

'What am I supposed to do, Steve? I don't have friends outside the job, not in this country anyway. I can only meet people from training school occasionally because our shifts clash. You and Ken are busy these days. Who else am I going to go out with? Spider?

'I'll still go for a drink with you sometimes. Emma wouldn't mind.' Steve said.

'Are you sure she wouldn't mind? Because by your standards that could be seen as a date.'

'I trust her and she trusts me,' Steve declared.

'Well, Gary and I trust each other,' I snapped back.

'Does he know the water fairy is sniffing around?' Steve asked.

'He's not sniffing around. We're just friends,' I insisted.

'I think you're going to have to make a choice quite soon. A man who is thousands of miles away, or an old flame who is right here and obviously interested in you,' Steve said.

'Oh, shut up! You're talking rubbish. Chris isn't an old flame, he's just a fellow emergency worker and a friend.' I strode off, too cross to talk to Steve anymore.

'Flame or not, there is a definite spark there. Don't say I didn't warn you,' Steve called to my back.

If I had to make a choice, it would be Gary. It would always be Gary. I had fond feelings for Chris, but they didn't compare to the love I had for Gary, and I was not going to risk our relationship, but I did want a social life. I reasoned that if I kept Gary informed, I was not deceiving him. Steve could take a running jump.

So, still miffed by Steve's reaction, I met Chris outside The Ritz cinema as arranged.

Chris pecked my cheek, which made me pause. I told myself he was just being friendly like that time at the pub, and I relaxed.

'I've already got the tickets.'

'Then you must let me get the popcorn,' I said.

'It's a deal.' He took my arm and walked me into the cinema.

The film was good, but my thoughts kept slipping to Gary, and Steve. Steve had all but told me I was having an affair. It was total rubbish, Chris was just a friend, I enjoyed his company and, being honest, perhaps if I hadn't met Gary I might have responded to Chris' overtures, but I was loyal. Steve should judge me on what I did, not what he assumed. I was a little surprised when the closing credits came up. I hadn't noticed the film had ended.

'Let's get some tea, and you can tell me what's on your mind,' Chris said.

'Who says there's anything on my mind,' I countered.

'Do you think I didn't notice you were distracted?' He took my hand. 'Come and tell Uncle Chris all about it.'

We walked to The Square and went into the Golden Temple restaurant. Chris ushered me to a corner table and let me sit facing outwards.

'Constable Sam! I haven't seen you for so long. Where have you been?' Hari Kapoor, son of the owner came over to us.

'I've been busy, Hari.'

'Where is Inspector Gary?'

'Hong Kong,' I replied.

Hari's face dropped. 'I'm sorry. It's sad when love dies.' He turned to Chris. 'Who is this? A new friend for my friend?'

'Gary and I are still together, Hari. It's only a temporary posting. He's coming back so don't worry. This is my friend, Chris,' I replied. 'Chris, this is Hari Kapoor, son of the owner of this fine restaurant.'

'Are you a policeman too?' Hari asked.

'No, I'm a fireman,' Chris replied.

'I am pleased to meet you Fireman Chris,'

'And I'm pleased to meet you, Hari, heir to the Golden Temple.'

Hari laughed. 'I like your friend, Constable Sam. What would you like to eat?'

We ordered Tandoori Chicken with rice, salad, and garlic naan. Onion Bhajis on the side.

'We have a drink licence now. You can have alcohol if you want,' Hari said. 'My father was not enthusiastic, but I told him that many people like to drink alcohol with their food and it would make us even more popular.'

'Has it?' I asked.

Hari's smile stretched so far I could see his back teeth. They were as perfect as his front teeth.

'It has; business is very good.'

'I'll have a lager, please, Hari,' Chris said.

'Could I have a half pint of lager and lime, please Hari?' I asked.

'Of course. I will bring it over to you.'

'I expect to see the bill for this,' I told him.

'Yes, yes.' Hari waved a hand dismissively.

'Why would you not see a bill?' Chris asked me.

'He thinks I saved them from deportation. I have explained that all I did was report our bent sergeant who was blackmailing them.'

'So you did save them from deportation,' Chris said.

'No. It was never on the cards. It was something that he was using to threaten them in order to extract money.' Some might have taken advantage of that, but I felt awkward. It was the main reason I didn't go to the Golden Temple as often as I would have liked.

'You know, he'll call you Fireman Chris forever now,' I said.

'I can live with that.' Chris took my hand across the table. 'So what's bothering you? And don't tell me nothing is, because I won't believe you.'

I opened my mouth, closed it again then took a deep breath. 'I miss Gary.'

Chris let go of my hand. 'If you told him that, would he come home?'

'I wouldn't ask him to,' I replied.

Chris put his hand back over mine. 'He'll be home in 1981. Meantime, I am here.'

I looked at Chris' hand covering mine. He had strong hands. 'I know…'

'Take your time, Sam. When you're ready, I'll be right here.'

I looked up. 'You're a very nice man and you deserve a nice girl with no baggage.'

Chris smiled. 'I've found a nice girl. I'm just waiting for her to make a decision.'

In my mind, I could hear Steve laughing.

A few minutes later, Hari brought over the food on a large round tray and laid it out in front of us. 'I have added some tarka dhal. It's very delicious. On the house.'

'Hari…' I began.

'You did not request it, I thought you would like it, so no charge.' He held the large tray in front of him as if he expected me to punch him in the stomach.

'All right, thank you, Hari,' I said.

Hari nodded and left. We tucked in. The tarka dhal was indeed delicious.

'I'd like to see you again. Would you like to go for a drink again?' he asked. 'I'm on nights next week so it'll have to be the following week. Say Wednesday? Pick you up from home, say six?'

I hesitated. I should end this, whatever this was, right now. However, I liked Chris. He knew my position, and Gary knew I was going to the pictures with him. I ignored the warning in my head and gave him my address.

'Nice, right by the seaside,' he said. 'Do you have a sea view?'

'Yes, we do,' I replied. If he picked up on the "we", he didn't comment.

Chris gestured to Hari for the bill, waving away my offer of Going Dutch.

'Let me see, I want to make sure he's charged us properly,' I said.

Everything was there, except the dhal and the drinks. I gestured for Hari to come over.

'Is there a problem?' he asked.

'You haven't charged us for everything,' I replied.

'I explained that the tarka dhal was on the house.'

'Drinks?'

Hari smiled. 'Our thanks to you. My father would be offended if you refused.'

'We don't want to offend Hari's father,' Chris said.

I reluctantly agreed. Chris paid the bill and we left.

'You have told Gary you're coming out with me, haven't you?' Chris asked.

'Of course, he knows all about you,' I replied truthfully.

'Then you have no reason to feel awkward about it,' Chris said.

'I still miss him.'

'I know.' Suddenly, Chris bent down and kissed me. It was garlicky but nice and I unconsciously kissed him back. Then I realised what I was doing and jumped back.

'Chris, I'm sorry, I shouldn't have.'

He shook his head. 'No, I'm sorry. I shouldn't have kissed you.'

I didn't know what to say, so I stared at him as he scratched around for something to say.

'If you want to cancel next week, I understand.'

I should have cancelled, but I didn't.

*

Back at the flat, I stared out of the window at the white-topped waves. A sea view was nice, but it could look a bit bleak in the winter or on grey, miserable days, or if I was feeling… something. Feeling what? Guilt? Shame? I didn't feel guilty about living in Gary's flat, I paid my way. Nor did I feel guilty about having a social life. It was one of the things we agreed before he went. It was that kiss. I had ignored the warning signals, and I ignored Steve's warning, and now a friendship had crossed the boundary. Ashamed was too strong a word, so it had to be guilt. However, I still wanted Chris as a friend and against all good judgement, I was going to try to pull us back into friendship.

The phone rang and made me jump. It was Gary calling from Hong Kong. Was he reading my thoughts?

'How's life?' I asked.

'Pretty good. I have a busy day on today and I'm going out tonight.'

I had a niggle at the way he cut off the sentence. Perhaps I was projecting my own sense of guilt.

'Are you going anywhere nice?' I asked.

'A restaurant in a hotel near work. It's not geared to westerners, so I should experience an authentic Chinese meal.'

'Are you going with people from the office?' I asked.

'Yes.' He paused. 'Lin Yun.'

'Sounds female,' I said.

'She is. She is the interpreter.'

I wondered if telling Gary about Chris would seem like a form of tit-for-tat, but we had promised we would be honest.

'You have a great time. I look forward to meeting her when I come out there.' There, I had shown I trusted him and voiced my commitment by mentioning my trip to Hong Kong at Easter.

Gary laughed. He sounded relieved. 'You went out today, didn't you?'

I felt my stomach flip. 'Yes. Chris and I went to the pictures.'

'Any good?' Gary asked.

'Not bad. We went for a bite to eat at the Golden Temple afterwards. I smell all garlicky now.'

He chuckled. 'Did you have to fight Hari to pay the bill again?'

'I insisted we paid for the food, he insisted we had free drinks. Oh, and some tarka dhal.' I paused for a moment. 'He kissed me,' I blurted out.

'Hari did?' Gary had stopped chuckling.

'No. Chris.' I swallowed hard. 'I kissed him back.'

'I see.'

'No, you don't see. You think you see, but you don't. We had lager with the meal and I told him I missed you, because I do, very much, and he walked me to my car and kissed me and I think it was the alcohol but I kissed him back and I knew at once it was a mistake and I told him that so he apologised for kissing me and I wanted to be honest with you because we promised we'd be honest, didn't we?' I was babbling.

'Sam, slow down and breathe,' Gary said.

I took a couple of deep breaths.

'Right. Is this headed anywhere or a momentary aberration?' Gary asked.

'It's not going anywhere. I'm seeing him after lates and I'm going to have a good talk with him,' I replied.

'You're seeing him again?' Gary's voice was half an octave higher.

'Not in that way. I only agreed because I didn't want to part on bad terms. He's a nice bloke, so I wanted to have an honest talk with him.'

'Sam.' Gary stopped talking for a minute. I held my breath waiting for him to say something. 'Sam, I think you need to have a think about what you want. I'm so far away and I can understand that you get lonely sometimes. Have a think and let's be honest with each other.'

'I am being honest. I want to tell him face to face that there cannot be anything other than friendship between us. He's just a friend and I'm sorry I kissed him. I love you.'

This long-distance relationship thing was more difficult that I had imagined. I wondered if Gary would kiss Lin Yun. I was hardly in a position to object if he did. I hoped he would be honest with me.

'Think, Sam. If that—us—is what you want, perhaps it would be best not to see him again,' Gary said.

'You're right. I'll cancel our meet up and let him know some other way.' At that point I would have agreed to anything that Gary suggested.

'Up to you. Anyway, I should go. Speak tomorrow.'

I listened to the static for a moment before replacing the receiver. He hadn't told me he loved me. Damn Steve for being right.

Chapter Nineteen

Fleming had been immediately suspended as a special constable pending investigation. I knew that he would be dismissed, if he didn't resign first.

I was still curious about the PCMG. I thought that any club that allowed people like Fleming in was bound to be dodgy. I wanted to see what it was all about, so when I got a free moment, I nipped out alone and drove the short distance to the hotel.

It was a tired, once mid-range establishment that once had been in much demand as it was close to the railway station. Now it was in desperate need of a refurbishment. Worn carpet that might have been red, covered the floor. Frayed seats surrounded scratched and pitted tables. Desilvered mirrors lined the walls, but the black discolouring gave them a certain charm. The wallpaper was holding up okay. I supposed that had been replaced in the last decade as it would have been the cheapest thing to do.

'Need help, love?' the barman asked.

'Er, I'm getting married and I wanted to see what facilities there were for a reception,' I replied.

He showed me through a set of double doors into a large, once grand room.

'Plenty of room for a top table and loads of tables. We can cater for up to a hundred-and-fifty people.'

'Good gracious, there won't be that many,' I answered.

'If you need somewhere smaller, we can pull the dividers over.' He pointed out the wooden dividers pushed back against the wall.

'That sounds better,' I said.

'When are you getting married?' he asked.

'Next year, just after Easter,' I lied.

'You'd better get your skates on then. Everywhere will be booked up.'

Actually, that was something to bear in mind when Gary and I did set the date for our wedding. Secure the venue at once.

A notice on the wall caught my eye. *"Peninsula Men's Christian Group"*. PCMG. So they did meet here. I noted the date of the next meeting. The barman saw me looking.

'A social group. Is it well attended?' I asked.

'Men only, I'm afraid,' the barman said.

'It's for my fiancé. He's not long moved here and I thought it might be somewhere for him to make some friends.'

'In that case, he should pop along. They're always pleased to see new people.'

I took a final look around the room. 'This seems fine. Do you have a brochure I can take to show my fiancé?'

He walked us back to the bar and handed me a brochure.

'Thanks for your help.'

I tried to look like an eager bride-to-be as I walked back to the car. I threw the brochure onto the passenger seat and drove back to the station. I wanted to be in the Middleton Hotel when the meeting was on even if I couldn't get in, and I knew who I wanted with me when I was there.

I peered through the glass panel into the collator's office to make sure that Irene was alone. She was, so I tapped on the glass and pushed the door open.

'Hi, Sam. What can I do for you?' she asked.

I sat on the chair by her table. 'Do you fancy coming out for a drink?'

She eyed me with her head tilted to one side. 'Yeah, that sounds good. When were you thinking?'

'Thursday night? I thought we could go to the Middleton Hotel and sit in the lounge.'

'That's very specific. What are you up to?'

She knew me well. 'I thought it would be nice to catch up. It's been a while since we were able to have a good chat.'

'It would be good to catch up. I say again, what are you up to?'

'Okay, I want to check out a men's group, the PCMG, who meet there. Fleming's a member and I want to see what the clientele are like. People look suspiciously at unaccompanied women sitting in a hotel bar, so I need a companion. When we've done that, you can choose if we go on to somewhere else.'

Irene smiled. 'Is this your investigation or are you off doing your own thing again?'

'He was my lockup. This is just a little extra.'

'Okay then, but I'm going to tell Eamon. Also, it will be observations only. You don't get involved with anything, you don't go snooping and you don't try to crash the meeting.'

'I would never do that,' I objected.

'Who are you and what have you done with Samantha?' Irene joked. 'Oh, and you put your findings into a proper report and submit it to DI Webb.'

'Agreed,' I said.

'Lovely. I'll see you at the Middleton Hotel on Thursday. Say six-thirty?'

'Great. See you then.'

*

On the Thursday, I again parked in the car park of the Middleton Hotel. I couldn't see Irene's car, so I went inside to wait for her. I spotted a card that read *"PCMG"* stuck to the double doors that led to the function room. The barman was not the same person I had spoken to the last time I had been there. That was probably a good thing. He watched me walk towards the double doors, ready to spring into action if I tried to enter the hallowed masculine space. I sat at a table that gave me a good view, whilst mostly shielding me from the members.

I nodded to the barman, who came over. I was about to order a glass of lager and lime, but then I thought I should at least try to look sophisticated. My efforts were wasted.

'A spritzer please.'

'Wossat?'

'A spritzer.' I sighed at his blank face. 'Half white wine and half soda water.'

He grunted and wandered off.

Irene came in and looked around, unable to hide her dismay at the surroundings.

'Over here,' I called.

She came over and sat down. 'What are you drinking?'

'I've already ordered myself a spritzer,' I answered.

Irene turned to the bar. 'Two spritzers, please.' He held up two fingers. The barman gave no indication that he'd heard.

'I think we're a bit early.' Irene nodded towards the sign. 'The car park was practically empty.'

'It starts at seven, or maybe half past,' I agreed.

'Let's make these drinks last. I don't want to get puddled; Eamon's on a promise.' Irene winked at me.

'T.M.I.!' I watched the barman lay out our drinks. He seemed to have got it right. I took a mouthful. It was okay.

'I had to promise him something. He was all set to run to Webby when I told him what we were doing tonight.'

'Are we doing something wrong?' I asked. It didn't feel wrong, but I was conscious that there was a hierarchy, and I was just an aide. An aide with a reputation for following my own path. Maybe Webby would have preferred to send in a proper team. A man could have infiltrated the meeting. I shook myself. That wasn't what this was about. I was simply wanting to see who and what would go to this meeting.

Irene looked around the room. 'This place has gone to the dogs. I had my twenty-first birthday party in here, through those double doors in the function room, and it was lovely then. Quite posh.' She took a drink. 'I suppose that was a while ago now.'

Irene was about ten years older than me so that would mean her coming of age party had been about thirteen or fourteen years ago. A while.

A couple of men arrived and went through the double doors. I looked at my watch. Ten to seven. A few minutes later, a couple more arrived. Ordinary looking men.

'I'd say it will be a half seven start,' Irene said.

I agreed. Then I spotted a familiar face.

'Dammit!' I ducked down over my drink, but it was too late.

'Hey Sam,' Vic came over to our table.

I looked up. 'Oh, hi, Vic,'

'What are you doing here?' he asked.

'We stopped off for a quick drink before we get the train over to the city.' I held a hand towards Irene, who was watching Vic with interest. 'This is my friend, Irene. Irene. This is Vic. He's a fireman.'

'Pleased to meet you,' Irene said.

'Pleased to meet you.' Vic looked around. 'This place has seen better days.'

'I just said that, didn't I,' Irene said.

Someone came out of the room. 'Ah, there you are. Do you want to come in now and we can set up?'

'I'll be right there, brother,' Vic answered. He turned back at us. 'Got to go. I'm doing a talk on my church youth work. Remember, I told you about it?'

'I do remember.' I nudged Irene. 'He helps run residential courses for wayward kids.'

Vic laughed. 'We don't call them wayward. They're just kids who need a guiding hand. Anyway, I'd better go.'

Irene and I watched him disappear into the room.

'Dammit, I could have done without that,' I said.

'Mmm,' Irene was non-committal. 'I must say that I haven't seen anything that alarms me so far. The people going in all seem pretty normal, and a talk about a course for wayward kids is hardly subversive.'

'But Fleming is a member. Something's got to be a bit off with it.'

Irene shook her head. 'I bet the members are sad, isolated men and this gives them somewhere to go. I wonder who organised this?' Then Irene's eyes widened and she hunched over her drink much as I had.

A large man with thinning hair walked past, belly first. He looked my way, looked away without a flicker or a break in his stride, then went into the room.

'Who was that?' I asked when he was gone.

'I'm not sure it's someone you will have come across. Eamon had dealings with him years ago when he was new in the job. He was sent down for indecent assault and GBH. He must have been recently released.' She drained her glass. 'This is definitely something Webby will be interested in.'

'Maybe we should leave. We've both recognised people. Who knows who else will come in,' I said.

'No, I think we should stay a while longer. Like you said, who knows who will come in next.'

I stood up. 'I'm visiting the ladies. Keep me posted.'

I came out of the loo, just in time to get a sideways look at Roger Duggan. I shrank back but he didn't look around. Breathing a sigh of relief, I watched him go to the double doors and enter the PCMG meeting. I scurried to our table.

'Did you just see Roger Duggan?' I asked.

'Middle aged. Trying too hard to look flash. Looked at me like I was something on his shoe?'

'That sounds like him. He definitely knows me, so maybe we should leave. Much as I despise the man, I don't want another complaint coming in from him.'

Irene scanned the room again. 'This doesn't strike me as the type of place a bank manager would frequent.' She glanced towards the double door. 'Unless he's a member of that boys' club.'

'We should go. Do you want to go on somewhere for a proper

catch up?'

'Yeah, just for an hour. I'll meet you at the Gozzie Moggie.'

We stood up to return to our cars just as another man entered the PCMG room. For a second, I had a clear view of Roger Duggan talking to Vic. Maybe they were just discussing tonight's topic, or maybe not. I longed to be a fly on the wall in there.

*

Next day, Irene and I reported our outing to DI Webb.

'You went to the Middleton Hotel with Sergeant Kildea and saw Duggan there?'

'Yes, sir,' I replied. 'And a fireman named Vic. I'm not sure of his surname, and Sergeant Kildea recognised another person that I didn't know.' I'd got used to not knowing everything. I'd be included if it was deemed necessary.

Irene said a name that I didn't recognise. DI Webb did know it.

'That git is out already?'

Irene nodded. 'Large as life.'

'Sir, you have to wonder what sort of club it is to have such undesirables in it. At least two I know of have misogynistic views.' I remembered Vic. 'I'm sure some are okay, but they might become influenced by the others.'

DI Webb remained quiet as he thought.

'Do you want someone to try to infiltrate the club, sir? Shall I ask Eamon?' Irene asked.

'No, his accent is distinctive. If we do that, I'll ask Mike how he feels about mixing with the dross of society.'

'Not a problem, sir. May I suggest that we photograph people entering the hotel as well? We can perhaps do IDs on them afterwards, see who's known to us. Get a handle on who's linked to who. I can do intel cards on them all, in case they come up in future incidents.'

'Do we have sufficient reason? Our only interest in that club is that a couple of undesirables are members,' DI Webb warned her.

'I can just do a card on the PCMG, a gathering place for people known to the police, with a particular antipathy towards women. We can then add names as we prove they are members.'

'Good enough,' DI Webb said. 'Start a card, but let's hold off on observations for now. Include the information on the records of those already known to us.'

'Yes, sir.' Irene said.

As we turned to leave, DI Webb called me back.

'Sam, make sure you keep me in the loop. I would be very disappointed if you went off on enquiries and forgot to inform me.'

'Yes, sir.' I said. That was my card marked. I still didn't think I had been wrong though. I wondered if he would have been so accommodating if I had not included Irene in my visit.

*

I had been an aide long enough to have built a job list of my own. Not large, but it would grow the longer I was there. Nothing serious, except to the victims, but enough to keep me busy. We would take advantage of any quiet spells to carry out ongoing enquiries for the myriad jobs that came our way. Even if we didn't have good news, at least the victims knew they had not been forgotten. I thought that was important. If a major incident came in, Webby would select a few people to concentrate solely on that.

I was out with Eamon during one of these spells, working our way through a list of bread-and-butter incidents. Straightforward and easily sorted. I was feeling pleased with our progress, and we were in a relaxed mood as we drove back to the station.

Normally, we would have our radios on our own channel, but when Eamon and I were out together, we'd started to use one radio to monitor the divisional channel and the other the CID channel. It allowed us to keep track of what was happening on the block as well as our own incidents.

Today, I had the divisional radio while Eamon monitored the CID channel. I listened to Ray trying to rustle up a patrol to meet with the RSPCA who needed to access a house on Victory Street. Everyone was busy.

'Let's lend a hand. It'll only take a few minutes,' I said.

Eamon agreed.

I radioed up. 'DC Barrie to control, DC Kildea and I are just around the corner. We can assist if it's just to aid entry.'

'Thanks Sam. Yes, the RSPCA will deal once entry has been gained.' Ray confirmed the address, which I immediately recognised as Annie's house.

'Roger, en route.'

'I hate people who mistreat animals,' Eamon said as he drove us to the address.

'Most people do,' I replied.

Eamon pulled into Victory Street and parked next to the RSPCA van outside Annie's House. I tried to remember if the windows had been boarded up when I had last been there, but I couldn't say for sure. Two RSPCA inspectors, one a woman of a similar age to me, and the other an older man, waited on the doorstep.

'All right,' Eamon greeted them. 'What's the craic?'

'A neighbour reported whimpering and crying coming from the address. It locks abandoned. We need to get in and rescue any animal that might be in there,' the male inspector replied. 'We'll have to force entry.'

'Go ahead then,' Eamon invited them.

They smashed the small window by the lock and Eamon put his hand in to open the front door. Once it was opened, they went inside and started to search the downstairs rooms. Curiosity drove me to follow them.

Eamon followed me. He wrinkled his nose. 'It smells like the elephant house.'

I gaped at the scene in front of me. Someone had definitely been there, but there was no furniture except a rotten, bare mattress. The floor was covered with newspapers, mouldy food, opened and discarded packets, and the sharp stench of urine permeated everything. I looked into the kitchen which had cupboards hanging from the wall and debris across the floor. There was no way anyone could use it to prepare food.

'How can anyone live like this?' I said to nobody in particular. I heard a whimpering noise from upstairs. 'It sounds like an animal is up there. Poor thing must be starving. There's nothing to eat here.'

We all ran upstairs and followed the noise into the rear bedroom. This room was bare. No flooring, no furniture. A large crate was plonked in the middle of the room. It was too big to have been brought in through the door, so it must have been built inside the room.

'What's that on the walls? It looks like eggboxes.' I ran my fingers over the unfamiliar material.

'Soundproofing.' Eamon ran his hands over the material as if looking for something. The inspectors approached the crate.

'It's so dark in here. We could do with some light to see what state the poor creature's in,' the male inspector said.

Heavy curtains partly covered a wooden board that blocked the light. He opened the window and pulled off the board. It was brighter, but it would take more than an open window to dispel the stench.

I turned back to the crate and spotted fingers curled around one of the slats. Human fingers. They moved.

'Bloody hell!' I shouted. 'There's a person in there.' I leapt forward and pulled at the slat. The fingers withdrew into the crate.

Eamon abandoned the walls and pulled the slat with me. The RSPCA people pulled at the slats on the other side. Together, we managed to get the crate open and a filthy, emaciated woman slowly uncurled from the crate and onto the floor. The RSPCA officers jumped back.

'My God,' Eamon breathed. He had an impressive repertoire of swear words and used every one of them as he stared at her.

Meantime, I was on the radio asking for an ambulance.

'We're police. You're safe now. What's your name, m'darlin'?' Eamon asked in his most gentle voice.

The woman croaked an unintelligible answer. It sounded rusted, as if she hadn't spoken in weeks.

'Which fecker did this to you?' It wasn't really a question. Eamon took off his jacket and draped it across the girl. She clutched it around her. 'Sam, find out who is the registered tenant here.'

While Eamon spoke to the girl, I radioed in a request for Ray to contact the council and get the tenant's name ASAP, although judging by the state of the place, it looked as if it had been abandoned ages ago. I then went and peered into the other bedroom. It too was soundproofed and had wood across the window. Another large crate sat in the middle of the floor.

'Eamon, there's another crate here, but it's empty,' I called to him. I returned to the rear bedroom.

The girl began to cry. 'Gone,' she rasped.

'Gone? Who's gone? Gone where?' Eamon asked.

She shrugged her bony shoulders.

'Sweetheart, we need to know who you are.' Eamon said.

'Sharon,' she rasped.

'Sharon Hall?!' I exclaimed.

She slowly turned her head to me. It seemed to hurt her. 'Sharon Hall.'

'Your mum and Martin have been worried about you,' I told her. 'They're going to be so happy to see you again.'

'Martin.' Tears rolled down her face.

'Sharon, who was in the other crate? Where have they gone?' Eamon gently asked.

'Gone.' Sharon's eyes were fluttering.

'Sam, ask Ray to chivvy up that ambulance,' Eamon said.

I immediately transmitted as requested. The RSPCA inspectors were also liaising with their control, not that there was a lot for them to do here. Caged women were outside of their remit. It was useful to have another female around though, for chaperoning purposes. Once we had got Sharon to safety, we'd need statements from both of them.

'We'll soon get you checked out at the hospital,' Eamon said to Sharon. 'Sam, see if you can see the ambulance. Let them know what they're coming into. Keep the space in front of the house clear for them. Oh, and fend off nosy neighbours.'

I wondered if I was being sent out of the way for some reason, but the RSPCA were still there. Also, I too was a jack now— okay, an aide—so he was probably just securing the scene. I went outside and, as usual, several neighbours had come out to watch proceedings. I wondered if Bessie was back home. I hoped Freda would be able to keep her in if she was at home.

'What's happened?' one neighbour called over.

'An ambulance is on the way, please keep the area outside the house clear for them,' I replied.

'Is it a murder?'

'Enquiries are ongoing.' And that was as much as they were going to get from me.

Nellie came out and scurried towards me.

'There was a bloke burning something in the back yard yesterday. Looked like old clothing. I was doing the bedrooms and I could see across the yards into Annie's. We're not allowed to have bonfires in the back yard. I went out back and into Annie's yard to speak to him about the smell and the rats, and the smoke, but he refused to even look at me.'

'Was it the tenant?' I asked.

She shrugged. 'I'm not sure who lives there now. Waste of a perfectly good house. A family would have been glad of that place.'

That was interesting. 'Thanks, I'll take a look.'

Trevor in Mike Three accompanied by Andy drew up outside

the house.

'Move up a few yards. Make room for the ambulance,' I called.

'Just because you're out of uniform now, doesn't mean you can boss us around,' Trevor called back. His grin told me he was joking.

'Shift it,' I jerked my thumb to emphasise the need to move and smiled to show I wasn't being a diva.

Trevor moved up and they both got out.

'Can you hold the fort out here while I check something out?' I asked Andy. 'Basically, keep everyone away and don't tell anyone anything. Apart from the ambos.'

He took up position by the front door while Trevor went in to see Eamon, and I nipped up to the entry and around the back of the houses. Nellie had gone into her own back yard and was peering over the wall. She was a small woman so she must have been standing on a ladder or something. She pointed towards the house next-door-but-one to hers. 'There, that one. I can see it from our back bedroom. He's got one of those metal bins with holes in.'

She watched me walk along the entry and nodded when I reached the correct house. I tried the gate and was relieved it opened. I hadn't relished the idea of climbing the wall. I saw the bin Nellie referred to and lifted the lid. There was indeed clothing in there. I got a stick and shifted a few things around. All fire damaged, but still recognisable as women's clothing.

'What is it?' she called.

'Clothing, just as you told me,' I called back.

Then I caught a glimpse of something that had once been red. It was burnt, but enough remained for me to see some of the colour. I lifted it with my stick and pulled out what was left of a coat. It was severely burned but not totally destroyed. It looked like being at the bottom had protected it from worse damage. Then I noticed the molten remains of a plastic handbag. I rubbed a finger across the surface and got a vague impression that it might have once been pink or red. I looked back at the coat and saw the lapel, or what was left of it, was frayed. Suddenly, I got a mental picture of Ruthie Pritchard outside the fire station wearing her red coat and carrying her horrible pink handbag. I dropped them back in the bin and took a deep breath. I didn't want to check the rest of the clothing. I'd seen enough. I hurried back to the front and went inside to speak to Eamon.

The ambulance had arrived while I had been in the yard and they were checking Sharon. I beckoned Eamon onto the landing.

'Who's out front?' he demanded.

'Andy,' I replied. 'Listen, Eamon, a neighbour told me someone had been burning old clothing in the back yard yesterday. I went to check it out and the bin is full of burnt women's clothing. There's also what appears to be a pink plastic handbag and the remains of a red coat. It looked like the outfit I last saw Ruthie Pritchard wearing. She hasn't been seen for a while.'

I suddenly was unable to speak. Ruthie had been a thorn in all our sides. If the burnt clothing was hers, it boded ill for her. It would all have to be examined by SOCO, the Scene of the Crime Officer, but I knew in my heart she was dead. If it had been her in the other crate, where was her body? Even if it hadn't been her in the crate, where was she?

'Okay,' Eamon said. 'Radio in and get SOCO to go through the bin. We're going to need a lot of forensics on this. You should also go and speak to Nellie when you're free. We'll need a statement that she told you about the burning and that's how you found the clothing.'

I don't know how I managed to keep my voice steady as I requested SOCO, but somehow, I did.

While I had been on the radio, the ambulance crew had transferred Sharon to a stretcher. They lifted the stretcher as if it weighed nothing and carried it out to the ambulance.

'The general?' Eamon asked as they passed.

'General,' the front one confirmed.

'Sam, go with them and remain with Sharon until someone else arrives,' Eamon said. 'DI Webb and Mike have been informed and are on their way here.'

I followed the ambulance crew out and went with them to the General Hospital.

Chapter Twenty

Sharon came to with a jolt. She looked at me, scrabbled to the top of the bed and stared at the drips in her arms.

'Sharon, it's okay. You're in hospital and you're safe. My name's Sam. Do you remember? I was one of the people who found you.'

She slowly relaxed as she took in her surroundings.

'Safe?' she croaked.

'Safe,' I echoed.

She began to weep. I wasn't certain of the protocol here, but she was a fellow human in distress. I sat on the edge of the bed and put my arm around her shoulders. I hesitated before speaking. I was about to share something that I normally preferred to keep to myself.

'I actually do know what you're going through right now. When I was fifteen, I was abducted. I managed to escape by jumping from the moving van in front of a car that was following us.' I lifted my fringe and showed her the scar that ran along my hairline. 'I was left with this. That same night, they abducted another girl in my place. She wasn't able to escape. She was raped and murdered. That should have been me and I still carry the guilt from that.'

'Not your fault,' Sharon whispered.

'I understand that now, but…' I tapped over my heart to convey what words couldn't. 'What happened to you, Sharon, wasn't your fault and you must not hold a single ounce of guilt about it. Be angry, be unforgiving, be sad, but don't feel guilty.'

A nurse came in and paused at the scene.

'She's a bit upset,' I explained somewhat unnecessarily.

'I'll get sister.' The nurse vanished.

'Try to remember as much as you can. Someone will be in to speak to you as soon as you feel strong enough,' I told Sharon.

'Mr Duggan,' she rasped.

'Martin's dad?' I asked.

She nodded and I waited for more, but she didn't say anything else.

'What about Mr Duggan?' I asked eventually. 'Do you want him to visit you?'

She frowned as if making an enormous effort, which she probably was, and shook her head. 'It was him.'

'Roger Duggan locked you in a crate?' I needed clarification.

She whispered, 'He took me.'

My mind was spinning. I knew it wouldn't be right for me to take a statement off her while she was in this state, but I needed to get this down. I'd incorporate it into my own statement until she was fit to be interviewed.

'You're saying, Roger Duggan took you but didn't put you in the crate?'

She nodded. Her eyes looked heavy as if it had taken all her energy to tell me this much.

The sister came in. 'Sharon, you're awake. How are you feeling?'

Sharon croaked something unintelligible.

The sister turned to me. 'You need to stop questioning her. Tell your people that she can't be interviewed until she's much more alert.'

'Don't worry, I will,' I replied. I stood up to go back outside but Sharon clutched at my hand.

The sister eyed her. 'She seems to have bonded with you, so you may stay in here if you wish. Do not try to take a statement.'

'I wouldn't!' I replied. Honestly, what did she take me for? 'It's okay if she wants to chat, isn't it? I wouldn't want to be accused of trying to interrogate her.'

The sister pierced me with a look. 'Chatting is fine. Her family are on the way I believe.'

'Hear that, Sharon? Your mum is on her way,' I said.

A fat teardrop slid down her face. The sister half smiled and left.

'Sharon, how did Roger Duggan manage to take you?' I asked in a low voice, in case anyone was listening.

'Car. Said we should talk. I got in.' Her eyelids flickered, but I had enough to piece together what had happened. If I had it correctly, as she walked to work, Roger Duggan—who disliked Sharon and blamed her for his son's refusal to obey him—had pulled up in his car. He had enticed her into the car by saying they should talk. Then she was taken to the house where we found her. Sharon had said he hadn't caged her, so he had to have passed her over to someone else. Neighbours would have seen any commotion in the street, so I believed that Roger Duggan had taken her into the house, which would explain how she had entered the house without a struggle.

'Sharon, when you feel stronger, we'll need to take a statement from you. We need to hear the full story from when you left your house. Everything, even if you think it's not important. Can you do that?'

Sharon nodded. It seemed speaking took too much effort, so I sat and held her hand until her mother and Martin arrived. Then I slipped away. Poor Martin. He disliked his father, but I bet he had no idea what Roger Duggan was capable of.

*

Back at the station, Ray called to me as I went past the control room towards the CID office. 'I have details of the tenant of that address.'

I took the scrap of paper that Ray held out to me. My stomach dropped when I saw the name. Walter Hodgeson. Walter the Weeble! He rented the property where Sharon had been left to die and another girl, possibly Ruthie Pritchard, had already died.

'What's wrong?' Ray asked me around his cigarette.

'I know this person. Not well, but I met him a few times at the fire station, and that charity dance.'

Ray snorted smoke down his nose. 'As Webby always says, you follow the evidence where it leads, even if it goes somewhere you don't expect.'

'I didn't expect this,' I admitted. I left Ray to it and hurried upstairs and knocked on DI Webb's door. When he admitted me, I launched straight into the story.

'Sir, while I was waiting with Sharon at the hospital, she told me that Roger Duggan had taken her off in his car.'

DI Webb raised his eyebrows. 'Please tell me you didn't interview her.'

'No sir. It would be inadmissible evidence because she is still pretty well out of it.' DI Webb would have been well aware of that, but I wanted to show him that I also knew when not to wade in. 'She woke up and just told me. I know nothing more than that at the moment. Also, Ray has got the name of the tenant of the address in Victory Street. Walter Hodgeson. We need to speak to him and Roger Duggan. May I be a part of that?'

DI Webb watched me for a moment. 'Didn't you have some kind of run-in with Roger Duggan?'

'Yes, at a domestic. I locked him up for theft. He complained. Then he deliberately set of the PA at the bank and I reported him to their security.'

'Is it a good idea for you to be involved with him?'

I grinned. 'Oh yes. And I have been part of this job from the very beginning so it wouldn't be unusual for me to take part in the interview now Sharon's found. I can't wait to hear how he's going to explain this one.'

'He'll think you're out to get him.'

'Yes, sir, he probably will.'

DI Webb grinned back. 'DS Finlay will decide who he wants

to be involved with the interviews. We'll speak to Sharon first, then DS Finlay can decide who he wants in first.'

'Yes, sir. I also need to go back and speak with Nellie Hayes. I need a statement about the burning clothes…' I faltered as I thought about the original noise complaint.

DI Webb watched me for a moment. 'What aren't you telling me?'

'Nothing relevant, sir.' Damn that man's bullshit radar.

'Tell me.' He leant back and put his feet up on the desk.

I decided to take the chance to unburden myself. What was the worst that could happen—apart from a charge of neglect of duty?

'A little while ago I attended an incident in Victory Street.'

'I saw the job sheet. Nellie and Bessie are still at it.' DI Webb chuckled.

'Yes, sir.' I took a deep breath. 'When I was waiting for the doctor to come and see to Bessie, Nellie told me about animal noises and smell and rats coming from the house.'

'Environmental Health,' DI Webb said.

'Yes sir, I did advise that.'

'So what's the problem?'

'I meant to check around the address when I was finished with Bessie, but we were diverted to the Peninsula Bank.'

'Roger Duggan's alarm?'

I nodded. 'I intended to do a brief incident report and perhaps ring the council or Environmental Health people myself when I got back, but I forgot. I remembered next day and phoned it in.'

'I repeat, what's the problem?'

I hung my head. 'Maybe those noises Nellie heard were Sharon, or Ruthie. I could have brought this to an end then. I should have gone back and checked again,' I said. 'I should have phoned Environmental Health or the RSPCA at least.'

'Why? You told Nellie to do that. Didn't the other neighbours hear anything? Why didn't they ring' DI Webb watched me for a moment. 'Would you feel guilty if there had been no further incident at that address?'

Something else I hadn't considered. 'I suppose not. It's the thought that someone was suffering there and I could have saved them.'

'Samantha Barrie, saviour of the world.'

Was he mocking me?

'I don't mean to come across as arrogant, sir.'

'Look, Sam, this is not the telly. We aren't all sitting around waiting for this week's job to come in. We cannot deal with the volume of work that comes in here and not have something slip our minds occasionally. There was nothing to suggest that the original report was urgent or was even something the police would deal with. You gave the correct advice at the time. What happened since is terrible, but not your fault. The sick bastard who left a girl to die in a crate is the one to blame.'

'Sir, you know what the media is like. If the papers hear about this, they'll say that someone reported it ages ago and the police ignored it. They'll say the police are to blame for Sharon Hall and the other girl because I forgot. I'm to blame!' I could feel my heart racing as I worked myself into a state.

DI Webb rolled his eyes. 'The police didn't ignore it. The police gave the correct advice before they were diverted to an urgent and potentially life-threatening incident that was occurring right there and then.'

Actually, that didn't sound so bad at all. DI Webb hadn't even suggested putting me on a charge. My breathing slowed and I started to relax.

'Yes, sir. Thank you.'

'Now, bugger off, I've got work to do. Go speak to Nellie.'

'Yes, sir.'

Strangely enough, despite his blunt manner, or perhaps because of it, DI Webb had made me feel better. Then I remembered that I had not cancelled my outing with Chris. My stomach flipped as I remembered the difficult conversation we would have to have. I had promised Gary that I would cancel, so

I felt I had to stick to that. I was a bit too busy now, but it had to be soon.

*

I took the beige Ford that was becoming my usual car and drove to Victory Street. Nellie was outside mopping the pavement. A task that was fast falling out of favour these days. I could see why she did it. If I had to step straight into my living room from the street, I'd want the area outside my house to be clean too.

'Hello, Mrs Hayes,' I called as I got out of the car.

She stopped swabbing and peered at me. She smiled as she recognised me.

'Hello. Constable Barrie, isn't it? Are you here about Annie's house?'

'Samantha.' I walked over to her. 'I need a statement that you told me about the burning clothes, to add to the file.'

She nodded. 'Yes, okay. The kettle should be almost boiled. Do you fancy a cup of tea?'

'That sounds lovely.'

Nellie tipped the soapy water into the gutter and carried the mop and bucket into the house. I followed her through the living room that had come straight from the 1940s, into the kitchen. I could see that this was where most of the living was done. A couple of cottage chairs flanked the fireplace. A table that served as both a preparation area and a dining table took up the space in the middle of the room. A sink was positioned under the window and the cooker sat beside it.

'Sit down.'

I sat at the table that was currently set up as the prep area and protected with newspaper. A gutted rabbit lay on a plate under a mesh dome that protected it from flies. Breadcrumbs and herbs spilled from its belly. Later, the paper would be discarded and a tablecloth laid out. I set out a statement form and a pen while Nellie took the mop and bucket into the yard then came back to make the tea.

'I like to take a break about now. It gets a bit hectic when the lads come back from work.' She moved the rabbit to the draining board then put a cup of tea in front of me and settled herself opposite.

'It shouldn't take long,' I said. 'I just need you to describe what you saw in the back yard of Annie's house and how you told me about it.'

'When I first mentioned it, you told me to ring the Environmental Health. I wish I had done then… That poor girl.'

I had meant the burning clothing, but it seemed I wasn't the only one feeling guilty. I decided to go ahead and include the original conversation with the statement, because we had nothing to hide. As DI Webb said, none of us could have had any idea of the horror that was going on just a couple of houses away.

'Nobody could have known, Mrs Hayes,' I said. 'None of the other neighbours said anything to us, not even the houses on either side, so they couldn't have thought much of it if they had heard anything.'

'No, I suppose not.'

We sat for a minute silently drinking our tea and working through our respective guilt, then I made a start on the statement. It was straightforward and we quickly finished. Nellie signed it. I popped it into my bag and picked up my cup to finish my tea.

'Annie would turn in her grave if she knew about all this,' Nellie said.

'I believe she had a son,' I said, pleased to have the opportunity to confirm the connection between Annie and Walter.

'Yes, Walter.' She paused as the front door opened. 'Who's that?'

'Only me, Mam,' a jovial voice called out.

'You're early, Don.' Nellie glanced at the large, dark wood clock on the mantelpiece.

'Work was done so they sent us home. Have I caught you

with your secret fancy man?' A man with dark, Brylcreemed hair and startling blue eyes bounded into the kitchen. 'Gotcha!'

Nellie laughed. 'You daft ha'porth.'

I smiled. It was nice to see a happy family. Not everyone I dealt with had that.

Don had to have been well into his fifties, but he looked to be in his early forties. A slim physique and tanned skin, callouses on his hands. An outdoor worker. Handsome by anyone's standards. He rolled his sleeves up, revealing muscled arms and tattoos on his fingers. I read "MAM ♥" across one hand and "DAD ♥" on the other. It didn't seem particularly military-based, so I wondered if this had been a teenage rebellion. Not much of a rebellion; I had seen much more colourful language permanently marked on people's skin.

'Hello, who's this?' Don asked.

'Samantha. She's a policewoman. We were having a cuppa. The pot's still warm if you want one.'

'Ta, Mam.' He poured himself a drink and leant against the sink. 'Has Bessie been kicking off again, or is it Annie's house?'

'Annie's house. Poor old Bessie's still away,' Nellie answered. 'We were just talking about Walter.'

I got the distinct impression that no matter who, if anyone, lived there in the future, it would always be known as Annie's house.

Don snorted. 'That useless tub of lard. He always thought he was a cut above everyone. Watch it when you speak to him. He's such a liar.'

'Don't be unkind, Don,' his mother admonished.

Don was unrepentant. 'Mam, if Walter Hodgeson told me that Christmas Day was on the twenty-fifth of December, I'd find a calendar to check. He's always been like that. He had his mam believing he was top of the class at school. Then, when he started work at the shipyard, he told his mam they'd promoted him to foreman within a month. He didn't last long there. Nobody was prepared to put up with him.' Don started to chuckle. 'Hey, Mam, tell her about the girl from Woodcock's.' Before Nellie had a chance to answer, Don ploughed on with his story. 'It was a good few years back now, Walter told everyone he was dating the girl that cut the bacon.' He turned to me. 'You know Woodcock's?'

I nodded. Everyone knew Woodcock's. It was a large grocer's store on the main shopping street. The most notable thing about it was that there was a central cashier. She'd sit in a wooden cubicle against the rear wall and all money would be sent to her via a system of pulleys that would shoot cannisters over the customers' heads. She'd send change back the same way. It had been cutting-edge technology once, but was a bit slow and dated now. Great fun to watch though.

Don continued. 'Like I said, Walter told everyone he was dating this girl. It went on for so long that Annie began to wonder why he hadn't brought her home. He always made excuses. In the end, Annie took matters into her own hands. She went into Woodcock's and invited the girl to Sunday tea. Of course the poor girl had no idea why a customer was asking her to tea. That's when it all came out that Walter was lying—again. God knows how he was supposed to have met a girl; he never went anywhere apart from that club at the Middleton Hotel.'

All that fitted with my experience with Walter the Weeble so far. I paused. Don had said the Middleton Hotel.

'Do you mean the Christian men's group?' I asked.

Don tipped his mug towards me. 'That's the one.'

'Nothing wrong with attending a Christian group,' Nellie said.

'No,' Don admitted, 'but it's hardly the place to meet a girl.'

That was true. Walter Hodgeson was, or had been, a member of the PCMG, and was the tenant of Annie's house. Roger Duggan was a member of the PCMG and had taken Sharon to Annie's house where she'd been locked in a crate. Walter and Duggan were linked, and Fleming, but only by virtue of him also being a member. As far as I knew, he had no connection to

Annie's house, but he did have some archaic views on women.

'She was a nice girl, her that cut the bacon. I used to wonder if she'd be a good match for you, Don,' Nellie murmured.

I looked at Nellie's Hollywood-handsome, well-groomed, blue-eyed son. I didn't think that he would have been interested in the girl that cut the bacon. Or any girl for that matter.

'I've only got room for one woman in my life.' Don kissed his mother's cheek. 'You know I'm not interested in marriage and all that palaver. I'm a free spirit.' He ran his cup under the sink and put it on the draining board. I was momentarily astonished to see a man from the Trafalgar streets washing a cup. 'Don't bother with tea for me. I'm meeting Ron, we'll get chips or something when we're out.'

'Hey, did you find it?' Nellie asked Don.

He paused at the foot of the stairs. 'No, Mam. I think that someone might have stolen it. I wouldn't mind so much if it hadn't been Dad's.' With that, he hurried upstairs.

'What has Don lost? I can check our property book when I get back,' I offered.

'A mallet. He followed his dad into the shipyard to train as a shipwright. When Oliver retired, he passed his tools on to Don.'

'Oliver is your husband?' I asked.

'That's right. Gone five years now.' Nellie unconsciously crossed herself. 'He gave us a good life. All my children have done well for themselves. I'm a lucky woman. Don has started a spot of moonlighting. He said if it takes off he might go self employed as a handyman or such like.' She thrust out a foot to display her slipper. 'It seems to be paying off. He got me these from a proper shoe shop. None of your market rubbish that fall to pieces in a week.'

'They are good quality,' I agreed. 'They'll last.'

Don reappeared in a clean shirt. 'See you later, Mam. Don't wait up. Nice to meet you, Samantha.'

As the front door slammed, Nellie shook her head. 'I worry he's going to end up lonely.'

'One of my great aunts never married and never regretted it,' I said.

'It's different for a man. They need looking after and I won't be around forever.' Nellie eyed me for a moment, her thought process clear. She evidently decided I wasn't suitable for whatever reason and started to clear up.

I stood up and gathered my things. 'I'll get off then. Thank you for the tea. I'll see myself out.'

I would make sure that Hodgeson, Fleming and Duggan were all included on Irene's card on the PCMG. If they were involved with this, I wanted all the strands to come together and tie them in a neat little bow.

*

A few days later, DI Webb gave the go ahead for observations on the Middleton Hotel. Mike would not be required to infiltrate it yet. I sat with Eamon and a SOCO, who had refused point blank to let anyone else near their precious camera, peering through the blinds in an office on the first floor of the department store opposite. Webby had done well securing this place for us. It offered an excellent view of the car park and the entrance without us being in view.

'While we're waiting for the members to arrive, I'm going to the ladies,' I said.

Neither of them answered me. I knew that they didn't really need me, The SOCO would get the photos and Eamon would watch the goings-on. Nevertheless, I hurried to the loo.

'Have you recognised anyone yet?' I asked Eamon when I got back a couple of minutes later.

'Not so far,' he replied.

'I have,' the SOCO said.

'Who?' I asked.

'You wouldn't know them.'

I could hear the condescension, and it annoyed me. I might

have been young in service, but I still resented being pushed aside. Maybe this was what Wilfred felt like when he was left out.

'Who?' Eamon repeated.

'I don't know his name. I've just seen him around.'

Eamon and I exchanged a look.

'That's helpful,' Eamon muttered.

A few men arrived, none of whom I recognised, then I spotted Roger Duggan getting out of a car in the car park. He stopped and chatted with another man and the pair walked into the hotel.

'Little prick,' Eamon muttered.

Vic was next, then the big-bellied man that Irene had seen.

'Bloody hell! I didn't expect to see him again,' the SOCO exclaimed.

'Unfortunately, he has recently been released on licence,' Eamon replied.

'Should have thrown away the fucking key.' The SOCO snapped a photograph several times.

'You're not wrong,' Eamon agreed.

While they talked, I was wondering what Vic was doing there again. He had gone to do a talk the last time I had seen him there. Had he become a member? Did he realise the type of people that attended this group?

I recognised Fleming striding through the car park and Vic left my mind.

'Get him!' I barked. I didn't mean to sound abrupt, but it would be useful for the Fleming file.

The SOCO glanced at me then snapped Fleming. He kept on snapping as Fleming went into the hotel.

'Sorry about that,' I said. 'I knew he was a member of the group but it's good to get a photo too.'

The SOCO grunted.

After a time, there were no more arrivals, so we packed up and returned to the station.

'I'll let you have the photos as soon as they're ready,' the SOCO said.

'Thanks, and thanks for your help today,' Eamon said in his soothing voice.

'Yeah, thanks,' I added.

'Let's get a cuppa, then meet Mike in the office to discuss what's next,' Eamon suggested.

'Sounds good to me.'

We went to the refs room and I made two hot drinks and carried them to the Formica table. It was not scoff time so the room was empty.

'Quite a cross-section of men,' Eamon commented.

'Yes, I didn't recognise most of them. Will they all have to be spoken to?'

'Possibly. It depends on how this pans out.' Eamon said.

'Follow the evidence wherever it leads.' I sipped my drink.

'Exactly. Without fear or favour. It's in the oath.'

I relished the challenge of unravelling this case. I couldn't wait to see Sharon get justice. Maybe I'd get a few answers on the whereabouts of Ruthie too.

Chapter Twenty-One

We received notification that Sharon Hall was up to speaking to us the following day. Eamon, DI Webb and I went up to the hospital and sat in Sharon's hospital room with Sharon and her mother, listening to Sharon describe her ordeal. She looked a whole lot better than the last time we'd seen her. She'd been bathed and wore clean nightwear. She was still attached to a drip but she'd lost that awful grey pallor. She was still weak, however, and lay back on white pillows that her mother kept plumping up and adjusting. I smiled inwardly. Mrs Hall was reacting just like my mother did after I had been abducted. I wondered if Sharon would be subject to the overprotective mothering that I had endured. She would like it at first but it would soon rankle, especially if she were still planning on marrying Martin and emigrating to New Zealand.

'So, Mr Duggan pulled up beside you and told you that you two should talk?' DI Webb asked.

'Yes. We don't really get on. Martin hates him, but I thought that it had to be better if we were at least communicating. I got into the car. I wouldn't ever normally get into a car with a man, but it was Mr Duggan.'

We all nodded. Why would she suspect him of something so horrible? Poor Sharon wanted to do the right thing and he had utterly betrayed her.

Sharon continued. 'I thought we were going to talk about Martin. I know Mr Duggan blames me for Martin wanting to move away, so I thought he was going to tell me to stop seeing him. He drove off, which surprised me. He drove into town and we went to a house with boards on the windows. Mr Duggan got out and told me to follow him. I refused because it all seemed very odd. The house was horrible, all tatty and boarded up.'

I felt that niggle at the back of my mind. What was it trying to tell me?

'What did Mr Duggan say?' DI Webb asked.

'He said he thought I'd be more comfortable and willing to listen if we went to the house. It belonged to someone he knew from church. I thought that maybe he had started to rent the place since his breakup with Martin's mum, and perhaps hadn't had time to do anything with it. I know the council board up windows of empty properties to stop the kids smashing them. I thought if it belonged to someone from church, then it must be okay. I got out of the car and he told me to go into the kitchen. I stepped through the front door into a disgusting, abandoned front room. I turned to Mr Duggan, but he was walking away. There was another man behind the door...'

She wiped the tears from her eyes with a shaking hand and took a deep breath before continuing. 'He grabbed me and put something over my mouth. I tried to scream but I was being smothered.'

'Who was this man?' DI Webb asked.

'I don't know. I didn't get a good look at him. I was so disorientated and he was behind me most of the time.'

'I'm going to find him and I'm going to kill him,' Mrs Hall snarled. 'Both of them.'

'I understand your feelings, Mrs Hall, but let us deal with it and keep yourself out of trouble. Sharon needs you here, not in prison,' Eamon said.

'Are you able to tell us what happened next, Sharon?' DI Webb asked.

'The man pulled my coat off and dragged me upstairs and I thought... you know.'

Yes, we knew. So did Mrs Hall who gasped and brought her hand to her mouth.

'Did he hurt you?' DI Webb asked softly.

'Not like that.'

We all breathed a sigh of relief.

'He shoved me in the crate. Then he left. That was it. He left and didn't return until the next day. I shouted and shouted but nobody came.'

'He just left you? No food, no water?' Eamon asked.

'Nothing. I was gasping for a drink the next day. A man came. He had a beaker of water.'

'The same man who put you in the crate?' DI Webb asked.

'I can't be sure,' Sharon replied. 'Like I said, I didn't get a good look at the man who put me in the crate, and the man with the water wore gloves and had a handkerchief around his face. He held out the water and quoted from The Bible. He made me repeat it to get the water.'

'What was it he quoted?' Eamon asked.

'*"Father, I have sinned against you and am not worthy to be called your daughter. Be merciful to me, a sinner."* I remember it because I had to recite it before I got any water.'

'What's that from? It might be relevant. Find out, Sam, book, chapter and verse,' DI Webb said.

'As soon as we get back, sir,' I replied. I jotted down the phrase.

'What happened if you didn't recite it?' DI Webb asked.

'He poured the water away in front of me. That happened the first day. He never said anything to me apart from that. Then I realised that he expected me to repeat it, and next time I got the water.' Sharon reached for her glass of water and took a sip as if to reassure herself that this water would be freely available.

'Can you describe the other man to us?' DI Webb asked.

'Six feet maybe. Dark hair. Strong-looking. I couldn't see his face properly because of the hankie around it.'

'What sort of build?' I asked. If it had been Walter Hodgeson, she would be sure to mention his size.

'Athletic. Quite slim but muscley.'

Not Walter Hodgeson then.

I could almost hear Mrs Hall's teeth grinding. Her hands were curled into fists. I wanted to punch him, too. Sharon had been put in a crate and left there to die, but not too quickly, hence the water, but not enough to sustain her forever.

'You said there was someone in the other bedroom?' DI Webb asked.

Sharon nodded. 'I never saw her but I could hear her. She made a lot of noise, wailing and shouting. I don't know how the neighbours didn't hear.'

'Soundproofing on the walls,' Eamon said.

'You're sure it was another girl?' DI Webb asked.

'Yes, from her voice. I tried to talk to her but she wasn't really coherent most of the time. Then I stopped caring. Then she went quiet.' A tear leaked from Sharon's eye. Her mother dabbed it with a tissue.

If that had been Ruthie, as I suspected, she would have been dealing with withdrawal symptoms on top of thirst and hunger. Little wonder she had been incoherent. I could hardly wait to meet Roger Duggan in court. Our theft case was coming up. Mind you, he would probably be in custody before then.

Questions whirled around my head. I had a little think and jotted my thoughts onto a sheet of paper. Was this a result of the domestic incident? Martin intended to get a trade then emigrate, and he refused to do his father's bidding with the birthday money. Roger Duggan identified Sharon as a reason for his disobedience. Would that be a motive for him trying to dispose of her? If that was the case, could the incidents be merged and dealt with as one? Roger hadn't put Sharon in the crate, so at least one other person was involved. Probably not Walter Hodgeson. What about Ruthie? Assuming the other girl had been Ruthie. Was Roger Duggan connected to that or was that the work of someone else? Was Roger an equal partner in these crimes or did he just make use of someone he knew? How did he know this other person? Church? Just because he told Sharon the house belonged to someone from church, didn't mean that was the case. However, Roger Duggan had to have been aware of the other person's activities to know to take Sharon to him. Was I overthinking this? I would have a chat with Gary next time he rang. He always gave me good advice.

'What are you writing?' DI Webb asked.

'Just some thoughts, speculation, questions,' I replied.

He held out his hand. 'Let's see.'

'I haven't thought them through yet, I might be completely wrong about some things, sir,' I said.

'Okay, let's look anyway.'

I handed the sheet over and watched him read what I'd scribbled.

He nodded, folded the sheet and put it in his pocket. I didn't know if that was a good thing.

'Right, let's leave Sharon to rest,' DI Webb said. 'We will need to come back again, probably several times, but don't you worry, Sharon, Mrs Hall: we'll put this bastard away.'

Sharon nodded.

'Thank you,' Mrs Hall said.

Eamon and I followed the boss out and back to the station.

Back at the station, I rummaged around until I found the station copy of The Bible. I blew the dust off, went into the report writing room and started to flick through it. It was an impossible task. Would I have to read the entire thing to find one verse? Would the library be able to help me? Perhaps there was a book that sorted Bible quotes into categories. That would shorten my search. Maybe I should approach a vicar. I rested my head on the heels of my hands and groaned.

'Found God?'

I saw Mr Hunter standing in the doorway.

I stood up as one did when a very senior officer entered a room. 'I need to find a verse, sir. DI Webb wants the book, chapter and verse because it is relevant to the Sharon Hall case. I have no idea where to start. I'll have to read it all.'

'My brother is a bishop. I'll ask him. Even if he doesn't know the verse, he'll probably know where to look for it.'

I didn't even know he had a brother, never mind that he was a bishop. How little I knew about Mr Hunter. I jotted down the quote and handed it to him.

'Thank you, sir. I do appreciate this.'

'It might take some time,'

'Of course.' However long it took, it would be quicker than me having to trawl though the entire Bible. I didn't even know which testament it came from.

He continued on his way. I returned upstairs.

'Mr Hunter's brother is a bishop and he's going to help track down that quote,' I told DI Webb.

Webby grunted. He then got out the sheet I had jotted at the hospital.

'There are some good thoughts here. How do you propose to investigate them?'

That caught me off guard. I was still conditioned to people taking interesting things from me.

'I think we need to speak to Walter Hodgeson as the tenant of the address, and Roger Duggan because Sharon named him, before we can do much more. I would like to try to establish if there is a connection with Ruthie Pritchard, and I would like to get an ID on the mystery man or men at the house. I think we should go for Duggan first, as he's directly involved in the kidnapping, then we should bring Walter Hodgeson in. We can decide any further action depending on whether anyone else is named during the interviews.'

'Okay, speak to Mike.' DI Webb turned and went into his office, leaving me with my mouth hanging open. I was actually being trusted to be a proper part of a major investigation.

Mike agreed with my plan of action, so I grabbed a set of car keys for us to go and arrest Roger Duggan. I wanted him brought in ASAP before he had the chance to tip off anyone else involved.

Mike eyed the keys in my hand. 'Do you think it's wise for you to be involved with this, given your history with Duggan?'

'Without fear or favour. I don't fear him and I'm going to do him no favours,' I said, paraphrasing part of our oath. 'And doesn't DI Webb say to follow the evidence, wherever it might lead?'

'Duggan will think this is personal. We don't want him to be able to use anything that might help him in court,' Mike said.

'That man's beyond help,' I said.

Mike smiled. 'Even so, it will be better if Eamon and I bring him in.'

Did DI Webb know Mike would say this? Of course he did. I reluctantly handed the car keys over.

'May I at least take part in the interview?' I asked.

'It'll wind Duggan up, so: no.'

My disappointment must have showed.

'You can take the lead on Hodgeson.'

'Really? Thank you.' I felt much better then.

'Let us get Duggan out of the way, then we can bring Hodgeson in,' Mike said. 'Make yourself useful here meantime. You can start by returning those files.' He nodded towards a desk almost hidden by paper. 'And I know you have some non-urgent follow up enquiries. Get rid of some of them before they do become urgent.'

'Yes, Sarge,' I said with more enthusiasm than I felt. I was conscious of making a good impression. I wanted them to want to keep me when my time as an aide was over. Maybe then I wouldn't be left out.

*

'Sam,' DI Webb bellowed across the CID office as I arrived a couple of days later. 'Mr Hunter's been on about that Bible verse. *Luke 15:18*. Does that mean anything?'

220

I trotted over to his office. 'I can't see it being especially significant, apart from that quote.'

DI Webb pursed his lips. 'I'll give it some thought.'

He dismissed me and I went over to Mike's desk. He and Eamon were poring over a pile of photographs.

'How did it go with Duggan the other day?' I asked.

'He really is an unpleasant little gobshite,' Eamon said straightening his back. 'Mike made the right call asking you to step back from him. He is going to sue us all. Oh, and he thinks you personally arranged for him to be arrested at work because of the bicycle incident, so he's suing you too.'

This was too good. How I wished I had been there. 'What did he say in the interview?'

'A whole lot, most of it irrelevant. Despite his solicitor trying to focus his answers, he kept going off into rants. In a nutshell, he wanted to talk to Sharon about Martin. He was concerned at his son's recent poor attitude. He thinks she has influenced him because he was never normally like that. He took her to the address of someone he was told runs some course for young people. He hoped by talking to this person, Sharon would realise that she should not influence Martin and then everything in the Duggan garden would be rosy again. He had no idea that he was putting her in danger.'

That itch at the back of my head started again. 'Did he name this person?'

'No, he said he was never told his name.'

'We need to try to find him,' I murmured.

'Why didn't I think of that?' Eamon snapped his fingers in mock frustration.

'Okay, sorry, Mr Mentor. Remember, I'm still fairly new to this, and I was mostly thinking aloud,' I said. 'Anyway, moving on, Sharon was missing for quite a while and it was well publicised. He didn't come forward with information about where he left her.'

'I know, I know, but apparently, he felt too scared to come

forward because of the personal vendetta some police officers had against him,' Eamon said.

'That's his entire defence?' I was incredulous. 'We should be able to demolish that very quickly. Where is he now?'

'Bridewell, then remand. There was no way he's going to get bail with the charges he's facing.'

'I'm supposed to be in court with him very soon over that bike theft,' I said.

'I'm not sure that will go ahead at all now. It might be TIC, but it seems unimportant given he's facing charges of kidnapping and conspiracy to murder.'

I could see that theft of a bicycle being *Taken Into Consideration*, that is, acknowledged and added to his record, but no further action taken because the punishment would have no effect on the overall outcome, was probably the best thing in this case. Martin had his bike back and there was no punishment that was going to make a difference, seeing as Duggan was facing a very long prison stretch.

I nodded at the photographs. 'What's happening here?'

'We have the photos and forensics from Victory Street back,' Eamon replied without taking his eyes from the photographs.

I joined them, rummaging through the photos. A very few years previously, they would have been black and white. Now most were in colour, which was much more useful, especially when I saw the half-burnt red coat and the pink handbag. Someone had prised open the melted plastic bag and had been able to retrieve a house key, which lay alongside the ruined bag in the photo.

'I bet that key fits Ruthie Pritchard's house,' I said.

'We'll have to try that later on.' Eamon held a photo out to me. 'Here, look at this. Can you see what's on that bracelet?'

I took the photo and stared at it for a moment. The writing was worn but I could just make out the word.

'Carol, I think,' I said. 'There's a design either side of it.'

'As in Carol Shilling,' Mike murmured.

I got a mental picture of Reverend Shilling and the broken Mrs Shilling in the front office.

'Is it a silver bracelet?' I asked. 'It's hard to tell from the photo.'

'We haven't seen it yet. It's been booked into property,' Mike said.

'With your permission, I'll go and take a look. Carol Shilling's parents came in to ask about a silver bracelet their daughter had been wearing the night she disappeared. Her late grandmother had given it to her. It has enormous sentimental value to them.'

Mike nodded. 'Get that key, too.'

I hurried downstairs and looked up the property reference number. As it was jewellery, it was stored in a safe. I located the property bag and peered at the bracelet. It was listed as white metal. Property officers didn't like specifying a type of metal as there were so many good imitations out there, it would be easy to list something as silver or even platinum when in fact it was nickel or some other low value metal. The inscription was easier to see.

♥ *Carol* ♥

Carol Shilling had been wearing this when she went missing, and now it had been found in a bin amongst the ashes of women's clothing. Carol had been in that horrible house with the crates. It was reasonable to assume that she had also ended her life in one of those crates. Why was she the only one to have been found burnt? And what had happened to Ruthie?

I took the bracelet back to the office along with the key. DI Webb was talking to Mike and Eamon and took the bracelet from me. He turned it over in his hand.

'It is silver, it has a hallmark. There's no doubt that the name Carol is engraved on it.'

Eamon sagged. 'That poor, wee girl.'

My thoughts were with her parents. Would they want to know the details of their daughter's suffering? She might not have burnt to death, but her death had not been easy.

'Right,' said Mike. 'Sir, we're going to Ruthie Pritchard's

house. Sam thinks there's a good chance the key will fit her door.'

'Why is that?' DI Webb asked.

'I saw her with a red coat and a pink, plastic handbag just before she went missing.' I held up the photo of the ruined bag with the key beside it.

'I suppose it doesn't hurt to try,' DI Webb agreed.

Mike signed out a car and he, Eamon and I went to Ruthie's house.

Chapter Twenty-Two

Ruthie's was another house that would be more suited to a small family than a single, penniless drug addict. Elsie Pritchard had brought up her two girls there before being sent to prison for trying to sell her underaged youngest child on the docks. Terraced, two bedrooms and bathroom upstairs, main living room and kitchen downstairs. I don't think one window of Ruthie's house still had glass in it. The broken fence sagged into the tiny front garden and wild grass grew through and around the boards.

Eamon took the key and inserted it into the lock. It turned and the door opened. I felt a mix of satisfaction that I had been right, and sadness that we had now forensically linked Ruthie to Annie's house

'Well, bugger me, it worked,' he said. 'Let's have a quick look around while we're here.'

Mike and I followed him in. Despite knowing Ruthie for some time, I had never been inside her house. Trevor hadn't been kidding when he'd described the house as a midden. In fact it was insulting to middens everywhere. It stunk worse than anywhere I could think of, and I had been inside Annie's house. Everywhere was filthy. The carcase of a sofa leant against one wall, a wobbly table against another wall. The kitchen was destroyed. Every cupboard hung open. There was not a crumb of food in the place. There was a hole where a cooker had been. I wondered if it had been stolen, or sold by Ruthie to pay for her habit.

'Mike, perhaps we'd better ask the gas board to come out to

check this has been properly capped,' I called.

Mike came into the kitchen. 'I used to be a gas engineer before I joined the job.' He peered at the pipes. 'It seems okay, but let's get the council onto it, then we can't be blamed if it goes boom.'

'It might be me, but we do seem to have to do a lot more back covering these days.' Eamon commented.

'You're not wrong,' Mike replied.

I climbed the bare, wooden stairs. Facing me was the bathroom. The toilet was smashed, and several days' worth of excrement lay in the bath. Flies covered the mess, the window, the walls. I put my hand over my mouth and nose and turned my back.

'Don't go into the bathroom,' I called.

I went into the rear bedroom, which was empty, then looked into the front room. Apart from a bedframe holding a stained, ancient mattress, that too was empty.

'Jesus Christ Almighty!' Eamon shouted.

'I told you to stay out of the bathroom,' I called to him.

'How could anyone live like this?' he said as he came into the bedroom. The question was rhetorical.

Mike, meantime, had pushed the loft access back and was balancing on the banister to peer in.

'Nothing here. The roof's knackered. A lot of slates are missing.' He jumped down, making the dust swirl.

I was certain that Ruthie was dead, but we couldn't write her file off without more evidence to support that. Finding the key was compelling evidence in my mind, but it could be argued that she had had her bag stolen. However, I wasn't sure how anyone would explain the coat also being there. When we got back, I would update Ruthie's misper file that another search had been carried out on the address with no result. I would log that her key had been found in the bin at Victory Street, and I would link the files. In the future, I didn't want anyone to say that Ruthie had been forgotten.

As we made our way back to the station, we followed transmissions from a fire that broken out in Marigold Way. B Block was on duty and were handling it. We happened to drive past the fire station and I spotted Chris. I still needed to speak to him.

I tapped Mike on the shoulder. 'Stop here please, I need to speak to that fireman.'

Mike pulled over and I got out of the car. 'Chris!'

Chris looked over and waved to me. 'How's it going?'

'Not bad, thanks.'

Chris came to meet me halfway, not that we were very far apart. He put an arm around me and pulled me into a side hug. I was aware I was being watched from the car, so I sidestepped away and paused to gather my thoughts. 'I needed to speak to you about something.'

'Sounds serious.'

Before I could answer, the klaxon sounded in the fire station. One of the men running to the appliances called to Chris. 'Marigold Way.'

'Got to go, talk later.' Chris pecked my cheek and ran to the fire engines and, almost as soon as he'd shut the door, they moved off. I could see him shrugging on his fire jacket as they went past me.

That peck on the cheek was confirmation that I had to end things, even if it meant I lost his friendship. I was frustrated that I hadn't been able to say what I needed to say to him. I had wanted to get it out of the way, but it would have to wait until later. We had exchanged numbers, but I didn't like to ring him in case I woke him after a shift. He hadn't phoned me, so he probably felt the same.

I walked back to the car. Eamon and Mike remained remarkably quiet about what they had seen as we went back to Wyre Hall. I sat in the back and didn't enlighten them. Instead, I listened to the transmissions that centred mostly on Marigold Way. That more appliances had been sent and our patrols were involved indicated that this was a significant fire. Ray started pulling patrols from their beats and directing them to the flower streets.

Mike One, and Ken, who were on the other side of town, would try to maintain normal policing in the town while everyone else was dealing with the emergency.

In the CID office, I settled down to type up a report on our visit to Ruthie's house while Mike and Eamon got on with other things.

A short time later, DI Webb called Mike into his office. It wasn't unusual, they normally discussed the situation with ongoing jobs, however, after only a couple of minutes, Mike came back out and called Eamon and I over to his desk.

'We need to attend this fire in Marigold Way. It turns out one of the residents is a gardener or something, and there's all sorts of chemicals illegally stored in the basement. The fire brigade needs to make it safe. We need to bring the gardener in. There are no uniformed patrols to spare.'

We arrived at Marigold Way, one of the original roads that were there before the council estate had been built. It had large houses, mostly divided into flats now, but there were one or two desperately clinging to the grandeur of past times. The fire was at a house that had been divided into flats.

Several disgruntled residents milled around, complaining to every uniformed person they ran across. I could see smoke rising, but I had seen worse. It was the hidden danger that was the worry.

Bert came over to us. Instead of the jovial station sergeant, we were seeing the efficient and capable boss. It had been some time since he had been operational, so it had been easy to forget that Bert had once been out, managing incidents on a daily basis.

'Apparently, each flat has storage space in the basement. One chap has told the fire officers that he's a gardener and business hadn't been going too well so he lost his secured lock-up. He decided that it was a good idea to put his chemicals in his storage space. We haven't established in which flat the fire started but it's spreading quickly. The fire crews have kicked out all the neighbouring residents.'

'Are dangerous fumes likely to spread out?' I asked.

Bert thought for a moment. 'It's possible, but I think they're more concerned about combustion. Apparently there's potassium nitrate and sulphur and other things which can be used in weedkillers that are also explosive.'

I had heard of terrorists using weedkiller bombs. 'Bert, could this be a bomb factory?'

'He probably had the chemicals legitimately, although his choice of storage was definitely illegal,' said Bert.

'It is something to bear in mind though,' Mike added.

I liked that he hadn't dismissed my suggestion outright.

A couple of ambulances arrived and parked up. So far, nobody had been hurt, but it did no harm in having them on standby. Another fire appliance arrived. I wasn't sure exactly how many fire appliances there were at the scene, but there were enough to let me know they considered this a serious incident.

'Your chap is with a fire crew over there.' Bert waved a hand towards a command vehicle that was parked a short distance away. Far enough not to get in the way. 'It would be best to take him back to the station and interview him there.'

'Thanks, Bert,' Mike said and led us over to the command vehicle.

The gardener sat in the vehicle. A more forlorn person I had yet to see. The senior officer came over to us as we approached.

'He's being very cooperative.'

I liked cooperative. It saved everybody's time.

We went to the command vehicle, and before any of us could say a word the gardener launched into a timeline of how we came to be there.

'I'm sorry, but I had no choice but to keep it all there. I still had to work, I needed to make money, but business has been bad. I didn't know this would happen.'

'You run your own business, but you didn't bother to learn the law relating to chemical storage?' Mike asked.

'I did…' the gardener's voice trailed away. 'I knew I shouldn't, but I thought it would be okay.'

Eamon swept an arm towards the damaged building. 'Does that look okay to you?'

The gardener hung his head.

'Let's just be grateful that nobody has been hurt,' Mike said. 'We need to get you back to the station.'

It looked like the fire crews had put out the fire because there was much less smoke. I started to relax. Once the fire was out, the fire crews could make the chemicals safe, and the residents could return to their homes.

Suddenly, I heard a huge crack louder than any thunder, followed by a deep rumble and a plume of black smoke rose up into the sky. Instinctively, I dropped to a crouch, as did everyone else. People near the scene shouted and there was an urgency in their movements. The ambulances trundled off closer to the scene. I hoped they wouldn't be needed. I stood up and stared at the renewed glow of flames. I guessed that at least some of the chemicals had ignited in the heat. The gardener whimpered. We stared towards the house.

I desperately wanted to find out what had happened, and more importantly to check on the welfare of B Block, but I knew better than to clog up the airways. The constant transmissions told me little, and I couldn't hear the fire or ambulance transmissions.

We eventually dragged ourselves away from the scene and put the gardener in the rear seat of our car for transportation back to Wyre Hall. I saw Steve walking towards us, and I felt relieved that he was safe. We didn't do sentimentality, so I nodded as he approached.

'All right?' The cover-all greeting. Even when disaster struck and everything was obviously not all right.

'All right,' he said. 'Bert sent me over.'

'Is the house still standing?' I asked.

He shook his head. 'The houses either side of it are damaged too. All residents are safe, but they might not be able to go home for a while.' He stopped speaking and stared at his boots.

'You've destroyed people's homes with your ignorance,' Eamon snarled at the gardener.

I noticed how pale Steve looked, and a nasty ball of worry squirmed in my stomach. 'What?'

He tried to meet my eyes but failed. 'The fire was pretty well dampened down and the fire officer felt it was okay to let a few of his people go in to check on the chemicals...'

'But?' I asked.

'Chris was part of the team that went in. Then, there was the explosion and the house just fell like a pack of cards.'

My brain refused to accept what he was telling me. 'Is he okay?'

'No, Sam, he's not okay. When the house collapsed, a joist fell on him. The rest of the team are injured but accounted for...' Steve took a deep breath. 'Chris is dead. They say he died instantly. They still haven't been able to get him out.'

I sagged as all the air left me. Steve put his arms around me and sat me down on the ground.

'That's fucking manslaughter!' Eamon shouted at the gardener, who wept and blew his nose on his shirt. While Eamon screamed the necessary formalities at the gardener before arresting him, I spoke to nobody in particular.

'I was talking to him just a short while ago. I was trying to tell him...' I knew it didn't make sense, but I could still see him waving to me, feel him hug me, feel him kiss my cheek. Chris was gone. I felt an enormous pain in my chest. We would never have that talk and I would never have to disappoint him. I felt guilty for the frisson of relief that gave me. Another bundle to put on my guilt pile. It had been getting a bit smaller recently.

I stood up and walked towards the obliterated street. Mike and Steve tried to stop me but I just shrugged them off. A fire crew saw me coming and one nudged the other. I heard him say, 'It's his girlfriend.' I didn't correct him. It didn't matter now.

The scene before me resembled an old *Pathé* newsreel of the town following a bombing raid. It smelt like bonfire night. Where did anyone start to put this devastation right? I continued walking towards the worst of the ruin.

Bert was talking to an ambulance crew and a fireman. He saw me and broke away. 'Sam, I know you were friends with the lad. They're about to bring him out. You shouldn't be here.'

I stopped walking. 'Are they sure it's Chris Atherton?'

The fireman Bert had been talking to came over. 'It is him, love. Listen to your boss and stay away. Remember him as he was.'

Steve and Eamon came up behind me. Eamon took my elbow and Steve put his arm around my shoulder to stop me walking further. I didn't fight them. It suddenly hit me why they wanted me out of the way. Chris was horribly injured by the joist, and burned maybe. I suddenly felt nauseous. I broke away and threw up beside a lamppost. They looked on sympathetically but did not move away.

When my stomach was empty, I stood up and wiped my mouth on my sleeve. Eamon and Steve took an arm each and, gently but firmly, they pulled me away back to our vehicle.

'If you try to leave again, I'll 'cuff you to a lamppost. Understood?' Steve said.

I nodded and sat where I had been sitting a short time previously.

Steve sat next to me. 'I love being a policeman, but sometimes it's shit.'

I was unable to speak past the lump in my throat.

'Did you tell the boss about Chris?' he asked.

I knew he meant Gary. He still couldn't think of him as anything other than the boss. 'He knows all about him. Chris was only ever a friend.'

Steve watched me for a moment. 'Sure.'

I had been using the tongue pressing trick since I had heard Chris had been killed. It didn't do for the public to see police officers blubbing, but finally the tears came. Steve hugged me to him, and I sobbed onto his chest as Eamon and Mike looked on.

*

I couldn't justify taking time off to mourn Chris. He wasn't family, so compassionate leave was out of the question. I continued to work as normal and dragged myself through my shifts. It was a good move. We were still working on the Sharon Hall case. I was still thinking about Ruthie, and other work kept coming in that needed attention. I didn't have time to sit and brood, and I could see life moving on. I talked to Gary, of course. We discussed how hard it is to lose friends, but I couldn't speak of my desolation. I told myself that I would have felt the same if it had been Steve or Ken that had died, maybe more so; but sometimes, in the quiet, small hours, I lay awake in the dark and wondered what would have eventually happened to Gary and me if Chris were still here.

Chapter Twenty-Three

Roger Duggan had been packed off to the remand centre pending his trial. Despite the evidence, he just could not accept that he was in the wrong. He couldn't or wouldn't name names. It was annoying, but Sharon had named him so we had enough for him to be charged. If he chose to carry the whole load, that was his problem.

We had no proof that Walter Hodgeson was part of Sharon's kidnap but, as the listed tenant, he needed to answer some tough questions. He was invited to present himself at the station to assist with our enquiries, which he did. The alternative had been that we went to get him, and he didn't fancy that.

Mike Finlay took the call that Hodgeson was in the building and instructed the caller to put him in the interview room.

'Sam, Hodgeson is here. Come on.'

I eagerly followed Mike from the room and down to the bridewell. As promised, he was letting me take the lead.

'We need to remember that Walter has a reputation as a liar,' I said.

'So are many of the people we interview.' Mike chuckled. 'You crack on, and I'll step in if necessary.'

Walter was sitting at the table in the interview room. He looked up when DS Finlay and I entered and sat opposite him.

'You're the one that was seeing Chris Atherton, aren't you? He was a good lad. Destined for higher things.'

'He wanted to be a fire investigator. I miss him,' I admitted. Maybe Walter would be more open with us because we had a link through Chris.

We remained silent for a moment before I spoke again. 'First of all, you are not obliged to say anything unless you wish to do so, but anything you do say may be taken down in writing and given in evidence.'

'That sounds official,' Walter said. 'Do I need legal representation?'

'I'm required to tell you your rights before I ask you questions about this incident,' I explained. He would have known this basic fact if he had actually done the training he had claimed he had done. 'You can have a solicitor if you feel you need one.'

'I see,' Walter replied. 'Never mind. Carry on then.'

'Do you know why we asked you to come here today, Walter?'

Walter sighed. 'I've a good idea. Have you nothing better to do than pull me in for this load of rubbish.'

'This is hardly a load of rubbish, Walter.'

'Since when have the police been interested in a bit of subletting? I don't see what the fuss is about. Why does it matter who pays the rent as long as it is paid? It's not like I'm committing benefit fraud.'

I glanced at Mike. Police wouldn't normally become involved in subletting, because the council carried out their own investigations and their own prosecutions when it came to tenancy and rent matters. We'd only be brought in in cases of persistent or maybe high value fraud. I began to wonder if Walter was aware of the crates, or if he was doing an excellent job of lying again. I decided to run with the subletting narrative to see where it led us, and extract as much information as possible before putting him right.

'You're down as the tenant of the address,' I said.

'Yes, but I don't live there. It was my mum's address. I took it on when she died last April.' He sighed again.

'Who is your tenant?' I asked.

'Does it matter? I'm the listed tenant so it's my neck on the block.'

'Unfortunately, it is,' I said. 'We still need to know the name of your tenant, though.'

'Ron Winger.'

I jotted the name down. I'd run a full check later.

'Ron lives there?' I asked.

'Yes.'

Having seen the state of the place, I doubted Ron Winger or anyone else lived there. I also suspected that, despite his reputation, Walter might truly be clueless about what was happening at his late mother's home.

'Look, you need to speak to Ron. He's been paying me, and I've been paying the council. Nobody's out of pocket, so no harm done.' Walter rested his elbows on the desk.

'How long has he lived there?' I asked.

'Three months or so,' Walter said. 'I'd have to look at the rent book for an exact date.'

'Have you been to the address recently?' I asked.

'Not since about June. I grew up there, so I was reluctant to let it go. I suppose I should have.' Walter straightened up. 'Oh no, has the stupid berk damaged the place? Is this what it's about? Well, any damage is down to him, not me.'

'How does he pay you?' I asked.

'Cash every month on payday.' Walter answered. 'I mark it in the rent book. We did it properly with a real rent book I bought at the stationers.'

'How did you get to know Ron?'

'Work.'

'He's a fireman?'

Walter nodded. 'He's a newbie and he was looking for somewhere in town that wasn't too expensive. I wanted to rent Mum's house out to make a little extra money. It made sense.'

'Did he approach you or did you go to him?' I asked.

'I was talking about it in the recreation room and he asked if he could rent it. He's a good lad, so I agreed.'

'Do you know Sharon Hall?' I asked.

'Who?'

'How about Ruth Pritchard?'

'Never heard of either of them. Has Ron been taking girls back to the house?' Walter laughed. 'He's a young lad, so it's to be expected I suppose. I'll have a word if it's annoying the neighbours.'

'Carol Shilling?'

Walter shook his head.

'Roger Duggan?' I asked.

'I don't think Ron swings that way.' Walter laughed but stopped when Mike and I didn't join in. 'Never heard of him.'

Odd, seeing as they had the PCMG in common.

'Walter, are you a member of the PCMG?' I asked.

'I used to be,' he replied. 'I don't bother these days. What's that got to do with anything?'

Without answering Walter, I indicated to Mike that we needed to speak outside.

'We'll pause the interview here,' Mike said. 'We'll be back shortly.'

We stood up and went out.

'He's got no idea what's happened,' I said to Mike when we were out of earshot. 'Although how he's never heard of Sharon Hall or Carol Shilling when they've both been well publicised, I don't know. Also, how could he not have heard of Roger Duggan when they both belong to the same club? He's either oblivious to what's happening around him, or he's lying.'

'Maybe Walter left before Duggan joined,' Mike suggested. 'Either way, we need to pick up this Ron Winger ASAP before Walter or anyone else can alert him,' Mike said. 'I'll speak to Webby and get that organised. Can you ring the fire HQ and find out Winger's duty roster and get a home address if possible?'

'Will do.' I went to the control room while Mike went upstairs.

After about fifteen minutes, we met outside the interview room again.

'The fire control room were reluctant to hand out information on the phone. I wasn't surprised. They're going to phone it through to our control room,' I told Mike.

'Great. DI Webb is aware now. When we get Winger's information, we need to go to Winger's home or to his workplace and bring him in.' Mike paused. 'I'll get Eamon to come with me.'

'Can I come too?' I asked.

'Not if we have to go to the fire station. You seem to have a good relationship with them that might be useful later on. If you're in on the arrest, you might lose that goodwill.'

'If he's well thought of, we might lose goodwill anyway when he's arrested,' I pointed out.

'Not when they find out what he's done,' Mike said. 'Let's break the news to Walter.' He led the way into the interview room.

Walter was examining his cuticles. 'I thought you had forgotten me.'

'Sorry to keep you, I had to speak with our boss,' Mike turned to me. 'Sam?'

He wanted me to break the news to Walter. I hadn't expected that.

I paused, wondering where to begin. 'Walter, was your mother's property furnished at all?'

'No. Ron was going to bring in his own stuff.'

'Right. There is actually no furniture there. The council received a call to attend the property because it was neglected and smelly and had become a breeding ground for vermin. The neighbours heard faint noises and thought animals were getting in.'

Walter's jaw dropped. 'Mum kept that house pristine. It was her little palace. I'll kill him!'

'There's more,' I said. 'We went in with the RSPCA because they had received a report that an animal might be trapped in there. We found two crates—'

'He's been mistreating animals?!' Walter roared, cutting me

off. He jumped up. 'He can find somewhere else to live. I want him out today. Wait until the lads hear about this!'

'Sit down, Walter. I'm afraid it's even worse than that.' Walter slowly sank onto the chair, his eyes wide. I continued. 'Are you sure you haven't heard of Sharon Hall?'

Walter paused. 'Actually, the name does sound familiar, but I can't think where I heard it.'

'Sharon Hall was a missing person. She was found in one crate. She had been put there and left to die. Another girl had been in the other crate. From clothing we found, we believe she was Ruth Pritchard, who is missing,' I told him.

Walter stared at me. 'Is she okay? The girl, Sharon, is she alive?'

'Sharon is poorly but she'll recover,' I replied. 'We don't know what happened to Ruth, if it is her, yet.'

Walter slumped back in his chair. 'I didn't know. I swear to you, I didn't know.'

'I believe you, Walter.' I did believe him. Nobody was this good a liar.

'Vic's a nice bloke. I would never have believed that he'd do something like that.'

'You said your tenant was called Ron,' Mike snapped.

'Vic's his nickname,' Walter explained.

I knew then who Walter meant. 'His dad's a vicar. That's why he's called Vic.'

'How do you know?' Walter and Mike asked together.

'I met him at the charity dance,' I replied.

'Oh right. Like I said, he's a nice bloke.' Walter put his head in his hands. 'I thought he was a nice lad. Christ! What's he done?'

'He's taken at least one young girl and imprisoned her in a wooden crate to the point of death. We believe he's killed another woman. There may be more,' Mike said.

Walter stood up.' I have to go. I have to see what he's done to Mum's house. Then I'm going to kick his arse around town.'

'Walter, we cannot allow you to leave right now. Please sit down,' Mike said.

Walter froze. 'I can go if I want to. I'm not under arrest, am I?'

Mike also stood up. 'Walter Hodgeson, I am arresting you on suspicion of conspiracy to murder. You are not obliged to say anything unless you wish to do so, but anything you do say will be taken down in writing and may be given in evidence.'

I wasn't sure it was necessary to caution Walter again, seeing as I had cautioned him before he was questioned, but better safe than sorry. This case was too important to lose on a technicality. I'd have to refresh myself on that point when I got a moment.

'But I didn't.' Walter's voice was little more than a whisper.

I felt a little sorry for him, but we now could keep hold of Walter to question him further and we could be sure he wouldn't go off and unintentionally alert our suspect, which was probably why Mike had done it. When time was up, I guessed that Walter would be released without charge and left to get on with his life. I wondered what stories he would take back about his time with us. I suspected that we'd be the unbending, authoritarian bullies while he was the unflinching hero who refused to be intimidated, not the sad, bewildered man before us.

Mike took Walter's arm and gently led him out to the charge office.

B Block was on duty, so at refs I made a point of going into the refs room.

'Hi people,' I called as I entered.

'Aren't you too grand now to be mixing with the likes of us?' Steve grinned at me.

'Of course I am, but I like to keep tabs on what you plebs are getting up to.' I sat in my usual spot at the Formica table, where Steve and Bert were eating their meal and Ken was resting his head on his arms.

'What's happening?' I asked.

'Same old, same old,' Steve replied.

Ken opened tired eyes and blinked at me.

'How are Gaynor and little Amy?' I asked.

'They're okay. It's amazing how something so small can make so much noise and cause such mess. I had no idea you could be so exhausted and still function.'

Bert groaned and inhaled deeply.

I looked up at him and was alarmed by his grey complexion and the perspiration forming on his top lip. 'Bert?'

He wrapped his arms around his body. 'I don't feel well.' His breathing became shallow and fast. Whatever was happening was hurting him.

Steve stood up. 'I'm calling an ambulance.'

'Don't fuss, lad,' Bert said. He stretched his neck up.

'Is your jaw hurting you too?' I asked.

Bert nodded and tapped his arm. 'And there.'

'It's a bloody heart attack!' Ken shouted, suddenly alert.

'I'm getting an ambulance and no argument.' Steve strode over to the phone on the wall and dialled 999. Then he phoned the control room.

Meantime, I got an aspirin from my bag and pushed it into Bert's mouth.

'Chew that quick.'

'He might be allergic,' Steve said.

'I think we've passed the stage where that's a worry,' I shot back. 'Aspirin thins the blood.'

Bert tried to stand up but flopped down back onto his seat. He cried out and rolled from the seat to the floor. I knelt beside him and tried to make him comfortable by removing his tie and opening his collar button. Ken rushed and got some cushions off the chairs.

'Try to sit and lean against me, Bert. I heard that sitting up helps with the pain,' I said, but he lay on his side, panting, and he was too heavy for me to lift. Ken pushed a cushion under his head.

Steve ended his call and, less than a minute later, Ray crashed into the refs room.

'Bloody hell!' Ray knelt beside me. 'What happened?'

'He groaned, said he felt unwell, and it became obvious he was having a heart attack. I gave him an aspirin,' I replied.

The door opened again, and Mike Finlay came in with Eamon Kildea.

'What's all this racket…?' Mike began. He fell silent when he saw Bert, now lying still on the floor. 'Check his pulse!'

I hadn't noticed Bert's movements lessening. I frantically grabbed at Bert's wrist, then when I didn't feel anything, I pushed my fingers into his neck and got a weak pulse.

'It's very weak. Thready,' I said.

Steve ran to the window. 'Where's the bloody ambulance?'

'You only rang five minutes ago,' Ray said. 'They'll be on their way.'

'Not long now, Bert,' I said.

Bert sighed then was quiet. I felt for Bert's pulse again. Nothing. I tried again. Still nothing.

I pulled Bert onto his back and tipped his head so his chin pointed upwards. 'Someone do the compressions,' I shouted and blew into Bert's mouth. Ken pumped Bert's chest. In the stress of the moment, I forgot exactly how many compressions to how many breaths. As long as someone was doing something, I figured it didn't matter. Steve knelt beside Ken ready to take over when he tired.

The door opened again and Mr Hunter came in. Nobody acknowledged him, we were all too busy. He didn't say anything but stood quietly watching us.

Ken leant back and Steve took over the compressions.

'Here come the ambos,' Eamon shouted from the window.

'Eamon, get downstairs and show them the way,' Mike ordered.

He ran from the room. We continued CPR until the door burst open and an ambulance crew ran in. One gently nudged me aside and the other took over from Steve. We stood up, moved out of the way and waited. I felt a hand on my shoulder.

'Well done, young lady. I'll be in the superintendent's office. See me there as soon as you are able. Bring your friends with you,' Mr Hunter said. I just nodded, unable to speak.

A few minutes later, one of the ambos announced, 'We have a pulse. We need to get him to hospital ASAP.'

They moved Bert onto a stretcher, and Mr Hunter dispatched the rest of us to hold open the doors so nothing would delay them getting to the ambulance. Within minutes, Bert was on his way to the hospital.

Steve, Ken and I waited outside the superintendent's office. Mr Hunter, as a chief superintendent, was in charge of the whole division and had an office in Egilsby station, the DHQ, divisional headquarters. When he visited the subdivisions, he would use the superintendent's office. It was that or hang out with us plebs.

He called us in, and we stood to attention in a row in front of the desk. It wasn't a big office, so the desk was a modest size for a very senior officer, but Mr Hunter didn't need a big desk to display his command. He could have sat on an upturned bucket and still exuded power.

'Stand easy,' he said.

We didn't relax in his presence. It was unthinkable. We didn't stand to attention, but none of us slouched either.

'I just wanted to tell you that I was impressed by your efforts in the refs room. Your actions mean that Bert has the best chance of recovery.'

'Thank you, sir,' we said together.

'Hopefully, we will receive good news from the hospital. Meantime, I will be endorsing your service files with my personal thanks for your actions.'

'Thank you, sir,' we chanted.

It wouldn't do any of us any harm to have a chief superintendent's thanks on our records.

'That's all. Dismissed.'

We snapped to attention. Steve and Ken, who were in uniform, saluted and we left.

Chapter Twenty-Four

Chris's funeral was well attended. He received full honours from the fire brigade. All emergency services sent a delegation. I wasn't part of that; I was there in plain clothes as his friend, with Steve and Emma.

Chris' family arrived in a long car behind the hearse. His parents and sister got out of the car first. His grandmother, stiff with age, followed, assisted by Chris' father. I was uncertain what to do but I wanted to say something, so I approached them before we filed into the chapel.

'My name is Samantha. I'm so sorry for your loss.'

His mother turned to me. 'Thank you. Christopher often mentioned you.'

I caught Steve's eye, but he made a point of pretending not to listen.

'Are you alone?' Mrs Atherton asked. 'You're welcome to sit with us if you are.'

'You're very kind but I came with friends.' I indicated Steve and Emma. 'We wouldn't want to intrude.'

Pallbearers in full fire brigade dress uniform lined up to receive Chris' coffin. The funeral director ushered the family, followed by the rest of us, into the chapel. Then, to *Adagio for Strings*, Chris was carried in for the service. I would never be able to listen to that sad piece of music again without remembering this moment.

Someone slipped in behind and slid into the end of a back pew.

'Spider's here,' Steve whispered to me.

I didn't want to start twisting around as the service started. I would speak to her after the service.

*

When the service was over, we stayed in our places until Chris' family left, then we all filed out. I couldn't see Spider anywhere, but that might have been because of the tears that filled my eyes.

'Are you going to the wake' Steve asked.

I shook my head. 'I just want to go home. You two go, I'll call a taxi.'

Steve and Emma didn't want to go either. They dropped me back at the flat.

'Are you sure you don't want us to come up with you?' Steve asked.

'Thanks, but I want to be alone for a while. I'll see you at work.' I got out of the car and went inside. The phone was ringing but I didn't want to speak to anyone, even Gary, so I left it until it stopped. I ran a bath and sat in warm bubbles with tears running down my cheeks.

With the funeral over, it was time to look forwards. I would never forget Chris, but I needed to make a deliberate decision to put his memory aside. Christmas was practically around the corner and Gary would be coming home. I made myself a hair appointment and booked in for a waxing session and a manicure a few days before his arrival. I intended to show him just how much I had missed him.

'You didn't hang around at Chris' funeral,' I said to Spider when I spotted her in the report writing room. She looked warily at me, but I hoped my expression showed that I was not looking for a fight. We'd never be friends, but we didn't have to be at war.

'I just wanted to pay my respects with being at the scene, you know.'

'You could have joined us.' It almost killed me to say that, because I was glad she hadn't joined us. However, I was playing nicely.

She hung her head. 'I didn't want to intrude.'

We remained silent for a moment, but I felt that we both knew what the other was thinking and feeling. It was as if we were having a conversation without words. I wondered if she regretted her haughty behaviour.

'The gardener is dead, did you hear?' I asked.

'Hung himself, didn't he? Couldn't live with the guilt.'

I nodded.

'Not the worst way to go, I've heard,' she commented.

'I heard that too,' I said. 'I still wouldn't fancy it.'

'Me neither.'

We sort of ran out of words so, after a moment's silence, I continued on my way.

*

There are few things more frustrating than a "no comment" interview, but that was exactly what we had had once Winger had been arrested and brought in. Ron Winger, who I'd originally known as Vic, looked as innocent as a choirboy as he sat with his brief in the interview room. I wasn't taking the lead on this; it was too important. Winger was the main suspect of this case. DI Webb and DS Finlay were dealing; I was sitting in for experience.

'You rent the house from Walter Hodgeson?' Mike Finlay asked for about the third time.

'No comment,' Winger replied.

'You set up crates in two bedrooms with the intention of capturing females and keeping them in there?'

'No comment.'

'Those crates were too big to have been carried through the house, so someone must have built them on site. Was that you or did someone else do that?' Mike asked.

'No comment.'

'Did Walter Hodgeson have any idea what you were doing?'

Winger sniggered. 'He has no idea, full stop.'

That was the nearest we had had to a proper answer in over an hour.

'So, you say he didn't know you weren't living there and that you had women imprisoned there?'

'No comment.'

He knew we had him bang to rights, as the old saying went, so he had no reason to hide anything; but this person in front of us was so different from the friendly chap I'd met. The young man who helped wayward kids.

DI Webb stood up. 'This is getting us nowhere. I need a pee. I'm taking a break. We'll resume in ten minutes.'

He left the room and DS Finlay followed.

Mike paused at the door. 'Come on, Sam.'

I stood up but something made me turn back to Winger. It wasn't my place but I asked, 'Why?'

I saw a flicker in Winger's eyes. For a moment, I saw him laid bare. There was no respect for us or the girls, no remorse, just disdain. He thought he was in charge.

'Is this how you deal with people who "need guidance"?' I shook my head. 'Chris Atherton was so wrong about you. He thought you were a good bloke.'

Winger smirked. He smirked!

Before I could check myself, I snarled, 'You're just a dirty little pervert who likes hurting women.' I turned away and was surprised to see DI Webb just out of sight on the corridor. Had he and Mike planned this so they could eavesdrop on anything Winger said to his brief?

'They should've done as God ordained.' Winger snapped shut his mouth, but the damage was done. Ignoring his lawyer's frantic whispers, he called out. 'Remove this woman who thinks she has authority over men. *1 Timothy 2:11* says she must be silent.'

Did he know Mike and DI Webb were in earshot? Maybe he

had seen my surprise on seeing them.

'Resuming interview,' Webby said as he re-entered the room.

We all sat down again.

'You know The Bible well,' DI Webb said. He sounded as if he recognised the quote, but I suspected he was just going along with it.

'All good Christians should know The Bible and live by its teachings,' Winger said. 'It's quite specific about the role of women. Those who disobey God's word must be punished.'

'So, that is why you took those women and imprisoned them? They disobeyed God's word somehow. This is all your work,' DI Webb stated. 'You alone are responsible.'

'No comment.'

'A bit late for that, lad. Who brought them to the address?'

'Why is she still here?' He jabbed his finger towards me.

I cut in. I'd deal with the inevitable rollicking later. 'If it isn't you, who is really in charge? Who do you answer to?' I wanted to hurt his ego. I hoped to rile him into losing his control again. I wanted him to incriminate himself further.

After a moment where Winger tried to pierce me with a hateful look, he said, 'I answer to God and only Him.'

'How do you think God is going to judge you?' I asked. I might be agnostic, but I wasn't above using religion as a means to get information.

'He loves me. When my time comes, I will stand before Him and He will thank me for upholding His Word.'

I leant forward and quietly said, 'You've corrupted His Word. I don't think He'll thank you. I think God weeps when He sees you.'

Winger sprang to his feet and so did I. If he was going to attack, I needed to be on a level with him.

DI Webb banged the table and pointed a finger at Winger. 'SIT DOWN!'

Winger's brief pulled on his arm, but Winger was too full of bruised ego and indignation to pay attention. He pointed a finger right back at DI Webb.

'God hates women who dress as men, He hates women who take authority over men.' The finger swung my way. 'Women like you!' Saliva gathered at the corners of his mouth.

'God hates me for upholding the actual law?' I laughed aloud.

He sank into his chair panting for breath. 'The Bible clearly states the penalty for women who do not follow His Word. In Leviticus, it says that the daughters of priests who bring shame to the family should be burnt.'

A thought, a memory, suddenly pushed itself to the front of my mind.

'Daughters of priests should be burnt. An interesting notion. Have you burnt the daughter of a priest?' I asked.

'He's just spouting religious claptrap,' Mike said.

'Carol Shilling!' DI Webb got it at once.

'Well?' I inclined my head and waited for an answer.

'Answer the lady!' DI Webb demanded.

'It is in The Book. That is the penalty for those that bring shame to their holy fathers.'

'Did Carol Shilling bring shame to her father, a vicar?' DI Webb asked.

'Consorting with men outside clubs. Humiliating decent, Christian men. My flock.'

DI Webb stood up. 'Ronald Winger, I am arresting you on suspicion of the murder of Carol Shilling and the attempted murder of Sharon Hall.' I wondered if he would also rearrest Winger on suspicion of the murder of Ruthie, but DI Webb didn't do that. He just went on to caution Winger. I was disappointed.

'So you put Carol Shilling in a dumpster and set her on fire?' Mike stated.

'I'm not a monster,' Winger replied.

'Because you killed her first? You think you were merciful because you put her in one of those crates and left her to die?' I was disgusted.

Winger's brief whispered to him and he stopped speaking. Damned bad timing. I was convinced with a little more pushing we were about to get an unequivocal admission.

'When I saw you at the hotel, you said you were doing a talk about your work with young people. Are you more than a guest speaker? Are you a member, or their leader? Is that why you think of them as your flock?' I asked.

Winger raised his chin and smiled. Pride and vanity drove this man. He wanted, no, needed, to be recognised as the one in charge. Okay then, so be it.

'You tell "your flock",' I waggled my fingers, 'that women are lesser beings whose only worth is in how they serve men. What a load of rubbish!'

'Do not ridicule God's Word!'

I snorted, which caused him to half stand. His brief grabbed his arm and pulled him back down.

'You set yourself up to police the behaviour of women, then to punish them for not following your code. You put the women into the crate then left them without food or water or toilet facilities,' Mike stated.

'They had to be broken so they could be re-educated. I understand that, but I have not said that I did that.'

'Who gave them the water?'

Winger didn't answer that or any other question.

Winger was returned to his cell. DI Webb, DS Finlay and I returned to the CID office.

'I thought the idea was that you were there to observe, not to ask questions,' Mike said to me.

Here it came, the rollicking. I was a bit miffed because I had been the one to get any kind of response from Winger and I was going to say so.

'A good move as it turned out,' Mike said. 'It can be risky attacking a prisoner's ego, but it paid off.'

This didn't feel like a rollicking.

'Will we have to get Sharon to identify him?' I didn't think it was a good idea to have her in the same room as Winger.

'That will seal the deal because I don't think we will get a definitive admission. We could show her photographs of Winger and Hodgeson and see if she recognises them.'

'Can we show her all the photos we have from the PCMG?'

Mike thought for a moment. 'If there is a connection to the case, we can.'

'There is! All the suspects we have are or have been members. Who knows if there are more involved with this that we know,' I argued.

Mike couldn't disagree.

'What about Carol Shilling? She was the daughter of a vicar, a priest according to The Bible. She was burnt and he's pretty well admitted it. He should face justice for Carol's death,' I said.

'It's not a confession. He needs to be spoken to again,' Mike said.

'I want to throw everything at him,' DI Webb said. 'Let him argue in court that he had nothing to do with it. Murder, attempted murder, conspiracy to murder, conspiracy to kidnap, unlawful imprisonment, GBH. Anything else I can think of. He's dangerous. We need to get him banged up. I don't want him to see the outside world again. Sam, I don't think you should take part in any further interviews with Winger.' DI Webb stalked into his office.

'Ruthie Pritchard?' I asked.

Mike quirked his mouth. 'That's a little different. We don't have a body; we just have some personal items found in a bin.'

'With other items that belonged to Sharon and Carol. I believe she's dead, Mike, and Winger and some other person or persons are responsible.'

'It's too shaky to take to court as it stands. It'll be too easy to disprove. Try not to worry yourself about it. Winger's going down for life, possibly for a whole life sentence. Another possibly dead girl isn't going to make much difference,' Mike said.

'If it isn't going to make a difference, why not put it before the court and see what happens?' I asked.

'The prosecutions department will decide. Trust the system.'

I wanted to trust the system, I really did, but sometimes… However, satisfied I had not brought the apocalypse on my head by hijacking the interview, I went for a break.

Chapter Twenty-Five

A little later, I was in the report writing room trying to think how to word an official request for Ruthie to be included with Winger's charges, when Ray came in pushed a Rich Tea biscuit into my hand and placed a mug of tea beside me.

'No bourbons, I'm afraid.' He took a seat next to me.

'Thanks.'

'What are you doing?' Ray asked.

'I want Ruthie Pritchard to be included with a load of charges on a suspect,' I replied. 'I'm trying to word it nicely.'

Ray shook his head. 'Don't. It isn't up to you. You'll just piss off the boss.'

I knew he was right, which was why I was struggling.

Spider came in. 'Any news on Bert?'

'Nothing yet,' Ray replied.

She leant against the doorframe and crossed her arms. 'It was only a matter of time. You can't carry that sort of weight around forever.'

I was about to answer her when Shaun, our patrol sergeant, came in. He didn't have to say a word; his grim face told us everything.

'Oh no,' I breathed.

'I'm afraid so. Bert passed away a couple of hours ago.' Shaun said.

I had a sudden thought. 'What about the children's party? He's Father Christmas.' I realised what I had said. 'Sorry. What a stupid thing to think about.'

'There are worse ways to be remembered than as Father

Christmas. He made so many children happy,' Ray said.

'Yeah, he did,' Shaun agreed.

'He was always stuffing his face with rubbish. I'm actually surprised he lasted this long.'

We all stared at Spider for a few seconds, then I threw my uneaten biscuit at her. She flinched as it bounced off her face and landed in pieces on the floor. She was lucky I hadn't been holding my tea.

Spider stared at me, her mouth agape. 'You threw a biscuit at me!'

'Be grateful that's all I threw,' I shouted. 'I've never met a more unfeeling, unaware, heartless, self-centred creature than you. You're an absolute bitch and you're going to be a shit boss.'

'You'd better hope you never work under me,' she retorted.

'I'd turn down promotion if it meant being within a mile of you,' I snapped back.

'Stop it, both of you!' Ray barked. 'This isn't the time or place.'

Spider spun around to Shaun. 'Aren't you going to do something?'

'I agree with Constable Barrie's assessment of you. A well-respected officer died today and you evidently couldn't care less,' Shaun said.

The chief superintendent came to the door, no doubt drawn by the shouting, so we all shut up, but before he had a chance to say a word, Spider jabbed a finger in my direction.

'Sir, I want to complain about Constable Barrie. She has called me names and she threw a biscuit at me. Also I want to complain about Sergeant Lloyd, he refused to take my complaint against Constable Barrie seriously.'

'I heard. I think everyone in the station heard. Think hard about consequences if you take this action, Constable Leader,' Mr Hunter said.

Spider hesitated. 'I wasn't in the wrong...'

'Many of your colleagues are going to be upset at the news

of Bert's death. Your uncaring attitude, your sense of superiority and your ongoing unpleasantness towards people might cause some to consider making their own complaints. However, if you wish to continue with your complaint, I will deal with it.'

I don't think anyone had ever spoken to Spider like that before. Her mouth opened and closed a few times, then she said, 'I withdraw my complaint about Sergeant Lloyd, sir. However, I wish to go ahead with a complaint against Constable Barrie. I was assaulted with a biscuit.'

Strictly speaking, it was assault. I wished I had thrown something harder. The stapler was within reach but there were too many witnesses.

Mr Hunter eyed the biscuit crumbs on the floor and nodded. 'Are you happy for me to deal with it informally?'

'I am happy for you to deal with it however you see fit, sir.' No doubt she thought she would gain brownie points for that.

'Constable Barrie,' the chief superintendent said.

'Sir?' I replied.

'Don't throw biscuits at people again.'

Ray made a choking sound as he stifled a laugh.

'I won't, sir,' I replied. Next time, it would definitely be the stapler, or the hole puncher. Both were chunky bits of metal.

'Right, that's dealt with.' The chief superintendent turned to Shaun. 'I've spoken to Mrs Mason. There's a policewoman with her until her family can get there. The official announcement will go out with tomorrow's orders. I'll come and speak to the block when they finish the shift.'

'Understood, sir,' Shaun replied. 'I'll go and gather Bert's personal property ready to be returned to his family.' He went into the sergeants' office, leaving us in the report writing room.

The chief superintendent made to leave but paused. 'Miss Barrie, clear up those crumbs. It's not fair to leave them for the cleaner.' Charlotte sniggered. Mr Hunter raised an eyebrow. 'Miss Leader. With me, please.' He continued towards the stairs.

'I won't forget this,' Spider snarled at me as she followed him out.

I replied with two raised fingers.

Ray and I sat in silence for a minute. Then he said, 'Watch your back.'

'What do you mean?' I asked.

'I wouldn't put it past her to cause trouble for you, especially as it looks like she's getting a rollicking from the brass,' Ray replied.

He had a point. I would have to keep an eye on Charlotte Leader. I stood by what I said though. I toddled off to the cleaners' cupboard to get a brush to deal with the crumbs.

'What was that all that shouting about?' Derek asked when we went into the control room.

'Bert Mason died,' Ray replied. 'The brass will be making an announcement to the block at knocking-off time. The official release will go out with the daily orders.'

'And Spider doesn't give a toss,' I added.

'You made your feelings clear,' Ray said.

Derek didn't cry exactly, but a single tear rested in the corner of his eye. I'd never seen him shed a tear. My own emotions, part anger and part grief, boiled over and I felt my own tears run onto my cheeks. I scrubbed them away with the back of my hand.

'Why not take five minutes before you go back to the CID office,' Ray suggested.

I nodded and hurried to the ladies, to blow my nose and reapply some make-up.

I studied my reflection in the mirror and arranged my fringe to cover the scar that ran along my hairline. There was once a time that I couldn't look at that scar without feeling sick with guilt, but over time, and with support from my friends, and a spell of counselling, I came to accept that what happened then was not my fault. That didn't mean I wanted to display my scar to the world, I still preferred to keep it hidden under a fringe.

What would B Block do now? Benno was on leave of absence and now Bert was dead. That left Shaun. Previously, he had been the patrol sergeant, responsible for incidents and anything outside of the station; Bert had been the station sergeant, responsible for paperwork and everything inside the station. When Benno went on leave, Bert and Shaun covered the station between them while Bert became temporary inspector, managing the block. Shaun couldn't possibly do everything by himself. Someone else would have to come in. I wiped my eyes again. Bert was a decent bloke, I'd miss him.

*

The photographs of the PCMG members as they arrived at the hotel had come back several days ago, but I had been too wrapped up in my misery to have paid much attention at first. Mike and Eamon had gone through them with Irene and had recorded those known to the police.

DI Webb decided that it was time to ask Sharon to look at the photos, to see if she recognised anyone. I was pleased because he was going to show her all the photos, which upheld my point that the club was the connection.

'Take Sam with you,' he said. Whether that was to keep me busy, I wasn't certain. I didn't mind if that had been his plan. It was more interesting that staying in the office doing the filing and making tea. I didn't want to be seen as a burden though.

DI Webb phoned ahead and cleared it with her mother; then Mike Finlay, Eamon and I went around to Wherry Street with a large brown envelope, fat with photographs. Sharon's mother offered tea. We declined. We wanted to get this done.

'Has your mum explained why we're here?' Mike asked Sharon.

She nodded. 'You want me to look at photographs and tell you if I recognise anyone.'

'That's right.'

'What if I don't recognise anyone?' Sharon asked.

'That's okay m'darlin'. You're not being tested here. There is no wrong answer,' Eamon replied.

Sharon sat at the dining table. I sat on one side of her and her mother sat on the other side. DS Finlay and Eamon sat opposite. She tipped out the envelope that Mike handed to her and began to shuffle through the photographs. Slowly, she examined each one and placed it into one of two piles, that I mentally named "Known" and "Not Known". Inevitably, the "Not Known" pile was much larger. So far, Mr Duggan was the only occupant of the "Known" pile.

I was disappointed when she didn't know Winger, but I had been warned not to show anything by expression, word or gesture while she was going through the photos. She discarded a few others then she picked up one photograph, looked at it for slightly longer than the others, then added it to the "Not Known" pile. She reached for another photo, paused then picked up the previous photograph again. She stared for almost a full minute then covered the lower part of his face with her finger. She shuddered. Her mum rubbed her back. The photograph joined that of Mr Duggan. I longed to be able to pick the photograph up and have a good look to see who had caught her attention, but I stayed still as she worked her way through them all.

When all the photographs were sorted, Sharon sat back.

'They're the only two I recognise, I'm afraid. There was another man too.'

'That's great, Sharon.' Mike said. 'It's a big help.' He picked up the "known" photographs, studied them for a moment then put them down.

I took the opportunity to pick up the second photograph and take a good look. I almost fell off the chair. Don Hayes! I could hardly believe it. I hadn't seen him arrive. Perhaps he had been first, arriving when I had nipped to the loo. I'd have to speak to Eamon about it.

'Mr Duggan we know,' Mike said. 'Tell me how you know this other person.'

'He's the one who gave me water,' Sharon said.

'How do you recognise him?' Mike asked.

'His eyes. He had nice eyes.'

'Do you remember anything else about him. Any marks, birthmarks, tattoos, scars?' I asked. I was thinking of those tattoos on Don's fingers. If he had handed her water, she must have seen them.

Sharon took the photo from me and stared at it for several seconds before shaking her head. 'Sorry, no. I think I told you; he wore a hankie over his face, and gloves.'

That was so disappointing. 'He probably didn't want his fingerprints everywhere,' I said.

Sharon nodded. 'Sorry.'

'Don't be sorry m'darlin'. You've done really well,' Eamon said.

'Yes, this has been very useful,' I said. I would go through the forensic photos when we got back and see if there were any gloves found at the scene. I gathered up the photographs and put them back in the envelope.

'We'll let you get on. As soon as we get any news, we'll update you,' Mike said.

'Thank you.' Mrs Hall saw us to the door.

Back in the car, I leant forward between Mike and Eamon as Mike drove us back to Wyre Hall.

'You didn't tell them about Winger?'

'Not yet. He hasn't been formally charged. We've still got a little time. As soon as he is charged, we will.'

'I know that second man, It's Nellie Hayes' son, Don,' I said.

'Nellie, as in Nellie and Bessie? Are you sure?' Eamon twisted around in his seat.

'Positive. I've spoken to him a couple of times. When did he arrive at the hotel?'

'It must have been when you went to inspect the facilities,' Eamon answered.

As I suspected. 'Sharon did only see him with his face covered, so will the eyes be sufficient?'

'It's a start,' Mike said.

'It's enough to bring him in for interview,' Eamon agreed.

I sat back, uncertain how I should be feeling about that. I had liked Don and I didn't want him to have been mixed up with this horror story. Maybe there was an explanation. As I had the thought, I dismissed it. Sharon said he gave her water. How much more involved could he be? Nellie had told me that Don was moonlighting. Had Don boarded the windows or made the crates? How could Don, if it had been him, not have known, or at least suspected, what those crates were used for. How did he get mixed up with this mess? It was that club again. He was photographed going into the Middleton Hotel on meeting night.

The *Sharon Hall/Victory Street* file was quite thick with more statements and reports to come. In a wallet, photographs from the house had been attached, adding to the bulk. I shuffled through the pile looking for gloves or anything else that might confirm that Don Hayes was involved. I was out of luck.

I had another thought and kicked myself for not considering it earlier. Nellie mentioned that she'd seen a man burning clothing in the yard of Annie's house. I smiled as I realised that I too always referred to the address as Annie's house, even though I had never met her. Maybe, if we showed Nellie photographs of the suspects, she would recognise one as the man doing the burning. I hoped it would be Ron Winger.

I checked through the rest of the photos, didn't find any gloves or anything else pointing to Don. Then I went to DI Webb's office and knocked.

'I'm busy, make it quick,' he called.

'Sir, I want to show the photos of the suspects to Nellie Hayes. She told us about the fire in the back yard and she might recognise someone.'

DI Webb nodded. 'It wouldn't hurt to do that.'

'Thank you, sir. I'll let you get on.' I turned away.

DI Webb called after me, 'Speak to Mike.'

I took that as a nice reminder to stop bothering him with stupid requests and go to my sergeant. He also had told me to keep him in the loop. Never mind.

'Yes, sir.'

I went over to Mike's desk. 'I want to show Nellie Hayes the photographs of the suspects. She saw the man burning the clothing in the yard.'

Mike called across to Eamon who was working at his desk. 'You busy?'

Eamon looked up. 'Nothing that can't wait a wee while.'

'We're taking Sam to Victory Street. Show Nellie Hayes some photos. It'll be an opportunity to speak to Don Hayes, too.'

I looked at the clock. 'Don gets home from work in about an hour.'

'You get on with Nellie?' Mike asked. I nodded. 'You call there. If Don Hayes is up for being interviewed, give us a shout on the radio and we'll come in. If he gets difficult, we'll bring him in on suspicion of conspiracy to murder. I'll wait in the car, and Eamon, you hang around behind the houses. I'll give the control room the heads-up we might need a spot of back-up if they're not too busy.'

One of the useful things that police powers gave us was the power to arrest on suspicion. It might not lead to anything in the end, the suspect might not ever be charged with the full offence, but it gave us a chance to question them.

'Take the photos of the clothing and such, too. She might recognise something from when the person was burning it. It might give us a timeline,' Mike said.

I thought that, just because clothing was burnt at a certain time, didn't mean that whoever had been in those crates died at that time. It might have been ages before the suspect disposed of the clothes. However, it was a line of enquiry and we would be remiss if we ignored it, although it might not lead anywhere.

At Victory Street, Mike positioned himself a little way up the street in the unmarked car. Eamon nipped down the entry in case Don did a runner through the back.

Nellie answered my knock and invited me in. She was as warm and welcoming as ever.

'I'm sorry to just drop in, but I wanted you to look at some photos and see if you recognise the man you saw burning clothing,' I said.

'Of course. I hope you find the sick bugger, whoever he is.' Nellie sat at the table, which had been cleared and set for a meal.

I took the envelope of photographs from the file in my bag and laid the pictures of Winger, Hodgeson and Duggan out for her.

She picked up one photo. 'That looks like Annie's son. I haven't seen him for a while.'

I took the photo from her. 'I just wanted to be sure it wasn't Walter clearing up his mother's house that you saw.'

'Definitely not him. I know him.' She shuffled through the other photos but then sat back and shook her head.

'I'm sorry. I didn't get a good look at his face so I can't be sure he's one of these people.'

'Never mind. Thanks for looking. Would you mind looking at some other photos? They're pictures of the items found burnt in the bin, and around the yard at Annie's house.'

I got out the other photos and laid them on the table. Nellie picked one up.

'You've found Don's mallet!' Nellie exclaimed. 'Did someone hand it in?'

And just like that, she'd confirmed to me that Don was indeed connected to this mess. I fervently hoped that this was just a peripheral connection and he was not part of the horror. I needed to plug the gaps. I wanted to apologise to her. She was a good woman and I was about to shatter her world.

'Are you sure it's Don's?' I asked.

Nellie tapped at the photograph. 'See those initials? O. H.? My Ollie did that with a hammer and nail before Don was born. Tools are expensive, so the men always marked their stuff or someone would have off with it.'

I peered at the photograph. The initials were made of a series of small holes driven deeply into the wood. They were a bit hard to make out, but Nellie was certain.

'I bought him the mallet for his birthday one year. We couldn't afford to get the full set all at once, so we got him bits year by year. In the end he had a good tool bag. It's Don's now. Can he collect it from the police station?'

I skipped over her request. 'Mrs Hayes, has Don ever lent it out to someone?'

'Good Lord, no. It never left his workbag.'

'Could it have been stolen from him, perhaps while he was at a job?'

She rubbed her chin. 'Maybe. He did wonder about that although it couldn't have been one of his workmates. If anyone were to be found with someone else's tools without permission, they'd be in serious trouble, and I don't mean from management.' She chuckled, then her face fell. 'You say these things were in Annie's yard?'

I hesitated for a moment, but it was all going to come out shortly anyway.

'Yes.'

Her face froze as she processed this information. Nellie was old but she wasn't stupid, she knew the implications of this.

'Maybe whoever stole it threw it over the wall. Maybe they wanted to return it but got the wrong house.' Nellie was clutching at straws.

I nodded, acknowledging the possibility. 'Yes, but I need to ask him about it.' I didn't tell her that he had been identified by Sharon. That was something for later.

'He'll be home shortly.'

We sat in almost silence, just exchanging the odd word and listening to the clock tick until the front door opened and a familiar voice shouted, 'Only me, Mam.'

'In here, Don,' Nellie called back, her voice flat. 'There's someone here to speak to you.'

Don peered into the kitchen, as handsome and jovial as before. 'Hello. You're that policewoman. Samantha, isn't it? Why do you need to speak to me?'

'We found your mallet. We need to know about any local jobs you've done,' I picked up the picture of the mallet and held it out to him. 'Can you confirm that this is yours?'

Don looked at the picture, to me, to his mother, then back to me, turned tail and ran through the front door. I took off after him.

'Headed your way, Mike,' I radioed.

Don spotted Mike, darted down the entry into the waiting arms of Eamon, who brought him down. Mike quickly handcuffed him and they both hauled him to his feet.

I stood before him. 'Donald Hayes, I'm arresting you on suspicion of conspiracy to murder. You do not have to say anything unless you wish to do so, but anything you do say may be taken down in writing and given in evidence.'

'I didn't conspire anything or murder anyone. I was paid to build crates. I thought they were going to keep animals,' he wailed.

That might be a defence. We'd have to interview him carefully to explore the depth of his involvement, but he was going to have to work hard to explain how Sharon recognised him as the man who brought her water.

I turned around and saw his mother standing at the end of the entry. Her hand covered her mouth and tears ran down her face. My heart broke for her.

'I never thought I'd be jealous of Bessie, but she can hold her head high when she speaks of her children. I'm ashamed to call you my son.' She walked away.

'Mam, no!' Don shouted. 'Mam!'

Nellie didn't return. Eamon and Mike put the weeping Don in the back of the car. He was completely compliant. Eamon sat beside him and I took shotgun beside Mike, who drove us to the bridewell.

Chapter Twenty-Six

There was no reason to hang around so, once Don Hayes was processed, we offered him the services of a solicitor to sit in during his interview. He accepted. He seemed crushed. Mike, Eamon and I had a quick discussion before the interview and decided that Don was undoubtedly the weakest link.

'I think we should just get him confused. Everyone fire questions at him and see what his answers are. I bet he'll tell the truth in the first ten minutes,' Eamon said.

Mike thought for a moment then nodded. 'Okay. If a question comes to you, just ask it.'

We trooped into the interview room and sat in a row facing Don and his solicitor. I felt a momentary pang as I remembered how Chris told me he'd felt like he was facing an interview board during the charity dance. I hoped this would have the same effect on Don.

Mike cautioned Don and started the interview, then we went for it. It didn't even take a minute for Don to crumble.

'We know that you saw Sharon Hall whilst she was held in a crate,' Eamon began.

'I had no idea he was going to trap women there,' Don declared.

'Women, plural?' I asked. 'Who said there were more than one?'

Don flushed. 'I mean I don't know how many there were there. I was asked to build two crates so I'm guessing.'

'Who asked you?' I demanded.

'Ron Winger. He paid me to build them. I thought he was

starting an animal breeding business.'

I felt a quiver of satisfaction. Two people had now named Winger. He was toast.

'Why didn't you tell your mother about it when she complained about the rats in Annie's house?' I asked.

'She wouldn't have liked it,' Don replied.

'Liked that you built crates for women?' I demanded.

'No!' Don insisted. 'I thought it was for animals. She would have been cross that I knew there was a breeding operation there. She's very fond of animals.'

'Sharon identified you as one of the men at the house,' Mike said.

'Why would she say it was me? I wasn't there.'

'She was quite firm it was you. You have very distinctive features,' I said.

Don looked at his hands and flexed his fingers. Mike had taught me to watch body language as well as listen to the questions. Don knew what I alluded to, although I was actually referring to the blue eyes that Sharon had pointed out.

'She couldn't…'

Eamon cut across him. 'She couldn't what? See your hands because you wore gloves? Why did you wear gloves inside? Was it to stop her from noticing your tattoos? They are so inconvenient when you're committing a crime, aren't they?' Eamon had slipped into bad cop mode.

'No! It was so I didn't get splinters.' Don tucked his hands into his armpits.

'Okay, so you admit that you did wear gloves?' Mike asked. He was businesslike.

'Well… Yeah. Carpentry can be a bit dangerous.'

'Are you a member of the PCMG?' Eamon leant forward onto the table.

'What?' Don was becoming disturbed by the different questions.

I flourished the photo of him by the Middleton Hotel. 'You

were photographed going in with other members.'

'I was meeting a friend.' Don looked deeply unhappy.

'Which friend? Would they be willing to speak for you in court?' Eamon asked.

'I, I don't know.'

'Don't know which friend or don't know if they'll speak for you?' Eamon demanded.

Don looked from Eamon to Mike than me, panic clear in his eyes.

'You're homosexual, aren't you?' Eamon asked.

'I don't see what my client's sexuality has to do with anything,' the solicitor said.

'We don't care whether he is or he isn't, but it's a reason for him not wanting to name the friend he was meeting,' Mr reasonable, Mike asserted.

Eamon turned back to Don. 'Your mum wouldn't like that, would she, Don?'

'I… I…' Don let his voice trail off. His hands fell to his lap and he slumped in his seat.

'I think my client needs a break,' the solicitor said.

We ignored him. Now was the time to double down.

'Not to worry, we'll seize the membership records. We'll get everyone's names,' Mike said to Eamon and me.

'I'm a member,' Don muttered.

'Why did you lie?' Eamon asked.

Don shrugged.

I adopted good cop to counteract Eamon. I wanted to appeal to the Don who loved his mum.

'You know the type of person who goes there,' I said to Eamon. 'Don probably didn't want to be lumped in with them.' I turned to Don. 'Is that right, Don?'

Don looked at me with something akin to hope and nodded.

'Who commissioned the crates?' I asked.

'Ron Winger,' Don answered without hesitation.

'My client has already answered that.'

I glanced at the solicitor but didn't answer him. I was deliberately trying to confuse Don, nicely.

'What did you think when you saw Sharon starving in the crate?' Eamon leant his elbows on the desk and glared at Don.

'I didn't,' Don almost whispered. If he had leant any further away from Eamon, his chair would have fallen backwards.

'Yes you did, you lying gobshite. You admitted you wore gloves around the crates. How would Sharon know that if she hadn't seen it?' Eamon demanded.

Don's eyes darted between us, but he didn't argue the point.

'That's right, you have been identified as the man who brought water,' Eamon said. 'We know everything. There's no point denying anything.'

Don hung his head without answering.

'You knew about Sharon,' Mike stated. 'She was reported missing. It was on the news and in the papers but you said nothing. That mallet proves you were there. Even if you weren't part of the kidnap, you knew she was there. You gave her water and you said nothing.'

'You must have seen her mother crying for her return. How do you think your poor mother would feel about you being involved with that?' Eamon shot at him. 'Oh wait, she does know and she said she was ashamed that you are her son.'

Don looked stricken. 'I didn't know she was Sharon.'

Bingo!

'Does it matter who she was?' Eamon retorted. 'A girl was in a terrible situation and you didn't feckin' care.'

'She says you gave her water.' After a couple of seconds of Don's silence, I quietly said, 'You kept her alive, Don.'

'Did you enjoy having power over another person? The power of life and death!' Eamon stared at Don waiting for his answer.

'She didn't die. You said she didn't die!'

'Sharon didn't but at least one other girl did.'

Don's eyes filled and tears tracked down his cheeks. 'I thought Ron was punishing them then letting them go. I didn't know they were going to die.'

I softened my voice. 'The other girl. She wasn't well, was she. What was her name?'

Don shook his head. 'I don't know. She just disappeared. I don't know what he did with her.'

Don had given up. We could ask him anything and get the truth.

'Don, why don't you tell us your story from the beginning?' I coaxed.

He scrubbed his cheeks with the back of his hands and took a huge breath in. 'I really thought that it was an animal breeding business, at first. I was paid to build the crates and I fitted soundproofing so the neighbours weren't disturbed. Then, after a little while, Ron told me what was really happening. He said they had gone against God's Word and he was teaching them their place. He said he'd pay me to take water in every day. The money was good. I could treat my mam.' He paused and wiped his sleeve across his nose.

'Your mum showed me her new slippers. They're good quality.' I smiled at him.

He half smiled back. 'I was saving up to get an indoor bathroom for her, and maybe a washing machine. It was going to be a surprise. The money was a help.'

A bathroom and a washing machine. Winger must have been paying him very well.

Don continued. 'I wasn't allowed to speak to them, I just had to make them say something from The Bible and then give them the water. I thought Ron was bringing in food. I came in one day and one crate was empty.'

'You didn't think to contact the authorities? You didn't think to call an ambulance? You just did as Winger told you?' Eamon was aghast. Even the solicitor looked sideways at Don.

Don looked almost pleadingly at me. 'I'm not like Ron. I'm not a bad bloke. It was just a job… I thought they were going to be released.'

'Lies!' Eamon snarled. 'You're every bit as bad as Winger.' Eamon half turned away in disgust.

'Did Winger ever tell you what he did with the one who vanished?' I asked.

'No! I told you; I don't know what happened to her.'

'There was a third person, Carol. Do you know about her?' Mike asked.

'Three?' Don seemed genuine in his surprise.

'Don, how many girls did you actually see in the crates?' I asked.

'Two in all. I didn't put them there.'

I supposed that was possible. It could be that Carol had been incarcerated in the period before Winger had employed Don to take water in. It was going to be hard to prove that Don had anything to do with Carol's death. However, he could testify against Winger. As Sharon was unable to identify the third man, he would be our main witness. Walter would confirm that he was subletting to Winger. If we could get Duggan to admit that he handed Sharon over to Winger at the address, that would be the cherry on the top of the cake. Winger was going down!

'Can you remember when Ron Winger asked you to take in the water?' I asked.

'About four weeks ago. Maybe a little longer. I'm not sure exactly.'

'Was it long after you finished the crates?'

'Not too long. A month perhaps.'

'I'm guessing that there aren't any receipts to prove the timeline?' Mike asked.

'He paid me cash in hand,' Don admitted.

'Who got the materials?' I asked.

'I did. Ron gave me the money and I bought them from the hardware warehouse on the industrial estate,' Don replied.

'Do you have those receipts?'

'I gave them to Ron.'

I wasn't sure if they would be any use to the investigation, but we knew who to speak to if we needed them.

'Right, I think that's enough questions. Thank you for your honesty,' Mike said.

'Eventually,' Eamon added.

Don turned pleading eyes to me. He'd evidently saw me as the softest touch there. 'Can my mam come to visit me? Please?'

'No, Don, she can't,' Mike said. 'You'll appear in court and then held in remand pending your court case.'

'I'll plead guilty,' Don said, probably in an attempt to persuade us to allow his mother in to visit.

'You'll admit that you conspired to murder?' Mike asked.

'Not that. I didn't do that. Something else.'

'You don't get to choose the charge,' Eamon barked.

'I know I'll have to go to prison but I'll tell the judge everything. I'll name names.'

'Don, you broke your poor mother's heart. You saw her. I'm not sure she'd come even if we said she could,' Eamon said.

Mike turned to Eamon and me. 'I think we're done here.'

'I loved Ron!'

We all turned towards Don.

'Is that why you blindly followed his instructions? Is that why you didn't report him?' I asked.

Don nodded. 'We met at the Middleton Hotel. We started out as mates, but things developed. I told him he was crazy but he kept insisting that God wanted us to do this. It was the only way to restore the natural order. I told him I didn't want to be a part of it, so he said he'd tell my mam about us and that he'd contact my work and tell them. I can't tell work that I prefer men.'

'It doesn't sound like he loves you,' I said. 'It sounds as if he was using you.'

'No, I don't think he ever did love me,' Don admitted. 'Thinking about it, I'm not even sure he's... he's like me.'

'What did you do then?' Mike asked.

'I told him that I would report him if he said anything, even though it would mean that I would be in trouble too. We ended up with this weird mutual hold over each other. He paid me, or maybe it was a bribe, to bring water to keep me involved so I wouldn't report him. I brought in water to keep him quiet. We both knew that if either one of us were careless, it would be all over for both of us.'

'That's useful to know. Thank you, Don,' Mike said.

'What about Mam?' Don asked.

'No, Don. Sorry.' Mike stood up and we walked out to the sound of Don's sobs. The bridewell officer took him back to the cell.

'A successful interview, I think,' Mike said as we walked back to the CID office. 'It's a nice complete circle. Sharon has named Duggan and identified Hayes. Hodgeson and Hayes have named Winger. Winger will probably give us Duggan and Hayes' names out of spite. Justice for Carol and Sharon.'

'Walter isn't being charged with anything, is he?' I asked.

'Not by us. It's up to the council if they want to follow up on the subletting and damage to the house,' Mike said.

'What do you think the final charges for Don will be?' I asked.

'Unlawful imprisonment. Maybe conspiracy to murder,' Mike replied.

'He was definitely subordinate to Winger,' I said. 'And Duggan was just a customer.'

'Duggan is going guilty on kidnap but not guilty to conspiracy to murder,' Mike said. 'We'll probably have to go to court over that, so make sure your desk diaries are well updated.'

In the CID, we had desk diaries rather than conventional pocketbooks, but they served the same purpose.

I spotted my old tutor constable, Phil Torrens, in the control room, sergeant stripes prominent on his arms.

'Phil! What are you doing here?' I was so pleased to see him; I wanted to throw my arms around him. I didn't because I didn't want to embarrass him.

He grinned at me. 'It's true then? I heard you'd defected upstairs.'

'Only my aides,' I told him. I tapped three fingers on my upper arm. 'Looking good, Sergeant Torrens.'

'I'm only on loan. I've been sent to cover until something permanent can be arranged.'

'You're the B Block sergeant?' I was surprised.

'Yep. Shaun is going to take over the station and I'll be the patrol sergeant. Someone is coming in from the city to cover until the inspector gets back.'

'Do you know anything about him?' I asked.

'It's not him, it's her. She was on my intake.'

That was going to ruffle a few feathers on B Block.

'We females are getting everywhere these days,' I quipped.

'I heard that she was an inspector in the policewomen's department. They couldn't demote her when that was disbanded,' Derek said. 'That'll be how she was promoted ahead of you, Phil.'

'Nothing to do with me not taking the promotion exams for years?' Phil asked ironically.

'What are you saying Derek?' I asked. I knew exactly what he was saying, Irene had explained it to me, but I wanted him to say it out loud. A lot of the older officers thought that women with rank had somehow slipped in through the back door. They had only been up against other women for promotion and therefore hadn't proved themselves in an integrated environment. Of course, with the passage of time, that would no longer be an argument. My generation had joined, served with, and would compete with, the male officers.

'I'm saying she's an unknown quantity. Will she be able to hack it at a serious incident? Will the lads listen to her?'

'She'll hack it, believe me, and if the lads don't listen, she'll kick their arses until they do,' Phil said.

'Respect the rank, Derek. The sisterhood is getting stronger.' I giggled all the way back to the CID office.

Chapter Twenty-Seven

The following day, I stopped off at Mum and Dad's house before work. We had had some interest, and I wanted to make sure that it was still in a suitable condition. One was a couple looking for somewhere to raise a family. The other was a young man. The estate agent said he had arrived alone and had pulled open every cupboard and drawer. Maybe they'd have a bidding war so my parents would get a good price, but I hoped the young couple would win. This was a family home in a good location for schools, shops and buses.

I picked up the letters from the hall floor, shuffled through them and tossed them onto the window ledge. There was nothing of interest there. Mum and Dad had paid to have their mail redirected to Aberdeen. I went into the kitchen and peered out through the back door. The garden could do with a last mow. It was a bit late now, but perhaps I'd come at the weekend and do a spot of weeding and tidying. I was almost certain that there was a mower still in the shed. If there wasn't, I could always ask Henry next door if I could borrow his.

A shuffling noise in the hall drew my attention.

'Hello?' I went to the hall expecting to see a neighbour checking who was in the house. The people around here had been good neighbours to my parents, and I was glad they would come and challenge visitors.

Nobody was there, but the front door moved slightly with the breeze. I mustn't have closed it properly. I reached out to close the door and that was the last memory I had until I woke up on the kitchen floor with a raging headache.

I could smell cooking and something else I couldn't place.

'Mum?' I called in my confusion.

No response. Oh, yes, Mum was in Scotland, wasn't she.

'Hello?' I called again to no avail.

I looked around and saw a chip pan heating on a full flame on the stove. I didn't recall seeing a chip pan that had been left behind when my parents moved. I hadn't put the pan on. Lord knows how long that lard had been sitting there if they had forgotten it, so I wouldn't want to cook anything in it. From the smoke, I guessed it had been heating for some time. A tea towel hung over the handle of the eye level grill that Mum had been so proud of. I didn't recall seeing any forgotten tea towels either. It took a minute, but the danger dawned on me. The fat would eventually catch fire; the flame would reach up to the tea towel and from there it could reach the blinds or spill over onto the linoleum. Then I realised that the other smell was coming from me. I was covered in what smelt like lighter fuel. If I remained where I was, I would fry.

I tried to stand but my hands were tied and my ankles tied to the legs of the cooker. I shouted for help with no real expectation of anyone hearing me. If I struggled too hard, the chip pan would fall, covering me in burning fat.

The fat ignited with a soft "whomp" noise. I watched the flame catch the tea towel and run towards the blinds. Then the window in the back door smashed in and Henry, the next door neighbour, I peered in.

'Bloody hell!' He furtled around trying to find the lock without success. Whoever had attacked me must have taken the key, and it could be anywhere now. Henry picked up a large rock from the garden, then banged at the kitchen door. Meantime, I could hear sirens in the distance. The kitchen door gave way and Henry filled the kitchen. He immediately switched off the pan. He then turned his attention to me. It was about then that I remembered that he was a retired fireman.

'Who the hell did this to you?' he asked.

'Dunno, they hit me over the head,' I replied, but I don't think it came out that clearly. My mind still refused to function at full capacity.

Henry leant down, produced a kitchen knife from his pocket and sliced at the ties around my feet. When they fell away, he picked me up and carried me through the ruined door into the garden and laid me on the grass. Age had not diminished his strength. He cut my hands free and I rolled onto the cool grass.

A fire crew ran from the side of the house towards us.

They nodded to Henry. 'All right, boss?'

Oh yes, I also remembered that Henry had been quite senior in the fire brigade before his retirement. It seemed he hadn't lost his skills.

'Obviously not. Get on to control for an ambulance. She's been hit on the head, I think.' He sniffed the air above me. 'She's been doused in accelerant, so no smoking around her.' He jerked his head towards his own house. 'Someone speak to my wife and let her know that it was Samantha in the house and we're both okay. Also, get on to control and ask them to contact the police control room as Constable Barrie has been targeted in an arson attack and is going to hospital.'

'Yes, boss,' they shot back.

One of the firemen ran back towards the appliance. The other ran to Henry's house.

'Thank you, Henry,' I burbled.

He sat on the grass beside me and patted my shoulder. 'I remember you growing up. You were always getting into a pickle. I knew I'd end up rescuing you one day, but I didn't expect this.' He looked around. 'Given your job, I'm guessing that you've upset someone.'

'There's always a disgruntled customer or two,' I replied.

'That young man I saw leaving, was he with you?' Henry asked.

'I was alone,' I replied.

Henry thought for a moment. 'No, I'm pretty sure that I

saw him come from your path. Then my wife saw smoke at the kitchen window, and I heard you shout when I looked out.'

I had never been more glad that our kitchen windows faced each other.

The ambos arrived and shone lights into my eyes. Henry insisted that they took me to hospital for a "proper checkup".

'Don't worry, I'll make sure the place is secure before I leave,' he told me.

I surveyed the broken window and the destroyed door. Still, at least the place would be safe. I'd have to get Henry something really nice to say thank you. I would certainly be dead without his help.

The fire hadn't spread too far, but it was going cost quite a bit to put right and the house would stink. I had no choice but to inform Mum and Dad so they could let their insurance know. Mum would probably break the land speed record on her way down here, where she'd go into hyper protective mode. Great!

*

I wasn't detained at hospital. A check-up, a short period of observation to make sure I hadn't inhaled too much smoke and a visit from High Lake CID, who seized my jacket as proof that I had been doused in flammable liquid, and I was discharged with a leaflet on how to deal with head injuries. I put it in the first aid box with all the other leaflets, and bundled what remained of my clothing into a bag to go into the rubbish.

The phone rang and I debated not picking it up. Gary would think I was still in work, so it had to be Mum. I didn't want to speak to my mother just yet. However, it rang and rang, so I snatched it up in the end.

'Where were you?' Mum asked.

'Bathroom,' I replied.

'Oh. Why aren't you in hospital?'

'Why are you ringing the flat if you thought I was in hospital?'

I countered.

'I know you would have discharged yourself, whether they said you were ready or not.'

'I didn't discharge myself, they let me go. I'm not stupid, Mum.'

Mum was silent for a moment, then said, 'Henry told me about the fire. He said you'd gone off in an ambulance. I'll be there tomorrow.'

I rolled my eyes, but then she did need to see the house.

'Is the damage very bad?' Mum asked.

'Just the kitchen. The rest of the house probably stinks of smoke. We'll have to get a structural engineer in to inspect the walls and make sure it's safe,' I replied.

'How did it start? Mum asked.

I mentally debated not telling her what really happened, but Henry or the insurance company might tell her, then she'd be annoyed at me.

'Now, I don't want you to freak out—' That was as far as I got.

'Freak out? Freak out! Now I am freaking out! What the hell happened?' Mum demanded.

'I was attacked by someone—'

'Who? Have they been arrested? Your father will want words with them,' Mum ranted.

'Mum, listen to me.'

Mum gradually ran out of steam and I could hear her breathing heavily down the phone.

'I went to check on the house and someone crept in behind me and knocked me unconscious. When I woke up, the chip pan was on the stove and it ignited. The flame caught the blinds and the fire spread. It's been crimed and investigations are ongoing.' I deliberately left out the detail about the accelerant.

'I should think so,' Mum said. 'You could have died!'

'Henry got me out before I was in any real danger,' I lied.

'What chip pan?' Mum demanded.

'The chip pan that you left behind in the move.'

'I've got my chip pan,' Mum said. 'You know what your dad's like for his chips. I wouldn't leave that.'

'Then where did this pan come from?' I asked. 'Did you have a spare?'

'No. I suggest you mention this to your colleagues.'

I certainly would. The only thing I could think of was that the offender must have brought it with them. The attack on me had been planned. I felt a chill go down my back. That little detail about them bringing a chip pan with them, and lighter fuel, brought home to me that whoever it was had fully intended for me to die horribly.

Mum's voice brought me back from my thoughts.

'Why didn't you shut the door after you? Why won't you say who it was?'

'I thought I had, and I don't know who it was,' I replied. 'The investigation is ongoing, like I told you.'

'Have you upset anyone recently?' Mum asked.

'Henry asked me that,' I chuckled.

'So he thinks it's a revenge attack! I said that job is dangerous.' Mum went off into another rant.

'Mum, calm down! I'm fine. The house needs some repairs, but it could have been worse.'

'Worse? How much worse? What aren't you telling me?'

Mum always had had a radar for lies, or omissions of truths.

'Never mind, I'm phoning your father. I'll get a neighbour to keep an eye on your nan. I'm leaving right now. I'll be there in a few hours and you will tell me everything. Does Gary know?'

'I haven't spoken to him yet. He's too far away to do anything anyway,' I replied.

'You need to tell him, he's your fiancé,' Mum insisted.

'Okay. I'll get the spare room ready for you.' I terminated the call. The phone rang again almost immediately. This had to be Gary. I sighed and picked up the receiver. I might as well get all the hysterics over at once.

Gary wasn't happy when I told him about events, but he was more logical than Mum. He asked intelligent, job-based questions instead of going off on one, but he had to admit there was little to be done other than let the investigation follow its course.

*

'What the hell are you doing here?' DI Webb demanded when I arrived at work the following day.

'I'm not injured; I'm okay to work, sir,' I replied.

He took me by the arm into his office and closed the door.

'Were you followed to your parents' address?' he asked.

'I must have been, but I didn't see anyone,' I replied.

'Didn't you see them when you heard the noise?'

'No, sir, I just saw the door was open and went to shut it.'

'Didn't it occur to you that the noise you heard might be a hostile?' DI Webb asked.

'No, sir. I thought it was a neighbour checking on me. If I had been in my own home, I would have been suspicious of any noises. I was in my parents' house and it is quite likely that the neighbours would check on an empty property.'

Eventually, he was satisfied that I was really okay and allowed me to stay. He put a gold response on the house and also the flat. This meant that any calls to either address would be a priority. He also had the owner details of my car blocked on the PNC. It meant that anyone checking it would receive instructions to contact the control room for details, where they would be grilled before receiving any information. I liked that. I didn't understand why all police personnel were not similarly protected, but it was reserved for people, not just police, with direct threats against them. I was less keen on being part of that club.

When we got a minute, Mum and I went to the house and inspected the damage, which wasn't as extensive as I'd feared. The house did stink though, and I would feel better when a structural engineer had done a report. Then we called on Henry with a thank you gift.

When he and Mum stopped chatting, I remembered something he had said the night of the fire.

'Henry, I want to ask you something. You said that you saw a man who appeared to come from our house. Can you describe him for me, please?'

'What man?' Mum demanded. I held up my hand to silence her so Henry could speak.

'He was fairly young, but everyone under forty looks young to me.' Henry laughed. I smiled at his joke but was keen to move on. 'He was white, average height and build. He had fair hair, moustache. He wore jeans and a leather motorcycle jacket. A bit nondescript, really.'

'This motorcycle jacket. What colour was it?' I asked.

He thought for a moment. 'Black with a design on the back. Red, I think. I couldn't see what it was because he had a backpack that covered it. There was a white logo on the front left side of that.'

Like a million other motorcycle jackets. Still, it was something to pass on to the High Lake team.

*

DI Webb really didn't like that someone had tried to kill one of his officers. Even though it had only been a very few days, he took it as a personal insult that no suspects had been traced and rang High Lake to give them the benefit of his advice and opinions on more than one occasion. Jerome Rigby, the DI at High Lake, probably dreaded hearing from him. Sometimes this happened. There would be few leads and what there were wouldn't lead anywhere. It was frustrating, but that was just the way it was. Maybe my case would be one of those that would never be solved. I tried not to mind.

I got a whole lot more vigilant though. I set up a security

camera in the hall of the flat, so anyone entering would be recorded, and I obsessively watched for vehicles following me. I sometimes took a different route home or, if I suspected that I was being followed, I would double back a short distance. As I watched a news report on the aftermath of a series of bombs in Northern Ireland one evening, I wondered how the police in the RUC could stand being on alert all day, every day. I had only been doing is a short time and it was exhausting.

Even Mum had to admit that I didn't need nursing or guarding. She reluctantly left me to supervise the repair work on the house and returned to Aberdeen. Henry offered to keep an eye on things when workmen were tramping through the house. I accepted, because it meant that I didn't have to be there so often. It didn't feel like home anymore. Whether that was because of the attack or the ongoing repair work, I couldn't say.

*

I went through a bit of a quiet spell at work for a couple of days. I don't think it was planned that way; it just happens sometimes. As per custom, I took advantage of the time to get rid of some of my less important jobs.

I was idly flicking through the prisoner property list as someone was alleging that his arresting officers had collectively schemed to steal a valuable family heirloom from him. As the heirloom was a *Skean Dhu* the knife that men in traditional Scottish dress, keep down their socks and he had used it to rob a couple of people, it had been seized as evidence. Little wonder that he had not had it returned. It had been correctly dealt with. A swift report and another job would bite the dust.

The bridewell sergeant came over. 'Hey, I don't want details, but did you ever sort out that membership card thing?'

'Yes. It was the Christian group that meets at the Middleton Hotel,' I replied. 'All sorted now.'

'Thought so. Is it a club for shirt-lifters as well?'

I sighed. He was letting his prejudices show again. 'That's a strange thing to ask. What made you think that?'

'Oh, I was just wondering. That bloke you arrested that time, the one whose card it was, he had a woman's lighter on him. At least, I thought it looked like a woman's. He said it was his so I thought he might be one of those.' He flopped his hand like Dick Emery.

'As far as I'm aware, it isn't specifically for gay men, but I suppose statistically some might be. I don't know. Why, are you thinking of joining?'

'Not bloody likely!' He wandered off to do whatever bridewell sergeants did.

I grinned. I knew that would wind him up.

My curiosity had been piqued. I flicked back to the entry from when Tony Fleming had been brought in, which seemed so long ago now but actually had only been a few weeks. At first glance it seemed straightforward enough, but something niggled at the back of my mind. I had not been present when Tony had been brought in; I had been dealing with Wilfred Wainwright and his broken leg. Someone had lodged my prisoner for me until I could get to the bridewell. I hadn't gone through the property myself; I had just accepted the property number attached to the file.

'What are you looking at, m'darlin'?' Eamon asked.

I hadn't heard him approaching, so jumped. 'Don't creep up on people like that.'

'What are you up to?' he asked.

I was offended. 'I'm not up to anything! I was legitimately checking for a *Skean Dhu*. Ask Mike Finlay.'

'You've seen something,' Eamon insisted. 'You've got that focused look about you.'

I didn't know I had a focused look. I tapped the charge sheet in front of me. 'This lighter.'

Eamon peered at the page. 'It was part of Fleming's property when he was brought in.'

'Yes, I can see that. The sergeant commented that he thought it looked effeminate, but Fleming said it was his. Can we be certain of that?' I asked.

'It was booked in as his. It's initialled,' Eamon said. 'See? L. F.'

My thoughts crystallised. 'The initials are wrong. Fleming's first name is Tony, or Anthony. T or A, not L,' I said.

Eamon pursed his lips as he thought. 'So maybe his official first name is Leonard or something, but he prefers to be known as Tony. Lots of people do that.'

I thought for a moment. 'It could be that it was a present from a family member who still thinks of him as Leonard or whatever.'

'Exactly,' Eamon said.

'Why would they buy him a woman's lighter?' I wondered aloud,

'Maybe he prefers pretty things, if you get my drift,' Eamon replied.

It was possible, but then… 'No, he's religious. Even if he was that way inclined, he wouldn't act on it, I don't think. The Bible discourages homosexuality.'

'But it's okay with incest?' Eamon said with a glint in his eye.

'Incest?'

'Adam and Eve. Who did their kids marry?'

'Eamon! you'll be excommunicated if you say that in church.'

'I'm a lost cause, m'darlin'. My mammy's always telling me that.' Chuckling to himself, he left me to it.

I grabbed the lost property book and flicked backwards from the date Tony Fleming had been brought in, for what seemed an age. I spotted a couple of entries for lighters, but one was the wrong colour and the other had different initials on it. Almost at the front of the book, I saw an entry for a lost handbag that contained a lighter that seemed a match for the lighter Tony Fleming had. It had been reported as lost by someone named Mary Jones while I was away on my driving course. An incident number was attached to the entry. I jotted it down and went into the control room.

Geoff was on duty. We'd had dealings before and he was not my favourite person, but competent enough at his job.

'Geoff, would you check this incident number for me, please? I need to know what it was and who was involved.' I handed him the scrap of paper.

Geoff took the paper from me. 'That's the date that girl was killed behind the nightclub. I was on duty then. We thought we had a murder, but it was just an accident.'

That was interesting. 'Could you check if this is the incident number for that, please?'

He passed the paper to the call handler. 'We'll ring you when we have the answer.'

'Thank you.'

Chapter Twenty-Eight

'Call for you, Sam.' Mike held out the receiver and I trotted over.

'Hello, DC Barrie speaking.'

'It's Geoff downstairs. That incident number is from the accident behind the club. The girl's name was Linda Fletcher. She was found by her sister, Mary Jones. I can request the job sheet from the archives if you need it. It'll have the patrols who attended and the jack dealing.'

'Thanks, Geoff, that would be very helpful.' I replaced the receiver. He wasn't such a bad old stick. Perhaps we had got off on the wrong foot. I should make more of an effort with him.

I went to Eamon's desk. 'Are you busy?'

'I'm always busy, m'darlin' but I can spare a moment for you.'

'You know that lighter I was looking at?'

'What have you done?' Eamon asked.

The flash of irritation came from nowhere. 'For God's sake!' I exclaimed. 'Why do you assume I've done anything? If I'm such a liability, why haven't I been sacked?'

Eamon just cocked an eyebrow at me. 'We want to see what you'll do next.'

I had to smile at that. I took a deep breath and continued. 'I checked the lighter on the lost property system and I think I got a match. I asked Geoff to check the incident number, and it was when the girl died behind the nightclub. I was on my driving course then.'

'The girl that died was Linda Fletcher,' Eamon said.

'L.F. Linda Fletcher, not Leonard Fleming. She was found by

her sister, Mary Jones, who reported Linda's handbag, containing the lighter, lost. Geoff is getting the job sheet from the archives for me.'

'Well, bugger me,' Eamon said.

'I'd rather not.' quipped Mike as he approached. 'What are you two plotting?'

'Young Sam here has just done a bit of decent detective work and found a link between Fleming, that special that was sacked, and that girl who was killed behind the nightclub a few weeks ago,' Eamon said.

'That means that the incident behind the club might not have been an accident,' I added, somewhat unnecessarily. 'We have the entries into the property system that he had a lighter engraved with L.F. in his possession when he was arrested. Also that Mary Jones reported Linda's handbag, with her lighter, lost on the night Linda died.'

'He might have just found it and kept hold,' Mike warned me.

'Theft by finding,' I said, but I thought there might be more to it than that.

'Yes, but we need to speak to him about it,' Eamon said. 'Do you have any connection to Linda Fletcher or Mary Jones?'

'None,' I replied.

Mike said, 'I'm taking this to Webb, keep him in the loop. Then you and I, Eamon, need to bring in Fleming for a chat.'

'Are you busy, Sam?' one of the jacks called from across the room. 'I need you to run an errand for me.'

I would have much preferred to remain to see what DI Webb made of the evidence, but I had to remember I was just the aide. I looked at Mike, who made a shooing gesture.

'Of course, what do you need?' I called back. Whatever it was, it wouldn't be as interesting as going to interview Fleming.

*

Mike and Eamon came back deep in conversation, and went into DI Webb's office. I was dying to ask how they'd got on, but I continued to type up a burglary whilst casting glances at the office.

'Sam, have you got a minute?' Eamon called from the doorway of Webby's office.

I pushed the typewriter aside and eagerly trotted over. 'I was just writing up a burglary.'

'We have Fleming downstairs. Want to sit in on the interview?' Mike asked.

'Yes, please. Has he been arrested or is it a voluntary thing?'

'Voluntary for now, but he's got a solicitor. Says he doesn't trust us anymore. Finish your burglary and meet us in the bridewell in fifteen minutes.'

'Yes, Sarge.' I went back and almost struck sparks from the keyboard in my eagerness to get the report done.

Fifteen minutes later, I was in the charge office. Mike and Eamon were preparing to interview Fletcher.

'He thinks we're going to talk about the Middleton Hotel,' Eamon said. 'We're going to try to blindside him with the lighter.'

I hadn't thought of that. Something else to remember for the future.

The bridewell officer came into the charge office. 'Your lad's ready. His brief is here.'

'Thanks.' Mike led us into the interview room. I sat slightly to one side, so the jacks could do the bulk of the questioning. Fleming and his solicitor sat on the other side of the table.

Mike cautioned Fleming.

'We're doing this officially then?' Fleming asked.

'Of course.'

'Lucky I thought to engage legal assistance,' Fleming said.

Mike launched straight into attack mode. 'Interesting that you thought you needed it. How did you end up with Linda Fletcher's lighter?'

Fleming blinked as if taken by surprise. I hoped he had been. Nobody talks more openly than a confused suspect.

'Who? I don't know her,' Fleming said.'

'You had her lighter in your possession when you were arrested,' Eamon snapped.

Fleming quickly caught on. 'I did borrow a lighter from someone in a club. It was heaving in there, so I lost sight of her.' He was quick on his feet; I had to give him that.

Mike pointed out. 'It's a nice lighter. Engraved. Did you steal it?'

'I'm not a thief! I had intended to return it. When I couldn't, I was going to book it into property but I forgot, then events overtook me.' Fleming glared at me as if it was my fault he had the lighter.

'That was weeks ago, though,' Eamon said.

Fleming shrugged. 'Stress can affect your memory. I was trying to cope with losing my status as a special constable, and as a result, losing my employment.'

'Status? Is that important to you?' I asked.

'Isn't it important to everyone?' Fleming retorted.

'I think it's especially important to you,' I replied.

'Linda Fletcher was the name of the woman who fell down the stairs behind the club on The Square and died,' Mike stated bringing us back on track.

'You're not pinning that on me. She was trying to break in. Her head hit the stairs as she fell and she broke her neck.'

'How do you know that?' Mike asked.

'It was in the paper. She died of head injuries,' Fleming responded.

'Her injuries weren't specified. You've been very specific. Nor was it released that she was trying to get in without paying.'

'I'm a Special… was a Special. I saw the report.'

'Were you involved with the case?' Eamon asked.

'No, but I saw the coroner said she'd died of head injuries.'

'Why did you need to access the file if you weren't involved?

The CID would have carried out any investigation.' Mike asked.

His cheeks grew pinker. 'I was curious.'

'Those are official documents, not a spot of light entertainment!' Mike exclaimed.

'A coincidence, don't you think. You have Linda Fletcher's lighter in your possession, a lighter that Linda's sister reported as lost on the night she died.' I cocked my head.

'I couldn't find her to return the lighter,' Fleming said. 'Now we know why.'

'If she was already in the club, why would she have been trying to force a door to sneak in from the outside?' I asked.

The solicitor sighed, leant back on his chair and rested an ankle on his knee. Never had I seen so much said without a word being spoken.

'I don't know. Maybe to let her friends in,' Fleming said.

'It would have made more sense to simply open the door from the inside,' I stated.

It was time to use silence. Most people didn't like silences and felt compelled to fill the space. I had no problem with it. I watched Fleming and didn't speak. He shifted in his seat, but we still didn't speak. I can't say it was a staring contest; we were just watching him, and he didn't like it.

'I don't know. Maybe the other girl saw her fall,' he blurted out.

Eamon pounced. 'What other girl?'

Fleming closed his eyes.

'What other girl?' Mike snapped.

'The one who called to her.' Fleming replied.

'You must have been there to know anyone called to her,' Eamon said.

'I wasn't right there; I was on the other side of the road. I was moved on by a policeman. I can give you the time and date. Ask him. He will verify I was outside the club, not behind it.'

'On the other side of the road, on the other side of the building from where Linda died. Too far for you to have heard

anything never mind being so sure someone called to Linda.'
Eamon leant forward, his elbows on the table.

Fleming said nothing.

Mike said, 'You were there. Her sister called to her and told us that nobody passed her as she went to investigate. You must have nipped over the back wall to get away. Did you mug her? Is that why you were there, you were robbing her? Is that why her bag was never found? You kept hold of the lighter. I bet you thought you'd get away with it because the initials are similar to yours. Do you have it on you now?'

'I don't have it anymore,' Fleming replied.

'Oh, what a shame. The officers I have dispatched to search your address will be disappointed to come away empty-handed.'

'You what?!' Fleming stood up. 'You have no right!'

Mike also stood up. He was a big man, a rugby player. Fleming immediately cooled down.

'I am arresting you on suspicion of the murder of Linda Fletcher,' Mike said.

Fleming's cheeks burned red as Mike cautioned him.

'How did she fall, Tony?' I asked.

'She probably resisted handing over her bag so he thumped her,' Eamon said.

'No!'

'Then how? The door she was trying to open was at the bottom of the steps so she must have come back up the steps at some point.' Eamon pressed on. 'Come on, Tony. We know you were there. We know you took her lighter. You can't hide anymore.'

'She was disrespectful,' Fleming snarled.

What was it with these men getting upset over women's behaviour? The PCMG was crawling with misogynists.

'Elaborate,' Mike demanded.

Tony sighed. He was ready to give us information.

'Okay. I saw her go down the alley so I followed her. She was trying to break into the club. I told her to come with me but she insulted me. I pushed her and she lost her footing and fell. It was an accident. I didn't mean to kill her.'

'You were reckless. Only an idiot would push someone at the top of steps,' Eamon said.

'I'm not an idiot,' Fleming growled.

'You must be to have done that,' I murmured. I could see from Fleming's expression that I was pushing him to the edge. His fragile ego could not stand a woman challenging him.

'I wish you'd died,' he hissed.

I gulped. I knew at once that he was referring to the fire at my parents' house.

The solicitor, recognising the seriousness, even if he was unaware of the fire that had almost taken my life, uncrossed his ankle and sat straighter.

'Say that again,' Mike said, his voice low but deadly.

Fleming looked at him, all innocence. 'Say what again?'

'Don't play that game. You will damn well explain yourself.'

As Mike spoke, I didn't need Fleming to explain himself. I couldn't prove it yet, but when I thought about Henry's description of the man seen leaving my parents' house, it all made sense. The motorcycle jacket. Black with red writing. The same jacket that I had seen Fleming wearing when he was going home after our disastrous shift together. Tony Fleming hated me to the point he wanted me dead.

'It was you. You set the fire in my parents' house,' I whispered. Shock had taken my voice.

'You were careless leaving a tea towel hanging on the grill.' Fleming gave me a nasty smirk.

'How did you know it was an eye-level grill? How did you know about the tea towel?' Mike asked.

'Stands to reason. Women like an eye-level grill. It makes their life easier, but they're such muddle-headed creatures, they don't think of the danger when they hang things from it. They need men to supervise them.'

'Bullshit!' I cried. 'You attacked me, knocked me unconscious, tied me to a cooker and left me to burn to death!'

Mike brought his hand down hard on the desk. Everyone turned to him. 'Fleming, I am also arresting you for the attempted murder of Constable Barrie, and assault on Constable Barrie, and burglary. You are not obliged to say anything unless you wish to do so, but anything you do say will be taken down in writing and given in evidence.'

'What have I ever done to deserve to die in such a horrible way?' I cried.

Tony's face twisted. 'What have you done? You ruined my life!'

'You did that all by yourself. You were seen leaving the house, you know.'

'All I wanted was to find a girlfriend. I got thrown out of the Specials and then I was sacked from my job. I lost my income and my reputation. You took everything from me.'

'Sam, you need to leave now. Tell DI Webb what's happened and ask him to come down, please.'

'But...'

'Now, Sam,' Mike said.

I abruptly stood up, causing my chair to fall backwards and fled to the CID office. Irene was there and spotted me charging in.

'Sam?' She abandoned her conversation and came over. 'What's happened?'

'It was Tony Fleming. He tried to kill me. He's just admitted it. Mike's arrested him.' I stopped speaking to catch my breath. I was going into a full-blown panic attack.

'What's going on?' DI Webb came over to us.

'Tony Fleming has just confessed to trying to kill Sam,' Irene told him.

'I thought you were interviewing him about Linda Fletcher?'

'We were,' I gasped. My breathing was slowing a little and I was feeling clearer headed. 'He knew too much about her not to have been there. Then he wished that I had died because I've ruined his life.' Then I remembered what Mike had asked. 'Mike says, could you please go down and speak with them, sir.'

'Want me to come, too?' Irene asked.

'No, stay with Sam.' He turned on his heel and strode from the office.

Irene walked me over to the rickety table that had become my regular seat and flicked on the kettle in the corner.

'A nice cuppa is in order, I think.'

Yes, the cure-all in every situation. A nice cup of tea. Irene put my drink beside me, pulled over another chair and sat opposite me.

'He's going to prison,' she said.

'I know.' I took a mouthful of tea. I didn't know what to say. I'd upset a few people during my service, and had come close to death a few times, but once the offender had been arrested, I carried on as normal. This one really got to me. Maybe it was the method he has chosen. The thought of burning to death horrified me. I didn't feel safe.

Irene seemed to be reading my thoughts. 'You've got a gold response on the flat and the house and a block on your number plate. He won't be able to hurt you.'

Gold response, at least if I did need to call the police, they would treat it as an immediate incident. Also, I could drive around without worrying about someone I'd upset seeing me and ringing the control room pretending to be a police officer to do a vehicle check to get my details. It had happened before to other officers. There was talk about introducing a password system. It couldn't happen soon enough in my opinion.

I needed to speak to Gary. I was seriously wondering about moving from Lyseby. How long until the next irate customer came after me?

*

After a time, DI Web, Eamon and Mike came back. DI Webb

caught my eye and jerked his head towards his office. I took the hint and followed them in. Irene followed me.

DI Webb turned to face me. 'I'll come straight to the point. When Fleming was being processed, the lighter was in his possession. It's now bagged as evidence. Fleming has admitted everything, the attempt to murder you, also the killing of Linda Fletcher, but I think the charge for Linda Fletcher will be manslaughter; we'll struggle to prove intent.'

Yes, that made sense. Better a conviction for manslaughter than having him cleared of murder for want of proof of intent.

'We'll be going for attempted murder for you. You said your neighbour saw him leaving, Sam?' DI Webb asked.

'Yes, Henry didn't name him or anything specific, but he saw someone fitting Fleming's description leaving.'

'Would he be willing to testify?'

'I'm sure of it. Henry saved my life.'

DI Webb nodded. 'Good.'

'Are you all right m'darlin'?' Eamon asked.

'I think so. I was just shocked.'

'He'll be an old man before he gets out of prison,' Irene said.

'I'll let Mary Jones know that we have her sister's lighter. She'll be able to have it back when the case is over,' Mike said.

'Everything goes back to that club, the PCMG,' I commented. 'Winger, Duggan, Fleming, are all members. Even Walter Hodgeson.'

'Walter wasn't a bad person, though,' Mike pointed out. 'Annoying, but not bad. He was released without charge.'

'And I'm sure there are others like him there, but the bad ones influence the rest. How long before another one who walks the line between good and bad comes along and is sucked in by their pseudo-religious, anti-women rhetoric?'

'I agree,' DI Webb said. 'Mike, we need to close that club for good.'

'There's a meeting tonight,' I said.

'Let's do it then,' Mike said.

'Should I book a car?' I asked.

'Irene.' DI Webb nodded in my direction.

Irene put an arm around my shoulder and pulled me out of the office. 'This is for the big boys. We girls would not be welcome.'

'But we're invested in this too!' I complained. 'It's not fair!'

'But it's the way it is,' Irene replied.

I allowed her to lead me away. I didn't doubt that, after tonight, the PCMG would be disbanded; but I also knew that it, or something like it, would pop up somewhere else. It was like playing whack-a-mole, and we'd never catch up.

Chapter Twenty-Nine

I was on the late shift for the next few days and wouldn't finish until midnight. I went out with Eamon to meet someone he needed to talk to. He asked me to remain in the car. It was interesting that he felt he wanted to have someone with him. We didn't ask too many questions about each other's informants. Snouts were a precious, closely guarded resource. I needed to get to know a couple of such people myself. Eamon and his informant didn't seem to entirely trust each other—their body language was borderline hostile—however, the meeting went off without incident and Eamon returned to the car.

'Right m'darlin', it's getting late. Let's get back.'

He didn't mention what was discussed and I didn't ask. He set off towards Wyre Hall.

As we passed the Kings Streets, I saw Wilfred limping under the streetlight. I hadn't heard anyone broadcast anything.

'Eamon, that's Wilfred. He shouldn't be out on his own, he's still recovering from a broken leg.'

'He should be in residential care if he's come out of hospital,' Eamon said, but he turned and drove after Wilfred.

'You know what Kitty's like. She probably insisted he went home when he was discharged,' I said.

Wilfred was dressed in pyjamas, with one leg cut away to accommodate the cast on his bad leg. He wore no slippers and no dressing gown or coat.

'He must be freezing. I'll let control know.' I picked up the radio handset. '4912 to control,' I transmitted.

'Go ahead.'

'I've spotted Wilfred wandering in his pyjamas. He's only in Charles Street, so Eamon and I will get him home.'

'Roger.'

Eamon parked up and I called out, 'Hey, Wilfred, hang on a minute.'

He turned towards me. There was something different about him. He was not the constable on the beat, he wasn't even the friendly ex-colleague. His shoulders were rounded, and he twisted his fingers around each other.

'I don't like the look of him,' I said to Eamon as we got out of the car.

Wilfred rocked from foot to foot as we approached him. He was a very different man from the one who helped me bring down Fleming.

'Are you all right, Wilf?' I asked.

He didn't reply in words; he gave a little whimper that alarmed me. I shone my torch on his feet checking for blood, then moved the beam up his body in case I had missed an injury. Perhaps he was just cold.

'You must be freezing, Wilfred.' I took his arm.

'Kitty's asleep,' he said.

'I should hope so. She'll be frantic if she wakes up and finds you gone, so let's get you home,' I said.

Wilf's rocking grew more frantic, and I caught a whiff of urine that was too fresh to have come from the gutter. Incontinence had not been one of Wilf's problems a few weeks ago.

I gently pulled him towards the car and thankfully he walked without any trouble.

'So, what are you doing out at this time?' I asked when he was safely sat down.

'I was looking for the bobby,' he replied.

'Well, you found us,' I replied. The rear seat would need to be disinfected before the car was used again. I was the aide, so it would fall to me.

Eamon drove us the short distance to Wilfred's home and

pulled up outside. The front door was ajar. We got him inside, then closed the door, put the snip on then slid the bolt across too in case Wilfred decided to wander off while we were distracted.

'Kitty's asleep,' Wilf repeated.

'I'm afraid we're going to have to wake her up. She needs to get you changed and settled into bed,' Eamon said.

'No, no, no,' Wilfred murmured. He resumed wringing his hands and rocking.

'I'll go and get her.' I turned on the landing light and hurried upstairs and knocked on the bedroom door. 'Kitty, It's Samantha. I'm sorry to bother you but I have Wilfred downstairs. He got out again. He needs fresh nightwear.'

Silence. My inner alarm started jangling.

'Kitty, I'm coming in.' I pushed the door open and entered the room. I felt for the light switch and put on the light.

It was the typical bedroom of a couple the ages of Kitty and Wilfred. Flowered wallpaper, chocolate-brown paintwork that was rarely seen any more. A heavy, dark wood wardrobe, two matching beside cabinets. A dressing table with mirror pushed under the window, and a surprisingly modern looking divan bed, upon which Kitty lay covered with blankets.

'Kitty?' Not a flicker of response. I went over and felt for a pulse. Nothing. Kitty felt cool but not yet cold. Her passing had been peaceful. Poor Wilf must have woken up and found her dead, then what was left of his failing memory must have driven him to wander off to find a police officer. My eyes stung but I held back any tears. In our job, dealing with death was commonplace, but it was normally distant. Occasionally we would be affected by a death, but it didn't usually touch us personally. I felt huge sadness at Kitty's passing.

Wilfred came into the room behind me, followed by Eamon. I hadn't heard him come upstairs. He made that little whimper noise again and sat on the bed. I remembered that he had wet himself. I opened a couple of drawers to find him some dry pyjama bottoms, but I only saw Kitty's things.

'Wilfred, where are your pyjamas kept?' I asked.

He stood up and pulled open a drawer in the dressing table. I pulled out a pair of bottoms, not bothering about trying to match them.

'Will these do, Wilfred?' I asked. I felt I should give him some choice now, as very soon he would have all choice taken from him.

I took his silence as affirmative. I left the room while Eamon helped him clean up and change his pyjamas.

When he was decent again, Eamon manoeuvred Wilf downstairs and left me to deal with Kitty.

'4912 to control,' I radioed in.

'Go ahead.'

'We've taken Wilfred home, but Kitty has passed away. I think Wilf must have woken up and found her like that. He's very confused. Could you ask supervision to attend and would you inform the doctor?'

'Roger. Mike Sierra Two.'

I listened to the radio beep as control passed on the address and confirmed that supervision was attending.

I went downstairs while I waited for Mike Sierra Two and the doctor to arrive. 'Why don't I put the kettle on and make us a nice cup of tea?' I suggested.

'Yes, a cup of tea would be splendid,' Wilfred replied brightly. He'd forgotten.

I went into the kitchen and switched on the kettle then set out the tray the way Kitty used to. I wanted Wilf to feel as normal as possible.

Both Phil and the inspector arrived together. I unbolted the door and let them both into the hall. It was the first time I had seen the new inspector. She was a pleasant-looking woman of about forty. Not a lot taller than me.

She held out her hand. 'You must be the Sam Barrie I keep hearing about. I'm June Baird.'

I wasn't sure how to take that, but I shook her hand and

smiled. 'Pleased to meet you, Ma'am. I'm currently on my aides' course.'

'Where is the lady?' she asked.

'Upstairs. Wilfred is in the living room. He's a bit confused,' I replied.

They went into the living room and introduced themselves to Wilfred. I went back into the kitchen and made more tea, while the boss and Phil went upstairs to check Kitty.

I carried the tray into the living room and put it on the little table.

'Oh, hello, lass. I didn't see you arrive. The woman inspector is talking to Kitty,' Wilf said.

I smiled at him and poured him a cup of tea. Maybe that was the wrong thing to do, I don't know, but it seemed kinder than reminding him that Kitty was gone. I heard a car draw up.

'That'll be the doctor,' I said and went to open the door. I knew the doctor; we often met him at incidents.

Wilfred followed me out. 'The doctor?'

Phil came down and greeted the doctor, who followed him back upstairs.

Wilf started wringing his hands again and rocking from foot to foot.

'Kitty's asleep, they'll wake her.'

'No, Wilf, they won't.' I guided Wilf back into the living room and sat him down. His mind must have been all over the place.

They came back down. I joined them in the hall and handed the doctor a cup of tea.

'There is no problem with the death certificate, I saw her just last week, but there's no way Wilfred can be left alone. We need to arrange care for him,' the doctor said. 'He'll have to go to the hospital tonight. I'll contact the duty social worker to see if we can place him somewhere more suitable until something permanent can be done.'

Poor Wilfred had no idea that these were his last hours in

his and Kitty's home, that he would never get into his own bed again. I radioed in the request for an undertaker. Wilfred sat watching us through the living room door, not comprehending what was happening.

'I'll message our welfare department; he's probably in the funeral fund and perhaps they can help with the administration side of things,' the inspector said.

We all crammed into the living room. The doctor perched on the arm of Wilfred's chair.

'Wilfred, I'm sorry, but Kitty has passed away.' He put a hand on Wilf's shoulder. 'It was peaceful, she went in her sleep.' He paused to let this sink in. Kitty hadn't suffered. 'I know your daughter is in America; is there anyone more local we can contact for you?'

'Kitty's asleep, don't wake her,' Wilfred said. He didn't seem to be coming back to reality as he used to.

'No, my dear chap, she's gone. She looks very peaceful. I know your daughter lives abroad, so I need to know if there is anyone else I can contact for you?'

'Wilfie, my son. He's in the Navy.'

I caught the doctor's eye and shook my head. The doctor nodded slightly in acknowledgement.

A tear leaked from Wilfred's eye, and he put his head in his hands. I blinked hard to keep a tear from escaping my own eyes. I had liked Kitty. Poor Wilfred, he would keep forgetting that Kitty was gone, he would have to be told again and again that his wife was dead. He would feel that awful jolt of pain at her loss every day.

While we waited for the duty undertaker to arrive, I searched the drawer in the telephone table in the hall to see if I could find an address book in the hope of finding some relative in this country, but to no avail. However, I did find the address and phone number of their daughter, which I passed on to the control room. Someone would have to get a message to her. Generally, we didn't like delivering news like this by telephone, so probably the local police would be informed and asked to call around. I estimated that it would be early evening in Boston. Wilf, meantime, would be shipped off into residential care, either at the hospital or in a home.

The doctor came out to speak to me.

'What's the story with his son?' he whispered.

'He was killed when his ship was torpedoed in 1944. He was only twenty when he died,' I replied.

'So the poor old fellow is totally alone now. Tragic.' The doctor returned to the living room. I hoped our welfare department would be good advocates for him.

*

The phone was ringing as I got in, later than normal. I kicked off my shoes and dumped my bag in the hall before answering. The neighbours probably hated me at that moment. Tough.

'Thank goodness. I was getting worried,' Gary said. 'It must be the early hours there. Where've you been?'

'Kitty Wainwright died. We had to sort Wilfred out. He's going into residential care,' I replied.

'Sudden deaths aren't normally dealt with by CID. Was there something a bit iffy about it?' Gary asked.

'No,' I replied. 'Eamon and I found Wilfred wandering and found her dead in her bed when we took him home.'

'Poor fellow.'

I couldn't say any more. My words wouldn't go past the lump in my throat. Tears ran down my cheeks. I sniffed.

'Are you all right?' Gary asked.

'Sad,' I croaked.

'About Kitty?'

'And Wilf. He didn't understand what was happening.' I wiped my tears with the back of my hand. 'I have to go.' I replaced the handset. I went to the fridge and took out the bottle of wine that had been sitting there waiting for Gary's return. I opened it and poured a large glassful. I would need help getting to sleep tonight.

Chapter Thirty

Only a few more days before Gary came home. I could hardly contain myself. I had started to think of it as Gary Day, or *G Day* as I wrote it on the calendar. I intended to show him how much I had missed him.

So much had happened in the months since he had left. I had passed my driving course. I had allowed my head to be turned by Chris. I could see that now. I was confident that I would not have been unfaithful to Gary even if Chris were still here, but it was worrying how easily I had been tempted.

I was finding my feet within CID. I was partway through my aides' course and had been part of what turned out to be a pretty big job with several arrests. I still had the more interesting parts taken from me, but I had learnt a lot.

I had been attacked—again. I was still dealing with the emotional fall-out from that, but my case had unexpectedly been solved, which was a plus point. I wish I could have said the same for Ruthie.

I called on Karen Fitzroy, who had reported Ruthie missing, to bring her up to date. I knew I could trust her not to blab. She showed me around her new home, now that it had been decorated to her taste. The lime green in the kitchen wasn't totally awful, but Karen was ecstatic so I made noises of approval. The view of the river from the back bedroom, which Karen used as a sewing room, was lovely.

We sat in the dining room, drinking tea. It would have been more comfortable to sit in the living room, but Karen was still enthralled with her dining room before and wanted to use it as often as possible.

'Is Sharon okay now?' she asked.

'Physically, she's recovering well, but there's always a psychological toll in cases like this. That could take a lot longer, if she fully recovers at all,' I said. I could talk openly to Karen.

'Yeah. Look at you.'

'I got there in the end.'

Karen remained quiet for a moment, then said, 'Let's talk about Ruthie.'

I swallowed a mouthful of tea and sighed. 'I'm pretty sure that she's dead, but that's only my personal opinion.'

'You saw her coat. You got her key. Why hasn't anyone been charged with her murder?' Karen asked.

'We know a coat similar to the coat she was wearing the last time I saw her was burnt, but nobody can say for sure that it was actually her coat. It's too badly damaged to say for sure. We know someone died, but there's no body. Sharon couldn't name her, neither could either of the offenders. Winger probably didn't even bother learning her name. Hayes was just a lackey who was told nothing.'

Karen sipped at her tea. 'Can't you charge them anyway? You have her bag and her key, surely that's enough.'

It was my turn to remain quiet. I thought Karen had asked a reasonable question but was finding property belonging to a missing girl enough to charge anyone with their murder? Possibly, but we could not prove it beyond reasonable doubt in a court. Nellie couldn't identify the person burning the clothes, so it could be argued that anyone could have put the clothing in the bin. Nellie would have known Walter Hodgeson and her own son, Don, so I was happy it wasn't them. Winger wasn't admitting it. Much as I wanted them to be charged, we didn't always get what we wanted. Ruthie would remain on our outstanding missing persons list until she, or her body was found, if ever.

'It isn't my decision,' I said. 'It would be very unusual for someone to be charged with murder without there being a body.

The good thing about this, is that Ruthie's profile has been raised. They're taking it more seriously now. I think the local paper is going to mention her in the next edition.' But I would bet my pension she wouldn't get the headlines or a press conference. Nobody was going to reenact her last known movements.

'Nobody will miss her,' Karen said. 'Not even Elsie or Bernadette.'

Bernadette. She was Ruthie's closest relative that we could contact. We were going to have to tell her that Ruthie was missing. I had pondered on adding the words "presumed dead", but DI Webb wouldn't authorise that. She was just missing until proven otherwise. I would speak to Irene about it. I didn't want to do anything to jeopardise Bernie's happy new life in Manchester.

*

In the CID office, everybody was discussing the Christmas celebrations. Some departments had a full-blown Christmas party somewhere, others had low key celebrations. Some had both. Our section fell into the latter category. A big party had been planned for the New Year, the location and the caterers were booked, but Mike and Eamon had decided that we needed to go out before Christmas to celebrate the conclusion of a successful job as much as Christmas. The men's group was closed, Walter the Weeble was not charged with anything and could go about his life, real and imaginary. Duggan, Hayes, Fleming and Winger were off the streets. I was personally pleased that Fleming was out of the way.

Don Hayes did plead guilty at his first appearance in court, and sang like the proverbial canary. He was in the remand centre, pending sentencing. He'd have to be careful. Pleading guilty is one thing, but ratting out other people was frowned upon amongst the prison population. I could imagine, once everyone had been sentenced, Don Hayes would have to spend a lot of time in solitary for his own safety. Duggan and Winger were also in custody, awaiting their trials at Crown Court. Duggan was still outraged at his treatment. We were well prepared and had no doubt that they would not be seeing the outside for a long time.

*

'I think we should go to the Gozzie Moggie.' Mike said.

'Nah, let's go to The Crown, they've got entertainment on,' Eamon said. 'Are you interested, Sam?'

'What entertainment?' I asked.

'People sing,' Eamon answered.

'Even those who can't,' someone else added.

'Sounds like fun,' I said. A night out was a night out, and I wasn't going to miss this one.

Everyone agreed on The Crown, a largish, old fashioned place with a nicotine brown ceiling and walls and worn benches along the walls.

We arrived early enough to grab a couple of tables in the lounge, and pulled them together to make room for everyone.

At the end of the lounge bar, a microphone had been set up with speakers either side.

About fifteen minutes later, a man in a loud shirt and silver dicky-bow, the compere, picked up the microphone and tapped it.

'Can everyone hear me?'

'Get on with it!' someone shouted from the back.

'Does anyone want to sing?' the compere asked. A couple of people raised their hands.

'Go on, Boss,' Eamon urged DI Webb.

'Behave,' he replied.

'Aw go on,' Eamon nagged.

The compere invited the first person to come up. A woman in a tight dress that did nothing for her.

'What's your name?'

'Beryl,' the woman replied.

'And what are you singing tonight?'

'*Build me up, Buttercup,*' she replied.

The music started and Beryl sang her song - badly. The audience were not shy about letting her know how badly.

The next singer was not that great either. The third one was better, but not great.

Eamon kept nagging DI Webb to sing. Eventually, DI Webb put his hand up and was invited forward by the compere.

'What's your name?' the compere asked.

'Norman,' Webby replied.

'Nice to meet you, Norman. What do you want to sing?' he asked.

'*Unchained Melody,*' Webby replied.

'Do we have that music?' The compere asked someone behind the bar. He paused for then answer then smiled. 'We do indeed. Over to you then, Norman.'

The music started, Webby sang the first notes and my jaw hit the table. Webby could sing! Really sing. He had a voice people would pay to hear. The chatter at the bar ceased and everyone turned towards him. People came in from the bar and stood quietly holding their pints.

When the last note ended, there was a moment's silence, then we, and the rest of the audience, all jumped to our feet and applauded and whistled our appreciation.

The compere came back out clapping his hands. 'Well, ladies and gentlemen, what can I say? I'd ask if anyone else wants to perform, but how do you follow that.'

Webby shifted from foot to foot, evidently uncomfortable.

Eamon leant towards me. 'I bet you didn't expect that.'

'I absolutely didn't expect that. He's fantastic.'

'He sang in the cathedral choir when he was a boy.'

'You're joking!' The cathedral had high standards; the choir was famous.

Eamon shook his head. 'No. He turned his back on music and became a copper.'

DI Webb sat down and glugged the remains of his pint.

'That was wonderful,' I said. 'I had no idea you had such a good voice.'

He shrugged. 'Thanks.' He finished his drink and put down the glass. 'Whose round is it?'

Mike stood up and went to the bar.

'If you do this again, would you sing *Moon River*?' I asked.

'Who'd want to hear that?' Webby asked.

'I would! Anyone would. I love that song,' I declared.

Webby half-smiled and almost blushed. 'Okay, I'll think about it.' He picked up the fresh pint that Mike had put in front of him and started drinking. It looked like it was going to be a late night.

*

D Day, or G Day as I had christened it, finally arrived. I had spent a fortune at the beauty parlour getting myself waxed, manicured and pedicured. My hair was neatly trimmed and now, the only thing to do before I left for the airport was to select a suitable homecoming outfit.

I took out my lingerie set with the French knickers and laid it on the bed. I remembered the first time I wore it. We had travelled to London for Gary's interview for the Hong Kong posting. Let's just say I wasn't wearing it for very long. I hoped the same would be true now. The fridge was full of snacks and a couple of bottles of wine, so we didn't have to leave the flat for a couple of days. My stomach rippled in excitement as I got dressed.

The arrivals hall at Manchester airport was busy as usual. A couple of planes were due in around the same time and there was an air of anticipation as we waited for our people to come through the sliding door.

The first flurry of people arrived and I watched them greeting their families, friends and for a couple, a stranger with a board with their names written on it, but I was only interested in one person. The next time it swished opened, there he was. I bounced on my toes and yelled Gary's name as I waved. He spotted me and waved back.

As soon as he was clear of the security area, I flung myself at him almost knocking him off his feet. He smelt so good despite travelling for hours.

'I've missed you so much,'

He hugged me close. 'And I've missed you.' He brought his mouth close to my ear. 'In fact, I've only been able to think about one thing on the plane.'

'Oh, and what's that.' I nuzzled into his neck. I could barely wait for us to get home.

'A big, fat bacon butty with brown sauce and a mug of proper builder's tea.'

THE END

Did You Enjoy This Book?

If so, you can make a HUGE difference.

For any author, the single most important way we have of getting our books noticed is a really simple one—and one which you can help with.

Yes, you.

Us indie authors and publishers don't have the financial muscle of the big guys to take out full-page ads in the newspaper or put posters on the subway.

But we do have something much more powerful and effective than that, and it's something that those big publishers would kill to get their hands on.

A committed and loyal bunch of readers.

Honest reviews of our books help bring them to the attention of other readers.

If you've enjoyed this book I would be really grateful if you could spend just a couple of minutes leaving a review (it can be as short as you like) on this book's page on your favourite store and website.

Acknowledgements

I would like to thank Si and Pete of Burning Chair for their support and for helping me turn my scribbles into a coherent piece of writing.

Thanks to the beta readers, their feedback is invaluable.

Thanks to Paul, my husband, who serves as a back-up memory on procedures from almost fifty years ago.

Thanks to the C and P gang. I wouldn't be here without your encouragement.

About The Author

Trish Finnegan has spent her whole life living on the Wirral, a small peninsula that sticks out into the Irish Sea between North Wales and Liverpool. She has always had an overactive imagination and enjoyed writing and reading, sometimes to the detriment of her schoolwork.

She first met her husband, Paul, in the charge office of a police station: where they both were serving as police officers. She has three grown up children and currently spends her time wrangling grandchildren and writing.

More From Burning Chair Publishing

Your next favourite new read is waiting for you…!

The Blue Bird Series, by Trish Finnegan
>Blue Bird
>Blue Sky
>Baby Blues

The Tom Novak series, by Neil Lancaster
>Going Dark
>Going Rogue
>Going Back

Killer in the Crowd, by P N Johnson

Run to the Blue, by P N Johnson

Burning Bridges, by Matthew Ross

Push Back, by James Marx

The Casebook of Johnson & Boswell, by Andrew Neil Macleod
>The Fall of the House of Thomas Weir
>The Stone of Destiny

By Richard Ayre:
> Shadow of the Knife
> Point of Contact
> A Life Eternal

The Curse of Becton Manor, by Patricia Ayling

Near Death, by Richard Wall

The Haven Chronicles, by Fi Phillips
> Haven Wakes
> Magic Bound
> Haven's Deceit

Love Is Dead(ly), by Gene Kendall

Beyond, by Georgia Springate

10:59, by N R Baker

The Other Side of Trust, by Neil Robinson

The Sarah Black Series, by Lucy Hooft
> The King's Pawn
> The Head of the Snake

The Brodick Cold War Series, by John Fullerton
> Spy Game
> Spy Dragon

The Great Big Demon Hunting Agency, by Peter Oxley

The Infernal Aether series, by Peter Oxley
> The Infernal Aether
> A Christmas Aether

About Burning Chair

Burning Chair is an independent publishing company based in the UK, but covering readers and authors around the globe. We are passionate about both writing and reading books and, at our core, we just want to get great books out to the world.

Our aim is to offer something exciting; something innovative; something that puts the author and their book first. From first class editing to cutting edge marketing and promotion, we provide the care and attention that makes sure every book fulfils its potential.

We are:
- Different
- Passionate
- Nimble and cutting edge
- Invested in our authors' success

If you're an author and would like to know more about our submissions requirements and receive our free guide to book publishing, visit:

www.burningchairpublishing.com

If you're a reader and are interested in hearing more about our books, being the first to hear about our new releases or great offers, or becoming a beta reader for us, again please visit:

www.burningchairpublishing.com